THIS
REBEL
HEART

ALSO BY KATHERINE LOCKE

The Girl with the Red Balloon

The Spy with the Red Balloon

It's a Whole Spiel: Love, Latkes, and Other Jewish Stories
(editor and contributor)

This Is Our Rainbow: 16 Stories of Her, Him, Them, and Us
(editor and contributor)

KATHERINE LOCKE

THIS

REBEL

HEART

Alfred A. Knopf
New York

THIS IS A BORZOI BOOK PUBLISHED BY ALFRED A. KNOPF

This is a work of fiction. Names, characters, places, and incidents either are the product of the author's imagination or are used fictitiously. Any resemblance to actual persons, living or dead, events, or locales is entirely coincidental.

Text copyright © 2022 by Katherine Locke
Jacket art copyright © 2022 by Aykut Aydoğdu
Map art copyright © 2022 by Virginia Norey

All rights reserved. Published in the United States by Alfred A. Knopf, an imprint of Random House Children's Books, a division of Penguin Random House LLC, New York.

Knopf, Borzoi Books, and the colophon are registered trademarks of Penguin Random House LLC.

Visit us on the Web! GetUnderlined.com

Educators and librarians, for a variety of teaching tools, visit us at RHTeachersLibrarians.com

Library of Congress Cataloging-in-Publication Data is available upon request.
ISBN 978-0-593-38124-3 (trade) — ISBN 978-0-593-38125-0 (lib. bdg.) —
ISBN 978-0-593-38126-7 (ebook) — ISBN 978-0-593-48766-2 (intl. pbk.)

The text of this book is set in 11-point Maxime Pro Regular.
Interior design by Cathy Bobak

Printed in the United States of America
10 9 8 7 6 5 4 3 2 1

First Edition

Random House Children's Books supports the First Amendment
and celebrates the right to read.

For my aunt Meryl, z"l

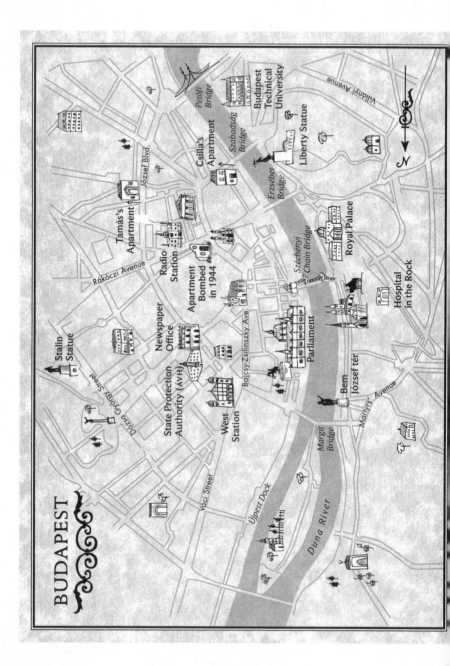

BUDAPEST

Stalin Statue

Dózsa György Street

Váci Street

State Protection Authority (AVH)

Newspaper Office

West Station

Bajcsy-Zsilinszky Ave.

Rákóczi Avenue

Radio Station

Tamás's Apartment

József Blvd.

Apartment Bombed in 1944

Csilla's Apartment

Szabadság Bridge

Petőfi Bridge

Budapest Technical University

Villányi Avenue

Liberty Statue

Erzsébet Bridge

Széchenyi Chain Bridge

Royal Palace

Parliament

Hospital in the Rock

Margit Bridge

Bem József tér

Martyrs' Avenue

Újpest Dock

Duna River

N

Let me fall if I must. The one I will become will catch me.

—Rabbi Israel ben Eliezer
(known as the Baal Shem Tov)

If all I have is magic, I'll come back.

—Miklós Radnóti, "Letter to My Wife"
(translated by Zsuzsanna Ozsváth and
Frederick Turner)

PART I

This is a story in the silt, says the river. Listen.

CHAPTER ONE

CSILLA

When she woke, she woke in pieces.

This happened often.

She had to pull herself together. In her sleep, Csilla Tisza's body drifted apart. Her hands were always farthest, reaching for the window that was bolted shut. The window that faced the Duna River.

She was invariably returning to the river.

She assembled herself, letting the skin knit edge to edge, seamless except to those looking for the seams of her. Her shoulder touched and bonded again to her upper arm, her upper arm to her elbow, her elbow to her forearm, her forearm to her wristbones, her wristbones to her hands. Only then could she curl her fingers against her palm, the fist sending a pulse of pain to her mind. That was how she knew she was connected again. The pain.

3

Her eyes never left her skull.

It was as if they knew better. They'd seen things out there, in the world, that they didn't want to see again. They'd rather stay here, beneath the quilt her mother had made, in the bed where her parents made her, in an apartment one-fourth the size it was when she was a child, when she was one-fourth the size she was now.

Csilla's hair stayed attached to her head too, moon-colored as it'd been since the day she was born. It was luminous, catching and throwing the light like a prism, every strand reflecting and deflecting light so it was impossible not to stare at the threaded lines on the walls that moved when she moved.

She wore the river on her head.

There had been little color left in Budapest since the end of the war. The Soviets marched in, and color marched out. (In truth, by the time the Soviets arrived, the only color left in Budapest was blue—the color of the sky, the color of babies' eyes, the color of the thread in her father's tallit, the color of her mother's favorite dress.)

Next to her, in the only bed they had, her aunt slept, mostly in one piece, as one body. Her aunt never drifted too far from herself.

Csilla took a deep breath, pressing her hand flat against her chest, just above her left breast. Her heart beat against her palm. She was alive. Somewhere beyond this bed, somewhere beyond this window, the river whispered to her.

She could feel the whispers in her chest, could hear them in her mind. When she was a child, before the war, before the river, her parents spoke to each other in Yiddish, a language they didn't share with her. This was how the river felt to her—a language that soothed her, a constant presence, but one she barely understood.

When she was a child and her parents spoke Yiddish, she wanted to understand. By the time she was old enough to understand that they'd use Yiddish to speak about her, or about things they didn't want her to hear, or to fight, they'd stopped speaking Yiddish. Her mother had continued to speak Yiddish with her sister, Csilla's aunt Ilona, but that was the entirety of the Yiddish left after the war, after the Shoah: soft words between sisters in the early mornings, over cups of coffee and in the bathroom, where one brushed the other's hair.

When her parents died, so did the Yiddish in their home.

Csilla had only the river left and its quiet, ceaseless murmurings.

Still, as she did every morning, Csilla waited, listening to the apartment as if she could hear it speak, as if something might have shifted overnight while the earth turned slowly. As if time would rewind.

She wanted time to rewind, but she didn't know where she'd stop it if she could. She'd go back to four years ago, before Stalin died, before her parents were detained and murdered by the Hungarian secret police, the ÁVH, for a crime she was sure they hadn't committed—the crime of dual loyalty, of Zionism. She'd go back ten years, to her father's joining the Hungarian Workers' Party and the security services, working alongside the people who'd murder him six years later. She'd go back to a time when she did not know her father's crimes, revealed to her only after his death. She had not understood what an architect he had been of other families' destruction until the place he built destroyed her own.

She'd go back fourteen years, to a time when they might have been able to flee Hungary, escape to Israel or Yugoslavia or somewhere less terrible, less painful, where they wouldn't have had to endure the things they endured in the war, where they would have been free to come and go as they wished. As she was not here.

Now, when she and her aunt escaped in two weeks, she'd be leaving the bodies of her parents behind, in a gentile graveyard, where she could not leave stones on their markers. She would say Kaddish for them in a different time zone, on soil they'd never know.

She would live somewhere else, and her parents would rest forever here in Hungary, a Communist country ruled by the strict and unwavering hand of the Russians.

You cannot change the world, she reminded herself. *You can only survive the one you're in.*

But sometimes the world around her changed, and survival in it felt different. Yesterday, this world, the one she was in, had teetered. This morning, she wanted to know what side it'd fallen on.

Yesterday, her parents, along with the others executed in the same purge four years earlier, had been reburied in a state funeral, exonerated of the charges against them, rehabilitated in the eyes of the State. She and her aunt had stood, blank-faced, as they'd practiced for the four years since Simon and Éva Tisza were killed, all in black, in a gray city, and watched bodies they'd never seen lowered into graves they had not chosen in a funeral that was not in any way Jewish.

Four years ago, her father had been declared an enemy of the People. What they could hurl at him, they did. And Csilla had grown up in the shadow of her father's crimes, both real and imaginary. A Jew. A Titoist. A Zionist.

He was reburied yesterday, and so the Party admitted that they'd arrested, tried, convicted and executed him on false pretenses.

A mistake, they said.

It wasn't a mistake. Mistakes could be rectified. Death could not be undone.

Only last night, when they were home, safe inside their own apartment, did Csilla and her aunt whisper the Mourner's Kaddish, just as they did every year on the yahrzeit of her parents' deaths. When her aunt went to sleep, tears still sliding down her cheeks like rain on windowpanes, Csilla had gone to their bureau and fished around in the top drawer. In the back corner, in one of her father's old gloves, were rolls of forint notes.

It hadn't been just one thing that made Csilla and Ilona think they needed to leave Hungary. It'd been, like most things were, the slow and gradual accumulation of hurts and wants and needs that couldn't be fulfilled by anything found here. And now that Csilla had graduated five months ago, it was easier to purport to travel—and to leave instead.

It stung to consider leaving Budapest, where her family had lived for hundreds of years.

It burned to consider staying in Budapest, where her family had died for hundreds of years.

But some time after they received notice that her parents would be reburied, Csilla realized that she couldn't put up with the charade any longer. She couldn't stay here pretending that everyone around her was not at fault, and she couldn't stay here pretending that she herself was not also at fault. Ilona had only nodded, a stubborn glint in her eyes, and together they saved their wages, Csilla from the newspaper and Ilona from cleaning the apartment building, the best they could.

She knew others who'd done it. There were agencies set up to help the Jews on this side of the postwar divide between East and West.

She thought no one would notice, or care, now that her parents' records had been expunged. It was good timing.

They had nearly enough, and they had train tickets to Belgrade, ostensibly to visit relatives, for November 1.

But Csilla had felt it in the crowd yesterday, the knife's edge of tension. She hadn't expected that. It terrified her. It could ruin everything. And at the same time, she wanted to slide her finger down the blade and see how it cut.

Csilla had heard everyone murmuring behind her yesterday, and when they'd walked back through the crowd, quiet and dark and appropriately mournful, a man had shouted, "What else was a mistake? What else was a lie?"

She could hear his words as clear as if he was shouting them in her apartment now.

What else was a lie?

He hadn't fired shots.

But a gun had been loaded.

Csilla wanted to be out of Hungary before that gun went off. They could be in Israel if everything went according to their plans.

If nothing happened. If her father didn't start fires from beyond the grave.

Careful not to wake her aunt, Csilla slipped from beneath the quilts and put her feet on the cold floor. When she stood, her nightgown, bunched around her waist, fell to her knees. She went to the window and pulled back the sheer curtain to stare out at the river. It was moonlight silver, pocked with dark waves. From here, it looked like fabric, bolts of velvet draped for miles between two old cities turned one: Buda and Pest.

She would miss the river.

But there would be other rivers.

(They would not be the same as the Duna. No river could be like the Duna. Not to Csilla.)

The river's whispers picked up in urgency.

Her gaze flicked down to the streets, where almost everyone was moving. Two children kicked a ball back and forth on one of the little side streets, and others walked in a stream toward the main avenues and the tram lines. Only one person was standing still. On the corner across from her apartment, a casually dressed man read a folded copy of *Szabad Nép*, the newspaper for which she worked. From where he was standing, he'd be able to see her.

And then he looked up, as if he could hear her thoughts.

She dropped the curtain and stepped back.

"Fool," she whispered to herself.

She'd thought that her parents' cases being cleared meant she could relax, that she didn't have anything to fear from the secret police. But here they were, right outside her apartment, watching her for the first time since her parents had been disappeared.

What had she done to catch their attention? Had they found out about her and Ilona's plans to escape? Csilla had made arrangements by letter with a Jewish man, a friend of a friend of a friend, who lived in Belgrade, who knew people at the Jewish Agency who could get them to Israel. She'd hoped that the letters wouldn't be intercepted, but they might have been. There must be a thousand secret police between here and Belgrade, on both sides of the border.

She turned her back on the river, trying to resist the urge to peer through the curtains. He'd still be there. The ÁVH didn't give up that easily. She forced herself to go through her normal routine. Her heartbeat pounded in her fingertips.

In the bathroom, Csilla ran her fingers through her wild moon curls and braided them quickly. She tied her hair off swiftly, tightly, so it would not come apart unexpectedly. Though there was no color in Budapest, Hungarians tended toward dark hair and dark brows, and so even in the city's seemingly permanent grayscale, her hair made her recognizable.

Across the hall, a door slammed. It jolted Csilla, making her drop a bobby pin into the sink. A shiver of panic ran up her spine. István, who lived across the hall, was better than any alarm clock. When she was a child, this entire floor had been her family's apartment. But when Communism came, the officials had nationalized the building and chopped up the apartments into smaller ones. István had the real kitchen and the real dining room, with the bay window she had loved more than anything. Across the hall, Rózsa had the east-facing bedroom that had belonged to Csilla's grandparents (z"l). István rose every morning at dawn and left his apartment every morning at a quarter to seven, slamming the door behind him. And if Csilla heard the door slam while she was still in her nightgown, she was late.

There could be no such thing as lateness. Not here. Not for Csilla.

The man across the street would know if she was late.

He could arrest her for—truly—anything he wanted. He didn't need a specific cause. But lateness could be one. They'd make up whatever charges they wanted, once they had her.

She couldn't give them an excuse.

She spent her entire life, every waking moment of every day, every step she took outside the apartment, being careful to not attract attention, to not make anyone look up her file with the police, to not make anyone question her loyalty and devotion to the Party or to Hungary.

In two weeks, she wouldn't need to worry about this.

But today, today, she still had to worry. There was still so much, *so much,* she could lose.

What else was a lie?

She pressed a quick kiss to Ilona's cheek, and her aunt's eyes fluttered open. She reached up and clenched her fingers around Csilla's hand.

"I'm late," Csilla whispered, her voice shaking. "And there are eyes outside."

Ilona's eyes widened, and Csilla saw her come fully awake and into herself. "Be safe," she whispered back. "We're so close—"

"I know," interrupted Csilla. "I have to go."

And then she slipped out of the apartment, locked the door, tucked the keys into her purse and trotted down the stairs.

Her hand touched the doorknob to the outside world. She took a deep breath to steady herself, but her fingers trembled anyway.

The river whispered to her.

She tried not to listen to it.

Outside, she did not look at the man on the opposite street corner. He followed her. Of course he did. She walked quicker, her footsteps as fast as the beat of her heart.

Around her, the buildings blurred against each other and the sky. It was misty in the mornings, which only made the gray of the city more disorienting.

Csilla was young—but she remembered some of the Before. Not just before the secret police, but Before. What stunned Csilla the most—in the rare moments when she slowed down to think about it—was how everyone had accepted the changes without much fuss.

She'd been four when the colors began to leach out of Budapest, running like rainbow streams through all the streets toward the river. There'd been articles in the papers and talk in the coffeehouses and whispers on the corners. There'd been inquiries and speeches and radio programs. People had congregated in the streets, watching the color drain as if from a face at the news of a loved one's death. It drained first from the buildings, the streets, the art on the walls, the clothing.

She remembered when it drained from people. She thought her parents were dying when they turned into moving sepia photographs.

People talked and talked, and the government convened panel after panel of experts, but no answers were found. No reasons came to light. And soon the people stopped congregating. The radio programs switched to more timely news. The politicians turned their eyes.

Life had continued.

People had still gone to their jobs.

People still married and celebrated and separated and died as if the world hadn't changed all the rules right around them.

By the time the war ended, she was seven, and Budapest was stained in sepia and sapphire. The blue stained walls and floors. The river was the color of a vein beating beneath the skin on the tender underside of a wrist. The longer the Soviets stayed, the more the sepia melted into gray. When the Soviets stayed for good, even the blue fled. It didn't drain like the greens and yellows and oranges and reds and purples before the war. It was just there, and then it was gone, leaving the people of Budapest wondering if it'd ever been there at all.

When the secret police came, they slipped so effortlessly into the fabric of society that the people wondered—not aloud, of course—if they'd been there all along.

Csilla remembered that too, as the secret policeman followed her through the city.

She remembered her father telling her, "Things will get back to normal."

But that was a lie, like so many other things he'd told her.

> Truth is a shadow. It's cast over everything, but it's hard to touch and impossible to hold.
>
> —The Journal of Simon Tisza, May 1943

CHAPTER TWO

CSILLA

October 17, 1956

He was still following her.

In her mind, she could hear her mother say, *Breathe in peace and exhale unrest.* She used to tell Csilla and Simon that every Shabbat, before she struck a match and lit the candles.

She couldn't think of anything other than that somehow the ÁVH had found out about her and Ilona's plans to flee Hungary. She didn't know how, but that was the only possibility.

Still, she knew as well as the next person that they didn't need reasons. They might not know, and they might disappear her anyway.

To her left, the river whispered to her incessantly, like a heart murmur she could hear in her own ears. Something tugged at her, like the river was reaching for her, and she could not ignore it. And she thought, if it came to it, she could jump into the river. Again.

She turned left, toward the river, past homes that had been bombed out or were still abandoned, their residents never coming home, and past houses that had once belonged to Jewish friends of hers but were now occupied by gentile Hungarians who had stood by when their neighbors were taken for the slaughter.

And all at once, the buildings ended and the Duna glittered in front of her in the early-morning light. The sight of the river nearly erased all the frenetic, desperate thoughts in her head.

The river sighed softly when she came into view.

She did not know if a river could miss a person, but if any river could, it would be this one.

This morning, the river appeared almost shadowed, a shade ever so slightly darker than silver. *Pewter,* Csilla thought. The color of a blade.

The world tilted, wobbling on that edge.

What else was a lie?

She'd seen the river glinting like this before. To escape the Nazis, when deportation finally came for the Hungarian Jews in May 1944, her father had jumped, dragging her mother and Csilla with him, from the Chain Bridge and into the silver river. She was six, and she still wore her hair in two pigtail braids tied off with ribbons that might have been as pink as a sunrise. When she saw the river, she could still remember the scream ripped from her chest on plummeting into the cold, cold water.

But the memory did not scare her.

The man still behind her did.

She crossed the tram tracks and walked along the banks. She

could see in the shadows on the silver river that the man, the secret police, had caught up with her. He was only a few paces behind her. The river hissed in her mind, and she felt the sound splinter across her ribs.

Her tongue was stuck to the roof of her mouth.

I'm so close, she thought again, dizzy. *We're so close.*

She'd done everything right. She had. She'd thought that her parents' exoneration would lift the cloud of suspicion that had hung over her for the last four years, provide the opening she needed to escape. But instead, here they were, the day after the funeral.

She could leap into the river if she wanted to. If she needed to. It'd save her again. Maybe it was a sign that it was the same shade of silver as that day. Maybe it wanted her to jump in. Maybe it knew she'd need to leap.

But if she jumped, she and Ilona would never leave Hungary.

And if he disappeared her, she and Ilona would never leave Hungary.

He was only a few paces behind her.

No one else seemed to notice.

There was a car idling up on the road that ran along the river. She couldn't watch the car and watch the man's shadow on the river at the same time.

Her pulse pounded in her fingertips. The blood rushed out of her head to her belly, pooling.

She needed to cut back into the city. They could find her anywhere, but she might have a better chance of shaking him for now if she could get back into the city. Then she could make a plan. She couldn't plan now, with him this close behind her. The only choice she had here was the river.

"Csilla!" called a voice.

She flinched instinctively, but the voice wasn't coming from behind her. A young man with moppish hair and long, gangly limbs waved to her as he jumped down the small wall and strode toward her, an easy smile on his face and a casual gracefulness to his walk.

"Csilla," he said warmly, even though she did not recognize him.

Secret police, she thought desperately.

But she was frozen.

All this time surviving, all this survival she'd already done, and it'd be a waste because she couldn't make herself move. She couldn't make herself go into the river or scream or run away.

The new young man took her hands in his, squeezing them. He kissed both of her cheeks, and on the second cheek he whispered, "Play along. I can help you."

And then his lips grazed her cheek again.

She breathed in steadiness. She exhaled unrest.

She lifted her face to him, forcing lightness into her voice. "I'm sorry I'm late! I overslept."

He slipped her hand into the crook of his elbow and began walking her away from the secret police behind her. "It happens. You needed the rest. Good work comes from good rest."

In the shadows on the silver river, the secret policeman was falling behind her. She exhaled.

The stranger squeezed her hand a bit and whispered, "You must continue talking."

She swallowed and raised her voice. "You're right, I know you're right. I'm sorry, comrade."

There was no reason to trust this man. He might be secret police too, leading her to the car or to somewhere else she didn't want to be. But she had the choice of the river, the man behind her and the man who sounded reassuring. Something in her tugged her forward with the stranger.

She listened to the river. It wasn't hissing as it'd done for the secret policeman. Its murmurs were warm and soothing.

The stranger raised his voice, telling her some story about his parents and their adventures to acquire a bottle of pálinka the night before and his little brother's ruined school uniform. He was filling the space, she thought, and she wasn't sure how much of this was true, but he was a gallant speaker. The more she listened to him, though, his Hungarian wasn't quite right. He said her name in a slightly drawn-out way, *chee-lah*, like he was lingering over the first syllable, while everyone else she knew said it like a bite. His Hungarian was too perfect, lacking any dialect, any accent.

It's learned, not native, she realized.

He could be secret police. Or he could be a spy, and she could be in more trouble than she thought.

But if he was a spy, he wasn't trying to lead her astray. He started to slow down, and she realized, dizzy with relief, that he'd led her to the steps of the newspaper. They stopped there and didn't continue across the street.

The newspaper building was drab and uninteresting, flat-faced and droll like all the postwar buildings. And right across the street was 60 Stalin Street, the headquarters of the ÁVH, the security forces of Hungary, her father's former place of work and the place where both of her parents died.

Her father's hands had shaped this country, its brilliance and its evils.

And this country's hands had shaped him, his brilliance and his evils.

And those hands still worked and shaped and killed in that building.

"Csilla," said the stranger, pulling her gaze back to him. He was so close to her, still strangely charming and beautiful, his cheekbones chiseled in his face and his eyes bright beneath his moppish hair. He looked familiar, but she couldn't place him.

If she hadn't been watching him so carefully, she would have missed the way his eyes slid off hers for just a heartbeat, noting the secret policeman behind her.

"Still there," he murmured, his lips not moving. Then he smiled, and she knew it was a smile for the policeman's sake, but she wished he was smiling like that at her. It made her want to smile back.

"I'll pick you up after work," he told her loudly. "We'll talk more then. Promise."

She frowned at him, and his eyes pleaded with hers. He wanted to talk to her—about what? Who he was? Another secret-police tail? She didn't know if she could take the risk—but he'd saved her from throwing herself into the river or being disappeared this morning.

She felt like she owed him.

"If you insist," she said, trying to make her voice sound playful. But she hadn't any practice, and it came out high-pitched and squeaky, like she was panicked.

He didn't seem to mind or notice. He kissed her cheeks again. This time he whispered, "Walk in with someone. Be safe. See you later."

And he let go of her hands. He gave her an encouraging smile, and with great effort, though he was still a complete stranger to her, she stepped away from him. She turned, scanning the other people heading into work, hoping to see one of her friends. But most of the faces were unfamiliar, and she could not risk the unfamiliar.

She caught sight of someone whose name she knew, even if she didn't know him very well, and she called out to him, "Comrade Szendrey!"

CHAPTER THREE

AZRIEL

OCTOBER 17, 1956

He waited until the door had shut behind Csilla, knowing that her safety in the newspaper building was an illusion he was willing to buy into temporarily. When he finally turned, the secret policeman was there, just as Azriel had known he'd be. He was a thin and sallow-faced man with cruel eyes. He wasn't one of the men who worked for the secret police because it was a good job, the way Csilla's father had.

This was one of the men that Azriel was sure he knew from the war. This man had undoubtedly been a member of the Arrow Cross, Hungary's Nazi Party. This man joined the secret police because he liked being cruel.

"Hello," Azriel said calmly. "I suppose you'll want me to follow you."

The man growled like he was disappointed that Azriel wasn't going to fight. But Azriel had no reason to fear this man, and so he had no reason to fight the man. He followed the man willingly, right across the street into the belly of the beast.

There is a selfishness, a hunger and thirst for power among some Party members that disgusts me. It pulls them away from what they should be working for: the People. Do they not understand that government is merely a tool? When will they realize it? It's a contagious worldview. I feel it creeping into my colleagues too—András in particular. And sometimes I think about myself and what I have done and created and supported, and worry it has crept into my own work. But I still sit in every meeting and fight for the People, for the Revolution, for all the things I can be. The short-term outlook is grim, and dire, and ugly. But all things are. Nothing good can be seen up close. I have to believe that by continuing to sit amongst these craven men, bearing their insolence, I can be an advocate in the long term for what is righteous.

—The Journal of Simon Tisza, December 1950

CHAPTER FOUR

CSILLA

October 17, 1956

Márton Szendrey was mostly harmless. He was middle-aged, perhaps the same age her father would have been if he was still alive. He was rounded in every possible direction and mostly bald. Among the staff, he had a reputation for being a congenial fellow, if a bit daft. He wrote fluff pieces for the paper, which meant he wrote fluff pieces for the Party. She was often assigned to type up his work, but they'd never interacted directly.

"Good morning, Comrade Szendrey," she murmured.

"Good morning, Comrade Csilla," he said, sounding wary and surprised.

He knew who she was, and the familiarity of her name on his tongue disconcerted her. That was unexpected. His eyes were more keen than his stories tended to be.

Maybe, she thought to herself, *he is an informant.*

Her body tightened. This felt suddenly dangerous, like thin ice, and she didn't—couldn't, not this close to freedom—fall through. She'd barely escaped this morning. Good girls, quiet girls, harmless girls didn't get angry, didn't raise their voices, didn't step outside the lines.

But almost as soon as she'd found the right soft and gentle and soothing words to apologize for bothering him, Szendrey seemed to realize how he'd sounded. He turned a careful smile to her. "You've had quite the week, comrade. I am surprised to see you here today. How are you, after yesterday?"

It was an olive branch in a city where no olives grew.

"I'm well, thank you," she murmured.

He glanced over his shoulder at the door. "I did not realize you knew me."

"I've been working on your stories for the last few months," she said. Almost since she started.

"I know," he said. Then his voice dropped low, and his lips barely moved, so if anyone was watching them, they wouldn't know he was speaking. "You look pale—paler, I suppose. Are you sure you're well, Csilla?"

There was no reason to trust this man, and in here, she couldn't hear the river whispering to her. She couldn't tell him she had been followed. "As you said, I've had quite the week."

He studied her with those keen eyes, but he didn't push her. "I hope you have a good day, comrade."

"Thank you," she managed.

He stepped away from her, holding his badge up to the security guards as a courtesy, though he was already sailing past them and up the stairs.

One of the security guards, Elek, hoisted his gun a little higher on his shoulder and gave Csilla a tentative smile. She wasn't quite in the mood for Elek's flirting, not after being tailed this morning and being saved by a strange stranger, but she didn't really have a choice.

"Good morning, Elek," she murmured, walking past the security desk.

"Good morning, Csilla," he said, a little too eagerly. His fellow guard, a burly fellow named János, snorted at him, but she didn't hear Elek say anything to him. He likely hadn't noticed. That was the thing about boys with guns. They felt powerful. That feeling could be dangerous.

"Csilla," Elek said again.

She turned around, hoping her face was a picture of bright expectation instead of mounting dread. His excitement flickered, and his brow knit in confusion. She wasn't pulling it off well, then.

"Would you want to—get a drink with me?" Elek asked quickly.

"Now? So early in the morning!" She shaped her words into a teasing tone so he'd think that she wasn't turning him down.

It worked. His shoulders relaxed. "Perhaps sometime . . ."

"Perhaps," she said, feigning coyness. "Ask me again soon."

There was a darkness to his cheeks, as if someone had taken a pencil and colored lightly over his skin, and she knew that this was called a flush, or perhaps it was a blush. It'd once had a color. He rocked back and forth on his feet. "I will."

"See you later," she said, ducking her head. A few moon-colored curls escaped her pins and fell in front of her face.

"See you later," he said to her, a little breathless.

Flirting was often a survival mechanism. Elek was sweet. He wouldn't kill her without cause, and he wouldn't turn her in without cause, but Csilla knew as well as most that just about anything could be cause.

This morning was the perfect example of that.

Upstairs, she slipped inside the typists' room and said to Mária, the typist in charge of the other girls, "I'm sorry I am late, comrade."

Mária had been opening her mouth to lambaste Csilla in front of the other girls, but she closed it, frowning, and nodded.

When Csilla took her seat, one of her two close friends, Aliz, leaned over to place a small toffee on the corner of Csilla's desk.

Csilla's fingers closed on it immediately, smooth to the touch and almost instantly sticky under the warmth of her hand. "Aliz! Where did you get this?"

Aliz gave her a secret, sly smile. "I have an entire bag of them."

Csilla popped it into her mouth, closing her eyes as the coffee and sugar hit her tongue. She sighed with relief. "Thank you. I needed that."

"I thought you might," Aliz said, giving her a small smile. It was the only acknowledgment her friend had made of the funeral. "Feri," she said, naming her husband, "got them for Tibor. He didn't know sugar would just make the baby cry louder."

"He doesn't know a lot of things about the baby," muttered Zsuzsanna, on the other side of Csilla.

Aliz shot her a look over Csilla. "He knows as much as he should."

Zsu's lips tightened around whatever she was going to say. Csilla was used to this tension. Aliz's views of motherhood were not modern ones. She still bore the brunt of her baby's colicky nature, while her husband slept in a different room. Zsu liked to call herself the modern girl among them. And sometimes that caused friction between her and Aliz.

"Enough," Csilla said to Zsu, who looked put out but still complied.

Zsu and Csilla had been friends for years, and they'd met and immediately befriended the ever-optimistic Aliz in June, when they'd started at the paper. She was four years older than them, but Csilla felt the difference only when Aliz talked about her son.

Of the two, Csilla was closer to Zsu, who'd lost her uncle

to the secret police the year before Csilla's parents were taken. Their adolescence had been marked by those disappearances, their social circles limited to the extended family of other dissidents and enemies of the People. Zsu didn't hold it against the ÁVH the way Csilla did, though. Her fiancé worked for them, and he didn't seem to think, or mind, that his impending marriage to Zsu would affect his promotions. To Zsu, the secret police was a symptom, not the problem.

To Csilla, it was the problem. Every inch of it was the problem. And it was just across the street, visible if she turned her head just a little to the right, her gaze moving past Aliz to the window.

"I thought you might not come today," Zsu whispered. "You could have skipped, I am sure."

She couldn't have, Csilla knew. But what would have happened this morning if she hadn't left for work? He wouldn't have followed her. Would he have moved to disappear her and Ilona in broad daylight? The image of his shadow on the river creeping closer to her trickled ice down her spine. She shuddered. The car had been so close. He had been so close.

Csilla glanced to see where Mária was in the room, and then she leaned over, whispering, "I was followed today."

In Hungary, she did not have to say by whom.

"Goodness!" Zsu exclaimed, and immediately crouched in her seat, grimacing as she glanced around. Some of the other typists were glaring at them, but no one scolded them.

On Csilla's other side, Aliz leaned in. "But why? They were exonerated."

"I don't know," Csilla whispered. But that was a lie. She knew. She'd played by all the rules for so many years, but it'd been brazen to think that she could get away with escaping Hungary just because her parents had been exonerated posthumously.

"They're worried," Zsu said, "because of Poland."

Poland seemed so far away, but the other country had been dealing with unrest all summer, and it'd continued into the fall. Like others, Zsu had clung to the news about Poland eagerly. Csilla hadn't, worried that reading too much of it would cause suspicion.

"Oh?" she asked lightly.

"Don't worry," said Zsu, with false sweetness. "Gerő would never let that happen here."

Ernő Gerő was the Party secretary, and despite assurances in the wake of Stalin's death three years ago that things would change, the Hungarian Working People's Party secretaries, and thus the prime ministers, had stayed firmly in the pocket of Moscow, something that never sat well with anyone in Hungary. The current prime minister, András Hegedüs, was young but ineffective.

At least Hegedüs was better than Mátyás Rákosi, the prime minister they'd all grown up with. Rákosi had fashioned himself into the Hungarian Stalin—in all that that meant. And while he'd lost some power after Stalin's death, he'd spent a majority of his energy ensuring that his successor, Imre Nagy, was unsuccessful at reforming Hungary.

It was on Rákosi's orders that Csilla's parents were tried and killed. And though he was far away in Russia now, his fingerprints and his legacy covered everything. Csilla didn't think there was a Hungarian alive who didn't know someone who had been arrested, convicted or disappeared during Rákosi's reign.

That included her friends. No one talked about it much, but Csilla knew they'd understand how frightened she'd been of being disappeared. She wasn't the only one with that fear.

She wasn't sure if she should tell them about the stranger that had helped her, but she did, leaving out any details other than that he'd pretended to know her. She did not tell them he seemed familiar. She did not tell them he knew her name.

"I just thought they'd leave you alone after the reburial," murmured Aliz at the end of the story.

"Aliz!" Zsu snapped. "We talked about this."

Csilla straightened. "What did you talk about?"

"The funeral," Aliz said, casting Zsu a nervous look. "Zsu thought we should ignore it."

"Because it must be so painful," Zsu added in clarification.

Pretend it never happened. Ignore it. Actively forget it. The idea was bitter in Csilla's mouth. And then, with a start, she realized that was what she'd been doing all morning, since the moment she woke up. She'd been hoping to continue as she had, an act of forgetting, of unremembrance.

What else was a lie?

"It is painful," Csilla said quietly, keeping her eyes on the pile of paper in the tray beside her typewriter. "It is." She looked up. "Thank you for coming, Zsu, and you too, Aliz." She gave them a watery smile. "Thank you. It means a lot to me. It means *everything* to me."

She did not share her parents with anyone still living but Ilona, the river and the Communist Party. It felt strange to be speaking of them here, even without their names. Just their bodies, in wooden coffins, in a gentile graveyard. But she did not want to pretend that yesterday hadn't happened, not any more than she wanted to pretend that she hadn't been rattled by the secret police this morning.

She knew that her mother had never committed any crimes and that her father's crimes were not the ones for which he was put to death. And she knew that she hadn't committed any crimes. And she knew, though the Party would never say this, that if they decided she had committed crimes, then the truth wouldn't matter.

Still, there were things that were true and there were things that were not. The river could sometimes save people. That was true. The man who saved her today was not a native Hungarian. That was also true. She had narrowly escaped being disappeared this morning. That was true.

She needed just two more weeks. November 1, they'd be on a train to Belgrade. It'd be that easy. It would be that hard.

That was true too.

"You're welcome," Zsu said, while Aliz said, "Of course we were there. Of course."

They turned back to their work just before Mária, their supervisor, walked down the aisle with her quick, alert steps, and for the time being, Csilla pushed the secret police, the stranger and the river out of her mind.

She'd worked as a typist since she'd graduated from secondary school in the spring, and while she couldn't say she liked her job, it kept her mind from wandering, and it gave the illusion that she was a good citizen of Hungary. She'd joined the Communist Party the way that they wanted her to, even though she could hear her mother's quiet insistence that they couldn't pass a law requiring one to be a member of the Party and that forced allegiance undermined the Party's own mission. She'd joined because it was safer. Layers of protection, like armor, keeping her safe. And alive.

The room was already full of the *flackery-clack* sound of typewriters, and in a certain rhythm, it reminded her of chattering teeth. She dared not close her eyes when the memory floated to the surface. She always waited a moment, holding her breath, and it'd pass.

It did not pass. It lingered for hours, a biting memory that fogged her focus.

At lunch, Zsu returned to the story Csilla had shared this morning and started digging for details on the stranger. She wanted Csilla to sketch a picture of him.

"She can't sketch him," hissed Aliz, appalled. "What if he's a wanted man and someone turns her in? She's on some sort of watch list! Zsu, be serious. She needs to stay safe."

Csilla wished she knew why the ÁVH was interested in her now. She wished she could ask Zsu to ask her fiancé, who worked across the street.

"Perhaps he's mad," Zsu whispered, with the kind of awe that suggested she read only the most romantic takes on madness.

"Perhaps," agreed Csilla.

But she did not think he was mad.

"What if he's a spy, Csilla?" Aliz said suddenly.

They were always being warned about Western spies who'd weaken the revolutionary spirit. Csilla didn't think she was likely to be a target of a spy—surely they went for people who worked in government or some such thing—but she didn't want Aliz to keep digging. "I thought about that too."

"If he's a spy, you ought to turn him in," Aliz said. "Then you'd be back in the ÁVH's good graces. I heard from Júlia that her sister did that and it worked."

In a place where information was currency, gossip like this spread like wildfire. This was all they had. And if it was true, Csilla could not blame Júlia's sister. It was the way Hungary was constructed, on past mistakes and believed lies and the kind of acceptance that comes from a line of tanks, a gun, a bag over one's head, a family member who never comes home. One's own safety was more important than someone else's safety.

She could see why a lie was often more valuable than the truth.

In this colorless Hungary, no one wanted the truth.

And so Csilla was glad she'd withheld the information that she had promised the stranger to meet him after work. Especially now that Aliz thought she should turn him in as a possible spy.

"She can't accuse him of being a spy," Zsu said, shocked. "They'll hang him."

"If he's a spy, I hope they hang him," Aliz said fiercely.

Csilla loved Aliz, valued Aliz's friendship, but there were parts of being a good Party girl that Aliz clung to a little too fiercely. She did all the right things. She went to school, she got a job, she got married and she gave Hungary a son. That she did not have a happy marriage didn't seem to be an issue. Maybe that too was in service to the Party. She saw good in the Party and in Hungary, where Csilla could see only history and one bad decision after another. Aliz would stay, always, in Hungary and for Hungary. Csilla could only think of leaving. Of surviving until November 1.

If she survived the next two weeks, and that was no longer a given, she'd have to leave Aliz and Zsu behind forever. She could write them once she was abroad, but she couldn't tell them ahead of time. It'd put them in danger from the same man who had followed Csilla that morning. Her heart ached to think of the betrayal they'd feel.

"That seems to be assuming many things," Zsu was saying. "For one, that he's a spy."

Csilla swallowed. She needed to change the subject. "Didn't you think it was unusually warm yesterday? It barely feels like October."

"I heard we'll get our first snow this week," Aliz said.

"Who'd you hear that from?" Zsu asked.

"A woman on the tram this morning," Aliz said cheerfully.

"If I ever want to know what anyone in this city said at any given point," Zsu grumbled, "I'll just ask you."

Aliz laughed.

And just like that, they moved on.

But Csilla did not. Csilla could not. Her spoon moved in slow circles through the gray broth of her halászlé, the fleshy white of the fish floating to the surface, and her mind slipped back to yesterday's funeral, the anxiety of hoping Ilona kept herself together, the roll of bills in her drawer that would pay their way out of Hungary and the thud of the dirt against the wooden casket.

What else was a lie?

She wished she'd seen who shouted that yesterday.

She knew what she'd say in reply now.

What is the truth?

That was the question they should be asking.

That was the question she wanted to ask the stranger this afternoon. She wanted to know his truth. She wanted to know why he'd saved her today. She deserved the truth, she decided.

Some part of Csilla hummed, a vibrant thrill that ran through her body, like the moments before a symphony, when the orchestra was warming up. She wanted to talk to him again. She shouldn't. She knew that. She was vulnerable, as was her aunt, and there was a wad of cash at the back of her sock drawer along with two tickets out of Hungary.

What is the truth?

"And Csilla's in, of course," said Zsu cheerfully, interrupting Csilla's thoughts and jolting her back to the cafeteria.

Csilla raised a single eyebrow in her friend's direction. "I'm in for what?"

Zsu widened her smile. "Dancing tonight. I hear Elek's going to be there."

"I feel suddenly faint with fever. I might have to go home," Csilla said with a grimace. She pressed a hand to her forehead and turned to Aliz. "Don't I feel warm? I feel warm."

36

Zsu slipped her arm through Csilla's, giving her a quick squeeze. "We'll find you someone worth dancing with tonight. Promise me you'll come out, Csilla. Please?"

Csilla could never resist Zsu's pleas. "Oh fine."

In two weeks, when she left, her promises would turn to lies. At least tonight, she'd give them a true one.

It feels strange that this time last year, I could not work outside of the ghetto. I spent my days teaching mathematics to children to give them the illusion of normalcy. Most of those children are dead, I think. When I dream, I dream of their faces. I should have taught them something useful. Something real. I don't know if it would have saved them. It is still so soon after the war. Perhaps people will come home still. Éva spends most of her days writing letters, looking for her family. She might still have family. She might never forgive me for taking her and Csilla into the river and leaving the rest of her family behind to go on the train. But I only have two hands. I only have two hands.

I need to get back to a new normal. Csilla is back in school, and I am applying for jobs. I do not want to go back to the university. I feel called (though perhaps *dragged* and *pulled* and *forced* would be better words) toward work in the new Communist state. I remember only a few years ago when it was dangerous to be a Communist in Hungary. Now it is a point of pride to say I've been a Communist longer than most of the people currently joining the Party.

I applied for a job in the security services, as I know György works there and he can put in a good word for me. Besides, the security services have never had an issue with hiring Jews, which I suppose is a mark in my favor. Even after the events of the last couple of years, this country seems loath to hire Jews.

I do have some ideas on how to reform the security services, especially in the wake of the war. It is absolutely vital that the security services be an institution of trust among the People, their arm to rooting out the evil that seeks to undermine the People's Revolution. The People cannot be distracted from their good work and goodwill to do this, and so that is what the security services must do. Secure the Revolution for all the People. It doesn't do this yet, but I believe that with some attention, it could become one of the most honored bastions of the People.

We must find a way forward out of the despair of the last few years.

And by that I mean that I need to find a way forward out of the despair of the last few years.

—The Journal of Simon Tisza, August 1945

CHAPTER FIVE

CSILLA

O**CTOBER** 17, 1956

As the day wore on, Csilla replayed the events of the morning. In some moments, she remembered the stranger as older than her, and in some moments, she remembered him as younger. She thought of him on Stalin Street and thought perhaps his hair had a color. She couldn't decide what color it was. Sometimes when she thought of it she was sure his hair had been red. Then she'd think about it and decide it must have been gold. He was kaleidoscopic, a rainbow, in her memory.

It frightened her, the way that he appeared slightly different in her own mind each time. Here, in a place void of color and full of secret police and information as currency, she could trust very little. Truth was invented by the powers that be, and sometimes lies were truth and truth was lies. But through all of that, she'd always been able to trust her own mind, her own memory.

She'd lost something that morning. And she wasn't sure how to name what was gone.

And worse, when she thought about what he said to her at the end, at the doors to the newspaper, she thought he might have spoken in English.

That was impossible, of course. She did not speak English. She wouldn't have understood him. She'd remember not understanding him. (Wouldn't she?)

She'd only heard English once before, many, many years ago, on the dusty floor of the attic of the apartment building, where they shouldn't have been playing. Her best friend in the ghetto, Nati, had lifted a piece of glass to the sky and thrown a glint of light around the room. In accented English, she'd said, "Let there be light."

She'd taught Csilla that phrase, and that phrase only, in English. Nati said she learned it from her father, who had been taken and shot by the river, so Csilla hadn't been able to find out why that phrase.

She'd asked her own father, who'd said, "There doesn't need to be a reason."

And when she asked her mother, her mother had said, "Maybe that is a message from God that we should go to America. Or England. Somewhere else."

If it'd been a message from God, it hadn't mattered. There was no going to America, or England, or anywhere else.

The window of opportunity had closed with the clang of a gate, and the last bit of hope drowned in the river.

There'd been a time after the war, before they'd known that Ilona was the only other surviving family member, when Csilla thought they would leave.

But then her father got a job in the new government the Soviets set up during their occupation, and he started to rise.

And now he would never leave Hungary.

Csilla had learned her lesson. Another window of opportunity had opened, and she wouldn't miss it. Neither would Ilona.

At the end of the day, she followed Zsu and Aliz out into the fading light. She was oblivious to her friends' chatter as she scanned the corner and streets for the stranger from the morning. But he was nowhere to be seen.

He wasn't coming, she realized with a jolt. The knowledge burst the bubble of excitement and curiosity that'd been growing throughout the day. She deflated, and Zsu noticed.

"Are you well?" Zsu demanded. She didn't wait for Csilla to reply. "You've had quite a few days. Go home and change. Dancing will do you good."

Csilla took a deep breath. "You're right." She mustered a smile. "I'll see you shortly?"

"Do you want me to walk with you?" Zsu asked. "It's only a little out of my way."

If she were to be disappeared, she wouldn't want Zsu there to be swept up in it. Csilla shook her head with a pasted-on smile. Her friends kissed her cheeks the way that the stranger had this morning, but they didn't whisper to her, and she knew that their hair was in grayscale and they were not kaleidoscopic.

On the other hand, she thought to herself as she walked home, Zsu and Aliz had never broken a promise to her.

The stranger already had.

Walking home was strange, because she did not feel like she was home in Budapest until she stepped across the street into one of the Jewish neighborhoods, either here or on the other side of the river. She remembered the bakery and the kosher butcher on the corner, and this curved street with its two synagogues. Of those who'd survived and stayed, they'd mostly weathered the war in Budapest, in safe houses or with fake papers, or in Csilla's case, in the river. But even as empty as this part of the city felt, even as haunted as it felt, it still felt like a burden lifted from Csilla's shoulders. Here, she could still smile and whisper "Gut Shabbos" on Friday nights as she went home to an apartment that smelled like sweet challah. Home was more complicated than four walls and a bed.

She made it to the apartment without any ÁVH tail that she noticed, though she was sure she'd earn one with the paranoid way she'd looked over her shoulder every few steps. But the creeping, crawling sensation had lingered on the back of her neck, and she couldn't shake the feeling that her fear of people watching her had finally been justified after all these years.

When she opened the door, the apartment was quiet and still, caught in a photograph. There'd be so much she couldn't bring with her when they left. They could only pack one small bag each, nothing more so as not to attract suspicion.

She'd leave behind her parents' wedding china, which had miraculously survived the war, and Ilona would leave behind her children's clothing. They'd leave behind photographs and prayer books and tallits and Shabbat silver and things that held tangible memories. And they'd leave these curtains, lacy and moth-worn, on this window facing the river that she couldn't bring with her.

"Are you standing there all night?" Ilona asked from the doorway to the kitchen. Flour smeared her cheeks.

Csilla stepped in and closed the door behind her. "No one came today, yes?"

Ilona shook her head, wisps of dark hair escaping her bun. She had been a beauty at one time, and she still was. But the war and its aftermath were written all over her face and her body.

"Did he follow you the whole way?" Ilona asked, keeping her voice low.

Csilla weighed her options as she shrugged off her coat and hung it up. She could tell Ilona the truth, or she could tell Ilona something safe so she wouldn't worry.

She hated lying—it made her just like her father, it made her just like them. But sometimes, she thought, lying was a kindness. "He followed me, but that's all," she murmured.

She followed Ilona into the kitchen. Ilona was in the middle of baking bread. But she'd clearly been baking all day. Three loaves sat stacked on the windowsill, wrapped loosely in cloth, and another bowl was covered, with dough rising inside, Csilla suspected.

"Tante," she said slowly. "Did you use all the flour?"

Ilona wiped at her face with her arms. The kitchen was stiflingly hot despite the cool weather outside. "I thought," said her aunt falteringly, "I thought they might disappear you. I didn't know what else to do."

They wouldn't have enough flour for challah this week. It was fine, they'd clearly have other bread to eat, but it still ached a bit. God, if God existed, would forgive them. That was what her mother said about the way they'd had to change their observance in the ghetto.

"I didn't get disappeared," Csilla said gently. "I'm home."

Ilona pressed her hand to her chest, leaving a flour handprint on her dress. "Only two more weeks."

Csilla hoped Ilona could keep her wits about her for that time. She hoped she herself wouldn't get disappeared. She didn't know what Ilona would do if she did. Bake, apparently. It was almost enough to make Csilla laugh.

Ilona sighed. "You look just like her right now. Especially when you're thinking so hard."

Csilla knew that she looked exactly like her mother, except for her hair. She had her mother's cheekbones, her mother's large and deep-set eyes, the pout to her mother's mouth.

"I know," Csilla said softly. Then she gave her aunt a smile and said something that she rarely said aloud. "I miss them too."

Ilona's eyes glittered with tears. "Yesterday was worse than the day they didn't come home."

She knew what her aunt meant.

It'd been so final.

Final for her parents. For Ilona and Csilla.

It was strange the way that something that was final for them felt like it'd opened a crack in the facade of the country. There was opportunity in death.

Csilla knew that. Almost no one from Hungary came home from the camps after 1945. If they did, they rarely returned to Budapest. They emigrated—the United States, Israel, the United Kingdom, other places.

They did not return to the neighbors who'd turned them into ash.

Ilona did, because her sister and her brother-in-law and her niece had survived the war here in this colorless city. And she'd lost everyone. Her husband. Her children. Her parents. Her husband's entire family. Csilla's mother, Éva, and Ilona had been close as children, and they were close as adults. But Csilla's mother always said that Ilona had put a bit of herself into each of her children and everyone she loved. When they were incinerated, so were parts of her. She never came home all the way.

After the war, Csilla's mother wrote letter after letter, called office after office, searching for her parents, her nieces, her nephews, her sister, her brother-in-law. Csilla's father's family had been killed and buried in a mass grave in the countryside. He'd known even before the war ended that they were gone. Csilla's mother had hope, and it burned ferociously, like the oil after the battles of Chanukah.

Only Éva's sister had survived.

Ilona came home haunted. Tiny, wild with grief and almost entirely silent. Csilla remembered when Ilona began to speak again, when she began to eat, when she began to reminisce without sobbing—though she never spoke of her children or her husband. She only spoke of times when she was a child. It was as if she'd erased the nearly twenty years before the end of the war, as if those years hadn't existed.

Just when Csilla thought Ilona might recover enough to start thinking about her future, Csilla's parents were taken. And murdered. Ilona's sister, her best friend, and her brother-in-law, who had been nothing but kind and generous to her. And once again, there had been no bodies to bury.

Her aunt had begun collecting when she'd come home from the camps. It'd started with shoes, hats, scarves. Things easily stored and hidden. Then it'd become dolls. There were dolls, bought from other people and found in abandoned apartments and squirreled away from God only knows where, all over the apartment. Then it'd been cups and bottles—glass ones, nothing else—and those were stacked on every surface in the kitchen.

Csilla was too tired to care, truly, or argue, and what could she say? When she'd tried to throw something away once, her aunt had shrieked and sobbed, holding her stomach as if Csilla had ripped a child from her arms.

And her children *had* been ripped from her arms.

Csilla let her collect, let her try to fill the bottomless hole of grief inside her. There was nothing else to do. She couldn't ask for more from her aunt.

It wasn't like she didn't do the same thing, trying to cope in her own ineffective ways.

"I'm going to go out with Zsu and Aliz," Csilla said softly. "Will you be okay here, on your own?"

Her aunt hesitated. "Do you think it's wise?"

"If they're going to come for me," Csilla said, her voice so low she wasn't sure Ilona could hear her, "they'll come wherever I am."

"And you want to savor these last moments with your friends," said Ilona to herself. She said, "Well, I can't stop you."

Csilla didn't move. "If you want me to stay, I will."

Ilona shook her head. "Go. Let them follow you there. Let them see your joy."

"The audacity," whispered Csilla, smiling as she kissed Ilona's cheek.

"So bold, so brave," Ilona said, and it sounded sardonic. But they both knew it wasn't. "Make sure you ask them to dance before they put you in the car."

"Can you even imagine their faces if I said that?" Csilla actually let out a laugh now.

Ilona's smile was as wide as the Duna. "It'd be almost worth it."

September 12, 1945

Dear General,

    I received your name from an American soldier who was briefly stationed here in Budapest. I do not know you and you do not know me. I am a Jew who survived the war. But the fate of my family is not known. I understand you are overseeing the displaced persons camps in Poland. I am looking for my family. Here are their names:

    Ilona Rosenfeld Frankel, age 32

    Isadore Frankel, age 34

    Zsófia Frankel, age 11

    Béla Frankel, age 5

    Oszkár Frankel, age 3

    Eszter Rosenfeld, age 67

    József Rosenfeld, age 70

    Ábrahám Rosenfeld, age 72

    Rút Auspitz Rosenfeld, age 58

    Sándor Auspitz, age 58

    Regina Rosenfeld Berger, age 37

    László Berger, age 38

    Rózsi Berger, age 17

    Pál Berger, age 12

With hope and faith in G-d,
Éva Rosenfeld Weisz Tisza

CHAPTER SIX

CSILLA

OCTOBER 17, 1956

Csilla found Zsu and Aliz by the bar, slipped in between them and leaned her head against Zsu's shoulder. Zsu tipped her dark head against Csilla's light-colored one.

"You made it!" Zsu said, her voice carrying over the noise.

"I'm sorry I'm late," Csilla said, grateful for the presence and warmth of her friend.

"I just got here too. Had to make sure my mother was set with Tibor," Aliz said, which meant that her husband was coming out too instead of staying home with the baby. Aliz brushed a dark gray curl out of her face. "I thought we'd never get out today."

Csilla laughed. "You say that every day, Aliz."

"Well, I feel like it every day," Aliz protested. "Did you have a tail?"

Csilla shook her head. "Not tonight."

She leaned close to Csilla, but she couldn't whisper in the din of the bar. She shouted into Csilla's ear, the volume chasing the singsong nature out of her words. "Are you sure? That man in the corner. He's watching you. Maybe he's an admirer."

Csilla's heart slammed to a stop, pressed against her ribs so hard she was sure she'd bruise. She gripped the edge of the smooth wooden bar until her fingertips hurt. "Where?"

Zsu grabbed her hands. "He isn't ÁVH, Csilla. He's been here since before you came in. He's not here for you."

Csilla thought that might be wishful thinking, but Zsu continued.

"He just thinks you look pretty. Because you do." She nodded, eyes over Csilla's right shoulder, toward the door. "There."

Csilla twisted, rising on her toes to look for the admirer. A young man with thick, ruffled dark hair leaned against a wall with a handful of other young men. Students, Csilla guessed, by their clothing. The top buttons of their shirts undone. Ties slack around their necks. Their sleeves rolled up. Their jackets tossed unceremoniously over a chair. The man watching her seemed about her age, maybe a year or two older, with a chiseled jaw, sharp cheekbones and a thick brow.

The corner of his mouth quirked up.

Csilla turned away, her cheeks heating. She'd been caught staring.

"I like Zsu's theory. Maybe he's an admirer. Or is he your stranger? Do you know him?" Aliz asked excitedly, reaching for Csilla's hands.

Csilla shook her head. "No. And I don't care to. He could be ÁVH."

Zsu rolled her eyes. She pressed a glass of wine into Csilla's hand with such firmness that there was no room for dispute. Not that Csilla minded. The challenge would be not drinking the wine too quickly. She offered one to Aliz, who declined.

"Are you pregnant again?" Zsu asked Aliz.

Aliz grimaced. "I hope not." She glanced around quickly, looking for her husband. But he wasn't there yet and couldn't overhear her admission. "Wine makes me itch."

"If you drink enough, you might not notice the itch?" Zsu suggested.

Aliz kicked at her. Zsu yelped, but laughed. Csilla couldn't help but smile as she sipped at her wine.

"Do you see Elek?" asked Zsu, scanning the room. "I told him we'd be here."

"You said he was already planning to come!" Csilla protested. "Did you invite him?"

"I did not say he was already planning to come. I said I heard he was going to be here," Zsu said mischievously.

Csilla groaned. "You two are terrible."

"You can't marry if you don't meet anyone," Zsu observed.

"Exactly. And marriage is great," Aliz chimed in.

"I've only ever heard you complain," Csilla replied.

Aliz waved away the worry with a loose hand. "Oh, you know. That's part of the charm."

Then someone bumped into Csilla, sliding into their circle. Gábor, Zsu's fiancé, and Feri, Aliz's husband, both arrived to much fanfare. Feri put a hand on Aliz's back and smiled at her, but that was as far as they went. In contrast, Gábor pressed a kiss to Zsu's cheek and whispered something in her ear. Her cheeks darkened with rough gray at his words.

"Hello, ladies," Gábor said cheerfully. "What's new in the newspaper world today?"

"There's a shortage of ink," said Aliz with a sigh. "So we have to cut articles to their bare minimum."

"There's no shortage," said Gábor calmly, but with an edge to his voice.

The group stilled for a moment, Feri's hand pressing into his wife's back. Aliz brightened and said, "No, of course not. We are being more efficient with page space."

Gábor nodded a little bit, and Csilla exchanged a look with Zsu. Gábor kept his voice low when he said, "I don't care, Aliz. Truly. But you must be careful."

Csilla felt as if she'd swallowed enough river water to make herself sick.

They couldn't say there was an ink shortage, because that would suggest that the Party couldn't adequately control the supply chain and produce enough, and that would suggest that the Revolution—such as it was in Hungary—was a failure.

"I know," Aliz said, flushing gray in the dim light. "Thank you."

"Well," said Zsu airily, "being efficient with page space is giving me a headache."

And they all laughed politely and with relief at the change of tone in the conversation.

"Excuse me," said a quiet tenor next to Csilla.

Her head jerked up, and she stared into the face of the handsome boy from the corner of the room. His mouth quirked again, but quick this time. She almost missed it. His dark eyes scanned her face, and then he held out his hand. "I'm Tamás."

"Just Tamás," she said, without thinking. "You're that well known."

This time he smiled all the way. "Tamás Keller."

She took his hand and shook it. His hand was warm, his handshake confident and firm, and she relaxed, despite her anxiety. "Csilla." She hesitated and then said, "Csilla Tisza."

There it was, the flicker of recognition across his eyes, but it cleared immediately. He reached with his other hand, plucked the wineglass from her hand and handed it to Zsu. Zsu took it, wide-eyed with surprise. Csilla's friends, as well as Feri and Gábor, were silent, watching all of this.

"Can you please hold this? It'll be easier to dance with Csilla if she's not holding wine," explained Tamás.

Csilla raised an eyebrow, instinctively pulling back the hand he still held. "Oh? Am I dancing with you?"

Tamás gave her a coy look. "You stared back. Wasn't that a yes?"

She wanted to scowl at him. It wasn't even close to a yes.

But he could be ÁVH. And she could not say no to the ÁVH.

They might have known she was coming here. One of her friends might have told them. Gábor was ÁVH. He might know about Csilla's morning tail. He might have tipped them off.

But she didn't think Tamás carried himself like ÁVH. There was something authentic and earnest about his posture, the clothes he wore, the smile on his face.

And the way he asked, just shy of a command, rushing her into a dance in which her friends couldn't overhear them, made her nervous and curious in equal measures. This was about more than flirting.

Just a dance, she told herself as she tried not to panic.

She let him draw her out of the circle of her friends. She glanced over her shoulder only once at Zsu and Aliz. They shooed her, laughing, and Csilla turned back to Tamás as he pulled her onto the dance floor. His hand slipped around her waist, his other hand lacing their fingers together. She stiffened. She couldn't remember the last time she had been touched like this, that she'd stood this close to a man. This was closer even than the man this morning.

She turned her face away from Tamás's as he stepped closer, and they began to sway to the music.

"Quiet, aren't you?" he said softly.

She risked a glance at him, then looked away. His face was so close she couldn't bring him into focus. "You invited me to dance. You ought to start the conversation."

"Ah," he murmured, and Csilla shivered at the sound reverberating down his arms and into his hands, to her lower back and into the palm of her hand. "I'm sorry. I missed that social nicety."

She couldn't help but smile. "They don't teach that at university?"

It was his turn to be surprised into a brief silence. "How'd you know?"

"Only students look so casually elegant and disaffected at the same time." She looked back up at him, relaxing a fraction. "Where do you study?"

"Technical University," he said, and she knew that they were watching each other's reaction.

Her father had taught at the Technical University before he'd joined the government. It'd been long before this boy was a student, but the careful way he said it told her that he knew who her father was (who didn't, after all?) and that he had taught there.

She swallowed and looked away again. "What do you study?"

"Engineering," he said, spinning her around the dance floor.

It could be worse, Csilla thought to herself. *It could be architecture.*

"I want to build bridges." He ducked his head close to hers. "I mean that literally and metaphorically."

Csilla tilted her head back a little bit so she could see his face, smiling in spite of herself. "Where do your metaphorical bridges go?"

"I don't know yet," he said simply. "Where do you think they could go?"

Anywhere, she wanted to tell him. *Everywhere.* But she didn't say that, because that was dangerous without knowing what the metaphor was. Still, she said softly, "A noble profession."

"Good for the People and the cause," he added, a sudden burst of caution coloring his words.

She was so *tired* of being so wary of everyone and of everyone being so wary of her.

"Good for the People and the cause," she repeated dutifully.

She could feel the river whispering, and she wondered if it was whispering danger to her. She could smell his cologne, and she wondered where he got it. *I had a tail this morning, and a stranger who knew my name saved me,* she thought, *and now a different strange man's asking me to dance.* The hairs on her arm stood up. The music faded into the background. She could hear only him, the river and her own heartbeat.

He pulled her a little closer, like he could feel her adrenaline spike. "Where do you work?"

It was exactly the wrong question. She stiffened, fingers curling into him. Leading questions about metaphors and bridges, and now questions about where she worked. Any other day and she might have cautiously laughed it off.

But she'd nearly been disappeared this morning. And yesterday, she'd watched her parents' bodies be reburied after they'd been disappeared. Today was not any other day.

She kept her tone deliberately light. "How do you know I am not at university too?"

"You're not so . . ." He paused, finding her words. "Casually elegant and disaffected."

She didn't want to know if she fell short on the *elegant* or the *disaffected*. She mostly wanted to slap the Csilla of a few minutes ago, who had let this boy flirt his way past her common sense and good defenses.

"I'm not a student," she admitted. He'd already know this if he was ÁVH, and this question was textbook ÁVH. She was in over her head. But she knew how to hold her breath. "I work at the paper. I'm a typist."

He spun her again and drew her back to him. His hand splayed over the small of her back, and she felt like there'd be a hot, sweaty palm print on her blouse. Her palm felt slippery in his hand, and she wasn't sure if it was her nerves or his. And it was only too late that she realized he'd been working her around the dance floor farther from her friends and their careful, watchful eyes, and now she was in a darker corner, a mass of people between her and the bright lights above the bar.

"I am sorry to ask this so soon after your parents' funeral. I need your help, Csilla Tisza," Tamás murmured, his voice low and tense.

Was this a test? He *must* be ÁVH. Did he think that she was like her parents? Did he have information from someone? They'd failed to get her this morning, so they'd come for her here. They'd disappear her right in front of her friends. She had never put a foot out of line. She was so careful. God. She had been so careful.

She was so close to escaping, and so far.

Csilla gripped his fingers too tightly. "You cannot be that sorry. I am sure I cannot help you."

"One of my friends was taken by the ÁVH yesterday," he whispered to her, urgency pulsing through every word. "I need to find out what's happening to him, if he's okay, if they're going to release him."

She was nearly a kilometer from the river, and yet it roared into her ears, surrounding her. She gritted her teeth hard enough to crack them against the cold, dark-pewter water welling up around her.

"Please," said Tamás. "You must still know people in the ÁVH. There were people in there sympathetic to your father, and now that he's been exonerated, surely they—"

Csilla pulled away from him, wide-eyed. "I can't help you."

He insistently pulled her back close to him. "Please. Please don't draw attention to us."

It's too late for that, she thought. It felt as if the entire city was watching them. She wanted to brush the curls out of her face where they stuck to her forehead and cheeks. She wanted to pull away from him, but he was holding her too tightly. It started to occur to her that he was holding on to her the way she held her breath. Like she'd save him.

Maybe he wasn't ÁVH. Maybe he was a foolish, pretty, charismatic boy.

Maybe she was wrong. But maybe she wasn't.

"I have no access to those records," she whispered. "I work at the paper."

"I think you can get access to those records," he replied. "Please. I wouldn't ask if he wasn't important to me."

They were all important, the people who were disappeared and taken. They were all important to someone.

"You knew who I was," she hissed, trying to yank out of his grip.

But he was ready for her this time. He kept her crushed against him.

"You planned this."

"I did," he whispered, desperate.

Fear prickled her belly. Men were not rational when they were desperate.

"I thought you'd understand, Csilla. Please."

She dug her fingers hard into his lower back. He grunted in surprise and pain, but it let her put some space between them so she wasn't crushed against him. She couldn't think that close to him.

She hissed, "I can't take that risk." It wasn't the safest answer. She should have left it at no. But she was in deep now. "Not for someone I don't know."

"His name is Márk Dobos. He's my best friend," whispered

Tamás hoarsely. "He grew up in southern Hungary. Most of his family's in Vojvodina now, in Yugoslavia. He was studying to be a mechanical engineer. He's the worst singer I've ever known, but he's enthusiastic. Sometimes he rides the trams just for fun, because he never grew out of that phase where little boys love trains."

"I can't help you," she repeated, her heart a fist in her chest. It didn't matter if Márk Dobos was important to him. What he was asking for was treason. What he was asking for would have her dead, drowned with her head in a bucket and her hands behind her back. She didn't want to die. Not here in Hungary. She didn't want to die and leave her aunt like that. She wouldn't. She'd spent too much time staying within the bold lines of the rules to fail here just because a boy asked her for a favor.

Even if the favor was someone else's life.

What else was a lie?

What was the truth?

She swallowed the urge to change her mind.

Tamás was quiet for a beat, for four steps. Then he sighed, his body loosening. Csilla had never felt defeat beneath her hands before.

"If you change your mind," he said quietly, stepping away from her, "come find me at the university." He still held her hand, and she had not pulled it away from him yet.

She said, "I will not change my mind," and her voice was not nearly as cold as she wanted it to be.

He swallowed hard, the knot in his throat bobbing up and down quickly. "Understood. I'm sorry that I asked, Csilla."

"Please let go of my hand," she said. If she stayed here any longer, she'd change her mind. She didn't want to change her mind.

He dropped it immediately. They each took a step backward. The other dancers moved around them, and they were attracting confused glances. Too much attention. Csilla spared Tamás one last glance, then brushed by him as she hurried off the dance floor. She reached her friends and scooped her wineglass out of Aliz's hands.

Her friends started to ask her questions, but stopped when Csilla took two big messy gulps of the wine and then put the glass back down on the bar, hard enough to make it slosh. Her hands didn't stop shaking, though, as she picked up her coat and slipped it on.

"Csilla?" Aliz asked tentatively.

"Was he inappropriate?" Gábor asked roughly, glaring at Tamás over Csilla's head.

He must be walking back to his friends, Csilla realized from the track of Gábor's eyes.

"I'll get him."

"No," said Csilla sharply.

Aliz and Zsu were both looking at her in surprise. That wasn't good either. She needed to regain that balance between maintaining her rules, her boundaries, and avoiding suspicion. She took a deep breath.

"I'm going to go home," she said with a forced smile, making her voice as soft and placid as she normally kept it. "I've had enough dancing, I think."

"Csilla, what happened?" Zsu whispered.

She should have known she couldn't fool Zsu.

"Csilla!" cried a familiar voice.

She closed her eyes, swallowing hard. Not now. She could not deal with Elek right now. But when she opened her eyes, he was there, beaming at her. She made her mouth into something close to a smile, but she must not have succeeded because he studied her, his smile slipping into a frown. "Is everything all right?"

"Csilla wants to leave," Aliz told him, her voice subdued.

"Let's go to this place I know in Buda!" cried Zsu, a little desperate. "Gábor and I love it."

"No," said Csilla firmly.

She would not cross the river. Not tonight. Not with the way its noise sloshed against her bones right now, not with the questions it was urgently pushing at her. She wanted to cover her ears. Had it been Tamás who made the river wild? Had it been this morning's stranger? Or was it her?

She shook her head. "I'm sorry. It's late. I need to get home. My aunt will wonder where I am."

Elek looked puzzled, but then he offered her his arm. "I'll walk you."

She did not want to accept, but it'd make everything easier if he remained enamored of her. She gave him a grateful smile and slipped her hand onto his arm. "Thank you. I don't want to ruin your night. . . ."

"I'd rather make sure you got home safely," he said gallantly.

Too much, she thought at him as she smiled again. "Thank you."

And as they left the bar, she very deliberately did not look at Tamás and his friends at the front of the room. But she could feel his gaze on her all the way down the street. It was as loud as the river.

Before the war, when I met Éva, she asked me why I was a Communist, and I didn't have a good answer for her. I think I said something to the effect that—in fact, I'm sure I said something along these lines—Communism would free us from the chains that had limited human society and innovation. When I rejoined the Party after the war, she asked me why again. I told her that I wanted to and that I didn't want to be questioned. It was such a weak answer, and I saw it in Éva's face, the way she turned away from me. Her expression was a slammed door.

The truth is that when I went to the office that day, I didn't think of any alternatives. Marx said that we ought to examine our life's calling, and once we've familiarized ourselves with its promises and with its burdens, and if it is still appealing to us, we must adopt it wholeheartedly.

That is how I feel about Hungary's future.

It seems so clear to me right now that the way forward for Hungary is the path of revolution, of deep and meaningful societal change. In the years after the empire, Hungary struggled because its leaders were averse to change. They feared returning to the empire, but they were too shallow-minded to think of themselves outside of it.

This is an opportunity. I want my daughter to grow up in an evolved society. A society in which people have more rights than their leaders, a society in which capitalism does not grind its people into dust. Capitalism begets nationalism. Capitalism begets patriotism. Nationalism leads to war between nations. Nationalism leads to labeling certain classes of people as other. Patriotism allows everyone to stand under one flag, with one common purpose.

I believe Hungary could be a leader in setting an example of how to step out from beneath the shadow of empire and two destructive world wars and start on a better path. If we can do it, then imagine all the countries that could follow in our path.

This will be worth it. Revolution is not easy, but it is always worth it. In the end.

—The Journal of Simon Tisza, March 1946

CHAPTER SEVEN

CSILLA

OCTOBER 17, 1956

On the walk home, Csilla could hear the river whispering to her, urgent, nonsensical words. Frantic. It sounded like radio static in her head that she couldn't turn off even though she mentally twisted the dials everywhere she could. She pressed a hand against one of her ears out of instinct, even though the sound wasn't strictly external, and out of instinct again, she looked over her shoulder every few blocks.

They were halfway there when she saw that they had a tail.

Her stomach sank. They wouldn't disappear them both, surely, but Elek was in danger now, just because he had shown her the courtesy of walking her home. She didn't know what to say to him. Could she warn him? Should she warn him?

Elek looked at her sideways, the concern etching his expression visible beneath each successive streetlight.

"Are you well?"

"I'm fine," she lied. She could feel in the taut beat between them that he did not believe her. They had another ten minutes to walk, and anything could happen. They might never reach her apartment. Elek might be in prison because he was walking with the daughter of executed Jews, and that daughter had plans to escape. Plans that might have leaked. She couldn't tell him. He might be ÁVH too. "I'm just tired."

Concern remained on his face, but the furrow in his brow smoothed. "Yesterday must have been exhausting."

She opened her mouth to deny this, then closed it. She'd almost forgotten that yesterday she'd buried her parents. It'd been exhausting, and it still was. She'd worked so hard to look and play the part she thought the Party and the State had chosen for her, dark dress and solemn eyes.

"It was," she murmured. She glanced up at him. "Were you there?"

"I was," he admitted. "I—I thought perhaps you'd need to see some friendly faces in the crowd."

She blinked, turning her gaze back into the dark. "Did I see you?"

His voice was gentle. "You answered your own question."

She'd looked at him and not seen him, then.

She glanced around as they walked. He'd taken her past a few parks, over crunching leaves and through the chill of autumn in the air. "I love this season."

He smiled at that, as if she'd said something very sweet and naive, as if he saw right through her attempts to change the topic. "Ah, you are a romantic."

"Hardly," she said, startled enough to laugh.

"Aren't you?" he asked her as they turned down her street. She did not ask him how he knew her address. "Autumn is a season on the precipice. You like it when everything feels full of potential."

There were so many kinds of potential. The world still felt as if it stood on the edge of a blade, and any slip would be blood spilled.

But this type of change, the natural order of things, the way day faded into night and night receded from day, the way that the river felt like possibility every day: she did love that. She was surprised he noticed. Change, for better or for worse, was the one constant in Csilla's life. That'd been true in all of the befores and all of the afters.

Yesterday, even through all her grief, she had been able to feel that possibility. That teetering on a knife's edge. A cracked door of opportunity.

Maybe that was why the stranger had helped her this morning. Maybe that was why Tamás had taken the risk to ask her to find information about his friend. Maybe it was why Elek felt the most real he'd ever felt to her, here when he was being gentle and honest instead of the shy and flirtatious boy with the gun at work.

Maybe she wasn't the only one who felt as if she were balancing on the edge of a blade. Maybe she wasn't the only one who thought anything could happen if they weren't careful.

What else was a lie?

What was the truth?

She wasn't sure the door of opportunity was still there, but she found herself hoping it was.

She gave Elek a small but genuine smile. "I suppose you're right."

Elek said goodbye to her at the door, and she could feel him wanting to kiss her. She turned her face at the last second, feigning shyness, so his mouth landed on her cheek. He didn't seem to mind, though. In the dim glare of the streetlights, she could see the gray flush of his cheeks when he stepped away from her. He shoved his hands into his coat pockets and looked up at the apartment building. Over his shoulder, she could see their tail step into the shadows. But he did not approach, and she did not hear the rumble of a car coming down the street.

"So that's good night, then?" he asked.

Csilla resisted raising an eyebrow at him. He was bolder than she thought he would be. She gave him a patient smile, though, one she'd mastered over the last four years, and said, "My aunt will be waiting for me upstairs."

He nodded in understanding.

"See you tomorrow?" he asked hopefully.

She found that she didn't have to fake the smile she gave him. "Tomorrow."

"Good night, Csilla." He backed into the shadows.

"Good night, Elek," she replied.

She waited until he started to walk away to make sure the tail didn't follow him. But the man stayed there, on the corner.

She looked at him but said nothing before she pushed open the main door to their building. She stepped inside the chilly, dark hallway.

There were two apartments on the first floor, then a flight of stairs and the mailboxes to the left, and the small hallway to another door that led to the courtyard of her building. She'd grown up here, lived here her entire life except for a handful of months during the war, and there was still something about the encompassing dark that unnerved her. The hall lights hadn't worked in years. Maybe not since the war. She couldn't remember anymore. All the residents had stopped complaining about it. There wasn't anything to do other than learn to walk as quickly as one could to one's apartment.

On the steps, to the side, sat a package wrapped in paper and tied in string.

Csilla picked it up, frowning at it.

Then Orsolya Varga, who lived in part of the first-floor apartment that'd once belonged to a family named Schwarz, opened her door, as if she'd been waiting for Csilla to come home.

"I don't like the man who brought that," said Orsolya. "I don't want him coming here again."

Csilla blinked at her. "Who was he?"

"I don't know, but I didn't like him." Orsolya sniffed.

"I'm sorry," Csilla offered her, even though she had nothing to apologize for.

She glanced down at the package in the light coming from Orsolya's apartment.

Csilla Weisz
Apartment of Her Birth
Budapest, Hungary

She nearly dropped the package.

"I'm sorry," she repeated hurriedly. "It won't happen again."

"Who's it from? Who was he? What's in the package?" Orsolya asked, her tone a mix of the sister emotions of suspicion and curiosity.

"Books I ordered," Csilla lied. The package seemed book-shaped. She couldn't stop staring at the address. At the name. "I'm thinking about going to university."

Orsolya made a disappointed noise.

Maybe she knew Csilla was lying. Maybe Orsolya had opened the package. Maybe someone else had. She couldn't inspect the taped edges here in the dim light and with Orsolya watching.

"Have a good night, comrade," Csilla said, as calmly as she could manage.

She took the stairs two at a time.

Apartment of her birth. True. But so few people knew that these days.

Csilla Weisz. No one had called her that since 1945. No one had called her that in eleven years. As far as her father was concerned, the Weisz name died in the war. (It might as well have died then. It wasn't like anyone who kept the name survived and stayed in Hungary.) He'd made their name Hungarian when he applied for his government position, and soon all of their papers changed, and what was done was done.

As far as Csilla was aware, the only person who knew the surname she'd carried at birth was her aunt.

She unlocked their apartment door with shaking hands.

Her aunt was there, reading the newspaper by the window. She set down her mug and looked up at Csilla. Her smile slipped away when she saw her niece's face. "What's wrong, sheifale?"

Csilla set the package down on the table.

Her aunt's eyes fell to the paper package. Her mouth tightened into a small frown as she studied it. "You're back sooner than I thought you'd be."

Csilla went through the motions of pouring herself a glass of pálinka. Her aunt made it at home, and Csilla had to admit that she was good at it. She liked the sweet liquor at the end of the night. She sat back down. "Yes."

Her aunt's eyes snapped to hers, sharp and bright. "You were careful."

The unsaid words were right there—*We are almost free, don't make a mistake now.* It was a question wearing the mask of a statement.

"Of course," Csilla murmured. "I am always careful."

She had been. She hadn't done anything that might account for the tail this morning. And she hadn't asked to be saved by a stranger, and she hadn't asked for Tamás to ask her to dance. She hadn't asked for Elek to walk her home, and she hadn't asked for another ÁVH tail, a man out there in the shadows.

She'd been careful, but danger found her anyway.

Ilona exhaled slowly. "Good girl."

They kept careful the way they used to keep Shabbat.

Ilona touched the package with two fingers. "This?"

"On the stairs when I got home," Csilla murmured. She hesitated, but decided to be fully transparent. "Orsolya saw them."

Ilona started to shrug, and then she leaned closer and looked up at Csilla, wide-eyed. "It uses your name!"

Her aunt never called it her old name. She always called it her name.

She had not changed her name. Ilona Rosenfeld.

It'd been a terrible fight between Simon, Csilla's father, and Éva, Csilla's mother.

"She almost died for being Jewish, they took everything from her, and now you want to take her Jewish name too!" Éva screamed.

"Changing her name does not make her less Jewish!" Simon roared back.

"She survived, Simon," Éva said bitterly. *"It is her name. It is all of our names."*

And in the end, Éva had won. Her sister kept her maiden name, as Jewish as it was, and the five-digit tattoo on her arm.

"Do not open it," Ilona said now, her voice urgent and low as Csilla picked up the package and examined it. "Csilla, sheifale, Csilla, Csilla, I beg you. Do not open that package."

The river whispered louder and louder, growing more insistent like a whistling teapot in the room that she could not ignore. She clapped her hands to her ears. "Stop!"

The river quieted, and her aunt whispered, "What did you do, Csilla?"

"Nothing," she said shortly, pulling her hands from her ears. Her hands were shaking again.

She paused. That wasn't entirely true, and she did not want to lie to Ilona. "This morning—"

She slumped a little in her chair. Her aunt reached across the table and wrapped her paper-thin hands around Csilla's. "Tell me, Csilla."

So she told her aunt about the stranger who had known her name and saved her from the secret policeman who had nearly disappeared her this morning, and the different stranger who asked her to dance. Halfway through the story, her aunt got up and made a new pot of watered-down coffee. When she sat back down, she traded Csilla's pálinka for the coffee.

"You need this more than you need that," her aunt said, setting the sweet Hungarian spirits to the side. "Someone found out about our plans."

She kept her voice low, but Csilla still flinched, glancing at the window. "I'm worried about that."

"Who?"

"It could be anyone," Csilla said grimly.

"That doesn't explain this," Ilona said, looking at the package. "Maybe it's from this morning's stranger."

"Then why didn't he show up at the end of the day?" Csilla wanted to know.

Ilona fixed her with a hard stare. "You don't *want* him to show up again! No trouble, Csilla."

"Maybe it's from the ÁVH," murmured Csilla, picking up the brown paper package again. Or from a charismatic young man who happened to attend the same university where her father had taught. But he was still at the bar when she left. Wasn't he? She'd seen him.

She did not like coincidences.

Not when the world teetered as it did.

She didn't think the package had been tampered with—the flaps of the paper were firmly taped down, and the string was tied in such an intricate manner.

"There was a boy this morning," her aunt said thoughtfully. "There was a boy kicking stones around the courtyard. I told him to scram."

Csilla gave her aunt a sharp look. "You did not."

Her aunt sighed. "I did not."

Her aunt never told the children to scram. Csilla supposed she was lucky her aunt hadn't started collecting children on top of everything else.

Ilona had been taken from her home when they took her to the trains. They threatened to shoot her children, and that'd been when she'd stopped screaming and started complying.

They'd killed the children anyway, of course. All of them, on arrival at Auschwitz. They'd gone straight into the gas chambers. It was a fallacy that everyone went to sleep in the gas chambers, that it was a peaceful death. The Nazis—or any of the Jews' enemies—would never be so kind. The gas killed them, but they knew they were dying. She'd heard her babies screaming. Sometimes she still did.

Maybe Csilla had imagined the stranger that morning. Maybe she'd saved herself.

Ilona frowned. "If there's anything in it . . ."

But Csilla knew what she meant. "I'll turn it in and report it."

Her aunt nodded, relieved.

Csilla untied the bow on the front beneath her name and pulled the string off the package. She slid her fingers beneath the flaps and popped the tape off. Carefully, she unfolded the paper. In the middle lay four black notebooks, their edges frayed and worn as if they'd been well loved and read many times. Something tickled the back of Csilla's mind, but she frowned at the notebooks. There was no card. There was no explanation.

She looked at her aunt, who was lighting a cigarette. "Do you recognize them?"

Her aunt shook her head silently.

Csilla picked up the first one and opened it cautiously.

On the first page it read

The Journal of Simon Weisz, 1930–1939

Csilla inhaled. She set it down, grabbing the next one and opening it.

The front page read

The Journal of Simon Weisz, 1940–1942

The third journal's first page read

The Journal of Simon Weisz, 1942–1945

And the fourth journal read

The Journal of Simon Tisza, 1945–1951

"Apu," she whispered, then switched to Yiddish. "Tati."

She shoved back from the table, sending her coffee flying. Her aunt screamed in surprise as Csilla's chair clattered to the floor, but Csilla was already at the door of the apartment, throwing it open. She tore down the stairs, her hand burning from the friction against the railing. In the main hall, she yelled again, "Tati!"

The dark screamed back at her, and so she pulled the door open and ran out into the damp, chilly night. She could smell the river, could feel the magic slipping off of it into the night air, but she didn't care. She turned wildly, chest heaving, looking for her father. Down the street, a figure stood in the shadows, smoking, and she began to run toward him, tears streaking down her cheeks.

"Apu," she called, instinctively switching to Hungarian. "Apu!"

The figure didn't move.

She was flying down the street, and nothing was fast enough until she reached the figure. "Apu! It's me, Csilla."

She could barely speak through her tears and her gasping.

Then the man said softly, gently, "I—I don't think I'm who you're looking for."

Now that she was close to him, she could see that he was much taller than her father, and his hair was too light. He'd tucked a notebook hastily inside his coat. ÁVH. The man who'd followed them back from the bar. He looked at her sorrowfully from beneath the brim of his hat. "I'm sorry."

Csilla whispered, "Did you see him? My father? He was just here."

The man shook his head and dropped his cigarette to the street. He crushed it with his heel and began to back away from her, as if sensing that all wasn't well here. "I'm sorry. I haven't seen anyone else around."

And as he retreated, Csilla spun, looking up and down the street.

"He was just here," she repeated in a whisper.

It had to be her father, didn't it? The name. The address. The careful wrapping.

His journals.

Who else would have his journals?

Why didn't she remember the journals?

Who had brought them to her?

She pressed her hands to her mouth to stop herself from trembling, but her whole body was shaking. She wiped the backs of her hands over the tear stains on her cheeks.

The magic in the night air was thick against her tongue, and she could hear the river whispering to her.

She spun to face it, west, the river, the castle on the cliff, the silver waters that shimmered even on moonless nights. Though she could not see the river itself, she balled her fists at her side and screamed down the street. "What do you want from me?"

The river whispered, whispered, whispered, but she couldn't understand it. It babbled nonsense at her, as frantic as it'd been all night, and as unknowable as it'd ever been.

"Stop," she begged the night, the river, the city, God, she didn't know. "Stop. Leave me alone."

But the river kept whispering.

There was a hollow part of her in the center of her chest, and she pressed her fist against it as if she could fill it from the outside, but it ached and pulsed like a second heartbeat inside her. All her life she'd skirted the edges of absence and loss, defined her life by what it was missing, what it could have been. In her adolescence, it had sometimes felt as if that gaping hole in her childhood would swallow her whole.

She lifted her face to the sky and breathed in the night.

Her father was not here.

Her father left her four years ago, without any warning, and he wasn't coming back. He was dead. She hadn't needed to see the body yesterday to know that they'd exhumed him from some nameless plot and put his remains in that wooden coffin, burying him next to the same people who had tried to kill him years before, during the war. She'd been there for the funeral.

Her father had been many things, including many unlovable things, but if he could come home, she knew that he would, the way she knew that the world used to have color, the way she knew her own name, the way she could braid her hair in the dark.

He wasn't coming home.

She didn't know who had brought the journals, but it was not her father.

She looked around for the ÁVH man, but he was gone too. She was alone on the street.

She walked back to her apartment, where her aunt was reassuring neighbors in the hallway.

"Long day," Ilona was telling Rózsa and Orsolya. "Her job is very stressful, and the funeral yesterday, it took so much out of her."

Rózsa was nodding, but the frown was still fixed on her face.

Orsolya said, "It's those books. That's what book learning does to a girl's head." And she shut her door.

Ilona looked relieved to see Csilla back in the hallway, the streetlight illuminating her worried gaze. The door shut behind Csilla, and for once she was grateful for the dark so her neighbors could not see her tears, her hands over her ears, the heartbreak that must be playing out across her whole face.

"I'm sorry," she said in explanation. "I think I'm overtired. I'm going to sleep now."

"Of course, dear," said Ilona, not using her normal Yiddish pet names out here among the goyim.

Csilla's steps back upstairs were heavy and slow. The door to the apartment was still open. She collected the journals from the kitchen table and took them into the bedroom.

But she couldn't bear to open them. Not tonight. Because no matter what was in those books, her father was not coming back to her.

She lay in bed, arms around the black books, and stared up at the ceiling. She thought perhaps that she could smell the scent of his favorite brand of cigarettes lingering on the pages, in the leather, in the binding. And it was still not him.

She pretended to be asleep when her aunt came in and climbed into the other side of the bed. Sleep did not come for a long time.

Éva, Ilona, Izzy, Yosef and I tried to build a golem. We had clay, water, everything that Yosef managed to find on Kabbalist teachings in the synagogue library (these were limited due to the feelings of the good rebbe, who does not know what we attempted). We didn't have another choice, though. We couldn't not try. Regina watched the children while we worked. It took us nearly three days, and much arguing, and then I watched as Yosef carved the Hebrew letters into the forehead of the golem.

I have never been so hopeful in my entire life.

I have never been so destroyed in my entire life.

The golem we built did not come to life.

Around me, the Rosenfelds argued about why—was the aleph crooked? Had Yosef's hand shaken? Was the water not good? Was the clay spoiled? But I could not get off my knees.

I don't want to die here, in the ghetto, or in Poland or on a labor assignment. I don't want to die here.

The ghetto feels unmoored from Hungary. It feels as if it floats in space, distant from all outside of these walls. We are lucky to have the same apartment, to stay where Éva and her family have always lived, but the world has shrunk to this small, cold, gray space. If it weren't for the blue sky, I wouldn't be sure that we were on earth still.

I want to die with my feet on the ground.

But I won't get the chance, because the golem never came to life.

—The Journal of Simon Weisz, October 1944

CHAPTER EIGHT

AZRIEL

They kept trying to kill him, and he kept not dying. He could see it was rattling the men who'd interrogated him, everyone except the man in charge. Tóth, or something like that. Admittedly, Azriel hadn't been paying much attention. He'd told them who he was—or at least what he was—and they'd laughed, but he could see they were starting to believe him now, after they had shot him and stabbed him and hanged him and drowned him and he did not die.

In his line of work, he did not do the dying.

Tóth, though, hadn't been alarmed. As the other men began to panic, Tóth grew calm. The more they panicked, the calmer he grew. It was an admirable trait in a hero.

But this wasn't Azriel's first time in this position, even if it was his first time in this chair, in this room. He knew Tóth was no hero. There weren't that many heroes in Budapest these days, but he really doubted they'd be working here, for security services.

He sat in the chair, hands bound behind him, wishing that one of his hands was free so he could sweep the wet hair out of his face. At least he hadn't come to Budapest with long hair this time. That would have been more of a mess now. The bullet holes had healed, as had the stab wounds, and though he thought he could still feel the ache in his neck from the rope, it didn't bother him much. He'd inhaled no water, because on a very technical level, he didn't need to breathe. He breathed out of habit, so while his head was underwater, he simply stopped.

Being picked up by the secret police wasn't part of the plan, of course. Normally he was more prepared than this. But he'd just been in Egypt, and he'd been called back to Budapest in a hurry, as if no one had expected what was happening to happen, but as far as he could tell, nothing had quite happened yet. He shouldn't have interfered with Csilla and the secret police—that wasn't his role—but he had wandered the city, pulled by the golden thread drawing him to her.

Csilla.

She'd lived.

That was unexpected.

And against the odds, certainly.

He hadn't anticipated her survival.

The whole day of not-dying and he'd nearly forgotten how she'd grown up, still silver-haired and big-eyed. When she'd been a child, she'd been incessantly curious, like knowledge was water and she'd never get enough to drink. She'd take anything. Stories, facts, numbers, lies. It didn't matter. But yesterday morning she'd been different. She'd wanted to ask a thousand things, but she hadn't.

He wanted to know who had stolen her curiosity and her impulsivity from her.

In this very city, a long time ago and yesterday all at once, when he'd stepped into a different form to be with a forgotten city, he'd known her.

But when he'd seen her, he couldn't let them take her. He didn't know what they'd do to her—not then. He knew now—but he couldn't let it happen.

So he'd let them take him into custody. He'd guessed what they'd do next. They'd snap his photo. And they'd inform Western intelligence services that they'd apprehended a spy and that they should claim him or let him die. And surely those Western intelligence services—MI6, CIA, the usual suspects—frantically contacted all of their assets and officers behind the Iron Curtain, particularly inside Hungary, and searched their files for anyone who looked like him. And coming up blank, they informed Hungarian intelligence services and the KGB that he wasn't theirs.

One by one, he was not claimed.

And so they tried to call the bluff of those intelligence services and kill him. They wanted to send a message. Don't meddle in our affairs, or something like that. That was, after all, essentially the entire point of counterintelligence. Snitches got snitched.

As long as they forgot about Csilla.

He'd told them in all fairness who he was, and they'd ignored it at their own peril.

The man in charge, Tóth, reappeared in the interrogation room. He sat down across the table and lit a cigarette. He stared at the wet, bound young man with the terribly, unfortunately pretty features.

"Who are you?" he repeated.

Azriel sighed. "I've told you."

"It isn't real," Tóth said dismissively.

But in his eyes, the truth flickered.

After all, the young man hadn't died.

"Let me go," said Azriel. "You can't kill me, which makes keeping me indefinitely rather boring. And you don't know what else I could do." He considered Tóth. "If it helps, I'm not here for you."

He meant not *just* for you. He was not so exacting. But Tóth didn't know that.

There, a flicker of relief across Tóth's face.

Tóth pressed a button on the desk. "Stop recording."

The young man had to work not to smile.

After a moment, Tóth sat back in his chair and tapped out his cigarette in the ashtray. It was barely burned down. He looked at the young man across the table from him and said, "We'll let you go out the back door. We'll destroy all the records of you having ever been here. If you say you were here, we'll deny it. If you name anyone here, we'll deny it. If you try to talk about what happened here, we will pick you up and put you in Siberia for the rest of your life, which appears to be eternity. Are we clear?"

"Crystal," said the young man.

He'd already lost precious time, over a day inside the building. A day of not-dying.

Everything there moved quickly, as if all sides wanted to put this behind them as soon as possible. He was swept out the back door into an alley, wearing the same clothes he had been wearing when he arrived, with a few new bullet holes, knife holes and bloodstains. He didn't feel the light rain, though, and he smiled up at the low gray sky. Behind him, Tóth snorted and the door slammed shut.

Azriel was free again to conduct his business, and then he could leave Budapest. Hopefully for a good long time.

My heart is like Margit Island. The river flows around it, forming it, caressing it, lifting it up. I stand between two cities, a part of them and apart from them. Everything upriver is blue. Everything downriver is red. I don't know if I am the transformation or not.

I wake because Csilla is crying again in her bed. She cannot sleep without a light. Not since the river.

My choices gave my child these unceasing nightmares.

—The Journal of Simon Tisza, December 1945

CHAPTER NINE

CSILLA

October 18, 1956

When she woke, she woke in pieces.

This morning, however, she did not pull herself back together right away. She lay there, disembodied and disenchanted. She watched her hands drift off into the air in front of her, as if they were floating in slow motion. They floated toward the huge window facing the river, where rain pattered against the glass, sliding down the panes sloppy and slow. She felt like that right now. Sloppy, slow. Rainlike. Rainy? She didn't know how to describe this morning. The corner of a journal dug into her cheek, but she didn't move her face. It was a strange feeling, this apathy that felt deeper than her bones. It reached back in time and yanked her emotions out by the roots. Unmoored. There was another feeling for this.

Her aunt rose next to her and said softly, "Do you want to talk about last night?"

"No," Csilla muttered into the thick hem of the quilt. Then she sighed. "I thought for a minute it might have been him."

They stayed there quiet for a moment, her aunt's back to her as she sat on the edge of the bed and Csilla remained beneath the covers, and then her aunt said, "Simon is dead."

"I know that," Csilla said softly. "Just for a moment, I hoped—"

That the bodies they'd never seen weren't her parents and her parents would come home. But she knew it was a foolish, childish wish.

Ilona turned back to her. "Do not draw attention to yourself, Csillagom."

"Don't call me that," she said, her words hoarse and thick, her tongue sticking to the roof of her mouth.

Her aunt ignored her, pulling the blankets off her. "Pull yourself together, child. We have thirteen days."

And then she went into the kitchen. Csilla heard her starting the stove, the familiar *click click click* of gas.

Csilla shifted her face off the journals and into her pillow, the sudden rush of blood coming back to the numb parts of her face and making her dizzy. She wanted to stay home and read her father's words, and she wanted to throw the journals into the river and pretend they'd never existed. But to do either, she would at least need her hands.

She pulled herself together. They had thirteen days.

In the bathroom, she washed her face and braided her hair. She picked a dress from her closet. She rolled her nylon stockings up her legs. She pulled on a coat that used to be her mother's and a black scarf to protect her hair from the rain. Her hair liked the rain too much, as her mother used to say. The rain made it wild and hungry.

She gathered the journals from the bed and tucked them under one arm. She walked over to the entrance to the kitchen, where she stood watching her aunt move about her morning. "Thank you."

Ilona turned, giving her niece a faint smile. This morning, she looked thin and far older than her forty-seven years. Her dress sleeves were rolled up, the numbers on her arm as bright and bold as they'd ever been. "This city can be a burden, yes?"

"Some of it," Csilla said quietly.

A burden, yes, but more than that. She felt as if she carried this city all the time, its stone walls of guilt, its nooks and crannies of joy, its boulevards of sadness. She'd tried to lay the city down, to walk away from it a time or two, but then she'd turn a corner and there it'd be: the fog slipping in from the mountains to lie low over the river, a mourning shroud over the bridges of Budapest, or children playing ball, or someone peeling an orange beneath a tree outside a church, and she could feel it slip back beneath her skin. In those moments—the fog, the ball, the orange—she loved this city. She loved it without needing to know whether it loved her back.

She loved it with a child's love, the reveling sort, the kind she knew she should have left behind in the Before, when the

87

city had color and her parents were alive. Before her mother had stitched the star onto her coat—even after her mother had stitched the star onto her coat—Csilla remembered being mesmerized by her own city, the way its streets twisted and turned, the way it had courtyards known only to its people and unknowable to outsiders, the way it surprised her with its windows and doors, its flower boxes in dark alleys, its turrets, its beggars and its wealthy, the fur coats and the dirty faces, the bridges and the sunsets and the dark waters and the way snow looked beneath streetlamps.

Those were the good days.

There were days when all she wanted was to love the city, and to be loved in return. She did not know what that would look like, that love, and she wasn't sure it'd be possible, but she ached for it.

There were days when she didn't want to love this city. She wanted to hate it. She had every reason to hate it. She'd lived through a war and through a genocide that her neighbors had perpetuated, had participated in. She'd lost her parents to this city, this country, these people all around her. She wanted to want to reject Budapest with every fiber of her being.

But she couldn't.

It was her city too.

And cities were more than the people who lived in them or built them. Cities were more than the words printed in newspapers and painted on the sides of buildings, more than gates locked and doors barred, more than smashed windows and shouted slurs, more than the scream of bombs and the scream of children, more than piles of rubble and destroyed bridges, more than their history books burning, more than declarations of peace, more than apologies spoken and unspoken.

Her father had told her that cities, to those who knew them best, each had a unique magic, a signature that was all theirs and very rarely matched by another (and even then, anyone who really knows a city can spot a forgery if they look closely). They had their own beats, their own rhythms, their own pulse, their own music, their own sunsets and sunrises—and the way light reflected through the streets belonged to that city and only that city. And that was magic.

When she was a child, before the colors left, before the war, before the river, before liberation, her father had told her, "In the way you are Jewish no matter what, this city is magical no matter what."

She remembered him tracing the blue veins on the back of her hand with his big, rough finger. "This is like a city all inside of you. You are magical, like the river is magical, Csillagom."

He'd always called her "little star" as a pet name, playing on her name. It felt like a hand crushing her heart to think of it.

She stepped out of the apartment building, and a man on the opposite corner folded his newspaper and tucked it beneath his arm. He wasn't the same one as last night or yesterday morning. This one was shorter, pudgier around the middle.

He knew that she knew who he was.

He made no move, standing there across from her, but it

unnerved her nonetheless. Thirteen days. It felt like a lifetime away, but it was so close. So soon. Anything could happen.

She should have made Ilona promise that if anything happened to Csilla, she'd still get on that train.

Csilla walked quickly, cutting to the river with the journals clutched to her chest. Her shadow followed her, but he didn't close the gap between them.

She'd nearly jumped into the river yesterday.

She could still do it today.

She waited for the stranger to reappear, but he didn't.

No one was coming to save her now.

When they'd jumped into the river—when her father had jumped and dragged her and her mother with him—in 1944, it had not been her choice. Her father had dropped their suitcase, grabbed both of their arms, and dragged them screaming over the side of the bridge.

Csilla remembered the water punching into her like a bullet.

But she hadn't drowned. The river had protected them. Though it was November, the water around them warmed up, almost to bath temperature. And though there was a current, the river didn't take them south.

Not safe, it'd told them. Stay here. And so they'd stayed. All winter, in the same water, treading it by instinct. The river would not let them drown. When they were hungry, the river provided. When they needed to rest, the river provided. When the soldiers shot into the river, the bullets never reached Csilla and her parents.

Since the war, she'd always known that if she needed to, if

she truly needed to, she could jump again. And this time, it'd be her choice.

She slowed by the Chain Bridge, her fingers curling around the edges of the journals. She hadn't opened them. Not even once. She glanced over her shoulder, and the ÁVH man was ten paces behind her. Their eyes locked.

She jerked her head back around, staring at the silver water.

Her father's journals.

Her father's words.

She was afraid of them—of his words, of the ÁVH man behind her, of all of it. And she was ashamed of her fear. She didn't want to know more about her father. She didn't want to have to reconcile new truths about what he'd done with the person she'd thought he was. She'd had to do that after he died. She'd had to hear about his crimes in the news, at the show trial, in the paper, on the radio, and in gossip on the streets. She'd had to find out that the man who'd been her kind, warm, storytelling father had pulled other families apart. She'd had to reconcile the father who, with an impulsive decision, had saved her and her mother during the war with the father who had made a series of deliberate decisions resulting in her innocent mother's death.

And then the Party had said that was wrong. That her parents shouldn't have died and that the Party had exonerated them.

What was Csilla supposed to do with that information? Which pieces were lies and which were truths? How could she fit the puzzle pieces of her parents back together?

She didn't want to do it anymore. She wanted to leave it all behind her and wipe the slate clean.

She did not want to read about her father in his own words and have more puzzle pieces and fewer answers. She wasn't going to get her father back, and his journals were just a pale imitation of him, an approximation, a shadow of the real man. She wanted her parents back, warm and real and whole, to wrap their arms around her.

She didn't want anything that fell short of that.

As soon as the crowd of people began to cross the street, she pushed through them toward the riverbank, putting some distance between herself and the ÁVH man.

Her strides were long and deliberate, purposeful and intentional, and for a split second, she almost considered it. Leaping in herself. Going over.

But at the last moment, she leaned against the railing and threw open her arms. The journals toppled from her embrace and fell, pages fluttering, into the pewter waters below. They splashed, bobbed and then began to float on the subtle current.

The river murmured softly, and she could have sworn that it was confused.

Behind her, the ÁVH man gasped. The sound of it made her jump, but she shoved her trembling hands into her coat pockets and began to walk as fast as she could. *Throwing things into the river is not illegal,* she reassured herself.

As if legality had anything to do with whether people could be disappeared.

She wondered if she should worry about him pulling the journals out of the river, but when she glanced back over her shoulder, they were already bobbing toward the middle. Their words would be ruined by the water, and after all, they were her father's words, not hers.

And they couldn't charge him with crimes now. They couldn't take back their exoneration.

The journals were in the river. Like she and her parents had been.

She turned her back to the speechless river and walked her usual route.

In the lobby of the newspaper building, Elek chatted with his colleague, but with one eye on the door: he was clearly waiting for her, because as soon as he saw her, he leapt up from his casual perch on the desk. He wiped his hands on his shirt, leaving sweaty dark streaks on the starched fabric, hoisting his gun a little higher on his shoulder. It kept slipping down. It was endearing, almost.

"Hi," he said shyly.

He'd been kind to her last night. A kindness she'd needed from him and had not expected. It wasn't hard for her to give him a smile. "Good morning, Elek."

Imre grinned behind them, winking at Csilla.

"I thought maybe we'd go dancing tonight," Elek said, and then added quickly, "somewhere quieter, of course."

She hesitated, then said softly, "I can't tonight. My aunt—" But she could not keep putting this off, and she didn't want to repay his kindness with more lies. "Next Monday?"

"Oh," he said brightly, as if waiting a week wasn't a wait at all. "Yes, next Monday would be wonderful."

Zsu came in while Csilla was hanging up her coat. Csilla didn't miss her friend's worried glance. "Are you well? Did you get home safely?"

"I did," Csilla said, giving her a reassuring smile. This, after all, was not a lie. She did get home safely.

"I was worried," Zsu told her.

Aliz was already seated, but she paused her work to say, "I'm sorry, Csilla."

"It's fine," she reassured both of them. "I was just tired." She needed them to move on from this. "Elek and I are going to go dancing next Monday night."

That did it. They were sufficiently distracted straight through to their midday break, fixated on the idea of her and Elek together. And Csilla was content to let them fixate. As they fussed about her hair, the dress she'd wear, her makeup, Csilla sank into a space in her head where she didn't need to work so hard to keep up appearances, where her interactions and responses were minimal, her mind deep in the task of turning the handwritten notes on her right into stacks of typed paper on her left. She could breathe there. A little better than she could anywhere else.

"Did you have a friend today?" Zsu asked, her voice low on their walk to the cafeteria.

Csilla's mouth tightened. "Yes. But he didn't follow me the whole way."

"I still don't understand why." Aliz sounded flabbergasted. "Your parents' crimes were erased."

In a way their deaths could not be.

"I don't know," Csilla lied. The family friend here, or his

friend in Serbia, or that man's friend who worked with the Jewish Agency: so many people who might not have kept the secret of her plans. So many people who might have spilled her secret to save their own skin. So many people who might spill her secret for a paycheck. "It's unnerving."

"They'll lose interest in a few days," Zsu reassured her.

"I thought," she said, faltering, "that things might change."

Aliz gave her a sympathetic look. "I think we all did."

"I heard there was a raid on the university the day of the funeral," Zsu said, keeping her voice low. "Gábor mentioned something, and then I heard talk in the washroom."

"Now who's the gossip?" Aliz said, amused.

A raid on the university the day of the funeral. Following people for no reason, arresting and disappearing people who had never committed any crimes—that felt like turning the clock back years. *Years.*

Had her parents' exoneration been a lie? Had it been an attempt to placate a population restless since Stalin's death and since Khrushchev's apology for Stalin's crimes? Had her parents' funerals been a political tool, the way their deaths had been?

Of course they had, she realized. She had just thought that perhaps, for once, it was an act of radical truth-telling instead of a farce designed to lead more sheep to slaughter. She just didn't realize that they'd use it as a distraction, a ruse, on the *same day.*

Then she remembered a boy, his hand splayed on her lower back.

"One of my friends was taken by the ÁVH yesterday. I need to

find out what's happening to him, if he's okay, if they're going to release him.

"I wouldn't ask if he wasn't important to me."

A university boy, stolen while her parents' funerals and exonerations served as political cover.

It took her breath away.

"Oh my God," Csilla said, her voice rising like a tide. "They used them. They tricked us. It was all a smoke screen."

"Csilla," Aliz said nervously. "Careful."

"I am tired," she snapped. "I am tired of being careful."

Her friends were silent in the wake of these words. Csilla closed her eyes, feeling herself sway, jostling against the walls in her mind. She'd reached this point of exhaustion before, but never in public, never with witnesses.

"I'm sorry," she said quietly, opening her eyes again. "The funeral—the man. I am overwhelmed. I am sorry."

"Of course," Zsu said smoothly. "That's understandable."

Csilla took a deep breath and let it out slowly.

They walked the remaining way to the cafeteria in silence.

Once they sat down at their tables with their trays, Aliz said brightly, "So Gábor seems pretty excited about the wedding, Zsu!"

Eyes swiveled to Csilla, like she needed to give them permission to change the topic, and she granted it, saying coyly, "Of course he is. Zsu makes too much noise in her father's house for any fun."

Zsu shrieked while Aliz laughed and Csilla smiled, letting the sound wash over her.

The world was a narrow bridge, and it grew ever narrower. That was, of course, unsustainable, but she could not fall off it out of negligence and willful impulsivity. She needed to be careful in her next steps.

So she laughed. So she smiled. So she did not think about the stranger who had saved her, or the secret police, or the boy who had danced with her, or the river, or her parents, or any of the befores, or all the missteps she had made.

She walked the narrow bridge.

CHAPTER TEN

CSILLA

OCTOBER 18, 1956

After their midday meal, the girls returned upstairs, where Csilla found Mária, their supervisor. "Comrade," Csilla said, ignoring Zsu and Aliz's confused looks, "I have a question for Comrade Márton Szendrey about his handwriting on this one note."

Mária stared at her and then nodded. "I believe he's down the hall."

"What are you doing?" Aliz whispered. "Show me, maybe I can figure it out."

"I'm sure Szendrey will be perfectly helpful," Csilla said, giving her friend a kind smile.

She picked a sheet of paper from her bin, making sure it was one of Szendrey's pieces in case she was stopped in the hall. Szendrey had some of the best handwriting of any of the men, which probably accounted for the look Mária had given her. And so Csilla, ignoring her friends' quizzical expressions, walked down the hall to the room where the journalists sat in a sea of desks.

She moved through the room to Szendrey's desk and put the paper in front of him. He'd been bent over a notebook, oblivious to everything around him, and he startled when she sat on the edge of his desk.

"Csilla," he said, caught off guard enough to forget the obligatory *comrade*. He looked at the paper. "What do you need?"

"Pretend I'm asking you a question about your handwriting," she murmured.

His eyes widened. "Csilla."

"Please," she added.

He glanced down, and she pointed to a random word, keeping her voice low. "I need your help. I need to find out about a prisoner across the street."

Szendrey exhaled slowly. "That's risky, Csilla."

The thing was, she knew it was risky. But she'd taken all the precautions she could while planning to flee, and she'd still ended up on their radar. She'd nearly been disappeared yesterday, and as far as she could tell, they were tailing her everywhere. She had so much she could still lose—Ilona, her window of opportunity to escape—but they'd used the last thing that was hers—her parents, exonerated—as a tool to continue their regime of terror, and she wanted to do one good thing before she left. She wanted to balance out what her father had done and what she'd done, in quiet, passive complicity for the last four years.

She could do one good thing. She could find out about Márk Dobos.

"There was a raid at the university, the same day as the funeral," she said quietly.

He looked up at her. "I know."

"They used my parents' funeral as a distraction," Csilla said, her eyes locked on Szendrey's.

His mouth tightened. "I know."

She took a deep breath. "One of those boys, he's a friend of a friend."

"Csilla," Szendrey said softly. "I'm sure they're already gone."

Dead, he meant, or on trucks going to labor camps.

"I want to know," she said softly.

He studied her, and then he looked back at the paper and her finger pressed against a word on his handwritten story about train schedules. He wrote next to her finger, *yes*.

"I have an interview with András Tóth," Szendrey said. "About the labor delays on the subway lines. Would you like to come?"

"When?" Csilla exhaled.

He looked at the clock at the front of the room. "Now."

She knew András Tóth. He'd been her father's deputy. She remembered being infatuated with him when he was a young, charismatic Party member rising through the security ranks. He'd been held accountable for not reporting her father's crimes—Titoist, Zionist, Jew—though he couldn't have known about them, as they were not real.

She nodded. "I'll come."

He gave her a wan half smile. "You are so like your father, you know."

She blinked, reeling. She hadn't expected that. "You knew him?"

"I did. He was a character. I'm sorry I didn't know your mother. She must have been an incredible woman to put up with Simon," said Szendrey with a chuckle, standing up and gathering his coat and his notebook.

Csilla gave him a smile in return. "She was."

She was brave right until the moment they arrived in front of the door to 60 Stalin Street. The wooden door was imposing and heavy, set into the stone wall. It looked like it'd seen the whole of the war without being damaged or burned as firewood, and Csilla couldn't decide if that was testament to the strength of the door or to the fear of this place in the hearts and minds of Hungarians.

Szendrey's hand touched her shoulder, and he murmured, "They will not disappear you right in front of me, Csilla. I promise you, I will not let them."

She swallowed, nodding. Then she stepped forward.

Before the war, and then during the war, this building had housed the Arrow Cross, the Hungarian Nazis. The same men who took her father and others from the ghetto to the edge of the river and shot everyone but him became his coworkers, became his employees as he soared in the ranks of this beautiful, terrible, violent space, and then, finally, did what they'd always wanted to do. They killed him.

Szendrey was not looking at her. He was speaking to the

guards, producing a letter about his interview with Comrade Tóth, and the guards were staring at Csilla like they knew who she was.

She closed her eyes. This was a foolish, impulsive mistake. Exactly the kind she'd told herself she wouldn't make.

The river whispered to her, and she could hear it even through the thick stone walls, soft and gentle. A caress. Her mother's hand on her curls, then her cheek.

Tamás's hand splayed on her lower back.

She hadn't wanted to take the risk. But she was here, and the risk seemed less now that she was behind these cursed doors. And at least if they were going to disappear her, she was making their job easier.

"Come on," Szendrey said quietly. "Let's go."

She followed, the dutiful girl ready to take notes and do nothing more than keep her head down and do her job, but her mind was whirring.

A handful of people sat in the lobby. Some thin young men staring at their shoes. A shaking woman with tear streaks on her cheeks, doing her best not to cry. Her loved one must be here, Csilla realized. And she did her best not to look around, not to take in the beautiful architecture, the glossy open lobby and the spiral staircases going up.

And going down.

Bile rose in her throat and she closed her eyes, willing herself not to fall or vomit.

"I wouldn't ask if he wasn't important to me," Tamás had whispered to her. Somewhere in here was his friend, dead or alive. Might be better to be dead.

Csilla shuddered.

With visitors' badges and an armed escort, they walked up the stairs to the second floor. They stopped outside an office. The guard told them not to knock but to wait until the door opened, and then he disappeared down the hall, lighting a cigarette on his way.

"I've known you all summer," Szendrey said to her quietly. "You've played by the rules and kept your head down the entire time. Why now?"

"I can't stand that they used the funeral to steal more people from their families," Csilla whispered, glancing around; but the hallway was empty.

"They probably weren't the only boys disappeared that day," Szendrey pointed out. "Why *this* one?"

I wouldn't ask if he wasn't important to me.

She hadn't come here when her parents disappeared. Neither had Ilona. They'd known what had happened. But maybe they should have come, even though it was risky. Maybe it mattered to show up, despite the risk, even if her parents wouldn't ever know that they had showed up.

She didn't know if Tamás had come here and inquired about his friend, but he had asked her. He'd taken a risk, and she could take one. Because this Márk Dobos: he was important.

"Because everyone's important and deserves to have someone ask after them if they're disappeared," she said softly.

Because before it had happened to him, her father had disappeared people, and she couldn't fix that. She'd been a child, and now she was not. This was something she could *do*.

Before Szendrey could say anything else, the door swung

open, and a young woman, looking a little flustered, stepped out, straightening her hair and giving them a quick smile.

"You can go in," she said.

"ENTER!" barked the voice inside the office.

Szendrey entered first, Csilla right behind him, and the flustered girl pulled the door shut. It snapped, making Csilla jump.

She knew who would be standing there, but that didn't mean she was prepared for András Tóth. He'd been the man who pretended to pull candy from behind her ear at parties for Communist Party members. He'd also been the man who testified against her father, and who trumped up charges on him, to avoid being charged with collaborating.

It helped that he was clearly unprepared to see her. He had stood to shake Szendrey's hand and left his hand in midair, staring at Csilla, his mouth slightly open.

"And of course you would know Csilla Tisza," said Szendrey lightly, as if he were introducing dance partners.

"Csilla," Tóth said faintly. "What is this?"

"I am here in a work capacity, Comrade Tóth," she said, ducking her head, trying to breathe. *Don't apologize,* she thought at him. But then, she wanted an apology from him.

"Are you?" Tóth asked, his voice still distant, and then Szendrey cleared his throat. Tóth snapped to attention. "You are?"

"Csilla is taking notes for me. She works at the paper," said Szendrey pleasantly, as if everything hadn't just been uncomfortable and tense. "But of course, you know that."

Szendrey chuckled, as if jokes about the secret police were lighthearted. Tóth and Csilla were silent. The river whispered.

"As you know, I heard that the ÁVH was why the subway

renovations on Stalin Street are held up. I'd like to talk to you about that."

"Why would the ÁVH have anything to do with subway renovations?" asked Tóth immediately.

"The subway repairs have been delayed considerably, affecting workers getting to the factories," Szendrey continued, but his voice was light and easy.

"You need Csilla here for this?" Tóth said, staring at her.

"Csilla is an excellent typist, and my handwriting is truly atrocious. It's better if she attends my interviews. It reduces work later and saves time. Efficiency," Szendrey explained.

He was so good at lying that Csilla nearly stared at him. Instead, she dutifully flipped open a notebook.

"The Államvédelmi Hatóság," Tóth said, his voice cold as he used the full name for the ÁVH, the State Protection Authority, "protects the People, the Party, and the goals of the Revolution. We must make sure that all of our assets are protected and not compromised physically or logistically by construction in the area."

"Ah," said Szendrey coolly. "So the cellar of ÁVH headquarters extends beyond its footprint?"

Tóth bit out his next words. "This is dangerous territory."

"Csilla, would you be a dear and go get us some tea? I believe the office with the tea is at the end of the hall, isn't it? Then Comrade Tóth and I can discuss potential ways forward. We don't need any note-taking right now," Szendrey said pleasantly.

Which was good, because Csilla hadn't taken a single note yet. She leapt up and, without lifting her head, scurried from the room. She exhaled in the hallway. Then she realized she didn't know which end of the hallway he'd meant, and she should have asked Tóth. But she was not walking back into that room. Not yet.

Finally, after walking hesitantly in one direction past two doors, she stopped another young woman, apologized, and asked where she could get tea. The woman smiled, pointed her in the opposite direction, and Csilla hurried there, her heels squeaking on the tile floor. She wanted to get out of here, out of this cold and terrible place. She heard a noise that sounded like a yell, and she jumped again, flinching a bit. But no one around her seemed to hear it.

Did they just hear torture all day? Were they immune to it?

At the end of the hallway, she found a small slip of a kitchen, and inside it was Gábor. She blinked, then stared at him. He looked up from the paper he was reading and startled.

"Csilla!"

"I'm here with a reporter," she said quickly. "He's interviewing Tóth."

Gábor winced, squinting at her. "I'm sure that's going well."

She looked at the tea. "What are you doing?"

"Getting tea for a colleague," he said, and then his voice dropped. "I could not stand to be in that meeting any longer. I needed to stretch my legs."

She shared a smile with him. She could understand that.

"Where do you work?" she asked, curious. She'd never heard Zsu name his specific office.

"In the records office," he said, jutting his chin at her. "Right across the hall."

Oh. Szendrey had sent her to the records office, not to get tea. He was helping her.

Csilla chewed her bottom lip. "Gábor, I need a favor."

He was smiling until he looked at her expression, and the smile slipped off. "Ah. I'm not going to like this, am I?"

"No," she admitted, "but I promise you, it's just a small favor."

She told him what she needed, lying by omission as needed, and his face grew more serious as she spoke. She was sure he'd deny her, or report her, but at the end, he just sighed.

"I've known you a long time," he said quietly. "And you've known Zsu longer. I know she loves you like a sister. So I'm going to help you as I would a sister."

Relief flooded through Csilla. "Thank you."

He took her across the hall. Just before he opened the door, he whispered, "Play along."

Before she could answer, he opened it and strode through with all the confidence of a man who thought he deserved everything he asked for.

The woman at the desk, glasses perched on the end of her nose, her hair a little out of place and wispy, looked up and gave Gábor a bright smile. "Hello, dear. I thought you were in that big meeting down the hallway?"

"I was," Gábor admitted. He tilted his head toward Csilla. "But this little mouse was in the hallway. She was scared to come in."

The woman's eyes flicked to Csilla as Gábor continued. "It's her first day, and she's filling in for Zoltán. You know, Tóth's secretary? Can you believe that's the assignment they gave her?"

The woman gave a sympathetic *tut* with her tongue.

Gábor nodded. "And of course, Tóth's busy today. She needs to pull a record for him."

The woman sighed. "I don't know why that office cannot keep their files in order. It isn't that difficult. What's the name?"

"Márk Dobos," said Csilla meekly.

The woman nodded. "Give me a moment."

She disappeared into a room of file cabinets.

Gábor turned to Csilla. "You won't be able to take the file out of the building. They'll search you. When she asks you to sign your name, sign a fake name. I'll take it from you and put it in the return bin in my office. Just read it. Understood?"

Csilla nodded, her palms clammy. She resisted the urge to wipe them on her shirt or skirt lest they leave a guilty stain.

The woman returned and said, "His file's here. But it has an expiration stamp." She *tsk*ed disappointedly. "Suicide." She continued as if she hadn't seen Csilla's insides turn to ice. "But no letter, so it's not complete yet. Once I get a copy from Ágnes, I'll add that to the file and close it."

She held out the file, and Csilla took it, hoping her hand wasn't shaking too much. "Thank you so much."

The woman turned a clipboard around for Csilla to sign. Csilla hesitated and then signed, too slowly, too cautiously, her cousin's name, Zsófia Frankel. A dead girl couldn't suffer consequences if she was caught. Csilla gave the woman a tentative smile, and the woman gave her a curious, but simple, smile in return.

"Have a wonderful day," the woman said, and then checked the clipboard. "Zsófia."

"Thank you," Csilla managed.

"Come on," Gábor muttered, guiding her by the elbow back into the kitchen.

He stood guard at the doorway while she flipped through the file, glancing at the neat typing. Arrested. Homosexuality and counterrevolutionary behavior. She chewed her bottom lip, thinking of the way Tamás had danced with her, his fingers splayed on her lower back, his voice low in her ear. She flipped past that and found the photo of Márk Dobos. He was—had been—a handsome young man with light gray hair, high cheekbones and bright eyes that sparkled even in his official photo. There was a quirk to his mouth, like he'd been laughing right before the photo had been taken.

Her heart ached.

"Suicide," she murmured.

"I'm sorry," said Gábor gently. "Did you know him?"

She glanced up at him. "Would I be in trouble if I did?"

He shook his head. "Not with me."

She handed him the file. "Thank you, Gábor. That meant a lot."

He tucked the file under his arm and nodded at the kettle. "You'd better bring your journalist and Tóth some tea now."

"I will," she promised.

He disappeared, and she leaned against the counter, closing her eyes. The river whispered to her, and she said aloud, "I know. I know."

She had to tell Tamás.

I miss him. I miss him like a piece of me that I carved out of my own heart. I saw him today. We met for coffee after work. He told me about his wife and his children, and I showed him a photo of Éva and Csilla. He told me he cried when he first heard I'd survived the war. He looks as devilishly handsome as ever.

I should not write this down.

I cannot keep pretending he is not a part of me.

—The Journal of Simon Tisza, September 1951

CHAPTER ELEVEN

CSILLA

OCTOBER 18, 1956

"Did you find what you needed?" Szendrey asked as they crossed the street back to the newspaper.

"I did," Csilla said, her mind racing.

She had to find Tamás. He'd said that he was often at the Technical University, but if she went over there and could not find him, what then? She could send a letter to him. How would she be sure it ended up in the right hands? In the wrong hands, they'd both be back in 60 Stalin Street, in the basement, with their heads held into buckets of water.

"How did you know my father?" she asked Szendrey.

He spoke carefully. "We were friendly. Before the war, though we kept in touch after. I hadn't spoken to him in a little while when he—when he died."

"It doesn't bother you? To go into that building?" she asked, keeping her voice low.

He gave her a sad smile. "No, it doesn't. Everywhere we walk in this city, we walk on ghosts. That building is no different."

"It bothers me," she said, a lump in her throat. "My father made that place what it is today."

Szendrey hesitated, and then he nodded.

She whispered, "And he died there. And my mother died there. She didn't do *anything*."

Surprise lit up in his eyes. "So you think he deserved to die?"

"No," she snapped. Then she pressed the heel of her palm against her forehead. "Yes. I don't know. He—he should have been held responsible for the crimes he committed. But those weren't the crimes for which he was executed."

"Csilla," said Szendrey gently. "The crimes you believe he committed are not crimes in the eyes of the Party."

They should have been. Her father helped to design and implement the State Protection Authority as it existed now, the ÁVH. He helped to create the institution that disappeared people from their families for crimes like having the wrong books on their shelves or listening to illegal radio stations. He deported people to gulags, like he hadn't thrown himself into a river to avoid deportation just a few years prior. She knew people—she knew people!—whose family members had died because of her father's orders.

She opened her eyes. They were in the middle of the sidewalk, people everywhere, a light drizzle falling steadily enough that she had to squint at Szendrey.

She tried not to think of her father's crimes, but they were everywhere around her. They shaped the country.

And it was his own crimes, his own policies and the things he shaped with his own hands, that had backfired on him and stolen her parents from her.

"They should be," she said softly. "No one ever gets held responsible here, Márton. Doesn't that drive you mad? What my father did—what they still do there—that's terrible. That shouldn't be legal. But the people who killed him had been Nazis just ten years before. And they weren't held responsible earlier. We just gestured and said that war was terrible and everyone made their choices, and pretended the slate was wiped clean."

"I know," Szendrey said.

"You *don't* know," she said.

"What do you want me to say, Csilla? I agree with you, but I can't know?" Szendrey's patience was finally fraying.

She stepped up onto the stairs of the newspaper building to get out of the rain, but it had the added benefit of giving her a height advantage over Szendrey.

"Hungary willingly collaborated with the Nazis," spat Csilla. "Hungarians—you? What did you do? How many Jews did you save, Szendrey? There is one member of my family who survived. One. My aunt. I lost five aunts, eight uncles, ten cousins, four grandparents, all of my great-aunts, all of my great-uncles. Every member of my extended family except one. I can count the Jews who came back to my neighborhood on my fingers, Márton, and they can say the same. The air I breathe is made from the ashes of my people that you burned."

Szendrey was pale. "Csilla, this isn't what I meant—"

"They took my father and other Jews from the ghetto to the river, lined them up, and shot some of them. Twice they did this to my father. Made him stand there on the banks, while people died around him. They took him twice, and spared him twice," hissed Csilla. "My mother lost everyone, and her sister came back a ghost, and my mother never lost her faith. Even when she lost my father to this place. And I'll never know if she kept it even when she must have known they'd kill her."

Szendrey swallowed. "Csilla."

"You don't know," Csilla said quietly. "You can't know. My family was dying in gas chambers and being incinerated in Poland like they were animals, like they were worthless and nameless and no one would ever miss them. And every single day I have to see the numbers on my aunt's arm that remind me that I am the lucky one. And no one is held responsible. Not for that, not for the crimes that have come after. When are we going to talk about what happened? When are we going to deal in truth and not lies? When will people be held responsible for their choices?"

"When you demand it," Szendrey said, stepping close to her. "Csilla, institutions do not have a vested interest in change. But people do. You do."

"I am not going to stay long enough for that," Csilla said, tears burning in her eyes. "I can't. I can't do it anymore."

"Don't leave," he murmured. "Csilla, if everyone who cared left—"

"They're killing everyone who cares," she said softly. "That's what that raid was, wasn't it?"

Szendrey pressed his lips together in a thin line. She knew she was right.

"Hungary's killed most of my family," she said at last. "I won't let it kill the last two of us."

She turned and walked into the newspaper building.

Szendrey did not follow her in. Csilla merely walked in, ignored Elek and went back to work. Because there was nothing else left to do. She could not go home. She could not cry. There was a boy not much older than her who had died in the basement of that building, perhaps because he thought death was better than whatever he'd get as punishment for his so-called crimes, or perhaps at the hands of others who would take no responsibility for their actions, and there was a boy across the river not much older than her who had risked everything to ask her to risk everything to find out information, a currency traded in the shadows here.

And somewhere in the city, a stranger had saved her life yesterday. He'd known her name, and then he'd disappeared. She wondered if he was in the basement of 60 Stalin Street too. She wondered if he'd been disappeared. She wondered if he'd ever existed.

The people in the city had moved on when the colors had left Budapest, and they'd moved on when tens of thousands of their citizens had been deported and turned into smoke, and they moved on every day when people were disappeared, for good reasons and for no reasons at all.

They'd accepted all the truths and all the lies and weighed

them equally against each other. But some lies outweighed some truths. Some lies were so egregious that refusing to acknowledge them was akin to committing the crime over and over again, every day.

She ached. Her bones. The marrow within them. Her empty stomach and her pounding heart. Every inch of her.

At the end of the day, when she stood, everything felt numb from her nose down, and the way that Zsu and Aliz were looking at her unnerved her. She touched her cheeks.

"Is there something on my face?"

"No," Zsu said gently. She glanced at Aliz. "I'll walk home with her."

Aliz nodded.

Like it was decided. Like she didn't have a choice. Like they'd been discussing something about her without her and agreed on something that she was sure not to like.

"I am not a child," Csilla said, and even to herself she could hear the whine in her voice.

Zsu shook her head. "It's not that."

Wasn't it, though?

Zsu, Aliz and Csilla pulled on their coats and made their way down the stairs in the din of the shift change. Csilla said nothing as they walked down the stairs and out the door.

When they were a few blocks from the newspaper, Zsu said, "What happened, Csilla?"

"Nothing," Csilla said automatically.

"Then why," Zsu asked gently, "do you look like you've seen a ghost?"

"It's nothing," she said, forcing a smile to her face. Even as she said it, she knew it was a lie. And that she was now one of the people who were perpetuating the lie.

Zsu must have felt it. "Are you sure?"

Csilla shook her head. "No. But I can't talk about it."

"Don't lie to me," her friend murmured. "We don't lie to each other. They lie, but we don't, Csilla."

She wished she could hug Zsu right then. But that wasn't something that was done in the middle of the street. She just nodded, because her friend was right, for the most part. They lied by omission. But never to direct questions.

They pushed through a crowd gathered on the street corner between the road and the path along the river.

Csilla heaved a sigh. "Why are there so many people tonight?"

"I don't know, but I wish people would just move," grumbled Zsu.

They got clear of the crowd and jogged across the tracks ahead of an oncoming tram. They crossed the road to where a crowd was gathered on the other side. The people looked around and down, anxiety etched on their faces.

"Stalin," murmured a man on one side of Csilla. He was speaking to another man, but the tension in their shoulders was clear, despite the joking tone. "From beyond the grave."

"Not his move," said the other man. "Coldest winter on record and no bread? That's more his style."

"There's still time," joked his friend.

"Stalin did what?" Zsu asked, but Csilla had suddenly realized how quiet her head was.

The river was not speaking. It was not whispering. It wasn't cajoling her. It was completely and utterly silent inside her head. She hadn't heard it since they left the newspaper building this evening.

Panicked, she pushed through the crowd to the front, where she nearly toppled over the wall into the—the water was no longer silver. The river was black as the night sky and just as still, as if the current had stopped, as if it'd been turned to stone.

"What happened?" she whispered.

And for the first time in Csilla's memory, the river did not try to whisper an answer she could not understand.

PART II

This is a story in my stones, says the city. Listen.

Dear Mama,

Budapest is the most beautiful city at sunset. It's all in gray, yes, but you could paint it if you wanted. The way the light cuts through the clouds, and it pools over the bridges and the river, and the churches and Parliament, and the statues rising high over the cliffs. I've been here a year and it still takes my breath away. And the river's always busy with boats going up and down. Sometimes I think about everything those boats have seen, going from Western Europe to Eastern and then down to Yugoslavia. It sees the whole world, doesn't it? Every way of life and all the scars of the war. But it's still beautiful, despite that.

I wish you would come visit. The city isn't so crowded if you know the right places, and there are plenty of parks in Budapest. It isn't the same as home, of course. And I miss your cooking, and I miss my siblings more than anything. It's lonely here, even though I've made friends. No one's snoring keeps me awake at night. Classes are going fine, I promise. I'm studying hard.

I'm sorry for the short letter, but Tamás invited me to a lecture tonight. He's one of my closest friends here. I hope you get to meet him soon.

Love,
Márk

—Letter from Márk Dobos to his mother, August 2, 1956

CHAPTER TWELVE

CSILLA

When Zsu and Csilla parted, they hugged tightly and quickly, the way they'd each hugged people during the war, when they'd grown up enough to know that they wouldn't see everyone the next day or the day after or ever again. They said very little, distracted by the river, and Zsu joined the crowd of cautious pedestrians climbing the stairs to the bridge, glancing over the side. Csilla watched her go and then turned toward home herself. She cut away from the river, and her head felt eerily quiet, as if she were walking in a dream. She couldn't remember a time when her head was quiet. When she hadn't heard the river. She knew when it must have been—before the war—but she couldn't recall the sensation.

She felt hollowed out. She kept pressing a hand to her temple as she walked, as if she could reach inside her skull and put a fist in the place where the river used to be.

It surprised her, the way she could miss something she did not understand.

Tonight, everyone was hurrying off the streets, speaking in low tones, their faces downcast, sloped and drained.

The river unnerved them all.

Not the river.

The stone slab between Buda and Pest, the two sides of the river joined together centuries ago, a beating heart of empires, the gateway from East to West.

What did it mean to solidify?

Csilla pushed open the door to her apartment building, shaking her keys free from her purse. Then she stopped. On the stairs, a stack of four black journals.

They were not wrapped in paper this time, and they were not addressed to her, but she supposed now they wouldn't need to be. She knew whose they were and to whom they'd be addressed. These were her father's journals, which she'd thrown in the river this morning, when it'd been the same liquid silver it'd been her entire life.

She took a step toward them, then another.

She looked around for the secret police, but she didn't see anyone. Cautiously, she turned back to the journals. This was a test. Surely it was a test. How had they gotten the journals out of the river? And why had they returned them to her?

She picked up the top journal and opened it.

There, in her father's hand, what she'd read last night.

The Journal of Simon Weisz

They were not wet, but the pages were wavy, as if they'd been soaked. The ink, though, had not bled. *Strange,* thought Csilla.

She closed the journal.

Yesterday, secret police and two strange men, both who'd sought her out.

Then the journals on her steps.

Today, secret police.

The journals in the river.

A trip to the ÁVH headquarters.

A river turned to black stone.

And the journals back on her steps.

Something itched in the corner of her mind, a desperate desire to connect these events. But she knew that was just human nature. Humans, her father always said, wanted to make order from chaos. And the last twenty-four hours had been chaotic by any definition of the word. Her mind was struggling to make sense of the chaos of her orderly, careful life.

"If you throw those in the river again," said a low, melodic voice, "I'll have to throw you in after to fetch them."

She spun, a scream on her lips, but it died as soon as she turned. The stranger from yesterday morning leaned against the wall, partially obscured by the shadows. He wore the same button-down shirt and slacks he'd worn yesterday, but there were holes in them now with dried blood. His coat was draped over his arm, folded neatly.

He looked younger in the shadows. And she still couldn't detect an accent. He was still too precise.

He was not Hungarian. But he existed. He hadn't been a figment of her imagination, and he hadn't been disappeared.

She stared at him, and the next words out of her mouth surprised her. "I thought I'd made you up."

He sobered immediately. "I know. I'm sorry I didn't show up. They detained me briefly and released me."

"Rare," she said, accepting his apology.

He smiled. "I am."

She knew he was. There was something about him that was ineffable, and she wasn't quite ready to put her finger on it.

"The river is stone," she said. "I couldn't throw them in if I tried."

"Ah," he said, sounding amused. "Well. It wouldn't be nearly as satisfying."

He didn't sound surprised to hear it was stone. Perhaps he'd seen it too. By now the news must have spread through the entire city.

"You knew who I was," she said softly.

"Yes," he said, and for the first time, he seemed unsure about what to say next. "We've met before."

She'd remember his Hungarian, she was sure of it. "I don't think so."

"No, we did," he said gently. "My name was Nati then."

She took a step back from him. "Nati died."

She could see his Adam's apple bob in his throat when he swallowed hard. "In a way."

"Nati died," Csilla said, raising her voice. "Along with my cousins and my grandparents and my uncle."

The man nodded sadly. "I know. I know, Csilla. I'm so sorry."

He still said her name in that strange and beautiful way.

She'd seen Nati's name on the death lists. Nati, her friend who'd spoken the first words of English she'd ever heard. Nati, who had played with her in the ghetto, all big eyes and long

125

eyelashes, like the ones on the man standing in front of her now. Nati, a tiny slip of a girl swallowed up in her shift dresses when Csilla's family had still been dressing her in ribbons and ruffles.

She couldn't understand it, but the river had turned to stone. "If you were Nati, who are you now?"

"Azriel. That is always my true name," said the young man. "You were, and still are, Csilla."

"I am," she said faintly, lacking anything else to say. Struggling to find her way back to center, she asked, "How did you come upon my father's journals?"

"They were in the river," he said simply. "And they belong to you."

"But where did they come from?" she asked. "Last night, when they were here on the stairs."

Azriel's expression sombered. "I don't know. But does it truly matter? You are your father's heir in all the things that mattered."

"The version of my father you knew in the ghetto," Csilla said softly, "is a very different version of the person he turned out to be."

"I imagine," Azriel replied, in a voice equally soft, "that's true for all of us."

Perhaps Azriel didn't know what her father had done. Or worse, perhaps he thought that what her father had done to this country, to this city, to her family and to her life was good. Perhaps he thought it was justified. Perhaps he too believed that he alone could bring order out of the chaos as her father had.

Perhaps he too didn't care if his daughter and wife were victims of his work, even if he himself did not have them detained, did not push their heads under water, did not steal a mother from a daughter, didn't disappear everyone who ever mattered to a girl who only wanted to live.

"Ah," murmured Azriel. "You're still ambivalent about the case of your father."

"He's not as uncomplicated as people would like to think he is, exoneration and all," she said defensively.

"No one is, Csilla," he said softly.

Csilla picked up the journals with shaky hands, stacking them on top of one another. "I threw these in the river for a reason. I don't know how you got them out, but I wish you hadn't."

"You need them," he said again, in the same patient, knowing tone.

"I do not," she replied.

"You do," he insisted. "Like you need your father. If you didn't need him, why did you run into the streets for him last night?"

She stopped on the stairs, her heart beating. She did not need her father. She swallowed hard past the lump in her throat. She wasn't used to lying to herself.

Azriel sighed. "You need those journals, Csilla. I don't know what's coming for Budapest. I don't know why I was called here again. But there's something brewing, and you are part of it. I know you are."

The knife's edge. They were teetering. Elek had called it the precipice of change. And she'd felt it after the funeral. It was a relief, in a way, to know she wasn't imagining it. "I'm not going to be here."

He blinked at her. "Oh."

She nodded. "We're leaving. On the first."

He looked surprised by this information, and she didn't know why it surprised her that he could be surprised. "Oh."

And she didn't know why it surprised her, the feeling of uncertainty inside of her.

"If it happens before then," she asked, unsure, "how will I know?"

She didn't even know what she was asking. But he hesitated and said, "I think you'll know. Or it'll just happen. I don't know, Csilla. I think that'll be up to you."

She didn't know what it was, or what she would know, or what was up to her, but the sensation of the unknown didn't feel uncomfortable for once. Her mind felt clear. "Are you a part of it too?"

"I'll be here," he said, which was an answer and not an answer all at once.

"I don't know how much I'll be able to do," she murmured. She needed to play it safe. She couldn't risk her and Ilona's one chance to escape Hungary. And she was being followed every morning now.

He ignored her words. "Read the journals, Csilla. Oh, and don't forget to find the boy. He ought to know what happened to his friend."

The questions tumbled together into a knot, tongue-tying her so that by the time she knew what to ask him next, he was gone into the night, and she was standing there on the stairs, clutching four crinkly journals written in her father's hand.

"Csilla?" her aunt called above her. "Is that you?"

"Coming, Tante," Csilla called back.

She started to climb the stairs. He knew about her father, the journals, Tamás and Tamás's dead friend Márk. She didn't know how he knew, but he knew. And he'd confirmed what she thought and felt. By admitting that her parents had been falsely convicted and executed, by giving them a state funeral, by deciding to acknowledge their wrongdoing, the authorities had put everything done during the war and after the war on the table.

Everything was up for grabs.

> I believe in this country, even though it is a fickle, angry beast. It does not know its borders, inflates its own history, destroys itself from the inside and makes the most damaging alliances. But I believe in it. I see the goodness and desire in its people. We only need to turn to the People instead of the archaic structures left in place by empire.
>
> —The Journal of Simon Tisza, June 1939

CHAPTER THIRTEEN

AZRIEL

OCTOBER 20, 1956

When he walked around the city, he tried to find the source of the fever brewing beneath the surface. But every turn he took brought him back to the river. The third time it happened, he blinked and swore softly under his breath. It didn't particularly matter in what language he swore, because he knew them all, but it was a language unfamiliar to those milling around him outside the church. They looked at him askance, shifting away from him. People moved in murmurations, like starlings, like schooling fish, like swarms of insects. He always forgot this. It took him a while to adjust to the idea that he ought to be moving among them.

Contrary to popular belief, he did not like to move among the people.

He didn't like to get attached.

It made it harder to do his job.

But so did returning to the same place for the second time in just over a decade.

He rubbed at his face. He could've gone another ten years before returning to Budapest. Another millennium would have been better.

He'd ended up on the other side of the city, in Buda, far from the place where he'd seen Csilla, far from the place where they'd tried to kill him before realizing that he couldn't be killed. He wandered down the steps and walked along the river—he'd forgotten how many bloody steps there were on this side of the city. Bloody. He'd learned that word in London, during the Blitz. He hadn't had time for a proper conversation last time before he was plucked from the river and handed over to the authorities.

He sat on the edge of the river, staring out at the expanse of stone that had once been water. If he could touch the water, he could speak with the river—rivers were used to speaking to angels—but this stone was a barrier not even he could cross.

He had been sitting there for a long time when he saw someone climbing down the wall and stepping onto the stone river. Azriel straightened on the wall, watching what he thought, based on height and build and dress, was a young man take one cautious step after another, half skating, half walking, as if he were shuffling across ice, toward the center of the river.

Azriel slid off the wall and landed on the stone river. He

walked—because angels did not *glide*—toward the young man, who didn't see him coming. As he grew closer, he could see the young man shivering, hands in his pockets, looking toward the lights of Pest.

"I'm a little surprised we're the only two out here," Azriel said lightly.

The boy startled, turning around. His hair flopped into his eyes, and he had to slide a bare hand from his coat to sweep it back off his face. He had a threadbare scarf wrapped around his neck, and his coat was too thin for this weather. (Azriel thought it would snow later that week, perhaps even tomorrow.)

"Am I in trouble?" he asked.

"No," Azriel said gently, thinking that having fear of punishment at the top of one's mind at all times must be a terrible, frightening and constricting way to live. "I'm here out of curiosity, same as you."

The young man looked down, tapping the stone with his foot. "I thought maybe it was ice. It'd crack beneath me. But it really does seem to be stone. I wonder if it's stone all the way through Hungary."

"I don't know," Azriel said. "That would be strange."

The boy's grin was quick and wicked. It made Azriel's heart beat faster. "Stranger than a stone river? It's the crossing of city limits that makes it weird for you?"

Azriel laughed. "I'm perhaps more comfortable with the odd than most."

The boy seemed to be considering something and then coming to a decision. He stuck out his hand. "Tamás. Tamás Keller."

Azriel grasped his hand. Tamás's handshake was steady and

warm, his hand dry, if cold. This was the boy whose lover had killed himself in the basement of 60 Stalin Street, the one Csilla would be seeking out. And just like that, Azriel felt, then saw, a thin golden line run from him through Tamás, and then it cut through the night, toward Pest, toward Csilla.

"Azriel," Azriel said pleasantly.

Tamás waited for a surname, but when none came, he laughed and dropped Azriel's hand. Azriel found he missed the feeling of Tamás's hand in his own. His heart ached a bit.

"What made you come out here?" Tamás asked, starting to walk around in the middle of the river.

"I saw you," Azriel said simply.

Tamás's look was cutting and all too aware. "Oh?"

"Yes," agreed Azriel.

Tamás looked back toward Pest, at a thin golden line he could not see. "I wanted to come out and see the city like this. I don't know how long the river will be stone, but I figured if it only lasts a night, then I'm going to see the city the way no one else has seen this city."

"By walking on water," Azriel said, amused.

Tamás laughed. "I suppose."

"Then let's walk," Azriel suggested, gesturing northward, toward Parliament and the Fisherman's Bastion.

Tamás gave him a wary glance. "All right."

Azriel knew that he shouldn't do this. It would be enough for whatever was to come to know that Tamás and Csilla were a part of it, that they were tied together and tied to him. He didn't need to bond with either of them. His contact could be minimal.

But he wanted to be here for this boy who had to pretend he

was not mourning anyone. This boy who could feel the change coming in the city but who would not face that change with the one person he'd assumed would be with him the entire way.

Azriel had been doing this work since—well, since the beginning, and he couldn't stand it. He was, in a way, too human. Too real. Called and beckoned where he needed to be, places of mass atrocity and mass suffering, and it hadn't hardened him. He wanted to touch the hand of everyone who needed his comfort, who needed to know that someone would be with them through the other side. But unlike the other angels of death, Azriel could not guide every one of his people over to the other side. There were simply too many in his line of work. He had to live, forever, with that knowledge.

He had told that man Tóth that he wasn't here for him specifically, because he wasn't ever called for one person.

If he said one name a day every day for every single person who had died between 1939 and 1945 in the world war, including the Holocaust, it would take him more than 230,000 years to say the names. He wasn't even entirely sure that angels lived that long.

But he wanted to know a few names, ones that he'd remember for the rest of his—life or existence, if they were not the same thing. He wanted to know who brought him here. He wanted to know the people who shaped the world to come.

They walked together.

"I'm new to Budapest," Azriel said quietly.

"I could tell," Tamás said. "Your accent."

Azriel would never understand how he could intimately

know all the languages of the world and still not get them right when he spoke to humans.

"I'm from . . ." He tried to remember a map of Hungary. The map of Europe had changed quite a bit in the last few decades. "The Serbian border."

Tamás made a noise like he didn't quite believe this, but he didn't ask any more questions. Azriel suspected that was more for plausible deniability than anything else.

"So tell me," he prompted Tamás. "Tell me what we're looking at when we're taking this once-in-a-lifetime chance to see your city from a stone river."

Tamás inhaled deeply and let out a long, slow breath. He looked over at Azriel. "I'm not from Budapest either. I'm from a farm. I grew up outside the city. Closer to the Austrian border."

Azriel felt like he should have known that. Tamás did not look at the city like someone who had lived here his whole life. He looked at it like he'd never quite get used to all the lights.

"That," Tamás said, pointing above them, "is the Liberty Statue. There's some bullshit on there about the Russians saving us. But the truth is, you can't be liberated from people you invited into your country. We allied with Germany. We ought to acknowledge that. Even if *we* were not the ones to do the inviting, or we did not agree with it."

Azriel looked up at the soaring figure hoisting a leaf over their head. "That must not be a popular opinion."

"No," Tamás said softly. "Both the Russians and my fellow Hungarians would hate me for that one."

"Why did you tell me?"

"I don't think you are ÁVH," Tamás said.

Azriel looked over at him, and Tamás was watching him. He gave Azriel a soft, sad smile, an action that drew Azriel's eyes. The angel looked away first, thinking of Csilla and thinking of the fact that Tamás had just lost his lover.

"Come on," Azriel said, his voice rough.

They walked beneath the bridges, and Tamás, an engineering student to his very core, paused to marvel at the size of the towers holding up the Chain Bridge. Azriel let him, and then they spoke as they walked.

Tamás nodded to the star on the side of the Fisherman's Bastion. "They hung those everywhere, like we could possibly forget."

"I have always thought that they hung the red stars everywhere so that *they* wouldn't forget," Azriel mused. "They are so far from the original vision, aren't they?"

Tamás paused, turning around on the dark stone. "It depends who you think has the original vision, I guess. But you know what really bothers me? I know it's red because they tell us it is red. So when I think of *red* in my head, I think of stars. Even though I read in books that blood is red, and so are some clothes, and sunsets. I know books call anger red and passion red. But for me, it is only stars."

Then he pushed off his foot, gliding forward on the stone. He nearly careened into Azriel, arms pinwheeling for balance. He laughed and whooped. Then he leaned back, lost his balance and fell, landing with a thud on the river. He laughed harder and stayed down.

Breathless, Azriel slid to his side, falling to his knees and reaching his hands out toward Tamás. "Are you hurt?"

"Oh God. In every possible way," laughed Tamás. "Except not physically. Not from falling."

He stayed down, hands folded on his stomach, staring up at the actual stars. "I don't know you, and you didn't give me a real name, and there's always a chance that I'll never see you again."

Azriel sat back on his heels. "True."

Tamás's head rolled to the side. "So do you want to tell me why you're really out here right now?"

"Do you want to tell me why *you* are really out here right now?" Azriel countered, feeling like a bit of a cheat turning that question around on Tamás.

Tamás's smile was very small. "Sometimes I want to feel very small in a very big world. It's a reminder of how insignificant I am. Not even talking about the whole galaxy right now."

"You want to feel insignificant?" Azriel asked. He'd always found humans wanted to feel very significant. It drove almost every major decision they made.

"If I am insignificant, then my mistakes are too," Tamás said softly.

Azriel thought about this for a long time. Then he stretched out on the stone river beside Tamás, looking up at the sky. Sometimes, in different places and different times, people asked him if he believed in God, if he'd met God, if he had weekly meetings in which God gave him an agenda of all the tasks and genocides and mass deaths he'd be attending over the next seven days. People asked him if, as an angel, he too rested on the Sabbath.

They'd thought him far more significant than he actually was. But for some people, at the exact moment they needed him to be significant, he was.

"I think," Azriel said slowly, "that in the grand scheme of time, our mistakes are insignificant. But our victories are not. And that the most important thing is to be significant at the moment when your significance can benefit the greatest number of deserving people."

Tamás considered that and then huffed out a frustrated breath. "So many considerations. Who are the deserving people? How do I know when I need to be significant? How does one choose to be significant in a moment? How are victories significant and mistakes not? Would they not zero each other out?"

"Our actions aren't a mathematical equation, Tamás," said Azriel gently. "There are no rules governing this science."

"It would be easier," Tamás said, "if there were. And then I get mad at myself for expecting a map for what's to come. I know there's not a map. It's just"—his hands rose and fell helplessly— "I wish I could calculate the risks. I don't care as much about the risk to myself as I care about the risk I'm asking others to accept. It's crossing a bridge into the fog for the first time, you know? You have to trust that the road continues and that there's something on the other side."

Azriel wanted to look at him right then, but he dared not. "You believe there's something on the other side."

Tamás rolled his head slowly. Azriel did not. Tamás sighed. "I do. And I don't know why I'm telling you all of this. Even if you're not secret police, you didn't ask for it."

It happened like this sometimes. Proximity to an angel of death loosened the lips of people.

"I just don't want to make a mistake," Tamás said, sitting up. Azriel could see him out of the corner of his eye, even though he kept his eyes on the stars. Tamás ran his hands through his hair and then slumped forward. "I made a mistake recently. And I am fearful that it was my mistake, a significant one, that had a person I loved taken out of my life."

Azriel wished that Csilla had already told Tamás, though he knew she could not have. He could not tell Tamás. And he thought that Tamás already knew the truth.

"I'm sorry," Azriel said, because that was all there was to say.

Tamás sighed. "Thank you."

Azriel got up as gracefully as he could on the slippery river and offered Tamás a hand. The young man accepted it, and Azriel didn't let go when he was on his feet. They stood so close, close enough that Azriel could feel Tamás's breath cross the distance to Azriel's cheek. He could close that distance if he wanted. So could Tamás. But neither of them moved.

"You are a good person, Tamás Keller," Azriel murmured. "And this risk was a good risk to take. I'm glad you did it. Remember that this was worth it."

And then he dropped Tamás's hand and began the walk across the stone river to shore, away from Tamás, and the red star, and all the things left to come.

> I am uncomfortable with grandiosity, but by God, I want to be someone this country remembers. Is that wrong? Should I be more humble? Sometimes I feel like the only person in this nation who dreams of its betterment. I know that isn't true, and it's hubris to think it. But I feel so lonely in my dreams. I don't know how to find people who want to make this country better. Should I just stand on a street corner with a sign? Should I take out an ad in the paper? How does one find others?
>
> —The Journal of Simon Tisza, October 1936

CHAPTER FOURTEEN

CSILLA

OCTOBER 21, 1956

Csilla could not shake Márk Dobos's fate and her need to tell Tamás Keller out of her head. It distracted her all of Friday, then during her day off on Saturday, and back at work on Sunday.

She once again considered sending him a letter instead of trying to find him at the university, but it was always possible that her mail would be read by the security services. And she thought that in this case, a letter would be impersonal and cold.

She knew, of course, firsthand.

She had received the news of her parents by letter.

When she came home from school the day of their disappearances, nothing had seemed amiss. Her mother was often out at a friend's house and would arrive home shortly to prepare dinner, while her father worked late hours—increasingly so. It'd only been long after dark, after eight p.m., that Csilla had begun to worry.

Ilona said, "She told me she'd only be gone for a little bit."

Her mother had taken her purse.

Csilla went down the hall and asked Mrs. Staller if she'd seen or heard from her mother. Mrs. Staller only said that her mother had had visitors earlier in the day, two men, and that she'd left with them but hadn't looked distressed. Csilla had gone back to her apartment on heavy feet, every step like lead falling from the sky to the ground. This time when she opened the door to her apartment, she could only see the things that felt wrong.

The book not pushed entirely back into the bookcase.

The unwashed glass in the sink.

Her mother's gloves by the door.

The eyeglasses in the middle of the table, as if they'd been taken off when she was interrupted. Perhaps she had been reading. Or sewing. Perhaps she'd been doing any number of things when they'd come.

But Csilla knew then, in a cold hard pit in her stomach, that the inevitable had happened.

Because six years earlier, when they'd jumped into the river, her mother had said it was useless.

"Sooner or later," she'd gasped, churning her arms to stay afloat, "they will find us. And they will kill us."

It hadn't been sooner.

141

It'd been later.

It'd been that day.

She sat down in her mother's chair at the dining room table and looked at her father's empty chair. At her own empty chair. Listened to her aunt's anxious humming in the kitchen, the way she washed the same glass over and over and over again.

Csilla took a deep breath, then let it out slowly through her nose.

Then she stood and went into the kitchen beside her aunt and lit the burner on the stove, where her mother had begun making their soup for the night. She put the bread in the oven to warm up, and she set the table for two people. Her aunt and herself.

Because she'd known then they weren't coming home.

She just didn't get the letters until months later. One after the other.

We regret to inform you that SIMON TISZA expired while in security custody during the investigation of his case. He was found GUILTY of being a Titoist, a counterrevolutionary and a Zionist, and his property will be seized.

We regret to inform you that ÉVA TISZA expired while in security custody during the investigation of her case. She was found GUILTY of Zionism, and her property will be seized.

We regret to inform you.

Now, here, thinking of that, Csilla knew she could not write Tamás a letter.

* * *

At the end of the day, Aliz and Zsu went to the market, and Csilla begged a headache so she could go home. She pulled on her gloves, trying not to make eye contact with her friends so they wouldn't see the anxiety in her face, wouldn't ask her any questions she couldn't answer.

She drew in a steadying breath. She'd acquired information illegally. She would now illegally share that information with someone else. This was the opposite of careful. This was the opposite of playing by the rules. Twelve days. In twelve days, she'd be on a train to Belgrade.

The bridge was so narrow it was a tightrope across the river.

But a letter wouldn't do.

She'd meet Tamás's bravery in seeking answers about his friend from her, the daughter of a newly pardoned ÁVH officer, with her own bravery.

In the lobby, Márton Szendrey was speaking with another journalist, one she didn't recognize. He waved at her, and Zsu and Aliz stopped their conversation, blinking in surprise.

"It's fine," she told them.

"Don't let him keep you from getting home and getting rest," Aliz said, sounding exactly like a mother.

"Comrades." Szendrey greeted them with a mocking inclination of his head.

They dropped their eyes and then glanced at Csilla, who nodded at them again. They left, but not before both of them gave Szendrey another long questioning look.

"They're going to think you and I are having an affair," Csilla said dryly.

"If I wanted to have an affair with you," Szendrey said with a snort, "I would. But you would not be my first choice. I wanted to ask you about Márk Dobos."

Csilla blinked. "How did you find that name?"

Szendrey ignored her. "Do you know what his crimes were?"

She did. But she did not know if she wanted to tell Szendrey.

"Homosexuality and counterrevolutionary behavior," said Szendrey, as if he didn't notice her lack of response. "The second we knew, of course. But the first—do you know what that means, Csilla? He had sexual intercourse with another man."

She hadn't thought much about Márk's alleged crimes, only that she needed to tell Tamás that his friend was dead, and Azriel thought she should tell him too.

"And anyone associated with him would also be under suspicion of this crime," Szendrey said, keeping his voice low.

Csilla had never known a man who had sex with other men. She wasn't even sure she strictly understood the mechanics of it. It wasn't something that one discussed, not then, not in her world. And in Hungary, it wasn't the inclination that was illegal but the actual act of having sex with another man. But she thought about the way Tamás danced with her, the way his voice broke when he asked about Márk, and she didn't particularly care about the legality of it all. It didn't really matter in that moment.

This was another thing that was a truth concealed as a lie. A great number of things that were terrible were legal, and a great number of things that were fine were illegal. She knew, being a Jew, that governments were not always the wisest of voices as to who was worthy of her respect and who was not, who deserved humanity and who did not.

She understood now why Tamás had taken the risks he had that night at the bar when he'd danced with her and asked her to commit treason. It was hardly the crime they'd hang him for. He'd taken risks enough.

She cleared her throat. "I am aware of the crimes alleged."

"Who asked you to find out about Márk Dobos?" Szendrey said, stepping closer to her.

She took a step away from him. "I will not tell you. Are you informing on me, Szendrey? Are you in bed with the ÁVH?"

He blinked, then murmured, "God no, Csilla, no. I was going to say—I know people who can help your friend. I know people who can get him out."

"Out?" she repeated.

"Out of Hungary," he hissed.

She stared at him. Márton Szendrey, the dumpy middle-aged man who just wanted to do his job, a doting father of two little girls, with a wife at home. Szendrey, offering her a secret. He knew gay men. Was he gay? Was this model-citizen act entirely fake, top to bottom? How did he know these people?

"I do not think," she said stiffly, "that my friend needs to leave the country, but if he mentions it, I will find you."

Szendrey studied her and then nodded. "I trust you."

She wanted to tell him that he shouldn't trust her. Of course he shouldn't trust her. She knew girls upstairs who didn't trust her solely because of who her father was. But maybe it mattered that Szendrey had known her father before the war. Her father had been eager, if overly ambitious, in climbing the Communist Party ladder. He'd associated only with the right people, and the right people were not newspaper journalists, especially ones like Szendrey, who had no ambition and no power at all.

So how *had* her father and Szendrey crossed paths?

Csilla's head spun. "You shouldn't."

"In my experience," Szendrey said softly as he stepped away from her, "the people who insist they can't be trusted can be, and the people who insist they can be trusted can't be. That is a truth this country cannot sweep under the rug."

He went back up the stairs, and it was another long moment before Csilla composed herself to step outside. She had places to go and people to see and, above all, a river to cross.

She'd leave Hungary on a high note, having done something good. Tamás wouldn't have to wait years to know the truth, like she had. And then she'd be gone, gone to somewhere where people weren't disappeared for real crimes or invented ones or ones that ought not to be crimes at all.

She ducked around the corner of the building, walking the long way down the block. She had a dozen opportunities to change her mind and turn back, a dozen opportunities to convince herself that this prisoner, this boy who'd danced with her, neither of them had anything to do with her. There was no reason for her to put everything at risk. Aunt Ilona. Her safety. Her job. Her friendships. The semblance of a life she'd constructed from the destruction of the last fifteen years. She was so close to getting out. She was *so close.* In ten days, she and Ilona would be in Belgrade, and from Belgrade they'd go to Israel. This could ruin everything.

She should walk back to her apartment, back to her aunt and their secrets and the names they used behind those walls and the memories they kept locked in the attics of their minds and the ash of bones that coated their dreams.

"It's time," she said aloud, startling herself and the woman next to her. They both stood at a street corner, waiting for the light to change, and when it did, Csilla let herself be swept up in the current of people walking up the stairs to the Margit Bridge. The bridge crossed the Duna at the northern end of the city center, with a good view of Margit Island and a glittering view of the setting sun over Buda. And beneath Csilla, the stone river blossomed, widening with every step she took. The river looked like it was made of marble, or of ice, as if she could skate across it. She would have been surprised no one was trying to walk on it or skate on it, but this morning, she'd seen the police and military roping it off. Now they stood every few feet the whole way down the bank, on both sides, as far as she could see.

If they came for her now, she couldn't jump into this river. The soldiers, and the stone below her.

It'd never occurred to her that it wouldn't be there when she needed it.

Keep your chin above the water, her father whispered in her mind. Her memory. Her mind. They were one and the same.

If we stay here, we will surely die, her mother said in her memory, in her mind.

If we let them take us, we will die, her father said hoarsely. *Stay in the river until they're gone. Then we'll climb out.*

Then what? Simon, you never think.

But that wasn't quite right. Her father was always thinking. That was his problem.

By the time she reached the other side, the sun had slipped below the mountains, and the air took on a damp bite. She began to walk along the river toward the university.

Her father had helped to build the facade of this country.

And his reburial had put a crack in it. People didn't like—and liked, at the same time—the admission of mistakes. But there'd be whispers now of how the reburial had been used as cover to disappear bright young men from the university. That crack would grow.

With every step Csilla took, she felt as if the city she knew was unraveling behind her.

The Technical University was far up the banks of the Duna, and her feet were tired by the time she reached it. She took a deep breath and followed her memory. After all, when she was very small, before her father had had grand ideas about architecture and the meaning of the images buildings gave to the world, before his ascent inside the Party, before he was a part of the secret police, he'd been a student here, then a professor. She remembered him riding his bicycle around on the grass between the buildings, remembered him letting her ride on the handlebars in front of him, his laugh deep and brassy in her ears.

She exhaled her memories. She might not find Tamás at the university, but she had an obligation to try. She made her way toward one of the academic buildings. The river remained silent, and she found that in this moment of anxiety and uncertainty, she missed the sound of it murmuring to her in her ears.

The door of the building opened, and a handful of young men spilled out. They laughed and joshed with each other on their way down the steps, and Csilla came to a stop at about the same time Tamás did so on the stairs, their eyes finding each other. One of the boys whistled at her, and Tamás absent-mindedly swatted him, his eyes never leaving Csilla's face. He crossed to her in two long strides, coming right into her space. His eyes roamed her face, and he touched her arm. It sent a spark up her spine, sending warmth from his fingertips right through her, and she curled her fists against the instinct to step closer to him.

"Come on," he said quietly. To his friends he called, "I'll catch up later."

"Who is she?" asked one of the boys, crowding close.

Csilla willed him not to say her name. She did not want to talk about her father right now. She wanted to keep a clear head.

"A friend," Tamás said shortly, in a way that declined to answer further questions but raised them nonetheless.

He settled a hand on her back like they were dancing again, and she let him steer her swiftly away from the boys in the grassy area. They found the front of the university again, with its imposing structure modeled after Parliament, and crossed the street to the river. He turned away from it, dropping his hand from her back and stuffing both hands into his pockets.

"You found out," he said, his voice low.

"He killed himself," she said with a lump in her throat. "I mean, I think. They say he did."

The knot in Tamás's neck bobbed up and down quickly. He looked up, squinting into the setting sun to hide the tears in his eyes. "Ah."

"I'm so sorry," she murmured. She didn't know what else to say. "I am so sorry. I didn't want you to find out by a letter."

"No," he said gruffly, tears in his voice. He scraped his hands through his hair, ruffling it. "Thank you. Thank you for finding out. I didn't know—how—"

"You didn't want to be picked up too," she said gently, and with clear curiosity.

He shot her a wary glance. "Yes."

She nodded. "How did you find me?"

"A friend of mine is friends with Elek's brother," Tamás said, and his cheeks darkened. He was blushing.

Csilla scowled. "Does Elek tell everyone about me?"

He snorted. "My understanding was you were practically engaged to be married. And you did leave with him that night."

"He walked me home," Csilla snapped. "That's all."

And then she closed her eyes, feeling the heat rush to her cheeks and wishing the ground would swallow her up or she could take back her words. She didn't know why it bothered her so much that Tamás might think she was seeing Elek.

But then there was also the risk that he'd tell his friend, who would tell Elek's brother, who would tell Elek, and then her one safeguard at work, her one safety net in case things fell apart, especially now that the river was stone, would disappear.

"I mean—" she hedged.

"You hold one of my secrets," Tamás said quietly. "I'll keep yours."

She opened her eyes and studied him. "That's not how it works."

He buttoned up his coat and put his hat on his head. It made him look older and smaller all at once, and she ached to take it off his head again, to see a boy her age instead of a boy desperate to be a man already. "Tell me how it works while I walk you home."

She shook her head. "I can walk myself home."

"I'm sure you can," Tamás said, oblivious. "But I want to walk you home. It's not every day that a man gets to talk with Simon Tisza's daughter."

She didn't want to be Simon Tisza's daughter, not to Tamás and not to anyone.

It'd be quicker and safer if she walked home alone. She could go back to her life, being careful. Tamás was a closed door now, and she could close the door on Azriel too. She could burn her father's journals, and then it'd be like this week had never existed.

She knew she was lying to herself. But she wanted so desperately to believe in this lie.

"Fine. But you can't ask me about my father," she said quietly. "Or my mother."

If she was going to keep taking this risk, then she wanted to be herself with Tamás. She wanted to be interesting enough on her own, without her parents' infamy.

His brow knit again. "Okay."

"Nothing about the war, either," she added.

The corner of his mouth quirked up. "Should I be taking notes?"

"It might be easier if you did," she said, and it took her a whole breath to realize she'd made a joke. That he was teasing her and she was teasing him. He slipped past her defenses again. So charming. He made her want to be charming too.

She had to turn away from him and begin walking.

He caught up with her and wisely said nothing as they walked. She liked the feeling of him next to her, a sudden steadiness to the world, at odds with the butterflies in her stomach.

For a brief moment, she thought he might offer her his arm. But no. Márk Dobos. On many levels, she didn't think Tamás would be offering her his arm. But they still walked close enough that their arms kept brushing and they kept bumping into each other and then scooting apart.

"I'm sorry," Tamás said the second time it happened.

"I don't mind," she said, and she meant it.

"Did you grow up in Pest?" Tamás asked abruptly.

"Yes," Csilla answered, surprised into the truth. "Always. And my mother grew up in the apartment I live in. My family has had it for decades now. You?"

"Baracska. I lived here briefly after the war, and then we moved back to Baracska," he said, naming a town outside of Budapest. Then he glanced at her. "Is that okay to say?"

"I don't want to talk about my experiences," she said, looking at the still, dark stone river. "I don't mind if you talk about yours."

"I know," he said softly, "that you are Jewish."

She flinched, waiting for the next lines.

"I'm sorry if you and your family suffered," he said into her silence.

She didn't expect that. She was used to the antisemitism of everyone around her. She was used to everyone justifying the antisemitism because of a few violent people of Jewish descent who'd led Hungary's Communist Party for a few years after the war.

She was used to knowing that in part, her father had died because the Hungarian Communist Party wanted to purge the Jews from their ranks, just as Stalin had done. That was why her parents were found guilty of Zionism—and why Zionism was a crime.

Antisemitism formed everything around her. She was used to knowing that the people around her would rather that she was dead, and if they didn't kill her themselves, they wouldn't stop someone else from doing it. It was part of being a Jew in Europe, her mother said. It was like that before the war, and it'd be like that for all of time.

She was not used to someone recognizing her Jewishness and not hating her for it. She rolled Tamás's reaction around on her tongue, savored the taste of it. It wasn't quite stardust. It wasn't quite bright. But it tasted sweet, like lemonade on a hot day. Refreshing and relieving when she hadn't realized how parched she was.

"Thank you," she said. She looked over at him and said, "I took a risk for you, you know."

His mouth was a flat line. His hands slipped back into his

pockets like that was the only way to keep himself from reaching out to her. "I know. And I cannot tell you how much I appreciate it."

"I did it," she said quietly, "because I know what it's like to have people important to you disappeared, and you took a risk asking me for that favor."

He looked at her curiously, and then he said, his voice low and uncertain, "I did."

"That was brave," she said, and it was a simple, delicious truth. She liked to say it aloud. He did not counter it, and she did not need to add to it.

He tipped his head toward the bridge. "Shall we?"

And together they walked up the stairs to the pedestrian pathway. It was there, as they turned slightly on the staircase and could see the path behind them, that Csilla noticed they had a tail.

She swallowed hard. She'd gotten Tamás in trouble. Or maybe he was under surveillance because of Márk, and now she was in trouble. Either way, she had to tell him.

"Tamás," she murmured.

"We're being followed," he said. "I know."

She looked up at him. The setting did beautiful things to the lines of his face, casting shadows down his cheekbones, slashing light every time he blinked. He looked like a painting.

"I've been followed a lot this week," she told him.

"I assumed they were here because of Márk," he replied quickly. "I apologize if I've put you at risk."

"I think I'm the one who put you at risk," she said miserably.

"What did you do?" he asked.

"I think they might have found out that my aunt and I are planning on fleeing," she murmured.

"Are you afraid?" he asked, after a long, steady pause.

It wasn't the question she expected him to ask, and it was such a dangerous question. They weren't supposed to be afraid. She resisted glancing over her shoulder at the secret policeman who was following them. She did glance down at the river, silent and hard. It was dark like the night, and she half expected to see stars in it.

"I am afraid all the time," she said quietly. "I can't remember not being afraid. I can't even imagine not being afraid."

It frightened her, the way she gave this stranger the truth more readily than she gave it to herself. She wrapped her arms around herself against the October chill. But fear had kept her alive. It'd kept her going. Fear was the reason she had money at the back of a sock drawer. Fear didn't always turn someone to stone. Sometimes it lit them up like a flame in the night.

"Do you remember the color red?" Tamás asked suddenly.

She blinked, then hesitated. She didn't want to answer this while the secret policeman was following them. She didn't know how far away he was. She started to turn, and Tamás grabbed her arm, tightening his fingers around her. "Don't look at him."

He was right, but it terrified her. She swallowed. "I do. I think. I'm not sure. I know what things are supposed to be red, but I'm not sure how I'd describe red, even in my memories. Do you?"

"No. And I hate that," he said. "I think sometimes that I

can remember all of the colors, but then other times, I'm not so sure." He glanced down at the river. "I've been wondering if it'll stay stone. If one day I'll forget what it was like as water."

"You think it won't change back?" she asked, surprised.

He shrugged. "That's what they're saying."

"It has only been a few days," she said, heart pounding. Maybe the river knew she was going to leave. Maybe her father's journals had done this. She didn't know.

"I am sure that's what they said when it turned silver too," he said grimly.

"You shouldn't say these things," she said, keeping her voice so low she wasn't sure he'd hear her.

If the river stayed stone, then what would she do when they came for her again? They'd already followed her twice this week. She didn't know if they'd stop there. If Azriel was not there to save her again, she might need the river.

"I know," he said. "But it's the truth, isn't it?"

"We could be arrested," she pointed out.

"There are worse things than arrest," he said.

And she thought at first that those were the words of a man who'd never been affected by arrest. But he'd just lost his—his lover—Csilla made herself think it through—and so he'd joined her in the most terrible, tragic fraternity behind the Iron Curtain.

At the base of the bridge, they turned again, and she could see the ÁVH man still following them. He walked with more purpose than anyone else this time of night, and he was watching them directly.

"We should split up here," Csilla murmured.

Tamás nodded. "You'll be fine getting home?"

She smiled. "Yes, thank you."

He gave her a crooked, sly smile. "You aren't afraid of the ÁVH man?"

"He ought be afraid of me," she said flippantly.

Tamás laughed, a big, full belly laugh that surprised her into a real smile. She wanted to make him laugh like that again. She wanted to tell him she wanted to see him again. She liked his steady warm presence next to her. She wanted to find out how her hand fit into his. But he was mourning, and she was leaving.

"I'm sorry again about Márk," she said, unable to find anything else to say.

The laughter faded. She'd ruined it. He gave her a sad smile. "Thank you. I'll see you around, Csilla."

For a brief moment, she wanted to rewind time and try again, to part as friends and without the grim reminder of everything they'd lost to Hungary and the Party. But she knew, better than most, that time could not be rewound.

So she just gave him her own sad smile and turned away from him and the river, her heart pounding with the urgency of its secrets and its pain.

She did not turn around, did not stop, did not take another breath until she reached her apartment door.

The ÁVH man followed her, not Tamás, the entire way.

> Éva Rosenfeld asked me tonight if I'd walk out with her. I do
> not know if I've ever been luckier than I am right now. Of
> course the first person I want to tell is M. I cannot tell M for
> all of the obvious reasons. I don't know why love has to be so
> complicated.
>
> —The Journal of Simon Tisza, February 1931

CHAPTER FIFTEEN

CSILLA

OCTOBER 21, 1956

Ilona watched the man from the window in the kitchen, clucking her tongue at him. Then she turned and clucked her tongue in disappointment at Csilla.

"I haven't done anything," Csilla protested, feeling suddenly young again. She remembered saying things like that, complete with foot stomping, a few years ago. When Csilla's parents were first disappeared, Ilona had tried to parent Csilla, because they both thought that was what Csilla needed. It'd taken them too long to realize that they got along better when Ilona remained her aunt, not her replacement mother.

Ilona raised an eyebrow at her. Csilla hadn't told her about 60 Stalin Street today, and she hadn't told her about crossing the bridge to see Tamás. She'd only said that the ÁVH man had followed her home from Buda, where she'd been with Zsu. It was a lie.

Ilona clearly knew it.

And they weren't used to lying to each other. But for some reason, some gracious reason, Ilona didn't push it tonight.

She came to the table and sat down, cutting slowly at the beef that Csilla had procured the other day. It wasn't kosher like the meat they'd had when she was growing up, but they'd long since given up on kosher.

"I suppose there's nothing to do but keep your head down," Ilona said to her plate. "Ten days, Csillagom."

Footsteps echoed on the stairs, and Csilla froze, looking up at her aunt. Ilona was still too. They listened. Csilla wondered if Ilona also remembered this type of waiting in the ghetto. They came then too. Sometimes they wore the uniform of the Arrow Cross, sometimes they did not. They took men and boys and women. Some returned, some did not.

If they came for Csilla tonight, she would be one who did not return.

"If they come," she whispered to her aunt.

Ilona shook her head. "No."

"If they come," Csilla insisted, "the money's at the back of the sock drawer. You can still leave."

Ilona's hands trembled on the table.

The footsteps stopped outside their door.

Across the hall, István opened his door and shut it behind himself.

Csilla's shoulders relaxed. It'd just been István, home late from work. That was all. The ÁVH would not come for her now. Maybe later, but not now. And that would have to be enough.

Ilona gave her a look and said, "I will not leave without you."

"If they took me, you'd have to," Csilla told her.

With a huff, Ilona refilled their tea and sat back down at the table.

"The day you were born," Ilona said, her voice shaking, either from speaking of the past or from the adrenaline rush of the footsteps, "the day you were born, the river burst its banks."

Csilla had grown up with this story. She knew it well. And perhaps a part of her said she ought to let her aunt tell the story for her aunt's sake, but there was something about the story that soothed her too. She did not mind then that Ilona wasn't responding directly to what Csilla had said. Perhaps they both needed this family fairy tale.

"The water wasn't silver before then," Ilona continued. "But as it crept over the banks in little waves, it turned to silver." She glanced out the window as she unnecessarily dunked the little metal tea ball up and down in the mug of hot water. "It was the strangest flood I'd ever seen. It went in no open windows and no open doors. It stayed in the streets and the parks."

The way Csilla's mother always told the story was, "The water was just enough trouble to mess up our plans." And it'd sometimes felt like an indictment of Csilla, the way she'd said it. But Éva had always said that she and Simon had prayed for a child for years before Csilla was born. They had been married for more than five years when she became pregnant, unusual enough to have Csilla's grandparents murmuring.

"Her water broke silver," Csilla said, interrupting the story.

Ilona blinked at her, pulled back into the present. "Yes. That's what she always said. And then you were born quick, silver hair and silver eyes."

Most babies were born with blue eyes, Csilla knew, even if she didn't remember exactly what the color looked like. She'd been born with silver but settled at brown eyes, like her parents' eyes.

"Your father wanted to call you Hajnal," said Ilona with a snort.

Csilla smiled a bit at the table, unable to look up. "So naming me Star was a replacement for naming me after the moon?"

"Éva didn't think it was a good name for a girl," Ilona said tactfully. She came away from the counter, holding the mug in her hand. She had to navigate around piles of newspapers to do so, and when she gave Csilla the mug, she used the newspapers as a seat, since a large radio occupied the second chair.

"Your father . . . ," began Ilona, and then she trailed off. When Csilla looked up at her, her aunt's face was clear and thoughtful. She was here, nowhere else, and yet still unreachable for Csilla.

"Yes?" Csilla prompted.

"He loved the river," said Ilona simply. "Sometimes I think Éva was jealous."

When she was a child, her father had told her that the river had burst its banks to celebrate her birth. Later in her life, he said it was because the Duna wanted to make headlines.

But that wasn't true.

The Duna didn't know it was famous. Rivers did not burst their banks because they were the second-longest river in Europe—and surely the Volga did not truly count, being in Russia— or because they touched so many lives, or for a newspaper headline.

Once Csilla asked her father how many people were alive because the Duna existed, with its fish and its trade and its barrier and its water, and he fell silent for seconds, if not minutes, something rare for him.

Then he'd spread open his hands the way his smile broke across his face. "Millions, and then those millions touch millions more lives, and so isn't it the whole world?"

Rivers were not people, Csilla thought. And perhaps that was where her father had gone wrong. There was some part of him that couldn't contain himself, couldn't play safely inside the rules. He always wanted more, overflowing his own banks and the confines he'd been given.

People were not rivers. Not even her.

Her father believed in the Duna the way her mother believed in God.

Csilla wished she knew what she believed in.

And Csilla knew that her aunt was right about Éva, and about Simon's love for the river. Her mother hated the way Simon spoke about the Duna. It was almost the other woman in their marriage. Her father called the river magical. He said it would save them. He said it knew everything, as if it was sentient. As if the river spoke to him, and as if he understood it. This was, of course, before the war. She remembered.

Her father, despite being the idealistic Communist, was always the whimsical one. At least he had been before the war. He was the one who told Csilla fairy tales, told her about magic, invented fantastic stories. He was the one who liked to retell the story at Pesach. He was the one who liked to tell her about the golem who saved the Jews. She wished he were there to tell her about golems now. She wished they were real, something that would protect her from the shadow men who followed her in the morning and the evening.

Her father changed after the war. They all had, of course, but she'd missed the father she'd known before the war. After the war, he was quieter. He was obsessed with work. He and her mother had argued for hours. She'd accused him of sacrificing his dreams and settling for something that fell short of them. And he'd accused her of refusing to accept any progress that wasn't the ideal. When the apartment that her mother had grown up in was nationalized and then carved up for four families, her mother hadn't spoken to her father for a week.

Csilla had felt like she needed to pick sides.

And she hated herself in retrospect, but she'd chosen her father. She didn't know what he'd done for work. She thought now her decision would have been different if she'd known. But at the time, it seemed like her father needed her more. After all, her mother had Ilona, and they whispered to each other in Yiddish and the secret language of sisters. Her father had no one else. She knew now that she had thought that she could love him back to her, the version of him she had before the war.

It didn't work.

"Tante," she began.

Ilona shifted on her chair of newspapers.

"Did you like my father?"

She'd never asked Ilona this before, and truly, she'd never thought of it. She'd attached herself to a static position, that Ilona must have liked her father, because she stayed and because he protected her from the State. He'd always been gentle with Ilona after the war. Perhaps that'd been survivor's guilt. He had, after all, saved only his wife and child. He'd left everyone else on the bridge.

Her aunt looked thoughtful. "Simon was . . ." She trailed off, looking into middle distance with a soft face. She took a deep breath, and Csilla let the silence drag on, waiting patiently. "Simon wanted to be much more than he was."

Didn't they all?

Ilona shrugged then, looking down at her hands folded on the table. The numbers on her arm peeked out from beneath her too-short sleeve. "Simon wanted to believe he could fix everything. He was always like that. Even when he was courting Éva. Some people are fixers. Your father was a fixer. And when he encountered something he could not fix, he did not know how to cope. He could not take the Shoah out of me," she said, pressing her hand to her chest. "And I think he blamed himself. But I also think part of him blamed me."

It was not an answer to the question Csilla had asked, but it was an answer to a question she hadn't known to ask.

"Sometimes," Csilla whispered, "I think I'll never forgive him. Everyone else thinks he is forgiven, but there are so many things left on his ledger."

Ilona gave her a small smile. "No one is asking you to forgive him, Csilla." She reached across the table and covered her niece's hand with her own. "And no one is asking you to carry his sins with you all the time. This world is hard enough without carrying more than you've been asked to carry."

In the quiet dark of the apartment, long after her aunt fell asleep, Csilla slipped out of bed and went into their sitting room, where she opened the first of her father's journals. Somewhere in the city, the river glittered, a dark stone. Below, in the streets, the ÁVH man watched.

On the first page of his journal, her father had drawn a star like the one on the bright white wall of the Fisherman's Bastion. She wondered if the one on the page was in red ink or in black, as it appeared. She ran her fingers across it. Her father wrote this. His hand was on this page. He'd sat, perhaps at this table, at this window, this late at night long after she and her mother had gone to bed, writing in this journal. Her parents had been in this apartment for their whole marriage, save for the months in the river. The ghetto wall had been built around them and then torn down, and then the walls were built within the apartment, both literal and metaphorical.

Csilla opened to the first page of writing.

She read and she read and she read, into the thin hours of the night. And when she was done, she closed the last journal and pressed it to her tear-streaked cheek. She wished her father, this one, from before the war and before the river, was here now. She could barely remember him, but she could hear these words in his voice, could almost hear the scratch of his pen on the paper. She could imagine him here at this table, bent over a low light, writing about his love for her and her mother as they slept in the next room.

She could imagine him all she wanted, but he was gone, and the man that he'd been in these journals had disappeared long before he had.

I asked Éva to marry me, and she said yes. This time, I did tell M. He celebrated with me, and though I wanted to kiss him, I did not. I belong to Éva now. I can now move past the shame of being a Communist before one was allowed to be a Communist, and look toward a time when the political climate allows us to return the country to the People. A revolution must come here.

—The Journal of Simon Tisza, August 1932

CHAPTER SIXTEEN

AZRIEL

OCTOBER 21, 1956

This city. Azriel loved this city. It'd been bombed to pieces in the war, both before and during the siege, and they'd rebuilt it lovingly, without the horrid architecture that dotted cities throughout the Soviet Union. Hungary loved itself. It loved itself whole again.

Almost. Almost.

The stone river had cracks in it, dark slabs twisting into the air like the tops of mountains, like hands rising out of the trenches of the Great War. The pressure was building within it.

The angel did not know what would happen if the pressure continued to grow.

The cracks were elsewhere in the city. He'd arrived after Simon and Éva's reburial, but there were piles of dead flowers on their graves from people who likely didn't love Simon or Éva but wanted to make a statement. And the Hungarians in Parliament kept their lights on late into the night. They strode from the building in dark clusters, heads together, murmuring about Moscow and Poland, about changes, about Khrushchev's misstep in apologizing for the crimes of Stalin and what it meant to admit mistakes.

What it meant to rebury Titoists and Zionists and admit that no crimes had occurred. That Simon and Éva—and countless others who didn't get exonerated but deserved to—had only committed the crime of being Jewish, or of being other in some other way in a state that wanted to consolidate power and feared any pull, any possible faith or power, greater than its own.

Azriel remembered Éva from the ghetto. She'd shone with her faith. And it'd never wavered. Not once. Not when they didn't have food. Not when her husband was taken from her multiple times to the river and returned to her a little more rattled, a little less himself. Not when her child cried.

Éva had faith enough for the rest of them.

And Azriel suspected, though he couldn't prove it, that as much as Éva and Simon could go for each other's throats, they loved each other, and that Simon loved Éva more than he loved Communism, or Hungary. If Éva had asked him to leave, he would have left, Azriel thought. That was dangerous too. The Party must have known that he loved her more than he loved them. He didn't believe in God, but he believed in Éva.

They must have been terrified of her.

Éva never asked him to leave, though, as far as Azriel could tell. Maybe she hadn't because she loved him too much to have him make the choice. He didn't know.

Trust, faith and love of something other than the Party were always a threat to the Party, and Azriel could see ripples forming here, beneath the streets and behind the fronts of buildings and under the masks all the citizens wore.

The Party had made mistakes and admitted to them.

Mistakes were opportunities for change. Mistakes could sometimes cut through the veils of lies and pettiness and propaganda. Mistakes could, in rare instances, expose the truth.

Azriel walked the streets, past the center of the city and into the outer stretches, to the smaller, cookie-cutter tenement buildings. He walked to the factories and back, crossed train tracks and bridges and roads, rode the subway and the tram cars.

And by the end, he was sure he was right.

The river groaned, and more fissures appeared.

CHAPTER SEVENTEEN

CSILLA

October 22, 1956

She woke in pieces, her hands plastered against the window. Outside, the river shivered, dark and ominous, cracking so slabs of stone clawed up at the sky. The river had risen, still stone, until it touched the top of the stone wall on each of its banks.

A new ÁVH man stood on the opposite corner.

She dressed, and wrangled her hair and pinned it into submission. She did not look at herself in the mirror. She thought about Tamás and how he thought the river would remain stone. She thought about the way she'd asked him not to ask her about her father, and about the father she'd discovered in the journals last night.

The Simon in the journals was not the father she'd known as a child, or the ÁVH man she'd known after his death, or the exonerated man she'd discovered in recent months. He was something altogether new and different, both proud and insecure, a dreamer who was trying, and failing, to stay grounded.

She understood this version of her father.

She was better at playing inside the rules, as her aunt said her father hadn't been, but this was a version of her father that she recognized in herself. But where he thought that he could achieve a better life here, where he thought he could be a part of it here, in the same place that nearly destroyed all of them, she wanted to leave.

She wished she could ask her father if she should leave.

"No," she said aloud to herself, sliding the last pin into place. She'd made up her mind. She'd come too far to stay now. They had tickets. They had plans. People were expecting them.

Her father would not understand.

But she wasn't sure how to understand all the versions of him that he'd been.

She did not understand.

He'd been prosecuted for the crimes of being a Titoist, of being a Zionist, of having allegiances that were not to the Hungarian People. She saw no evidence of that in the journals.

But she hadn't seen evidence of the real crimes of the ÁVH, either. The orders he'd given to have people arrested on false pretenses. The families he'd torn apart. The people whose lives he'd ruined. Those were his real crimes, and he'd done them in the name of the People and the Party. He'd been complicit. In this country of truth and lies, he'd lied even to himself about the power he had and the good he could do.

She didn't know how to hold all of her father in her mind:

the doting father, the dreamy storyteller, the idealistic Communist, the ambitious Party man. She couldn't justify what he'd done, even with his dreams and his ideals, and she couldn't forgive him for them either.

When she stepped out of the bathroom, Ilona was so still, so quiet in bed beneath the covers, that Csilla held her hand over her aunt's mouth to feel her breath. They'd done that in the ghetto during the war.

"Tante," Csilla murmured.

Ilona shifted and muttered, "Not now, Zsófia."

To dream of one's dead daughter and then to have to wake to the awful horror of reality again and again was the worst kind of torture, Csilla thought.

Csilla pressed a kiss to Ilona's cheek and left her.

She stood at the banks of the river, considering the black stone.

It was unmoving now. And it still did not speak to her.

She thought that once, she had remembered sunrises that were pinks and oranges, but she no longer quite remembered what pink and orange looked like, only that they were words she'd once attributed to the sky. Now it was grays. She hadn't known before how much gray was in the world, but the sky contained every shade imaginable.

She only had so many days left with the Duna. Only so many silver sunsets and only so many silver sunrises over its bridges, and the way it shone, metallic like the taste of blood on her tongue.

Like everyone in Budapest, she'd grown adept at finding

more than one word for silver. *Ashen. Stone. Pewter. Platinum. Oyster. Leaded. Smoky. Charcoal.* More than one word for things moon-colored, like her hair. *Frosted. Pearly. Ivory. Opaline.*

They raided other languages for colors. *Gris,* she'd heard people say. *Cinzenta. Kijivu.* And they, unlike her parents, were not called capitalists or Westerners or Zionists. There were only so many words for gray in Hungarian. There were hundreds of languages. Thousands, perhaps. Perhaps, somewhere, someone had counted all of the languages in the world. Perhaps right then, someone was inventing a new one.

This was the language she had. Scraps of Yiddish. A stomach full of Hungarian. A mouthful of Russian. A taste of every word for the only color she really knew.

And the river.

"I had no idea," said a smooth and oddly familiar voice, "that rivers were stubborn."

Csilla looked sideways at Azriel, who appeared a little more mundane, a little less beautiful, in the light of day. He would still stand out in a crowd. His eyes were softer on her, and while his voice was teasing, she did not think she was the target.

"Hello," she said. "So you don't know why it's stone either."

He shook his head. "I don't. I've never seen it happen before."

She glanced over his shoulder at the ÁVH man watching them from a distance. "I think they found out that I'm leaving."

"Perhaps," Azriel said, glancing at the man. "Perhaps they're just afraid of you. They are not the only ones who could use your parents' exoneration and reburial as a shield for their own motives. You could as well."

She blinked at him. "Me? What motives?"

"Imagine," Azriel said, "what you'll say when you leave here, when you aren't afraid of being disappeared."

She hadn't imagined. She hadn't even gotten that far in imagining life somewhere else. She'd thought about the lack of secret police, but she hadn't thought about living in a place where she could say what was on her mind without fear of reprisal. She hadn't thought about what she could say about Hungary, and the ÁVH, and the Party after she left. She'd been so concerned with leaving that she hadn't thought past that point.

What *would* she say?

"I told Tamás," she said to him, wanting to change the topic.

He sighed. "Good. I'm sorry you had to do that. But I'm glad. He needed to know."

"I know," she said quietly. "But what I don't know is how you knew about Márk Dobos and the journals, and how you survived the ÁVH and why they let you go. Why are they scared of you?"

"Ah," said Azriel. He frowned at the stone river, at the brightness of the day. The line where white sky met black river made them both squint. "My name is Azriel. I take different forms, and sometimes I need to use other names. I've taken on many forms throughout my life, and I'll take on many more. I go where I am called, and I've been called back to Budapest. The last time I was here, you knew me as Nati. This time I am taking the form most comfortable to me right now and most useful in this space. Do you understand?"

"You are . . ." She faltered, searching her memory for the familiarity of Azriel. "An angel of death. The angel of death?"

"An," he said firmly. "One of many."

"That's not in the text," she said, her voice faint. She struggled to pull up memories. She'd been taught this once, a long time ago, hadn't she?

"The text was written by man, and man is fallible," he said simply, as if he'd said that many times to many people. Then he added, "Actually, men are the most fallible of mankind."

"Why were you Nati last time?" she said, looking back at the river.

"Because the children . . ." And now he was the one who faltered. "I am an angel they send when there's going to be some mass event—war, genocide, terrorism. And in the Holocaust, especially for Budapest, the children bore the brunt of it. I wanted to be a child so I could get close enough to the children to soothe them when the time came."

Horror ran through her, a jolt to her system, as if she'd fallen into the icy waters again. Her jaw dropped open, her body went rigid, and she stared at the black river as if it had answers, as if it could make what he'd said make sense. She turned her head slowly to him. He looked miserable there, his hands in his pockets, his shoulders hunched, and he looked young.

He was an angel of death. He'd gone through the Holocaust as a child, from Budapest to the gas chambers of Auschwitz. If he stayed as Nati, stayed with the children of the ghetto until the very end, then he would have been there with her cousins. She wanted to ask him about that, if he knew them, if he had been able to soothe them as he said he wished to.

"Did you," she managed to say, "know my cousins? Do you remember them?"

He looked at the river. "I remember them all."

And in a way, she was jealous. She did not remember her cousins well. She remembered Zsófia's laugh and the way she bossed around all the younger cousins in their games. But Zsófia's face, and Béla's face, and Oszkár's face were blurry in her mind, chubby cheeks and curls, but without shape.

"Did—" she began, and then changed direction with her question. "How do you stand it?"

He grimaced, looking down at his shoes. "Not well."

Impulsively, she reached out, her hand gliding across his wrist. He slipped his hand out of his coat, and she wrapped her fingers around it. She didn't squeeze it or lace her fingers between his. She just held his hand, feeling his skin, warm and real, against her own, warm and real.

"I'm sorry," she said quietly.

He smiled back at her, a small and shaky thing, a leaf at the end of a branch. "You aren't afraid of an angel of death?"

"You aren't here for me," she replied, and realized she'd come to that conclusion a minute earlier. "I mean, you might be. But you aren't here for me alone."

"No," he said gently. "I'm not. Even if you wish I were."

It was the most honest and painful thing anyone had said to her in the last four years, even with everything Tamás and Ilona had said to her the day before. It made her want to cry, but she did not cry easily, so she held back her tears by sheer force of will.

She dropped his hand. "You were called back to Budapest. For whatever is coming."

He grimaced. "Something, yes. And before you ask—I do not

know. I am here to witness and to soothe those who are crossing over. That is my only role. I cannot know what is to come."

"So much for a heavenly messenger," she muttered, and she thought she caught a quick smile on his face.

"I thought when I arrived that the balance hadn't tipped yet, but the more time I spend here, the more I think I'm still catching up, that the balance tipped a while ago and I'm just figuring it out."

She felt that too. "I don't think you're alone there."

"When do you think it happened?"

"I don't know," she admitted. "When the powers that be admitted that they'd made errors, that Stalin had made mistakes and perpetrated crimes, then everything we were told was shaken loose. I don't know how to tell what's true and what's not anymore, and I doubt anyone else does. It feels—" She hesitated and held out her hand, tipping it side to side. "And this time, I want truth to win."

Her father had sought the side of truth too, but in doing so, had ended up abetting a system of lies.

Would she repeat that history?

"Truth will out," Azriel said. He tilted his head toward the street. "You'll be late to work. May I walk you?"

She blinked. Something was coming to Budapest, but she still had to go to work. That seemed incongruous. But she understood that it would not come today, or he'd be urging her in a separate direction, urging her elsewhere.

"Can you tell me when?" she asked as they began to walk. "Will I still be here, in Hungary?"

She didn't know why that mattered, but she felt curiosity bubbling up in her. She wanted to know what it looked like when truth overcame lies.

He hesitated. "Even if I knew, which I do not, I could not tell you. We are not to meddle in the affairs of men."

"This isn't meddling," she clarified. "Saving me from the ÁVH man, the journals, the warnings: also not meddling."

He held up a hand and tilted it back and forth, giving her a coy smile. "Depends on the definitions, and I am very good at arguing for my definitions."

"I bet you are," she murmured.

His laugh was a warm, soft sound that made her smile, though she hid it from him as they wound their way through Budapest and toward her office.

Éva has been trying to teach me Hebrew. I have been so ashamed that I grew up without learning any prayers. I have memorized the ones we do every week at Shabbat, but I want to know the ones that she does every day. I want to be able to do more than mumble on high holidays at shul.

She's written out all of the Hebrew letters on small cards.

When I guess the sound right, I get a kiss.

It's a very effective teaching method. She should write a paper about this pedagogy.

She is finally with child. She thinks the baby may be a Pesach baby. She looks beautiful, even if she does not feel her best right now.

I wrote to M and told him, and he phoned me back when he got the letter to congratulate us.

—The Journal of Simon Weisz, December 1937

CHAPTER EIGHTEEN

CSILLA

OCTOBER 22, 1956

"For someone who's never late, you've been late twice recently," Zsu said to Csilla. It was a question, and there was no subtleness to Zsu's way of asking. She was not, Csilla was realizing after all these years, a subtle person. Then she nodded, without waiting for an answer to her question, at the stack of papers in Csilla's in-box. "Bet you have what we all have. It's causing trouble."

Csilla picked up the top piece of paper. It was a handwritten note from one of their journalists in Warsaw. The next one was a telegram, also from Warsaw.

"What's happening?" she asked.

"The Russians are meeting with the Poles," Zsu murmured. "The Poles are getting what they want."

Csilla blinked over at her. "You know that from these notes?"

Zsu shrugged and gave her a smile that said *Oops*.

For someone in the secret police, Gábor had a loose tongue, Csilla thought. She stared down at her full box. "We can't write this story."

"We have to," Zsu said. "I'm writing it for some local paper in Tata," she added, naming a large city to the west of Budapest, closer to Czechoslovakia. Their paper was the State paper, and some of the international articles would be shared with whatever city needed them.

Csilla looked through her papers. She was writing the one for Budapest. The journalist, Attila Kis, was one of the younger men on the team, and they often sent him abroad, a sign that he was more trusted than most.

It probably also meant he was a spy, but Csilla tried not to think about that.

She kept flipping through the notes and papers. She couldn't write the article that these notes said Attila wanted her to write. These notes he'd sent her to piece together into the coherent story of a country under the thumb of a faceless empire, a country asking for freedoms due to it and freedoms it'd fight for. It was a good story, the kind that turned into folktales and fables, the kind that fathers would tell their sons when they were small, the kind that led to parades and flag waving and songs and national holidays.

This had been what her father wanted for Hungary.

Only now, reading these notes, did Csilla realize that this was what she wanted for Hungary too.

When she started at the paper in June, the Polish protests had just begun, but she only knew that from scraps of conversation she heard. The Polish news wasn't carried by the papers, especially not her paper. Her paper likely thought it would "undermine the Hungarian People's will." Whatever the reason, the Polish protests were rumors, unfounded, unformed and unguided.

What she held in her hand was proof that things were changing for Poland. The Soviets were to meet with the Polish leaders and decide the future of the country. Csilla could scarcely believe what she was reading. The future of the country was negotiable. The future of the country was up for discussion. It was on the table. Csilla couldn't imagine it, couldn't imagine Khrushchev saying that Hungary could discuss its own future with the Soviets and that there was a place for agreements.

A small part of her wondered if it was a trick, if the Polish leaders would all be assassinated or arrested for show trials elsewhere while pro-Soviet leaders were installed in Poland. But the Polish people wouldn't stand for that, she didn't think. She thought she remembered that people had died in the protests in June.

Change, she thought, relishing the word in her mind. She didn't often get a chance to think it. It was fall, and it was October three years after Stalin's death, and there was change in the air.

She knew where her father, the man she'd grown up loving and the man in his journals, would have stood on this issue. She also knew where her father, the politician and Party man, would have stood on this issue.

She wanted to believe in the version of him that he'd lost but she'd loved. She wanted to think about a world in which she wasn't so afraid all the time. But she was afraid of this story in front of her, begging to be told.

She read through the rest of the pieces, marveling at the bits of information. Wages going up fifty percent. The idea of sovereignty. *Szuverenitas.* She rolled the word around in her mouth, relishing the feel of it and all its syllables, feeling the weight of its meaning. It tasted like an orange, bright and surprising, sunlight on her tongue.

She had forgotten words could taste like something other than dry bread and ash.

She could tell this story in all its truths, with none of the lies or slanted truths she'd been forced to use before.

Attila would have to forgive her. And if he didn't, if he was given the blame, then at least he wasn't here to face the consequences. He could escape. He could stay in Poland.

She was the one in Hungary.

She was the one staying in Hungary.

She turned the last piece of paper out of her typewriter,

stacked the article together, fastened it with a paper clip and set it in her done basket on the other side of her desk. Almost immediately, Mária whisked down the aisle, picking it up along with all the completed articles in the other girls' baskets. She returned to the back of the room, and Csilla picked up her next task.

She was knee-deep into typing up the next article—the journalist had horrific handwriting—when Mária stopped by her desk.

"That was good, comrade," she murmured.

And then she was gone again.

For the months that Mária had been her supervisor here, Csilla had thought that she was a Party favorite, that she always played by the rules, that she would never bend or break them for anything. She'd been surprised by so many people in the last week.

At the end of the day, all the girls were gossiping at the doors.

"My article said there was to be a meeting today in the student union at the Technical University, in solidarity with the Polish students," said Marika, a ghostly pale girl who usually avoided Csilla and flinched every time someone used Csilla's last name.

Zsu brightened. "Oh, I'd love to go." She turned to Csilla and Aliz. "Are either of you free? I want to hear what all the news is!"

"We write the news," Aliz reminded her.

Csilla's first instinct was that this was a trap. Her second was she wanted to go too. And maybe she had learned something that the students didn't know. Maybe there was enough for an article tomorrow. Perhaps Szendrey would help her write it. "I'll go."

Zsu and Aliz looked at her in surprise, and then Zsu grinned. "Excellent!"

Aliz looked at them warily, and she didn't sound particularly sad when she said, "I can't. Baby."

"Right," Zsu said with a sigh. "Can't your mother watch him for a few hours? This will be fun."

Or end in their deaths, Csilla thought, reasonably. She was dizzy at the idea of defying the Party so openly. They wouldn't take kindly to this, not with all the news out of Poland right now. She felt delirious, drunk.

"No, but tell me all about it," Aliz said, still sounding wary. "Tomorrow."

"Tomorrow," echoed Zsu and Csilla.

Tomorrow. The word blossomed in Csilla's chest, a bloom of a word. Her fingers curled into her hands, her hands to her wrists. She wanted to hug herself, to hold that feeling inside of her. Selfish, perhaps. Perhaps someone else needed that blossom inside of their chest, but she didn't want to release it into the world.

Tomorrow. When had she ever looked forward to the next day? And what was it about the next day that felt—she unfurled her fists, searching out of instinct with an open hand for the word—promising? She didn't understand, but she found she wanted to.

Their walk across the city was unremarkable. The river was still stone. The people still gathered on the banks, but even today, the crowd numbered fewer than the day before. There were bigger problems in Hungary than the river turning to stone. Or perhaps, as with the colors, people had accepted what they shouldn't have.

A steady stream of students and other people flowed toward the Technical University, coats up against the damp October air. Csilla and Zsu stuck together, wary and alert in a crowd that was overwhelmingly male. A few of the boys joshed at the girls, but they both raised their chins and kept marching forward.

"You aren't students here," guessed one. "Why are you here? Spies?"

"ÁVH girls aren't that cute," said another dismissively.

"No, they're cuter," argued a third. "To get you into bed. Hey, unbutton the top of your dress. Just two buttons."

"Enough," Zsu told them, when Csilla couldn't speak.

The boys laughed, then elbowed each other and jogged ahead of the girls to another cluster of boys heading into the university.

Zsu and Csilla were silent as they stepped up and into the building. When they crossed the threshold and into the loud, crowded room, a thunderous, earthshaking noise rocked them.

And like a dam breaking, the river burst back into Csilla. She gasped, staggering into Zsu. The roar was a gushing of water and sound, words that babbled and didn't make sense, and the waves rocked inside of her.

Around her, people yelled and screamed, grabbing on to each other and the walls, the desks and the chairs, sinking to the ground.

"It's the Russians," gasped someone. "They're bombing us."

"It isn't the Russians," Azriel said, appearing at Csilla's side.

She opened her mouth to reply, but no words came out. His hand around her elbow was the only way she knew she was falling.

Ehyeh asher ehyeh, the river whispered to her. *Ehyeh asher ehyeh.*

And like she had dragged her fingers through the river silt of her memory, she felt the translation surface, bobbing and gasping.

I will be what I will be.

As if it knew she'd found the translation, the river settled in her mind, lapping at the edges like a boat against the dock.

"Csilla," said Azriel, his voice low and urgent. "Come back to us."

"Give her space," spat a familiar voice.

Csilla opened her eyes. She hadn't realized they'd closed. She was on the floor, with Zsu's pale face next to her and Tamás leaning over her, his face haloed by the overhead lights. The crowd was clustered around her, leaving her a small island in a sea of bodies. Azriel knelt beside her, her hand in his. He stared at her with such intensity that she thought he was willing her to her feet.

"Csilla," Azriel said calmly, without looking at Tamás. "You must get up."

And just like that, as if he'd poured strength into her, she knew she could stand. She nodded as best she could in her position, and he gripped her hand, hauling her to her feet. She staggered a bit, and Zsu caught her other hand. Tamás reached for her, but finding nowhere safe to put his hand, dropped it back to his side.

His forehead knit in a little cross. "You fainted." And then he blinked and added, before she could say anything, "You're here."

"You're the man from the bar the other night," breathed Zsu. "Csilla . . ."

The crowd, finding Csilla to be well and far less interesting when she was on her feet, began to murmur, filling in the spaces as they went back to their discussions and gossip around her. She caught heated words about student groups, new names, new acronyms, all with similar ideas.

Azriel dropped her hand and turned to Tamás. "Don't make a spectacle."

"Who *are* you?" Tamás said to him, and the way he'd said it, Csilla knew that they'd met before. Had they, too, met when Azriel was Nati?

"I'm fine," she insisted, leaning on Zsu. She was glad Azriel was here, but she was more glad that Zsu was here. "I'm fine. Let me be."

Both young men turned back to her, and Zsu growled, pointing a finger at both of them as if she were uncertain who was the real problem. "I don't know who either of you are, but if you hurt her, or if you're the reason why she fainted, I will kill you. I will rip you to shreds. I will feed you to the fish in that river."

Azriel was fighting a grin. "I understand."

"I don't mean her any harm," Tamás said, looking like he was calming down too.

Csilla said softly, "Zsu, they're fine."

Zsu gave her a doubtful look, and Tamás gave her a crooked smile. "Yeah? Just fine?"

She shot him a look. "Don't push it."

The smile faded. "Are you well? The earthquake—"

"The river," Csilla said. "It's not stone anymore."

Zsu sucked in a breath, but Azriel's eyes never left Csilla's face. "A little on the nose, don't you think?"

His tone was dry but his gaze serious. Still, his words loosened something in her chest.

"Azriel, I can understand it now. The river," she whispered. "There are words now."

Azriel's hand closed around her wrist, holding her in place, and the rush of water in her mind disappeared. She blinked, then exhaled. She hoped he wouldn't let go.

"Why?" she asked. She meant the letting go. She meant the river's words.

He shook his head. "I don't have answers. Maybe the river does."

The river hummed against her bones, scraping on her edges.

His eyes roamed her face. "Will you promise me something?"

"I can't make promises," she said automatically.

"I know," he said, smiling. "But will you promise me anyway?"

"No," she said. Who was she to make promises to an angel of death?

"Listen tonight," he said. He let go of her wrist, and the water rushed back into her mind.

Tamás said to Azriel, "What if this is a mistake? Bringing everyone here. They could arrest us all."

Azriel reached toward Tamás and then stopped himself, his

hand falling back to his side. "I don't know if it's a mistake. But it is not insignificant, Tamás."

Outside, the river groaned, like it was stretching. The people inside the room slowed, stilled, listened, and in the silence that followed, the conversation picked up again. Csilla listened to the river, felt it wash over her. It began in her sternum, ran right down the center line of her body and lapped side to side, over her breasts, slipping between her ribs as it rushed through all the twists and turns of her body, crested her hips and trickled down her thighs.

She touched her sides with flat, open palms, expecting to find herself soaked straight through by the warm silver water, but she was as dry as a bone.

Tamás looked at Azriel and Csilla. "Will you both stay? It means something to me, to know what you think."

"I see how it is," Zsu grumbled.

"Yes," Csilla said, surprising herself. She looked sideways at Zsu and Azriel. "We'll stay."

Tamás gave her a relieved smile and nodded to Azriel, and his smile warmed. A flash of jealousy went through her like lightning. Azriel was hers—he'd been Nati, her friend during the war, and he'd come back to her.

Maybe he'd been someone to Tamás too.

Tamás disappeared to the front of the room, and she wrestled the feeling back down inside of her. There was a time and a place for everything, and now wasn't the time for that feeling.

When Zsu was distracted by the commotion in the room, Csilla leaned over to the quiet, steady angel at her other side.

"Why is it when you touch my hand that I stop hearing the river?" she asked quietly.

Azriel made a small *hrmph*. "Interesting."

"Why?" she asked.

He sighed. "I don't know, Csilla. You're asking me to explain the unexplainable. Maybe it's because Tamás is more grounded than you. He's had to be."

Csilla thought that some part of that statement was probably insulting, but she decided not to think about it too hard. "That doesn't explain you."

Azriel gave her a wry smile. "It doesn't."

Zsu scanned the room again and said quietly, "I half expected Gábor to be here."

Csilla blinked at her. "Oh? Did he mention it?"

"No, but he said something the other day about students being a pain in the ass," Zsu said, keeping her voice low. "And he seemed stressed. We were sneaking off to his apartment at night sometimes, for privacy, you know? And he hasn't wanted to do that in a while."

Csilla didn't know, but she didn't need to know to understand. And now it made more sense: Zsu's sudden interest in politics came from a desperate attempt to understand her fiancé's job and personality switch. She didn't know how to tell Zsu that this was what the ÁVH did to people. They stole them from the people they loved. The ÁVH made them paranoid. The ÁVH made them bitter. And that effect stretched to everyone those people ever knew, ever loved, ever spoke with. It was contagious, this malevolent spirit that permeated Hungary from 60 Stalin Street.

But the thought itself was paranoid and bitter, wasn't it? Perhaps the system, from top to bottom and bottom to top, made people bitter and paranoid. Perhaps that was the role of the system. Bitter, paranoid people were paralyzed by their own thoughts. Bitter and paranoid people didn't try to change; they just tried to survive.

"Do you think he's having an affair?" Zsu asked.

"I think it has to do with where he works," Csilla said absentmindedly. "It isn't your fault, Zsu."

"I still thought maybe he'd be here," Zsu said sadly.

The room filled, and filled, and filled. Rivers knew their boundaries, but people did not. Csilla tried to count but lost track in the hundreds. There were easily ten times that number spilling out into the courtyard. She could only see people in every direction. The walls and architecture of the building disappeared until the only shape, the only structure, was bodies. The energy in the room shifted, moving like wind through trees, and Csilla swallowed away a lump in her throat. It felt like a powder keg. It felt like one sharp word would strike the flint.

She was no longer sure that she wanted to be the one who struck the flint, or that she wanted to be here when the crowd went off.

"There are so many people here," marveled Zsu.

Given how fast the news had spread around the typists' room, Csilla felt like she shouldn't have been as surprised as she was at the growing crowd. How many of them were here out of curiosity? How many of them were here out of hunger?

Csilla wasn't even sure why she was there, if it was curiosity, or hunger, or something more. It was the something more that rattled her.

"Is this going to get started?" she muttered, trying to turn away from that feeling.

She slipped away from Azriel and Zsu without warning and shouldered her way through the crowd to the front, where Tamás and several other men were chatting, heads bowed together. From what she could gather, they were discussing who would speak first.

She interrupted them. "You have a room full of people here, and they're waiting for something. If you're going to be leaders, lead. Otherwise, you'll lose them. We all showed up because we believe in something or we want to believe in something. We're here. Give us something to believe in."

"What if they don't want to hear what we have to say?" one boy asked.

"What do *you* want to believe in?" Tamás asked her.

She already knew. She was there because she believed that Hungarians who wanted change weren't alone, for the first time in a long time. They weren't isolated. Eleven years ago, during the war, that'd been true too. They might not have known it, but what happened in Poland rippled into Hungary. What happened in Stalingrad reverberated in Zagreb. Hungary was not just Hungary anymore. For better or worse, it was a part of something larger than itself. And that meant what happened in Poland mattered here too.

"What I want doesn't matter," she said. "But you have a

window of opportunity here. People won't stand here forever. The more you argue about student union acronyms and who gets to speak first, the more time you waste. Be more interesting than the river."

Tamás stepped forward. The crowd roared when he climbed up onstage, his face covered in rough gray patches. He was flushed, Csilla realized. And not from drink. From nerves, or perhaps excitement. He held up a hand. His voice echoed in the microphone, feedback cutting through the crowd.

Everyone fell immediately, utterly silent.

Like the river had, that day it turned to stone.

Csilla watched him in awe as he, a scrawny academic boy with hair flopping into his eyes, commanded the entire room.

"What happens in Poland affects us, and what happens here affects Poland," Tamás said, like he was reading Csilla's mind. "We do not exist without the comrades around us. We are lifted up and empowered by them for the cause."

Csilla scanned the crowd, and her eyes snagged on a familiar face. The ÁVH man who'd followed her that first day. He was listening too.

"Shall we follow our friends in Poland?"

A wild cheer went up, and Tamás nodded, like he'd expected that answer. He swept his hair out of his eyes with a hand. "What do we want?"

In that split second of silence, Csilla could feel the entire room realize that they didn't know what they wanted. They didn't know what they could have.

They only knew what they didn't want.

And she knew what they did not want. Things could not stay the same. They could not be as they'd been.

And then, somewhere in the crowd, someone called, "Why are the Russians still here?"

The room erupted between people who wanted to stay focused on solidarity with Poland and others who wanted to get to the crux of the problem. Csilla felt a knot in the center of her chest, a compulsion to say something or do something, but she didn't know what.

She could be her father's daughter and still right the wrongs he'd done. She could see the drive for greatness and not choose power. She could choose to tear down that power that he'd sought, that had corrupted him from the inside out, that had stolen him and her mother from her. She could choose truth over lies.

Before the war, her father would have loved these students and their energy and their desires. When he jumped off the bridge and took his family into the river to wait out the siege of Budapest and the deportations of the Jews, something had happened to all three of them. Her mother had gone inside of herself. Her father had gone outside of himself. And Csilla had become herself.

It'd just taken her years to realize it.

"We have to protest," she said simply. And when no one heard her, she raised her voice and said it louder. "We must protest."

For a brief pause, there was nothing but silence.

She repeated herself. "We must protest. If you want to show

true solidarity with Poland, if you want what is happening in Poland to succeed and catch fire, then we must mimic it here. We must send the Party a list of demands that echo the Polish students', and we must be prepared to take to the streets."

"They will not let us," said someone in the crowd.

She glanced at the crowd and said, "We aren't asking for permission."

Tamás raised his voice to gain control of the room again. "All in favor, say aye!"

It moved like a wave, like an earthquake, like the stony silence of the room had cracked open and the floodgates opened, first a scattering of *ayes,* then a tsunami. It washed over Csilla, and it was all she could do not to cry.

CHAPTER NINETEEN

CSILLA

OCTOBER 22, 1956

They stayed late into the night, hammering away at the specific goals of the protest. Someone had brought a typewriter, and Csilla had sat down to type, but she'd been too impatient, too eager to pace the room and think, to turn the ideas into words. Zsu had been the one who sat down calmly, her fingers on the keys. And in the end, they had sixteen specific goals.

Someone ripped the paper from Zsu's typewriter, and then it was gone, off to a printer, and the room had slowly emptied of people—but not of energy.

At the bridge, Zsu and Csilla kissed each other's cheeks and promised to see each other at the protest tomorrow, and then Zsu turned into Buda, the old city, where she lived with her parents. Azriel stayed on the Buda side of the river, walking off alone into the night with his hands in his pockets. He didn't even say good night. Perhaps angels didn't.

Csilla set off back across the bridge into Pest. Below her, the river was silver again, with chunks of black stone floating through it, bobbing up and down. The light glinted off the silver droplets clinging to the surface of the black rocks. She kept waiting for it to speak, but it said nothing more to her. Still, she could feel it in a way she'd missed when it was stone.

She could see the whole city spread out in front of her, and she could feel it at her back, and it no longer felt like a looming threat but rather like something she stood within and was a part of. She was swallowed whole by her own mind.

She wanted the city to open its palms, cradle her in its hands, whisper, "I will you to stay."

But a city would not ask her to stay, no matter how much she craved that. She would have to stay by her own choice, shaping the city and the country herself with her hands.

And more than she wanted Budapest to tell her to stay, she wanted her parents here. She wanted her mother's gentle wisdom and her hand smoothing her hair, and she wanted her father's whispered fairy tales. And she wanted to know that the choice she'd made was right.

Tonight, the city felt enormous and old, and she felt small and young.

She could not see the future—or whether the brazen words she'd said and written tonight would come back to bite her. She'd thrown caution to the wind, everything she'd held close for the last four years, since her parents had been killed. And she hadn't gambled just with her own life and her own future, she'd gambled with Ilona's.

There was still time to change her mind. She didn't have to

show up tomorrow. No one had to know. She and Ilona could go into hiding tonight. If she hurried, they could leave under the cover of darkness.

She didn't move.

The river murmured to her again, like it knew her doubt.

Ehyeh asher ehyeh.

I will be what I will be.

She had always thought that the Hebrew words connoted something static, something predestined, something fated. That she was made and set in stone and that was the only option. But now, for the first time in her entire life, she could hear a different reading of the words.

She could be whatever she would be. She could become whatever she would become.

Whoever she could become would guide her through the process of being.

She could see out of the corner of her eye the glint of the Soviet star on the Fisherman's Bastion. And the lights of Pest danced across the surface of the water like stars, like something trapped in the water.

Like possibility that she could unlock.

She delayed the inevitable until she could not delay it any longer. She climbed the steps to their apartment and entered. Her aunt was alone, as always, reading the paper by the window, the lamp the only source of light in the room.

Her aunt put down the paper, a smile on her face that faded quickly when she saw Csilla's expression.

"Csillagom," murmured Ilona. "What have you done?"

Csilla locked the door behind her and sat down next to her aunt, pulling her chair around so she could rest her head on her aunt's shoulder. "There's going to be a protest tomorrow."

Her aunt sat very, very still. "Csilla."

"Please hear me out," Csilla began.

"If you get arrested, if anything happens, that affects our train tickets," Ilona interrupted, her body tightening beside Csilla.

"I'm not leaving," Csilla said, not lifting her head. Her aunt smelled like spiced tea and sugar. She'd been baking again. "I want—I want to stay, and I want to see this through. I want to be part of the change. It's coming. Can't you feel it?"

"We promised each other," Ilona whispered, tears choking her voice.

Csilla raised her head. She could hear the river whispering *here, here, here,* in Hungarian this time, and the water felt as if it were rising in her chest. "Tante, you can still go."

"Go alone?" Ilona swatted her hands away. "No. I won't."

Anger flared, white and hot in Csilla's chest. "So you'll stay just to punish me?"

"And you'll stay just to torture me?" snapped Ilona.

Csilla swallowed. "I want you to be safe."

"You don't think I want the same for you?" Ilona cried.

"Tante," whispered Csilla, gesturing for her to lower her voice.

Ilona took a deep breath, letting it out slow. "Why now? Why could you not resist for a few more days? You are your father's daughter when you are like this."

"I'm my mother's too," Csilla whispered, ignoring the blow that had hit home. "And she stayed, didn't she?"

Tears trickled down Ilona's cheeks. "She did."

"I want to stay. I want to try for a better Hungary," Csilla whispered. There were tears, she realized, on her cheeks too. Rivulets. "But you don't have to want those things. You don't have to stay."

She wanted Ilona to live free and safe somewhere that didn't contain so many nightmares for her. She wanted Ilona to live in a place where her neighbors weren't a constant reminder of the children she had lost in the Shoah. She wanted Ilona to live in the safety and embrace of a Jewish community like the one they used to have here.

But Ilona shook her head. "I'm not leaving without you. You are my last relative. No, that's not what we do. We Jews, we belong together. I will not leave you. Perhaps this whole protest business will be over before the train departs. Perhaps you won't get yourself arrested or killed."

Perhaps. So Ilona felt the possibility too.

Csilla had to hold on to the possibility that the worst outcomes wouldn't happen because the alternative made her want to burst into tears. There were no easy choices, but there was one that made her feel hopeful for the first time in her entire life. And she wanted to make that choice.

> Just as each country's history differs, so does the struggle differ, and each people must decide through which lens the Revolution is seen, lived and made real. And so the world watches the Polish comrades with great interest, the East because it is a reminder that we are constantly making the Revolution anew, steering toward a better future, and the West because they may seize upon the opportunity if we are weak.
>
> Poland, our eyes are on you. Lead us into the light.
>
> —Excerpt from Attila Kis's article in the *Szabad Nép*

> Comrade Csilla Tisza assisted with this article, writing it from Kis's notes.
>
> —Appended note in *Szabad Nép*'s files

CHAPTER TWENTY

AZRIEL

OCTOBER 23, 1956

He was sitting on the edge of the river this time. The soldiers had been withdrawn when the river turned back to water, or perhaps in anticipation of the protests, and so the banks of the river were unoccupied and quiet. His mind did not look unoccupied. The streetlights cast an eerie glow on his face, all shadows and angles, like light ricocheting through a twisting alleyway.

"I didn't know you knew her too," Tamás said as Azriel slid down beside him.

"I knew her when we were both young." He did not want to tell Tamás what or who he was. Not yet. Tamás was not Csilla. He was not yet open to the unknown and impossible.

They sat there in silence for a while, watching the sky above Budapest, the tram cars crossing the bridges, the lights twinkling on and off, listening to the sound of people laughing and jostling each other on their way home. Azriel loved that about humans. They were capable of finding so much joy in places that seemed devoid of it. They created art in secret, scratched poetry onto cell walls, composed songs, preserved their cultures even in the midst of heinous crimes.

And here, under the heavy thumb of Stalin's legacy and Khrushchev's struggle to maintain control and balance, Hungarians were still fighting and laughing their way toward a future and an identity they couldn't see.

They were not unique among humans. Every people that Azriel had ever witnessed at their time of most painful suffering had done this. He loved them fiercely for it.

"I hope," Tamás said heavily, breaking Azriel's thoughts, "that we have done the right thing."

"What would be the right thing?" Azriel leaned back on his hands, curling his fingertips against the rough, cold stone.

"Honoring the legacy of the man who first turned my mind toward this." Tamás looked at him, his face animated with excitement and frustration. "Before, I accepted everything the government said as fact, you know? You're taught to trust. There's no room to question or to think for yourself. But all it takes is one person, right? One person who stands up and says that this isn't right, that things could be better."

"And you want to be that one person," Azriel clarified.

Tamás shook his head. "No. That person already existed. He was a friend of mine. Márk Dobos. He was the one who first opened my eyes to all of the legitimate complaints we had."

Azriel knew who Márk had been to Tamás on a personal level, but not on a theoretical, idealistic, philosophical level. The loss felt compounded now. "And he is not here anymore."

"And he didn't even die for this cause," Tamás said softly.

"Are you doing this for Márk?" Azriel wanted to know.

Tamás shook his head. "No. But I hope, in doing it, I do him proud."

That could be, Azriel reasoned, enough. It could.

Apu,

Budapest continues to surprise me.

I remember coming here when we were young, right after you came back from the war, and the horses that brought the ice into the city on sleds, and the way we sledded down the hill in the park on pieces of metal pulled off of tanks. We didn't know any better. We didn't know much about the war. You did.

I am sorry I was not a better son when I could have been.

I am trying to be a better son to Hungary, since I cannot make up my failures to you.

> *Love,*
> *Tamás*
> *October 22, 1956*

CHAPTER TWENTY-ONE

CSILLA

The next morning, Csilla woke in pieces.

But she did not linger. She assembled herself quickly, hands to wrists, wrists to arms, arms to elbows. Toes to feet, feet to ankles, ankles to legs, legs to hips.

In the bathroom, she brushed her hair, but she left it down, a shoulder-length mess of wild silver curls. She looked other-worldly. She did not mind. Not today.

She ran her fingers over the seams of herself, thinking about what her father had written about stitching himself together and remaking himself as an act of survival. Perhaps that was what she did every single morning. Stitched herself back together for survival. Or perhaps she truly did drift apart because she wasn't meant to stay together. Maybe she'd have to leap and fall to pieces to save this city and herself. From the Soviets, from itself, from herself.

Across the hall, István slammed his door. But she did not hear his footsteps. In her apartment kitchen, her aunt made her second cup of coffee. She hadn't drunk the first one. She'd forgotten. Or perhaps she was collecting cups of coffee now.

She puttered around in there.

Csilla's mind stayed on István's door. She listened, and heard nothing.

Curious, she listened while she changed into her skirt and blouse. She was sure he hadn't left his apartment. That was strange. She'd lived her entire life here, and István had lived here since the end of the war, and she'd never heard him not leave for work before she did. He worked at the train station. Doing what, she didn't know, but she'd seen his uniform once.

She stepped into the hallway, her purse in hand, and hesitated outside his door.

She would have walked by, because she had no true interest in István's life.

But there was something inside her that whispered, then knocked at her conscience, and it wasn't the river, but it wasn't *not* the river either.

She knocked on his door. Somewhere inside the apartment, she heard someone who was moving slow come to a stop, holding his breath.

"István," she said. "It's me, Csilla. Your neighbor."

And slowly, steps came to the door. István opened it, the chain keeping the space to only a few inches. He peered at her, his bushy eyebrows over deep-set, suspicious eyes. "What?"

"Are you well?" she asked. "You normally go to work before I do."

He licked his lips. "I don't know if— You should be careful today."

"What do you mean?"

"There's going to be trouble today," he muttered, his eyes dropping from hers. "I heard it. And you—you shouldn't get in trouble."

She stepped closer to the door. "István, I was at the meeting last night. It's only a march. They did one in Poland."

It was a bit of a lie, but a lie of the kind that might soothe István.

His eyes darted up and down the hall. "Poland's different, Csilla. They're Slavs. We are not."

She studied his face, trying to read the neighbor she'd taken such pains to avoid, and then said, "Do you have a radio?"

And that was how at seven in the morning, Csilla ended up in István's apartment, which used to be hers before the war, huddled around his tiny table, for what was once her dining room was now his bedroom, drinking bitter coffee and bent over an illegal radio.

"They said the march was illegal," István said, his hands shaking as he picked up his mug.

"Are you afraid?" Csilla wanted to know.

He snorted and shook his head. "No. I fought in the Great War," he said, like that was an answer. "But I have a bad feeling about this one." He lifted his hands helplessly.

"It's a march. We're standing in solidarity with our comrades. Reforms are not the antithesis of everything the Party stands for," Csilla said carefully. She didn't know why she was reassuring István. He'd never said another word to her, never greeted her, never helped her with her aunt other than to avoid turning her in to the authorities. She suspected he didn't like Jews. But here they were.

"Imre Nagy," she told him abruptly. He'd find out soon enough. The former prime minister who'd been bested by Rákosi at every turn. He'd been ousted in favor of someone Moscow liked better.

István frowned, glowering at the radio like it'd done him a personal insult. "Nagy?"

They'd known last night, when they were writing their demands, that they needed to pick someone to support who was well liked, not too far outside the establishment, but still pro-reform. Nagy fit the bill. And Nagy—Nagy could win over people like István.

"We're asking for Nagy," Csilla told him quietly.

István chewed on that for another minute. Then he looked up at her and said, "You will be careful out there, yes?"

She raised her eyebrows. "I will."

He grunted a reply. "I've no interest in taking care of your aunt. And if she loses another person, she might lose her last marbles."

"I'll be careful," Csilla said again. It would be fine today—the Russians had allowed the Poles to protest and march. They would have to allow Hungary. They were big on consistency, and if they hadn't wanted this to spread, they would have put down the Polish protests in June with a heavy hand. They hadn't.

He stared into his coffee and then sighed deeply, taking a long sip. "We'll both be late for work. Let's go."

Csilla had no intention of going to work.

She let István walk ahead of her, and then she crossed the street to the ÁVH man standing on the corner, where one of them had been every day for the last week.

"Hello," she said, sounding braver than she felt.

He stared at her, and then he swallowed. "Hello, comrade."

"You'll want to be careful today," she said, giving him the gift of warning that István had given her. She had no use for it. And she delighted in the wariness that exploded in the ÁVH man's face.

"Is that a threat?" he asked, stepping toward her.

She steeled herself, keeping a pleasant smile on her face and brightness in her voice. "No, comrade. It is a kindness."

And then she turned and marched away from him.

It should frighten her, the way she didn't feel fear, but she was not afraid.

The day was beautiful. Bright. Warm for October, and she knew that in another world, one where there was color, she was flushed from the sun on her cheeks as she wandered by the wall along the river, where twelve years ago, her father had stood, swaying, while Jewish bodies dropped into the water around him. She didn't know how to walk on the same places where people she'd loved had suffered and died, where people she'd never known and never would know had suffered and died. She didn't know how to stay in the present and love the feeling of the sun on her face and at the same time hold the knowledge that someone else had suffered here with the sun on their face. She did not know how to remember and move on at the same time. Memory and forgetting were two weights on a scale of history. One must forget just enough to move forward, and remember just enough to avoid repeating the horrors of history.

She didn't know that she'd found the balance yet.

She didn't know if she ever would.

The river hummed beneath her, silver and welcoming, but she didn't fall into it, didn't whisper to it and didn't listen to the whispers it shared with her. She wondered if some people heard the city whisper the way she heard the river whisper, and if the city and river were in conversation with one another. She wondered what they said.

She was making up stories, just like her father had. Maybe it was because of the feeling of the precipice again, the edge of the knife, the potential of the city tonight. It was easier, she thought, to see the city and everything that could come through story.

Her father always said that it was easier to believe the fiction of the city than the truth of it.

At a quarter to ten, she began to make her way across the Chain Bridge toward the university. The normal flow of people walked back and forth on the bridge, crossing to one part of the city and then the other. Csilla looked up at the towers as she passed them.

They'd jumped from the Erzsébet Bridge into the river, but that bridge hadn't been rebuilt yet, a ghost structure in the middle of the river. But they'd watched the Nazis blow up the bridges on their retreat. When they'd blown up the Chain Bridge, the chains and the roadway fell into the river, but the enormous stone towers had remained.

Csilla let her hand run across the stone when she walked past.

"They've seen a lot," said a quiet voice.

She jerked, looking sideways in surprise. She came to a stop. Azriel was in fresh clean clothes, his hair swept back from his face and damp, as if he'd gone swimming.

He gave her a thin-lipped smile. "I keep sneaking up on you. My apologies."

"I didn't realize you were there," she said, struggling for words.

"I caught up a bit ago," he said. "You seemed lost in thought. I was content to listen."

"To what?" she asked curiously.

He shrugged. "Everything."

People passed between them, but their eye contact did not break. Then she said softly, "I thought maybe you'd be gone. That I'd changed something last night, and we did not need an angel of death anymore."

The corner of his mouth tilted up, but his eyes remained sad. "I am still here."

"My aunt," she told him, "won't leave if I don't leave."

He watched her. "Does that change your mind?"

She hesitated, then shook her head. "Does that make me a bad person?"

"No," he said immediately. "She made her choice too."

A year ago, Csilla hadn't felt like she had any choices. A

month ago, she'd felt like she had only one choice: stay or go. Today, it felt like there were too many choices. She was overwhelmed.

"Is whatever's coming inevitable?" She wanted to know.

He shook his head. "Nothing is."

She looked up at the Liberty Statue overlooking the river, a palm leaf held aloft. "Then every moment could be a turning point."

"Every moment is a turning point," Azriel said.

She looked back at him. "Then we should get to the university before they get started without us."

He stepped forward between clusters of people and offered her his arm. She slipped her hand into the crook of his elbow and let him walk her the rest of the way.

When they reached the university, the courtyard was already packed with people. They parted for Csilla like a sea, and the farther into the people she walked, the more the chaos took on the shape of a circle and the cacophony turned into sharper, clearer voices. In the center of the circle was Tamás, with his ear against a radio as two other boys hovered around him. A little pale, he straightened when he saw her, and stepped toward her, his expression sliding between worry and wonder. But he didn't move his ear from the radio, and so Csilla waited.

"They've been going back and forth on the march the whole day, whether or not we'll be allowed," he said, watching her. He glanced between her and Azriel. A frown flitted over his face.

She ignored this. "And if they decide it is illegal?"

She looked around at the boys. They all shuffled, hands in pockets, looking down in the half circle they'd made around her.

Quietly she said to them, "What do you want?"

"You know what we want," one of them said, frustrated. "You heard the list last night."

"You say that like I am an outsider, like I didn't help you put that list together, but you stand here waiting for my opinion," Csilla said, letting a little ice into her voice.

The boy had the decency to look away from her, though he didn't apologize.

Do you know what the Torah is? Csilla's mother whispered to her. *It is only words. It only matters what you do with the words. If you live by them. If you love them. If you study them. If you will them into being.*

"But what do we want to happen from this?" she asked them, finding her footing in the dark of indecision. "It isn't enough to write sixteen things down. We must want them enough to fight for them. If we're not willing to fight for them, then it's just a waste of paper."

"I'm ready," Tamás said, voice strong. "We'll hold the line until we get what we want."

She turned to him, meeting his bright, unwavering gaze. "You're ready for that?"

She didn't know what she was asking him, because she didn't know if she was ready for that. But she'd already made the decision. While all the other boys looked around at each other, trying to summon courage for something they hadn't yet considered, Tamás didn't look away from her. She felt herself flushing under the intensity of his regard.

"I want to be ready," he said.

And that was a kind of courage all on its own.

He tilted his head. "My turn. Why are you here, Csilla?"

"I want to be here," she said. "It feels right to be here."

"You're not here because of your father, are you?" he asked, keeping his voice low. It didn't matter. The boys around them were hanging on every word. Csilla couldn't stop looking at Tamás. "Because I don't know that you can make up for the sins of your father, the ones of which he wasn't exonerated."

She was there because of her father's dreams, not his crimes. But she wasn't going to tell Tamás that, at least not in front of people. "I believe in this. I believe that Hungary has a right to the freedoms our Polish comrades have secured."

The boys around her clamored and shouted for her attention, arguing indistinctly, but Tamás and Csilla didn't move, a sun and moon at the center of the chaos around them. He smiled at her, slow, like the river in summer, his eyes shining bright. "Yes, we do. So your coming tonight has nothing to do with me, then."

She laughed. Joy filled his face. He was running his eyes over her like he was trying to read her, or memorize her, or figure out how she was assembled. She grinned at him. "Nothing to do with you."

And it was true, for the most part. But would she be here if not for him? She'd broken her own rules, had lied and stolen and retrieved information for him because he'd whispered in her ear and begged her. Was that yesterday or a week ago or six years ago? She wasn't sure anymore.

He stepped close, and for a second she thought he might kiss her, and she wasn't sure what she thought about that. But he didn't. He tilted his mouth near her ear and then whispered, "I am glad you're here. If Márk couldn't be here, I am glad you are."

She didn't want to take the place of a dead man, but she thought she understood what Tamás was saying. There was strength in having people near who knew the truth of you.

She wished she knew the truth of herself to share it with him.

"I'm glad I'm here too," she said honestly.

He opened his mouth to respond, but at that moment, the radio crackled again. They all turned toward it.

She listened closely as the announcer said, "Secretary Gerő and Prime Minister Hegedüs have agreed that the march in solidarity with Polish comrades will be allowed to proceed as planned."

Cheers erupted around them, loud and chaotic, but for Csilla, the world narrowed down to a point. She could feel them sliding onto one edge of the blade, choosing to cut through the lies, choosing to take a side.

She had chosen.

Csilla looked at Tamás and said, "Those sixteen points? You're about to read them for the world."

PART III

These are our voices rising up, say the people. Listen.

When spring came to us in the river, we wept. The river had kept us warm, but we'd been surrounded by snow and ice, and the city loses all dimension during the winter when the snow and sleet fall in steady waves. It was worse than the ghetto, the feeling of being unmoored.

I never realized how much I felt like I was drifting, grabbing on to any anchor I could find. I can see now, looking back at my life, that I've been trying to find ways to tie myself down for a long time. University, studying something tangible and hard like math and architecture—the design of perception. M, who is by his very nature a physical person. He takes up space. He took up my space and all my vision. And Éva, who is steady and reliable. I love her mind, but what I find I crave the most when I come home at the end of the day is an embrace, or a kiss, or a hand on her shoulder. She's an anchor. I keep coming home to her.

She tells me to be less afraid, but I do not think she understands that I am afraid of losing sight not of myself but of her.

—The Journal of Simon Tisza, May 1945

CHAPTER TWENTY-TWO

CSILLA

October 23, 1956

The university clock struck two, the deep bells ringing through Csilla's chest, and the chatter died down in the courtyard. People looked up at the clock and then at Tamás. He checked his watch, shifting his weight from side to side, and then glanced at the gates again. Csilla followed his gaze. It was if a switch had been flipped across the city. And if the rumors were to be believed, across the country.

Csilla remembered that when she was a child, at the end of Shabbos men poured from the doors of shul, and the streets were filled with black hats and white tzitzit as far as she could see. And here too, the courtyard of the university quickly went from a few dozen men to a few hundred, then a thousand, then more. They kept coming, a steady flow until the courtyard could no longer contain them and the street outside filled too.

A river of people. A flood.

"Is this real?" Tamás wondered next to her.

She wasn't sure of much, but she was sure of this. "Yes."

She glanced over at him, hoping to catch his eye, but he was still staring at the growing crowd. She wanted to tell him that he had done this.

But it wasn't just him. It was her too.

It felt big, wild, impossible, hard to hold. She kept reminding herself that they were marching, just as Poland had done, nothing more and nothing less. And the result of it would be perhaps—perhaps they wouldn't have to live in so much fear. Perhaps they wouldn't have to live with so many lies. Perhaps they'd know what was the truth and what wasn't. Poland had done it. Why not Hungary?

But Azriel was still there. His presence, both a comfort to her and a reminder that all might not be well, made her shiver, and Tamás turned to her in concern. "You're cold?"

"Excited," she lied. It was only a half lie, but a half lie was still a lie. She wanted this to work. She wanted to believe that this would be enough, that the government and Russia would see that they'd opened a can of worms in Poland and that Hungary, too, had come for her freedom.

That Csilla had come for her freedom.

The father in her journals would have been curious. He'd be here. The father of her childhood would have been leading the march, carrying a child on his shoulders. The father who'd worked for the ÁVH and who'd died at their hands—she wasn't sure. She wished she could stop wondering which version of him was the real one.

Her mother wouldn't have been here at the march—she did not like such ostentatious shows of political opinion, despite whom she married—but when Csilla thought about what her mother would say if she'd told her that she was coming here today, she imagined that it'd be, "Not everyone gets a chance to be David and slay Goliath."

Or some midrash Csilla had yet to read.

She found herself missing that right now, not her father's stories, but her mother's quiet, stubborn faith that the Torah and the Talmud and the Midrash contained all one needed to know to navigate the world.

What, she wondered, would her mother say about protest?

And then she found it, deep in the recesses of her memory, dusty from disuse.

Whoever can protest and does not is responsible for what happens without protest.

From the Talmud. Where, and who, she couldn't remember, but she remembered her mother teaching her this when she was young, when Csilla hadn't wanted to tell the teacher about an injustice that'd happened to someone else.

If you can stop injustice, you are obligated to do so, said her mother. *That's what we are taught. Whoever can protest and does not is responsible for what happens without protest.*

And that lesson existed in the annals of Jewish history too.

Where injustice was not countered, it continued. And people would suffer.

If she was caught today, her aunt would lose the last living relative she had.

If she was not here today, she'd be contributing to injustice.

Csilla stayed.

She didn't know what her father would feel about today, but she thought her mother would be proud. She was choosing her mother this time.

The courtyard was full of several thousand people now, and Tamás left Azriel and Csilla to confer with the other student leaders. Csilla and Azriel stood apart from the rest, an island of their own making.

"Are you here because people are going to die?" Csilla asked Azriel, watching him look over the growing, restless crowd.

He glanced at her. "People are always dying. That is, in fact, what you do."

She frowned at him. "You know what I mean."

He sighed. "I don't know much more than you do. I'm driven by instinct and a pull. And sometimes, I can see thin connections between people. That usually means that they're important to the reason why I'm here. But I don't know who, or when, or how. I only follow the feelings," he said, tapping his chest, "and try to be there for people when they need me."

"But you believe it's more of a *when* than an *if*," she said quietly. Nothing was inevitable except death. And death stood next to her, looking sad and pale and worried and strangely handsome.

"Yes," he said in return. "I do."

The march was a river of people. Thousands poured out from the university onto the streets heading toward Bem tér, the square named for József Bem, the Hungarian hero of the Revolution of 1848. More people joined them in the street. Car horns blared in the background, like the drivers hadn't realized that there wasn't a chance of them getting through. As far as she could see, heads bobbed, a flotsam of pale, excited faces on top of broad and narrow shoulders under dark coats. Then she spotted a few women, clutching Sixteen Points pamphlets, and dozens more toward the river. They must have seen the march on their walk home and joined it spontaneously. They caught sight of Csilla, and their faces exploded like stars at the brightness of finding other women in the crowd. Someone had found a wreath to lay at the memorial at Bem tér, and Tamás marched at the front, carrying it.

Then Zsu appeared out of nowhere, holding one of the pamphlets. She squealed and hugged Csilla, startling her. "There you are!"

"I can't believe you found me in this crowd," Csilla said,

laughing and hugging Zsu back. Some part of her felt lighter and less dizzy at the sight of a friend. She gripped Zsu's hand tightly. "I'm so glad to see you."

"I can't believe I'm here either!" Zsu said. She glanced around Csilla at Azriel. "Oh, and your friend is back. We weren't introduced last night, because I was busy threatening you. Csilla, introduce me to your handsome friend."

Csilla snorted, but started walking again. "Azriel, Zsu; Zsu, Azriel." She picked up her pace again. If she stopped in the middle, she'd break the flow. People were like water. If they weren't given banks, they'd flood in every direction. That wasn't the intention here.

But despite the movement of the people-like river along the actual river, there were eddies and spillovers. People tore Communist stars off buildings and walls, signs off signposts, breaking them and shredding them, tossing them into the street to be stomped on. It was symbolic, but it made Csilla catch her breath.

Zsu gripped her arm. The girls exchanged knowing looks.

They'd been told all their lives to be grateful, and apologetic, to the Soviets. The Liberty Statue overlooking the city was dedicated to the Soviets, ostensibly by the Hungarians. Sometimes the Soviets were liberators of the country and sometimes they were occupiers, beating down a force that had stood with the Axis powers during the war. The narrative shifted like winds to serve Moscow's needs at the time. Hungarians never controlled the narrative. They'd never been able to touch the Communist stars, literally or metaphorically.

The next time someone tore one down, Zsu grabbed it. She

spat on it and threw it, clumsily, into the river. The crowd cheered, men running up to her to shake her shoulders and shout their pride. Csilla watched Zsu glow under the praise, and watched her eyes follow the sign floating in the silver water.

She took Zsu's hand and whispered, "Gábor. Remember Gábor. Do not get in trouble, Zsu."

Zsu's eyes shone with the intoxication of being part of something like this. "He won't know! I promise. He'd never guess that I'd skip work. Not for something like this."

A cold stone formed in Csilla's chest. She knew there were ÁVH here. Even if they were here only for her, they'd see her and Zsu. Zsu would get trapped in the same net that Csilla was in. It would be Csilla's fault. She could see journalists—or regular citizens—capturing the march with cameras, capturing her with cameras. Those photos would be pored over in a darkroom at 60 Stalin Street to identify protesters.

Zsu's face softened, and she grabbed Csilla's hands. "I want to be here."

Csilla could only nod.

Around them, a chant started like a hum, rolling through the crowd. "Russia, go home!" And it repeated like an echo, a sound rippling back and forth from front to back through the crowd.

The river glittered at them, and Csilla swore the current picked up as it moved alongside them. It seemed brighter, more silver, this afternoon, even when compared to that morning.

As they wove through the old section of Buda, Csilla caught sight of the other half of the march coming over the Margit Bridge. Thousands of people. Maybe tens of thousands. So many more than she ever thought would march. The cold stone in her stomach grew. The back of her neck cramped with anxiety. And yet, hope blossomed inside her chest.

She wasn't the only one who was starving for hope, for the truth, for a life without lies. This was proof.

"Zsu," she whispered, tugging at her friend's hand. "Come on."

She pushed and elbowed and fought her way to the front, glancing sideways to see Azriel gliding through the crowd as if something about him had made people give way. She glared at him, and he gave her an easy smile.

At the front, she grabbed Tamás's arm, interrupting him mid-chant. "Did you see the others? Coming across the bridge?"

He looked, his eyes widening.

There was a palpable, peaceful energy running through the crowd, despite the anger that people clearly felt and Csilla understood. Had there not been official announcements first prohibiting the march, then permitting it, none of these people would have been there.

This mattered, she realized. Not just to her. She wasn't alone in how she felt. This mattered to a lot of people.

Bem tér wasn't a large square. It occupied a footprint the size of an apartment building, surrounded by buildings on either side, a statue of József Bem in the middle and the ghost of Erzsébet Bridge within sight. Farther up the river, the other students poured off the Margit Bridge and made their way to the square.

And the river was right across from the square. It whispered urgently, frenetically, to Csilla, and the blood in her veins sloshed in response, dizzying her as if she'd stood up too quickly. The crowd swelled, filling the square and breaking over, spilling up the sides of the buildings and onto the rooftops, into every inch of breathing room they'd ever been given.

"Here we go," Tamás said, his voice low enough that Csilla thought she was the only one who heard him. He sounded nervous, and when she glanced over, he was chewing on his lower lip. His eyes never stopped scanning the ever-growing crowd.

"Hey," she said, turning toward him so she blocked his view. His eyes dropped to hers, and his lip slipped free of his teeth. She held his gaze. They'd been unusually honest and brave with each other from the moment he introduced himself. She had no intention of stopping now. "The next part's easy. Momentum's on your side."

"And you?" he asked, searching her eyes. "Are you on my side?"

"I am," she said. She didn't know why it mattered, but there was a definite flicker of relief on his face. He reached out across the small distance between them, finding her hand. Despite his nerves, his hand was warm and dry and steady. He gave hers a quick squeeze and waited until she squeezed back.

Then, to her surprise, he turned to Azriel. "You'll be listening?"

Azriel gave him a small, patient smile. "Of course."

Tamás looked like he wanted to say something more to Azriel, but he didn't. He turned away from both of them and shouldered his way through the crowd.

"What's that about?" Csilla whispered to Azriel.

He hushed her.

Tamás climbed up onto the base of the statue. József Bem, who'd been Polish, who had fought so valiantly for Hungary just over a hundred years before. And here they were today, marching for reform, inspired by Polish comrades.

Tamás shouted, "Brothers!"

The crowd roared. Csilla smiled.

"Sisters!" shouted Tamás.

A smaller but still noticeable roar. Zsu screamed louder than everyone around them, and people turned, their faces ranging from amused to annoyed. Zsu didn't seem to notice.

"Comrades!" cried Tamás.

And everyone cheered.

Someone handed Tamás one of the pamphlets, and he began to read off the Sixteen Points.

We demand the withdrawal of Russian troops. The gasps made Csilla shiver, but cheers and hoots and hollers immediately drowned out the shock.

We demand a new government under Imre Nagy and that all criminal leaders from the Stalin-Rákosi era be put on trial.

Imre Nagy would get a second chance at reforms, and those who were wary of marches would be reassured by his name, Csilla hoped. She needed them to believe in Nagy, so that those who had had her parents killed after a show trial would—

We demand that Rákosi be returned to Hungary to stand trial.

—be held accountable for their crimes.

She did not think about whether or not her father would have been tried under this clause if he were alive today.

We demand elections by secret ballot across the country, with all political parties participating.

We demand that the Stalin statue be removed.

We demand complete recognition of the freedom of opinion and of expression, of radio and the press.

The points went on, and each began *We demand.*

It had been so long since they had *demanded* something. It'd been so long since they had thoughtfully decided what mattered, what really mattered, what the essential steps to freedom looked like—and written them down. And said them aloud. This reading was flagrantly against the law.

And yet, thousands were listening. And they were participating, cheering and applauding each point as Tamás read. The river sounded like spring to her, rushing with snowmelt.

Csilla twisted a little and found Azriel close to her. She swayed at their proximity, trying to bring him into focus. He caught her by both shoulders, steadying her, and she leaned into his touch, her shoulder pressing against his chest. He did not move away. The river quieted.

"This is tearing apart everything my father worked hard to build," she whispered.

"Is it?" Azriel asked.

And she thought about the journals, the dreams her father had put on paper that she didn't know he'd had. He'd thought he could shape the country from the inside and bring it closer to his dreams, his ideals. Maybe he'd been wrong. But maybe that didn't matter. Maybe he would have understood that everything happening here in Bem tér was exactly what he wrote down: the People searching for and striving for a voice in a system that had forgotten them.

But these demands Tamás was reading—these weren't her

father's dreams. These were hers. And theirs. A shared hope turned into words.

Then something changed in the crowd around her, a tangible shift in the energy, and she turned away from Azriel, trying to figure out what was going wrong. Tamás finished reading the Sixteen Points, and in the silence that followed, the crowd began to shift, a murmuring that grew into a movement of shifting bodies and fading attention spans. She glanced over at the other boys who had organized the protest, and they didn't step up. They looked as if this was it. They were satisfied. Walk down one street and read a piece of paper, and that would be enough.

It was not enough.

It wasn't enough to demand, if no one heard the demand.

A story, she knew, was completed by the reader. A demand was completed by the listener.

Csilla's hands itched.

"Azriel," she said. "Give me a boost."

"What?"

"Help me get to the statue," she said. "Please."

"So much for not interfering in the affairs of humans," he muttered to himself. But he took her hand and made his way through the crowd. They parted for him seemingly without even realizing it, shifting away at the right moment. No elbowing or pushing. Csilla let him pull her alongside him. At the base of the statue, he laced his fingers together, and she stepped into them and launched herself up onto the statue beside Tamás.

"Csilla," Tamás said, his voice a low hiss. Still, he dropped the paper and caught her, helping her steady herself. "What are you doing?"

She pressed herself against the bronze statue of a wounded József Bem urging his soldiers on and stared into the sea of people. The river glittered endlessly behind them. The people immediately around the statue gave her their attention instantly, but the wider crowd was already drifting. People stretched as far as she could see, to the banks of the river, to the steps of the bridge, and they hung from the windows of the apartment buildings around the square.

"Citizens of Budapest!" she called. Her voice cracked. She cleared her throat and started again. "My father said, 'My Hungary is free, prosperous, diverse, a jewel of Europe, which should have always been our place.'"

The people cheered.

She added, making sure not to let herself whisper, "My father was Simon Tisza."

There was stunned silence, a sea of blank, pale faces. Her father, the Party man. Her father, who had been unspeakably cruel to some of their families. Her father, the man just reburied, the first cracks in the facade of the Party.

Beside her, Tamás whispered urgently, "Csilla!"

He slipped from the base of the statue, moving between her and the unsure, volatile crowd.

But she gripped József Bem's hand, hanging on to the bronze statue for balance and hope.

"We are not only our past. We are our future too. We are not the bad decisions of our fathers and our mothers. We survived. We survived a siege. We survived the Terror. We survived Rákosi. We survived Stalin's reign. We can do more than survive. Survival is the lowest bar. It is easy to believe that outlasting a regime or a time is enough. It is courageous to say we deserve better. It is brave to demand a better life. It is natural to want a better future. But most of all, it is human."

The crowd roared with approval.

She held up her hand. "We cannot enact change."

The energy that had switched to her side a moment ago ebbed, wavering. People grumbled, shifting, looking confused.

"Csilla," Tamás said again, his hand reaching for her shoe.

She resisted kicking at him so he couldn't grab her foot and pull her down. She shook her head at him. "Trust me."

He didn't look like he trusted her to get him a coffee.

She continued, "We cannot enact change *on our own*. We don't make the laws. We don't work in Parliament. But our Polish brothers and sisters showed us the way. We need the ears of everyone in Parliament. You think they have not noticed this march? How could they miss it? How many are we? Ten thousand? Twenty thousand? More? How many gather here today? Alone, each of us is just another person who can disappear, who can be disappeared. But there is power and safety in numbers. All together, our voices will carry to the highest offices of Parliament. The Party is for the People. Let us remind them of that!"

In her memory, Csilla heard her mother whisper, *Ken y'hi ratzon.*

The crowd really roared then, and for a moment, Csilla's chest filled with terror. Their roar was louder than her heartbeat, louder than the river, and she was shaking so hard she thought she might shake herself right off the statue.

Then Csilla saw her, a woman about the same age as her

mother would have been, leaning out of a window with a Hungarian flag. But she'd cut the Communist crest out of the middle, and when she waved it, through the hole in the center, Csilla could see blue sky.

She knew it was blue because that was what the books said the sky was. But she'd forgotten what a brilliant thing color was. Blue. It dazzled her. It was endless and deep, and Csilla wanted to reach through the hole in the flag to touch it, because she was sure it felt like rain. *Blue,* she told herself, delirious with shock.

She pointed, and heads turned. There was a collective inhale, and Csilla knew that she was not the only one who saw the blue sky. A complete and total hush fell over the crowd, and this corner of this city in this corner of the world fell into a silence that rivaled the night the siege ended.

But back then it was a terrible silence. The long silence of suffering people who were too tired to go on but went on anyway. This was a different type of silence, though just as fathomless. Awe. Awe at a miracle performed right in front of them.

Color, the sharp, intrinsic brightness of blue against a gray sky, against the gray flag. Just a spot of blue, the size of a sleeping infant, waving in the wind.

Then the silence was broken when a woman sitting on a man's shoulders reached up, seizing the end of the flag, and the woman in the apartment let it go. The woman in the crowd cheered as she lifted it into the sky, and the whole crowd saw the rich—chestnut, Csilla decided—brown of her hair, and then the edge of a tree, with its green leaves, and then the blue sky again.

People began to weep.

And something inside Csilla whispered, *This is a turning point. This is a moment.*

But Csilla didn't know what to do. She couldn't tear her eyes from the color either. Tamás scrambled up onto the statue next to her, and in a quavering voice, he began to recite. "Talpra magyar, hí a haza! Itt az idő, most vagy soha! Rabok legyünk vagy szabadok? Ez a kérdés, válasszatok!"

Heads turned from the flag to him, mouths open. The poem was ostensibly banned, but most of them had grown up reciting it in school—some traditions the Soviets couldn't stomp out of the country—but to hear it here, at the statue of the man who had inspired the song, with tens of thousands of people listening . . .

Arise, Hungarians! Your country calls. Now or never, our time comes. Shall we be slaves? Shall we be free? These are the questions. Answer me! The words were so familiar to Csilla, and she'd never, not once, felt they applied to her before this moment. They'd belonged to Hungarians, and she was Jewish.

Right then, for the first time in life, she felt like she was both.

Csilla was dizzy. The river in her mind threatened to overtake her.

Then Tamás's hand landed on her shoulder, and her body steadied itself, came back to itself.

Someone else shouted "To Parliament!" and shook the flag over their heads, the blue sky appearing and disappearing as the hole in the center moved, and the rest of the crowd picked up the song.

The cry of "To Parliament!" was interspersed with cries of

"Arise, Hungary!" and "Russians, go home!" and the crowd shifted, turning its attention to the other side of the river, where the Parliament building was.

She looked into the crowd, and her eyes fell on a familiar face. The ÁVH man who had been following her. He stared back at her, and she stared back at him. She wasn't afraid of him. Not any longer. If he took her, if he wanted to disappear her, he'd have to disappear all of them.

Tamás jumped down, then offered Csilla his hand. She took it and stumbled off the statue into his arms.

She hated herself for how she was shaking, but he held her for a moment, warm and safe, and whispered in her ear, "You are a constant surprise, Csilla Tisza."

Last week, it would have killed her to be called a surprise. Surprises were dangerous. But today, she stepped back, away from him, and gave him a shaky smile. "And this is what you get for dancing with a stranger. Any regrets?"

He laughed. "Not yet."

She smiled up at him and then at the flow of people emptying out of Bem tér. "Let's go surprise Parliament."

He grinned. "Let's."

CHAPTER TWENTY-THREE

CSILLA

OCTOBER 23, 1956

Large groups of people usually do not move with much haste, but this one flowed with purpose to make up for its lack of speed. Almost everyone walked on the bridge in the same direction, from west to east across the silver river, except for a handful of people who were pushing through from the east.

"Paper!" shouted one.

"What?" Zsu craned her neck, reaching out her hand. Someone slapped a folded newspaper into it. She pulled it back, shaking it out as they walked so Csilla, Azriel and Tamás could see.

It was the State paper. Their paper.

And right there on the front page were the Sixteen Points.

Zsu pointed at the byline, and Csilla sucked in a breath. Márton Szendrey.

Brave, brave, stupid Szendrey.

"He's going to get himself fired for that," Zsu said.

"He's going to get himself hanged for that," Csilla said, fear in her veins. She looked at Tamás. "Who gave him the Sixteen Points? He must have gotten them last night to make this morning's paper."

Tamás shook his head. "I don't know."

She wanted to tell him that he had put Szendrey in danger, but then she thought about Szendrey and everything she'd discovered him to be this week. He knew the danger. He wouldn't have done it if it wasn't a risk he was willing to take.

Csilla had to trust him.

They began to cross the bridge a little before four in the afternoon, and Csilla knew this because someone showed her his watch, and because someone had tied the new flag to a broomstick, hoisting it high above their heads at the front of the crowd, and through the hole, they saw the sunset.

Pinks.

Oranges.

Blues.

Yellows.

Reds.

Purples.

They shared these words through the crowd as people sang songs punctuated by chants, and everyone shared stories of the last time they had seen colors. The crowd took the colors seen through the flag as a sign that God, the universe, the world was on their side, and even Csilla, unsure as she was of the existence of God, found herself unable to come up with another reason.

"I think I was five," Zsu said. "When did they leave?"

"1942," said a man near her. "Blue in 1945."

"I was four, then, when the colors left," Zsu said, and shook her head. She touched her curls. "My mother. She had red hair. I think I remember that. Maybe I have red hair too."

Csilla had forgotten that hair could come in other colors. Hers would always be moon silver, she thought, as it had been before the colors left.

There were words for everything Csilla could see, but she couldn't quite connect them with the colors she saw in the sky, just as she knew there were words for the emotions in her chest, but she couldn't quite draw the line from emotion to experience. She could only feel, and it was like drowning with a smile.

Word of the protest had spread. They'd expected the students. But they'd expected perhaps a thousand, maybe two thousand students if they were lucky. They'd gotten more than ten thousand students, a number that swelled to more than twenty-five thousand. By the time the first of them reached Parliament, the factories had let out, and the factory unions had declared alliances with the student unions.

Twenty-five thousand became fifty thousand.

Fifty thousand became a hundred thousand.

A hundred thousand became two hundred thousand.

Twenty percent of the city stood outside Parliament. More waved from windows and honked their horns, not in irritation but in support. The streets and bridges and plazas filled with people, the way the river once filled them. Cars inched forward until they could not anymore, and then their passengers tumbled free of the doors, swept up in the masses and the excitement.

"There are trucks," Zsu reported, elbowing her way to the front, where Csilla, Azriel and Tamás stood alongside the other student leaders. At first, the word *trucks* made Csilla clench her teeth in fear. Trucks took people away. But Zsu continued. "There are trucks bringing in people from the surrounding areas. They can't come very far, so they're dropping people off. People are walking in."

Someone brought a bullhorn, but it did not matter: with this many people, sound carried only so far. The message rippled through the crowd, and by the time it reached the people walking in from the suburbs and the factories farther out, it'd be a game of whisper down the lane. Who knew how it would be changed. Csilla wasn't sure it mattered.

Tamás elbowed her and pointed to the rooftops, where men stood, holding rifles.

She glanced at him wide-eyed, and then at Azriel, the angel of death in their midst. Azriel was watching the men on the rooftop too, a frown on his face. "Do you think they'll use them?"

"They won't," Tamás said confidently. "They can't. Not after Poland."

"But we're not Slavs," Zsu murmured, huddling close to Csilla. Just as István had said, there was a brotherhood among the Slavic peoples, and the Hungarians weren't Slavic. They'd prided themselves on that for centuries, and still did, but right then, the way Zsu said it, Csilla wondered if it was a liability.

She wanted some guarantee of protection.

She remembered reading about golems in her father's journals, and remembered his stories from when she was a child. She wished they had a golem now. Someone who could not be hurt, someone to protect them. But she didn't know how to build one. She didn't know where to get the clay untouched by man. She wouldn't know where to start.

It didn't matter that she could not build a golem right now, right there. The crowd did not fear the men with guns.

The chants rose and fell, moving from Russia to Poland to elections to specifics like trying Mátyás Rákosi, their former general secretary hiding in the Soviet Union, as a war criminal, but the words said didn't matter as much as the mood—in Bem tér, the mood had been cautious optimism. Here, outside Parliament, the mood began to shift to anger. Csilla could feel it. The rigidity of the crowd's movements, the tone of the chants, the chaotic way that the crowd spoke.

It was like the river turning to stone.

No one at Parliament answered the demands.

The sun set. And that was when things began to turn.

First, they turned off the lights at Parliament, as if the dark building meant anything to the protesters.

The people did not disperse.

So just after sunset, with hundreds of thousands of people, a fifth of the city, at their doorstep, they cut the lights to the entire district. They cut all the power. And the plaza was plunged into dark and chaos.

The people did not disperse.

Tamás swore, slamming his rolled-up newspaper into his palm. Csilla felt her knees going weak, and she sank toward the ground. She remembered this kind of dark.

Azriel knelt beside her, his warm hands on her cheeks. "Csillagom, Csillagom."

She sucked in a breath, and it rattled. The water rose higher and higher around her. The river clamored, and its words seemed nonsensical again.

The angel of death whispered, "Do you remember? In the ghetto?"

She did.

"And God said, 'Let there be light,'" Nati said again, in English, in a new voice, deeper and softer and older, but it was Nati again, holding her hands.

In the distance, and yet close enough to bump into her, Tamás said, his voice rising in urgency, "What's wrong? What's wrong with her?"

Her father whispered to her, "Do not be afraid of the dark, Csilla. Our people have known the dark."

"'And there was light,'" Csilla replied, covering Nati's hands on her cheeks. She opened her eyes and it was Azriel in front of her, and the edges of his beautiful face were fuzzy and bright.

Csilla remembered reading the passage, and she remembered the words. She remembered that God didn't know if the light would be good. God said, "Let there be light," before God saw it was good and before God separated the light from the dark.

And she remembered that when her father told her not to be afraid of the dark, her mother had said, "But that's why we light candles every week. You know what we say? 'Let us be a light unto the nations.'"

She did not need to be afraid of the dark or anything to come. She need only strike the match.

Her father had said that rivers knew what people did not

know. He said, "You must know who you've been so you know who you will become."

And her mother gave her the Hebrew. *Ehyeh asher ehyeh.*

I will be what I will be.

She surfaced from her memories, gasping like she'd just leapt into the river again.

"I have to go," she said, staggering to her feet, hands against Azriel's chest.

"Yes," agreed Azriel.

"Wait, don't go," Tamás said, his voice cracking. "Csilla."

"Give me your newspaper," Csilla said, already fumbling through the dark for it. She found it, wrapping her hand around it. "Please."

"Fine," Tamás said, baffled. He was bewildered, but so was she. She felt a pulse inside her, a decision, an action that she had to take, but she couldn't explain it to him.

She said to Azriel, "You know how you said you were guided by instinct? This is instinct."

"Where?" he asked, but she could tell he already suspected the answer.

The mass of people reached the riverbanks where her father once stood, his eyes closed. Did he pray? Did he ask the river to save him? Why couldn't the river save all of them as it had saved her and her family? Why hadn't the river saved them when they needed it the most? Why hadn't her father gone to the river the day he was taken?

Questions for another time.

Csilla reached the stone bank and fell to her knees. She rolled the newspaper into a tube and leaned down, touching it to the water's surface.

"Ehyeh asher ehyeh," she whispered to the river. "That's what you said to me, isn't it? But you weren't talking about yourself. You already know who you are. You are a blessing."

The river warmed against her hand in the cool October night.

"You were talking about me," she kept saying. And then she reached into her memory for a prayer she hadn't said in years, but she remembered it, her mother's hands on her hands. "Baruch atah Adonai, Eloheinu melech haolam, shehecheyanu, v'kiy'manu, v'higianu laz'man hazeh."

The prayer for auspicious beginnings. A prayer of gratitude.

Beside her, Azriel murmured, "Amen."

She sank the newspaper into the river as far as she could, and when she pulled it out, the paper burned like a torch, the flame flickering red and white and orange like a sunset, and it did not go out.

A light in the dark.

A light unto the nations.

She scrambled to her knees and lifted it up, careful not to touch it against anything and extinguish it. She could feel the heat coming off of it and illuminating her face. She stood, shaking, and held it in front of her.

The river whispered to her, *Chazak!*

But this was not the end of a book; it was a beginning.

Azriel's face was illuminated, ghostly pale in the flickering light, his dark eyes bright and knowing.

"What now?"

"We go back to Parliament," she said grimly. She held the burning paper in front of her as she returned to the edge of the crowd. The people parted for her, wide-eyed and solemn. She could feel them filing behind her, instinctively following the light; and the chants, which had disappeared when the lights were cut, rose again, demanding a new prime minister, demanding that Russia leave the country.

As she passed through the crowd, others with newspapers reached out with their rolled-up papers, touching them to her torch. And the flame spread from torch to torch, but it did not burn the paper. No sparks flew from it. It was light, without the danger. It burned fiercely, but it was not destroyed.

And the light spread from one person to the other until there were dots all around her, and just one torch, hers, moved through the crowd with any urgency as she tried to find the front again, where Tamás and Zsu were hopefully still waiting for her. Azriel took her by the hand, and she laced her fingers with his and let him guide her through the crowd, trusting that he knew where he was going.

The light caught Tamás's face, and he looked at her in disbelief, then at her torch. "Why isn't it burning down?"

"It is a gift," Csilla said simply. "From the river."

Tamás cast his gaze over the crowd, and Csilla turned, looking across the sea of darkness.

The people who touched their light to her light touched lights to each other now, and so the fire spread, torch to torch, a paper for the people, by the people, on fire in the dark. A hundred, five hundred, five thousand, ten thousand, a hundred thousand torches, and the glow lit up the square.

The windows all around them reflected the illuminated torches back at the crowd. Faces, half flame, half shadow, all looking forward and up, determination etched on them.

"What have we done?" Tamás breathed.

And it was bigger than they could have imagined, more people than they could have imagined, and the anger was growing, bubbling over. Csilla knew this feeling now, like they were balancing on the edge of a blade. Another one of Azriel's turning points.

There was, she realized, no coming back from this. She could not stop what she had set in motion. She could not pull the emergency brake on this train. She could not turn this ship around. No one could, she thought.

It was its own creature. It'd become its own animal.

Then a young man pushed through the crowd, reaching Tamás. He grabbed for Tamás's arm and shouted something Csilla couldn't make out. Then Tamás turned to Csilla, grim-faced.

"They're pulling down the Stalin statue."

"The one at Városliget?" she asked, a ridiculous question. Of course it was that one. The real question was *who,* but she supposed that didn't really matter. If people wanted to tear down a statue, they'd find a way.

He nodded. "And they're going to the radio."

Csilla felt the knife inside of her wobble, cutting through the dizzy wonder of the torches. "Why?"

"To read the Sixteen Points."

"That isn't going to end well," Zsu said softly. "They're not going to give up Radio Budapest that easily."

Tamás, Csilla, Zsu and Azriel stared at each other for a long time, and then Csilla said, "If we aren't there to make the decisions, to shape whatever this is becoming, then someone else will."

Tamás nodded. "Yes."

Zsu looked at her, in the torchlight, impressed. "Look at you. A mouse turned cat."

"I'll go to the statue," said Tamás, pulling his hat out of his pocket and down over his head.

"We'll go to the radio," Csilla said. Azriel and Zsu both nodded. Csilla tried not to think about the fact that Azriel was coming to Radio Budapest, the State's official radio station. She dearly wanted to ask him if he was coming because he needed to be there or because he wanted to stay with her.

Tamás grimaced. "Where should we meet?"

"We'll come to you," Csilla said. "Don't leave before midnight."

Tamás gave her a wry smile. "I don't think this is going to calm down before midnight." He leaned forward and brushed a quick kiss across her cheek. "Be safe, Csilla Tisza."

"You too," she said numbly, her hand coming up to her cheek where his lips had touched her skin. It felt as if it sparkled. She watched him disappear into the crowd, swallowed by the people and the dark, before she realized he didn't have a torch because she still had his newspaper.

"Csilla," said Zsu. "Let's go."

*   *   *

The scene at the radio station was ugly and chaotic, and the clamor of shouting voices drowned out the frenetic whispers of the river. Csilla's chest burned almost immediately when they arrived. She couldn't see her way through the situation in front of her. A crowd of thirty or forty people shouted at the building, or rather, at those inside. They carried some of Csilla's torches— paper that didn't burn down—but they also carried rocks that they threw at the windows of the radio station. The doors were barred.

"What happened?" Zsu asked someone.

"A few people went in to read the Sixteen Points," a protester told her. "Now they're being held. They won't release them, won't let them read . . ." He grimaced. "Not sure if they're still alive."

"They wouldn't kill them," Csilla said, turning her face up to the building. She could see the muzzles of guns peeking out the windows on the second floor. "They wouldn't dare."

"They might," said Azriel grimly.

The doors remained shut, and when faces appeared in the windows, it was only briefly. The people outside heard nothing from their comrades inside the building. Everything that the protesters did was ineffectual, and it only made them angry that they weren't getting any results. They weren't accustomed to protesting. They clearly held two vastly different thoughts at the same time. One was that protesting wasn't helpful at all, and nothing would change in Hungary, so why bother? And the other was that they were doing something, so they should get results.

But Rome took more than a day to build. It'd take more than a day to burn down.

Csilla's skin crawled. There was something about being here that unnerved her. She said to Zsu, "We shouldn't be here."

At that moment, the shouts grew louder. Zsu turned toward the building just as someone yelled, "Gun! Gun!"

Shots rang out, and people screamed. Csilla threw herself to the ground, and Zsu fell right next to her. Csilla looked around for Azriel but couldn't see him. Someone stepped on her hand in the dark as panic overtook the crowd and they scattered. A few more shots—*POP POP POP*—were so loud, Csilla screamed into the dirt and the corner of her arm.

She remembered, she remembered, she remembered. The scream of bullets next to them in the water. They didn't need to hit her to terrify her, though.

And then it was quiet. Quiet enough to hear the river. *Chazak, child.* Quiet enough to feel its touch in her chest. It was an unearthly, unnerving silence. And then, all at once, people began to move again. Someone nearby stood up, their shoes scuffing against the ground. Around her, people began to move again.

Csilla scrambled to her knees, running her hands over her face and body. Her torch was lying on the ground and still burning.

Everyone who could move was either fleeing the station or moving toward the too-still bodies on the ground. In the smoke-dimmed light of the torches, Csilla could see Azriel seeking those people too, camouflaged by the others, kneeling at a few to hold their hands for a brief moment before letting them go again.

She exhaled shakily.

"Zsu, it's over," she whispered. *Over* was the wrong word. It was the only word she had right now. The river was a riot in her mind, in her blood, in the spaces inside of her.

Zsu lifted her head, glancing around. There was blood on her face, but it didn't appear to be hers. There was a dead girl next to her, and Zsu screamed, shoving back from her into Csilla, knocking her over again. Csilla wrapped her arms around her friend, clapping a hand over Zsu's wet, warm mouth.

"Shhh!" she hissed. "Zsu. You must be calm."

Zsu kept screaming into Csilla's hand.

"You can't help her," Csilla whispered to her. "She's gone. Azriel will take care of her. Come on. Let's go."

Mentioning Azriel had been a mistake, but Zsu didn't seem to notice. Csilla dragged Zsu to her feet, and in the light of the river's torches, she could see the blood splattered all over Zsu's dress. They didn't have time for that now, though. Csilla needed to get Zsu away from here. She staggered to her feet, pulling Zsu with her. She didn't let go of Zsu's mouth until they were around the corner.

Zsu gasped for air, shuddering and shaking. Csilla grabbed her by the shoulders and shook her. "Zsu, look at me."

Zsu did, and she wasn't the girl who had sat next to Csilla for the last few months, the girl Csilla had known for years through school. There was none of the excitement or joy or anticipation on her face. Under the streetlights, Csilla could see only the shock on Zsu's face giving way to a blank expression.

"We have to go," Csilla whispered. "Come on. They'll send police or the army here next. We have to go."

Zsu nodded, still shaking. Csilla tugged her friend close. They hugged each other, pounding hearts slamming against their ribs, each of them trembling more than they knew.

"Come on," Csilla said, pulling away and taking Zsu by the

hand. There was a part of her that screamed for her to go to the river, to jump in and let the current take her far away from this place, let the river wash away the day, the decisions she'd made, let the river save her from herself and the things she'd done.

But she did not turn to the river. She turned away from it. She pulled Zsu through the streets. She wasn't even sure exactly where she was, but she hurried three or four blocks from the radio station before she felt they were safe enough to slow down and orient themselves. She held her torch up to the side of a building for the street name, read it and exhaled. They'd gone north. They'd need to cut east to find Tamás.

"Azriel," Zsu said, speaking for the first time in minutes. She twisted. "We left Azriel!"

"Azriel will be fine," Csilla said firmly, knowing it was true. Her hand was shaking in Zsu's, but she didn't think her friend noticed.

"I can't believe they shot her," whispered Zsu.

"I know," said Csilla quietly. "I can't either."

They stood there in the dark, the weight of the events at the radio station falling down on them. The river was faint here. Csilla hoped that it was merely distance from the river and that the river wasn't changing again. Then Csilla heard a car door slam up the block. It was strange that there were no police and no army on the streets yet, but the sound jerked her back to the risk of it. They couldn't stay in one place.

"Come on," she said. They cut across the city again, slicing through the night that shifted around them. The torch was not enough, and every few steps, one of them twisted, looking over her shoulder for followers, for police, for protesters, for the army, for phantoms and ghosts. Csilla's mind raced ahead of her, running up the walls and climbing to the rooftops. They needed to get control of the night. This wasn't what she imagined would happen when she'd suggested marching to the Parliament. She'd set something in motion. She did not know what it was or where it was going.

CHAPTER TWENTY-FOUR

CSILLA

The night was chaotic, the way that nights tend to be when the rules of the day have been thrown out the window and no one is sure who makes the rules anymore. Everything was rewritten at night, like the world was made over anew. But this world was chaos. There was no structure to fall back on as the scaffolding was on fire, burning like the radio building soon would, to judge by the men storming in the opposite direction, armed with the torches Csilla and the river had given them.

The river shivered, and Csilla felt it in her veins. A tiny earthquake of movement beneath her skin.

Even the air felt different—muggier, as if the fog that came into Budapest in the midmorning had arrived in the middle of the night, as if the sky was closer to the city, low to the ground and clinging to the sidewalks, the roots of trees, the foundations of the buildings.

Csilla could see the dead girl's blood splattered on Zsu's cheek. Her heart tightened. She hadn't even stopped to check the other girl. She hadn't even told Azriel they were leaving. But he'd know, wouldn't he? She'd told Zsu he would, but now she wasn't so sure. She wasn't even sure where she was going, or why she was going to the statue at the city park instead of home. Zsu could sleep on their sofa. She was small enough. She could go home tomorrow.

They ought to go home.

Csilla swallowed her own bile and guilt, letting it turn her stomach into knots.

She'd asked for this, hadn't she?

They came around a corner sharply, nearly running into a handful of boys—some so young that she wanted to cry when she saw them—pouring something liquid into milk bottles. They all froze, staring at each other, unsure.

Csilla found her words first. "Friendly."

They all exhaled.

Zsu leaned forward, her face still pale in the torchlight. The circles beneath her eyes looked like dark water. "What are you making?"

"Bombs," murmured one boy. Another boy elbowed him.

"Be careful," Csilla said immediately. She flushed when they looked at her. *Careful* didn't belong out on the streets tonight. That word had belonged to the daytime, to a different Budapest. She amended her statement. "Careful with where you throw those. Make sure you don't kill people on our side."

The boys relaxed, but still said nothing.

There was no way to tell who was on their side and who wasn't. And she wasn't even sure what she meant by "her side."

"We're going to Stalin Street," she said to the boys.

One nodded and stepped closer to her in the torchlight. She willed herself still. He drew on the pavement with a wet rag. "Up two blocks. Take a left, and then there's an alley about halfway down that block. Use that. The Russians don't know it's there. You'll drop out on Rippl Rónai."

She nodded. "I know that."

He smiled. "Good luck, comrade."

She met his gaze and smiled back. "You too."

She was surprised she meant it.

Zsu, meanwhile, was taking instruction in how to make a bottle bomb. She had no notepaper, but it did not matter. Her face was the picture of focus and intent while one of the boys, who must have been twelve or thirteen, showed her how to stuff the soaked rag into the neck of the bottle.

"Thank you," Zsu told the boy as Csilla tugged her away.

He blushed gray all over his neck and cheeks. Csilla kept tugging Zsu until they were out of earshot. "Bombs, Zsu?"

"If we'd had bombs," Zsu whispered back fiercely, "that girl might not have died at the radio station!"

"And others would have," Csilla reminded her.

"Others," Zsu said quietly.

Csilla understood what she was saying. She gripped Zsu's hand tighter. "Come on."

*　*　*

At the top of Stalin Street was the city park of Városliget, and along that was Stalin Square, where a statue of Stalin stood. It'd been erected in 1951 as a "gift" to the people of Hungary on the anniversary of Stalin's birth. They'd torn down a church to build the statue, and though Csilla had no particular attachment to the churches of Budapest, she disliked the way her memories of the area before the statue were hazy, fuzzy at the edges, and she could no longer remember the details of the church, the colors of its bricks, the stairs, the way people flowed to and from it on Sundays and holidays, the way it had brought people together.

The Stalin statue did not bring people together. The square was nearly empty all the time, desolate like Siberia, where they shipped Hungarian dissidents.

The statue faced west, toward the river and over the hills, as if it peered right through the city and didn't see it. And that had been the way Stalin looked at Hungary during the war—and the way that Hitler looked at Hungary.

To too many people, Hungary was nothing more than the gateway between East and West, into the Balkans and north into Europe. It was the crossroads.

And it was in the crosshairs.

Csilla and Zsu reached the statue, and now, finally, it had drawn people together. The two girls had to push their way to the front of the crowd.

The Stalin statue tilted forward, and men with tools that made sparks straddled it, dismantling this thing that did not belong to them—but did not belong here either. They were lit by a spotlight, by torches, by streetlights. The government hadn't cut the power to this part of the city, a sign, Csilla thought, through her pain and bleariness, that the government didn't know what to do. And where governments thrived on order, rebellions—perhaps even revolutions—grew like weeds in the cracks of the sidewalks. They sprouted up with the same wicked determination—and the same surprise that anything could grow where they grew.

She scanned the crowd, looking for Tamás or anyone familiar. But he found her first.

"Csilla!" yelled a familiar voice.

Csilla spun around, dropping Zsu's hand. Tamás looked wide-eyed and frantic, hoisting his torch in the air. She ran to him, not caring what he thought or who saw her. She threw her arms around his neck, and he caught her, stumbling backward.

He exhaled into her damp, sweaty neck. "Csilla. What happened?"

"They killed a girl at the radio station," she whispered. "They shot her and killed her. Boys are making bottle bombs. I saw them. We saw them. Zsu—"

"I'm glad you found me," he murmured, and released her, stepping back to a proper distance between them. The flame flickered, colorful and beautiful. He studied her in the flame's light. She wondered what he saw. Then he glanced over his shoulder as Zsu came up to them. "Killed a girl. That changes the rules."

"That's what I thought," Zsu said, wrapping her arms around herself. The torchlight caught the blood on her face. Tamás blanched, but Csilla shook her head quickly at him. It wasn't hers. Zsu didn't know it was there. Csilla didn't want her to know then, didn't want her to melt into the ground at the dead girl's blood on her skin. It was best she didn't know until she was home safely tonight.

"It doesn't change the rules," Csilla said quietly, glancing around at the crowd. "They've always been quick to kill."

"It changes the rules from what happened in Poland, Csilla," Tamás said tersely. "Calm down."

"Don't tell me to calm down," Csilla said sharply at the same time as Zsu said, "Don't tell her to calm down."

He winced. "Right. I know better. I'm sorry." Csilla accepted the apology, and he continued. "We need a better plan."

"There was a plan?" Zsu asked.

"There's no plan," Csilla said. They were outgunned and certainly outmanned. The river was chattering, its murmurings choppy as waves in her mind.

"What are you thinking?" Tamás said, his voice low and gentle. He played with her fingers, his eyes intent on her face. His touch kept her grounded. She hooked one finger around his and held on, and he let her, with a shy smile.

"We cannot win against them," she said finally. Before Zsu and Tamás could react, she added quickly, "Not like this. We're just going to put children into the path of a bullet."

"That's how you win wars," said Tamás. "You sacrifice."

"We don't need to sacrifice children. And this," she snapped, gesturing to the statue, "is not a sacrifice."

"It's a symbol, Csilla," Tamás said softly. "Symbols are important."

"They have tanks and planes," she said, still thinking. "We have chisels and a new flag."

"What if that's enough?" Tamás asked her.

"What if it isn't?" she replied. "We need a real plan, Tamás."

He grimaced, his fingers tightening around hers. "I know. I know. I just don't know what comes next."

"Hey," said someone in the back of the crowd. A familiar voice. "I know you."

And Elek pushed through the crowd to them. Csilla felt the blood drain from her face. She took a step back, dropping Tamás's hand. "Elek."

"Csilla," he said, looking confused and worried.

"Please don't report me," she whispered before she could stop herself.

He stared at her and barked out a laugh. "God, Csilla. Don't report *me*."

"You're the security guard," Tamás said.

"Elek," she murmured. "Tamás, Elek; Elek, Tamás."

An idea formed in her head, like a small bubble rising to the surface. "We only have chisels right now, but what if—what if we do something more?" She turned to Tamás.

His eyes lit up, but he kept the rest of his face flat. "Like what?"

She wanted to free Budapest. She wanted to free this city that had never loved her, that would never choose to free her. But she could give them something that she'd only read about in her father's journals, that she didn't know could exist here in Hungary.

"What if we let you into the newspaper building?" she whispered.

CHAPTER TWENTY-FIVE

CSILLA

O CTOBER 23, 1956

Elek strode next to her, his hands in his pockets. His strides were long, powerful, confident, whereas she felt as if she scurried along the streets like a mouse. She took two or three steps for each of his, but she kept pace with him as they proceeded down Stalin Street toward the newspaper building. Zsu and Tamás and a few others Csilla didn't know trailed behind them. The river was a riot in her mind, growing louder with every step. All this time it had been a whisper, and now it was a cacophony of rising and falling sounds, like a call-and-response to which she wasn't yet replying.

"I'm surprised to see you," Csilla said, trying to push the river out of her mind, as Elek held up his hand at one intersection, checking around the corner. For enemies? Who were the enemies? Csilla wasn't sure. The army. Police. But as she stared down the dark boulevard, she realized they were marching straight to the security services. They could be, or would be, arrested when they left the newspaper building.

He glanced sideways at her. "Because I'm a guard, you think I don't see the necessity of reforms?"

She flushed, pressing her hands to her warm cheeks even though he couldn't see her clearly in the dark. "You seemed like you played by the rules."

He gestured for them to follow him across the intersection. "So did you."

"I did," she said quietly.

"What changed?" he asked softly. When she didn't immediately answer, he added hastily, "You don't have to tell me if you don't want."

"No," she said quickly. "It's not that. I just—I need to think."

It was a good question. It wasn't a question she'd been expecting him to ask, and in a way, she wondered if by asking her, he was searching for what had changed for him, seeking answers through someone else's articulation. She recognized the desire, the need, to find oneself through the words of others. She'd done the same thing with her father's journals. She had thought she was looking for her father, and perhaps she might have been, but in part she'd been looking for herself. Some sense of purpose in a country on the precipice of change.

"I have spent," Csilla said quietly, "years of my life believing that I had no part, no space, no place in this country and this city. And maybe there are people who agree with that. Because I am Jewish, and because I am Simon Tisza's daughter. But this is my city—and the future of a city, or of any place, I suppose, is decided by those who do something about it. I am doing something about it."

Elek huffed out a breath that curled gray and smoky in front of his face. "I am atoning for the sins of my father."

"What did your father do?" she asked, even though she felt like her stomach's cramping told her the answer.

She could feel Elek's hesitation, but he had already committed to telling her with the little bit he'd let slip. "He was Arrow Cross."

Hungarian Nazi. He might have been one of the men who shot at them in the river, or who herded her aunt and cousins and family onto trains to their deaths, or who shot people into the river, sparing her father. And Elek, who had courted her, who'd smiled at her daily, was his son.

"There are many out here tonight, shouting at the Russians to leave, who would be Arrow Cross, if they could," murmured Csilla.

He sighed. "Yes."

"There are many who are here only because their hatred of Russia shapes everything they understand about being Hungarian," she added, thinking of her father's journal entries.

There was a pause, and he said, "I do not think I even know what it means to be Hungarian."

"Then maybe," she said softly, "that is why you are here. Not the sins of your father but the absence of your country."

His hand slipped out of his pocket and wrapped around hers. He gave her cold hand a quick, hard squeeze, just once, and then he dropped it as if he, like Csilla, could feel Tamás's eyes burning into their backs.

"Coming up on 60 Stalin Street," he murmured.

She tensed. "Do you think—?"

"I don't know. Lead them inside? I'll keep an eye out." He shook keys out of his pocket and handed them to Csilla. "These unlock the front doors." He shook out another one. "This one will open the printing room."

She took the keys, the metal warm from his pocket, and wrapped her fingers around them. "I am glad you're here."

"The feeling is mutual," he said. They were nearly at the corner. He stepped closer to her, and their shoulders brushed as they walked. He lowered his voice. "When you get inside, lock the door."

"But then you won't be able to get in," she said, panic rising in her throat. "I'll have your keys."

"I'll be fine," he said.

You don't know that, she wanted to say, but the words stuck in her throat. She just gripped the keys until they cut into the palm of her hand.

At the door, Elek swung around, crossing his arms and squaring his shoulders. She'd never noticed how broad he was, how intimidating he could be if he wanted to. She realized with a start that the Elek she saw in the mornings was perhaps the true Elek, shy and gentle, but a version of him that only she got. There was, after all, a reason he'd been hired as a guard. Her mind was still winding itself around this thought as she unlocked the doors and pushed them open.

The lobby was blissfully quiet and dark. Zsu stepped past

Csilla, giving her a ghost of a smile. Tamás followed, not looking at her, and then the others. Elek stayed at the door.

Before she let it shut, she said, "Be safe, Elek."

He nodded, not taking his eyes off the building across the street. "You too, Csilla."

She shut the door against his silhouette and turned the lock. She stood there for a heartbeat, wondering if she ought to disobey him and leave the door unlocked. But then she thought about Tamás and Zsu and the others. Elek was risking everything to let them work, to keep them safe. She couldn't make that potential sacrifice worthless.

When she turned, Zsu was waiting for her, a smile playing on her lips. "Come on, Csilla. Let's make a paper."

They led the boys up the stairs, heading for the typists' room, but at the very top of the stairs stood Márton Szendrey, smoking a cigarette as he leaned lazily against the wall. Csilla, Zsu and Tamás came to a stop, the other boys bumping into them. Csilla's heart beat in her chest, loud and disorienting. Szendrey gave them a slow smile.

"Well, well," he said softly. "Little revolutionaries."

"Don't report us, Márton," Csilla blurted out.

"Please," added Zsu.

Szendrey's eyes ran over them, pausing briefly on Tamás and then flickering back to Csilla. "Why are you here?"

"We're going to make a paper," Csilla said quietly.

The corner of his mouth tipped up. "Are you?"

"Yes," she said firmly. And then, recklessly, she added, "If you want to help, we'd welcome it. But otherwise, please let us pass."

The corner of his mouth fell flat again as he studied her.

Then he straightened up off the wall and said, "I think I will help you. I don't think any of you have used the press."

"And you have?" Zsu sounded doubtful.

"That's where I started," said Szendrey cheerfully. "Well, that's not entirely true. I started by sweeping the printing room floor, when I was very young." He looked around the halls and said softly, "This used to be my family's paper."

It was dangerous, to remember a time before nationalization, but here in the hallway at the top of the stairs, Csilla felt all of the young people breathe in Szendrey's words. They settled, warm and sad, inside of her.

Before anyone could respond, Szendrey shook off his admission and said, "Well, shall we begin? I've heard Gerő called for Soviet help. There will be tanks here by morning."

They had already begun, Csilla realized, as they started to put together the paper. Two days ago, their thoughts and ideas had been scattered, varying, diffuse and idealistic, perhaps. But they were honed now—the radio station, the size of the crowd at Parliament, the reaction of the crowd at the Stalin statue—had all sharpened the message. The Russians needed to leave. The current government must go—especially if they'd called for Soviet tanks to invade Budapest. Imre Nagy must be made prime minister. He would declare Hungary a non-aligned country like Yugoslavia, there would be free and open elections, and Rákosi would be returned to Hungary to be tried as a war criminal.

They wrote the articles and then took them downstairs to the press, a nervous energy coursing through each of them and picking up speed. The printing machine whirred to life, churning out papers, and the smell of fresh ink filled the air, Szendrey shouting instructions to them. It was hot in the room, and they swiped at their hair, foreheads, collars and arms, leaving streaks of ink wherever their fingers touched.

And when they were done, the boys, except Tamás, each took a stack with them, promising to distribute the papers throughout the city.

"We could hang for this," Szendrey said cheerfully, watching the boys depart from the loading dock on the back of the building. "Or perhaps face the firing squad."

"Maybe we'll get a choice," Csilla said softly, too tired to be afraid.

Tamás shot her a look and then stepped close, touching his ink-stained fingers to her cheek. "You look dead on your feet."

"I feel dead on my feet."

They heard a terrible noise on the street, and the four of them froze, listening to the distant rumbling that sounded like it was getting ever closer.

"Tanks," breathed Szendrey, looking pale. "That was quick."

"Zsu," Tamás said urgently. "Go. Get home now. You're across the bridge in Buda, aren't you? Go now in case they close the bridges."

"Csilla," protested Zsu.

"I'll take care of her. I promise," Tamás said.

Zsu narrowed her eyes at him, but whatever passed between them seemed to satisfy Zsu, for she nodded and jumped down from the loading dock, jogging out into the night and disappearing around the corner.

Csilla watched her go, and said, exhausted, "I wish she'd stayed home. She should have stayed home."

"She made her choice," Szendrey said sharply. "Same as you, Csilla."

And it'd been a choice. Tanks rolling in. Papers with seditious materials printed. Treason streaked in black across her face. Outside, she knew by now they'd have Stalin's statue on the ground, decapitated by the sheer force of the people's will, and in the radio station, there were bodies and the burning scent of tear gas in the air.

They'd just rebuilt this city after the war.

"We're rebuilding it anew," Tamás said, for she'd said it aloud.

"I hope we are," she whispered.

Students marched in solidarity with their Polish comrades, protesting the occupation of their sovereign nation by Russian troops.

"Hungary has the right to decide its own future," said Tamás Keller, student leader. "Hungary has a right to free and fair elections and to hold criminal leaders responsible for their crimes."

He referred to Rákosi here and to the students' desire for the leader who led Hungary from 1945 to 1956, during one of the darkest times in Hungary's history. Rákosi ruled as Stalin's right-hand man in Hungary, and Stalin had no love for Hungarians. Rákosi resides in Russia, where he is protected by Russian comrades.

"Free and fair," repeated Keller. "And the truth of what happened in Hungary's years after the war."

The government rejects these demands.

—Excerpt from an article by
Márton Szendrey and Csilla Tisza
for *Szabad Nép*, October 23, 1956

> Not everyone will agree with me, but the path is still through the Party. The Party is the river of the Revolution come to life in Hungary. I cannot even bear to entertain the alternative.
>
> —Letter from Simon Tisza to Márton Szendrey,
> July 1, 1951

CHAPTER TWENTY-SIX

CSILLA

OCTOBER 24, 1956

She woke when she heard a door open and shut, and it was a firm, precise click, not the click that belonged to her apartment, where the door needed to be urged back into its frame and she had to lean against it to lock it. She shifted on the unfamiliar bed, her eyes adjusting to the dim splash of light against a plain, unfamiliar wall. The room she was in was sparse, minimal and surely not home, where her aunt's belongings collected on every surface.

She was still in her skirt and blouse, her coat draped over her for a blanket.

And she was wholly herself. Her limbs had not reached for

the windows. She did not need to reassemble herself. She listened, warily, to the footsteps in the room. They were soft and careful.

Tamás came into the corner of her vision. He was sweaty and dirty, and there was a brush of darkness across his temple that she thought might be blood. Ink. The newspaper. She wanted to believe it was only ink. He sank wearily to the floor beside the bed, balling his coat up as a pillow. He sighed with relief as he leaned his head against it, and then his eyes caught Csilla's. He froze.

"I thought you were asleep," he whispered.

"Where am I?" she asked.

His brow furrowed. "You don't remember?"

She shook her head. He propped himself up on an elbow. "After the newspaper, you were so tired you were babbling. We didn't think it was safe enough to get you all the way home. This is my apartment—by the theaters. Azriel helped bring you here."

Azriel was back, then. A little shiver of relief ran through her. She let her body relax into the thin mattress. She remembered Szendrey printing the paper, and Zsu hurrying into the dark, and the tanks rolling into the city.

"I am afraid," she whispered to Tamás in the dark.

He lay his head back down on his coat. "Me too."

She was not ready to see this city torn apart by death and violence again. And she wasn't so sure she'd survive it this time. She'd always thought of the river as her last resort, the ace up her sleeve, but it had turned to stone—she couldn't be sure that it would always be there when she needed it. But that was beside the point. She used to think she wouldn't die for this city, that she fell apart nightly and that was enough. That was all she had to give to Budapest. But in the last few days, she'd given so much more. And now, she found that she didn't feel depleted by the act of giving to this city. She felt fuller, surer of herself.

In her mind, the river whispered warm and sweet, pooling in her belly, *hush*.

"Did you expect this?" she asked Tamás.

"Would you be mad at me if I told you I'd hoped it'd go this direction?"

She considered his words. She wouldn't be. She couldn't be. She'd been so limited in her imagination by her fear and her caution. She could only see the protest as the biggest action they could take. And she knew now that there'd been more power in their words, in their thoughts and in their actions than she'd known could exist.

She felt naive for not realizing that revolution was possible.

But Tamás didn't make her feel naive. He just said, "You knew you had it in you. Your heart's a rebellious one. I saw it the first time I met you. You just needed a little push in the right direction."

"I think you might have shoved," she teased back softly.

His laugh was low and gentle. She wanted to feel it against her skin. "Go back to sleep, Csilla."

She rolled over, nearly crashing right into Azriel, his beautiful angelic face slack with sleep. She hadn't realized he needed it.

She didn't know what made her do it, but she slipped her hand into his, laced their fingers together, and fell back asleep.

*　*　*

A faucet turned on in her dreams, and it took longer for her to realize it was in the waking world. The murmurs of two voices nearby, and then footsteps.

"Csilla." Tamás's voice was gentle and soft. "Drink some water."

She opened her eyes and sat up, her body stiff and pained. She'd stayed together. Her body was in one piece. It was strange, so accustomed she was to reassembling herself. She didn't know what to do without that morning ritual.

She took the glass of water from Tamás, drinking it down in gulps. She hadn't realized how parched she'd become. She couldn't remember the last thing she ate or drank. Azriel appeared in the doorway, his eyes dark and solemn.

Tamás sat, perching on the edge of the window. Csilla's skirt was above her bare legs, indecent, but she didn't fix it for either of them.

"Tanks?" Csilla remembered the rumbles from the night before.

Tamás nodded. "I don't have a count yet, but they're around Parliament, major roads, the bridges."

Csilla watched him turn to look out onto the streets below the apartment, and when she glanced away, she found Azriel watching her. He gave her a faint smile, which she returned tiredly. Yesterday had changed everything. They couldn't pretend they were still on a knife's edge anymore. They'd chosen a side.

So why did it feel like a precipice inside this room now?

"What's next?" Tamás asked finally, glancing between them. When Csilla turned back to him, she realized he'd been watching her and Azriel. The tension was palpable between them. She wanted to reach out and touch it, to find out what it was made of. What they were afraid of.

"I'm afraid that momentum might have been lost overnight. Numbers were on our side last night, but they may not be now," Csilla admitted. "What if people went home and realized it went too far?"

"Do you think it went too far?" Tamás asked.

She shook her head immediately. "No. I don't."

"Good," Tamás murmured, visibly relieved.

Csilla hadn't realized that her opinion mattered so much to him, and a mixture of pride, relief and embarrassment bloomed inside of her. She touched her fingers to her neck, wrapped them around the gold chain, pressed her knuckles against the pulse in her neck.

"But some people will," Tamás said.

"That doesn't mean it was wrong," Azriel said gently.

Tamás gave him a look that was hard for Csilla to interpret but reminded her that he and Azriel had known each other before they met at the student meeting. She felt a bit like an outsider every time they made eye contact.

"I know," Tamás said finally. He glanced at Csilla. "I'm going down to the theater—I heard some of the other students were holed up there. This feels like an opportunity, doesn't it?"

"It does," Csilla said, and Azriel nodded. "I need to check on my aunt. Should I grab anything from the apartment? Is there anything we might need?"

It wasn't the only question she was asking. *Can I come back here? Can I stay here?* She could tell by the way Tamás's eyes flickered to her, to Azriel and to the floor that he heard the unspoken questions too.

"If you have warm clothing, bring that," he said softly. "They say the temperature will drop."

She nodded. "Warm clothes. Very well."

Tamás gave her a relieved smile and then glanced sideways at Azriel. "And you, Azriel?"

"I'd like to see the city and get the scope of the protests," Azriel said slowly. "I could tell you what's happening in various neighborhoods."

Csilla hid her grimace from Tamás, but she could tell Azriel had caught it. If he felt called outside, then it likely meant people were dying. And she didn't want to think about that. That she was, in part, responsible for others' deaths. She couldn't dwell on it, though. Azriel would dwell on it enough for her.

"And then we'll come back here," Tamás said, and he sounded young then, hopeful that this trio would survive the day.

"And then we'll come back here," Csilla agreed.

"We'll come back," Azriel said.

When Csilla put on her coat, she realized that Azriel had slipped out of the room while neither she nor Tamás had been looking, and Csilla thought that it must be easier for him that way, to never have to say goodbye.

Sometimes I grow frustrated with myself. I could be better. I need to be better. But then I wonder if I'm setting myself up for failure. Maybe the work is inglorious and messy and dark. Maybe I simply lack perspective.

Or maybe I'm wrong.

Sometimes I'm afraid I'm letting Hungary down.

It could be so much more than it is.

We could be so much more than we are.

I could be so much more than I am.

My fear of failure holds me back, I think. It keeps me from myself.

—The Journal of Simon Tisza, October 1949

CHAPTER TWENTY-SEVEN

CSILLA

OCTOBER 24, 1956

Aboveground, when she listened, she could hear the sporadic sound of gunfire and the boom of a tank. She watched the sky and corners of buildings, waiting for the flashes and sounds they all held in their memories from the war. But none of it was happening in her section of the city.

The streets felt different in the bright light of morning—like the entire city remembered how to breathe overnight.

They inhaled occupation.

They exhaled revolution.

Most of life continued as if nothing had changed—people walked to work, and the corner stores hung up their signs, and beneath her feet Csilla could feel the subway rattling along its tracks. The trams were running, and the cars flooded the bridges.

But she tried to go down one street, and suddenly there was a rumbling tank right there, crunching the street beneath its treads, and someone threw something glass and flaming on it. It exploded, useless, on the surface of the tank, which stopped, its gun swinging toward an apartment building. She ducked back into another street, hurrying as fast as she could toward the safety of her apartment, when behind her there was a solitary boom.

Budapest had always been two cities, joined by bridges and a river, and now it was both a city at war and a city not at war all at once.

Her feet slowed as she approached the bridges, the river coming into view. A flicker of memory came back to her, like a movie playing in reverse. The newspaper office, the Stalin statue, the radio station, the river's gift of fire, the protest at Parliament, Bem tér, the march.

The river had saved her life when she was a child.

And last night, the river lit paper on fire, and the fire did not extinguish. The river gave her everlasting light, the kind of light that hung eternal at the front of a synagogue sanctuary.

The river that cut this city in half, that bound Buda and Pest together and tore them apart like a zipper, this magical river.

This river her father trusted with her life.

This river that could not save her parents.

"Miss, you're in the way," grumbled someone as he pushed past her.

She jerked, coming back to herself. She put her head down and hurried onward.

The river might be magic, but if this revolution was to survive, it would need to survive on its own.

The day still had the briskness of morning to it, and the fog and clouds crept in from the hills to blanket the inner city. She used to love this as a child, how bright mornings could fade into muggy, foggy, mysterious days. Her father used to carry her on his shoulders. He'd call up to her, "Can you see up there, Csillagom?"

She'd laugh and say, "No!"

And he'd laugh too and say, "One day you'll be so tall your head will be above the clouds!"

"Is yours?" she'd asked him, because she was just a child and she did not know any better.

"Oh, darling," he'd say, his hands holding on to her ankles, his walk confident and bold. "I am always in the clouds."

She didn't understand until now that that'd not only been a no, but an admission of guilt. He'd never been able to ground himself to get his mind out of that dreamer space. He'd never been able to see clearly. He'd always been mired in the fog. He'd hoped that she'd be the one to see clearly. But she didn't know that she could any more than he could. Maybe he'd meant her whole generation would be the ones to see clearly.

Yesterday she'd thought she'd been there for her father's dreams.

Now she was starting to truly believe that she'd been there for her own.

"Csilla!" called a familiar voice. Zsu bounced across an intersection toward Csilla, a box in her arms that rattled as she walked. Zsu looked bright and alive, her cheeks shaded gray and her eyes sparkling.

They kissed each other's cheeks, and then Csilla peeked inside the box. "Plates?"

"I had an idea this morning!" Zsu said exuberantly. "When the tanks started rolling through the streets last night, I remembered the last time there were tanks in Budapest. During the war. Do you remember?" She continued even though Csilla had not answered. "They'd covered the streets in land mines then. The Germans. They'd blown up a lot of Soviet tanks that way before the Soviets got smart. Do you remember the mines?"

She set the box on the ground and took out a white porcelain plate. Then she lowered her voice, still bubbling with excitement. "They looked like *plates*."

"Zsu," breathed Csilla. "This is brilliant."

"I figured we'd leave them across the streets to control where the tanks went, then to slow them down so we have enough time for them. And then I was talking to another girl—Nadia, have you met her? I can't remember her family name, so I suppose that's not too helpful—and she had the grand idea of oiling the streets to make them too slippery for tanks. So after I drop off these plates, I'm going to go collect kitchen grease."

"I'm off to my apartment," Csilla said. "Should I bring you grease?"

"Grease, bottles, plates. Anything you can spare," Zsu said, a wicked grin on her face. "The boys all think about guns and bombs, but this is our city too, you know, and our country. We women can fight for it, and we have other tools at our disposal."

Csilla squeezed her friend's arms. She did not warn her about Gábor now. Zsu knew the risks she was taking. She was a grown girl. "I'll bring you what I can. You really are brilliant, Zsu."

"Aren't you glad you know me?" Zsu said with a laugh, and then she picked up the box again, and they parted ways.

Her apartment building looked exactly as she'd left it. She didn't know what she expected, but she felt as if she'd been changed, and it was strange to see that the change didn't extend everywhere. She trudged up the steps, realizing how truly tired she was, and at the top her aunt opened the door, the chain pulled tight across the gap.

"Csillagom," she called. "Is that you?"

"It's me, Tante," Csilla said, too weary to care if anyone overheard her speaking Yiddish to her aunt. It'd be terrifying if it was her worst crime, but it couldn't possibly rank in the top ten after the last twenty-four hours. She couldn't believe her aunt hadn't been arrested, now that she thought about it, or that the ÁVH hadn't been waiting for her to return.

The chain rattled, and Ilona jerked the door wide open. She reached out and pulled Csilla forward into a hug.

She'd never felt her aunt hug like this—desperation and love pouring out of her like a dam had broken. It felt so incredibly as if her mother was home, as if these were her mother's arms she was folded into, that she burst into tears, collapsing against her aunt's thin body.

"Shhh, shhh, bubbeleh," murmured Ilona. "You are safe. You're home."

She pulled Csilla inside the apartment, shutting and locking the door behind her with one hand as Csilla clung to her, sobbing. They sank to the floor, toppling over a pile of books, newspapers and cups next to the door, but neither of them seemed to notice. They folded into one another, crying for a good long time.

When they finally untangled themselves, Ilona pushed Csilla into a chair at the table and made her a cup of coffee. They sat across the table from each other, staring into the dark liquid, and then Csilla began to tell her bits and pieces of the story that she'd been a part of. She told her about the flag with the hole cut into it and how they could see the sky through it, she told her about the river cracking and returning to silver when Csilla stepped into the room to plan the march with the students. She told Ilona about Azriel, the angel of death who had once been Nati, Csilla's friend during the war, and she told her aunt about Tamás, an engineering student two days ago, who went to the barracks to seize the opportunity they'd created.

"And so the boys who took notes in class yesterday take up arms in the streets today," murmured Ilona.

Csilla whispered, "None of us know how to fight a war."

"Yes, you do," Ilona said immediately. "You've done it before."

"Surviving isn't fighting," Csilla said, shaking her head.

"It is the same thing," insisted Ilona. "Surviving is a siege."

And with a jolt, Csilla realized why Ilona collected so many things. It wasn't because she had lost so much before—it was because she was still surviving. She was withstanding a siege, preemptive, perhaps, but a siege nonetheless. Like all the Jews who had come before her and all the Jews who would come after her, she was preparing for the past. Csilla had grown up hearing about it, whispers between the women as they cleared the table, offhand mentions of cousins who didn't exist anymore, reminiscences of villages wiped off the map in a single night.

But she'd also grown up in Budapest, where though anti-semitism existed, it was the casual, institutional, systemic type that kept people from rising too far in society, both before the Communist reign and now. Here in Budapest, with the exception of the Holocaust, the Jewish community had been largely insulated from the pogroms in the villages and rural areas and places like Poland, Russia, Ukraine, Moldova.

She'd forgotten. The cardinal sin in Judaism.

Her aunt had not forgotten. Her aunt held the memories of all the pogroms and all the genocides and all the Shoahs for thousands of years close to her, surrounding herself with every single object she kept in her house. She was prepared for what every Jew ought to know, if they hadn't forgotten: it would happen again. They would come for the Jews again. It might be the same—fire, and trucks, and guns, and dogs, and smoke, and starvation, and camps, and disease, and gas showers—or it would be something new. It would be a purge of the Jews from the Communist Party with accusations of Zionism, which had taken Csilla's parents and dozens of others. Or it'd be something Csilla didn't yet know about, or understand.

But it would happen again.

It was like they said at Pesach every year: wherever they were was eternally Egypt. But sometimes they weren't leaving. Sometimes they were staying.

"Surviving is a siege," Ilona repeated, somewhat to herself.

Csilla sipped her coffee. "They aren't coming for Jews this time. If they come this time, they're coming for all of us."

Ilona gave her a sideways look. "Even when they are not coming for us, they come for us."

She wasn't wrong.

"I haven't changed my mind, Tante," Csilla said softly. "It feels wrong to leave now, when I could do something good and real."

"Whatever you choose," Ilona said, "will be good and real, Csilla." She swallowed and looked at their clasped hands. "But I haven't changed my mind either. If you are not going, then I am not going."

She was taking something away from her aunt. She knew that. But she hoped she could give Ilona something of whatever they were giving to Hungary. There had to be something for Ilona and the other Jews who'd stayed or returned too.

"Ilona, can I ask you something?" She didn't wait for an answer. "You could have gone to Israel. You came back here because my mother stayed, didn't you?" When Ilona nodded, it was a confirmation of something Csilla had always assumed. "And my mother stayed for my father."

And she knew now from his diaries that her father had stayed because he thought he loved Hungary and thought he could make Hungary love him back.

He'd been wrong.

"It is hard to love places and people who have hurt you," her aunt said with a heavy sigh, speaking like she could read Csilla's mind. "But that doesn't mean you are wrong to love them. You love Budapest. You love Hungary. You love some Hungarians, even, I'd guess."

Zsu.

Aliz.

Maybe others. Maybe Tamás. Maybe Elek, in his own way.

And Ilona, who was Hungarian too, even if they and others didn't always believe it.

Maybe her father didn't have the wrong idea. Maybe he'd been right to fight for his country. And working from the inside, from within the Party, hadn't worked out for him—but she didn't need to try that. She could try to shape the movement in front of her the way she wanted to shape it. She could try to love the Budapest in her heart and mind into existence.

"I need to ask one more favor from you, Tante," Csilla said to her aunt.

"Anything for you," said her aunt.

"I need plates and some of your glass bottles," Csilla said.

Her aunt hesitated only for a moment, then nodded.

CHAPTER TWENTY-EIGHT

CSILLA

October 24, 1956

When she kissed her aunt goodbye, she promised her that she'd be home as soon as she could. Ilona gave her a brave smile that shook at the corners, but she didn't try to stop Csilla from leaving. Csilla wove through the backstreets, the little alleys and cutaways too small for cars, where only pedestrians and bicycles could fit, where the walls smelled damp and where it felt like she could feel the secrets of the cities in her fingertips when she touched the bricks and stones.

She reached Dob Street and cut through the old market in the old Jewish Quarter, a corridor between Dob and Király Street. There were a few other people out on the street, but she kept her head down, unsure of what was happening and whether she was in danger of being picked up by the ÁVH. In her bag were all four of her father's journals, and she carried an entire box full of bottles and plates and a sealed bottle of cooking oil. She'd have a hard time explaining any of it to the interrogation officer.

She left the box in Tamás's apartment, but no one was there. She wandered back out, wondering where everyone was. The streets seemed suddenly empty.

On Király, two students jogged past her, laughing and whooping.

"What happened?" she called to them impulsively.

"Nagy's been made prime minister!" they called back.

They'd won. They'd achieved one of their objectives. She grinned to herself and skipped a few steps.

Then she heard the boom of a Molotov cocktail and a distant scream. She hesitated and then turned toward the noise, following the sound of shouting.

She turned a corner, smashing right into a man. She hit the ground, sprawled. The man caught himself before he landed next to her.

"Elek," she said faintly.

Elek had something too close to blood speckled across his face, and he looked like he'd been in a fight. He reached down and pulled her up, steadying her until she found her footing. "Csilla."

"Do you hear that?" she asked.

"Where are you trying to go?" he asked. "You shouldn't be out here."

"Nagy's prime minister," she protested. "I thought people might be celebrating somewhere."

She almost said aloud, *It's over, isn't it?* But the look on his face stopped her.

He nodded grimly. "Not everyone's happy about that. Come on, I'll walk you back to headquarters."

She hesitated. "But the shouting. Someone might need help."

He sighed. "Fine."

They followed the sound of the shouting until it grew louder, and they came to a street where a crowd had formed around the entrance to a building. The area smelled of smoke and something acidic Csilla couldn't identify. A body was slumped against the base of the building.

Csilla lurched forward, but Elek caught her by the shoulders just as someone else was dragged out of the building by a handful of men and to the waiting group.

The man they'd dragged out was pushed into the center, and Csilla was horrified, horrified—the kind of horror that made her feel as if she'd plunged once again into a river in January—to see that it was Gábor.

Sweet, infatuated Gábor, looking confused and terrified as he was shoved around between people. And then there was a roar, and she could no longer see his face, his expression, as the mob descended on him. They kicked and punched and struck until the man fell to the ground, where they stomped on him.

Csilla screamed. "Elek! We have to stop them."

He grabbed her elbow. "He's ÁVH. Let them have him."

"I know him!" She struggled against his grip on her arm. "I know him! He's just a secretary. He's not ÁVH! He doesn't kill or kidnap anyone!"

Elek kept a grip on her arm and dragged her away. Csilla fought him, thrashing and twisting so she could keep an eye on Gábor on the ground. He was so still now. So completely still.

"Gábor!" she screamed.

He did not lift his head.

"Elek, let me go!" she cried. "You met him! You know him! He's Zsu's fiancé."

He said nothing to her.

They went around the corner, and Gábor was out of view. She felt cold all over, a cold she'd never felt before. She looked up at Elek's blood-speckled face. Then she whispered, "What did *you* do?"

He glanced down at her. "Nothing you wouldn't do. Didn't they take everything from you too?"

They had. They had taken everything from her. But mob justice—she shuddered. Gábor. It'd been Gábor. Surely someone would bring sense to the mob out there. They'd get Gábor to a doctor.

Elek pulled her into the entrance of the tunnel and deposited her there. "She's here for Tamás."

And then he, the once sweet, shy boy who blushed when he said her name every morning, was gone, and the wide-eyed boy holding a gun bigger than himself at the entrance to the tunnel pointed her in the direction of Tamás.

She pushed past the boy with the gun, but she couldn't run anymore. She half staggered, half walked to the stairs and descended to where a door was propped open, leaking sewer air into the hallways. She hesitated for only a split second, then descended into the subway tunnel under construction beneath the theater.

They had a makeshift office down there, a lamp swinging overhead, and Tamás stood beside a desk with a handful of other men, looking over a map. He looked like he'd grown up in the few hours since she had seen him.

He glanced up and blanched, reaching for her. He cradled her face in his hands. "What happened?"

"They are killing people," whispered Csilla.

"I'm listening." And he was. The rest of the room faded away, the men coming and going, the smell of sewage and dank air in the subway tunnel, and it was just his dark eyes on her light ones, his hands on her face, the low pitch of his soft voice.

"There are mobs. They're pulling out people they think are ÁVH."

Their eyes met, and he was so close when he whispered, "You're really going to defend the ÁVH?"

She didn't want to. "How will they know if the person is actually ÁVH? Tamás, it was Zsu's fiancé. Gábor. He wasn't secret police. That's just where he worked."

"If he worked there, if he supported them, then he was ÁVH," Tamás said.

"We're going to be better than they were," Csilla told him firmly. "We must. If people have done wrong, they will stand trial. We cannot have vigilante justice on the streets."

He hesitated and said, "I'll talk to some people."

She nodded, stepping away from him. She needed a little distance right now. "I'm going to go to the paper."

He frowned. "Quick to leave."

"It's not like you're trying to give me a reason to stay," she shot back, and immediately winced. "I'm sorry. I'm sorry."

"No, you're right," Tamás murmured, his mouth tensing. "I've no right to set restrictions. If you'd like to go to the paper, or home, or wherever you'd like to go, I can take you there. It's going to get worse out there before it gets better, and my guess is you don't know how to fire a gun."

"And you do?" she asked, surprised.

He shrugged. "Grew up on a farm. Did a year in the army. We got hold of some stock today."

"Just mysteriously liberated into your hands, eh?" she asked, when it didn't seem like he'd give her any more.

He laughed. "Yes. Something like that."

She shook her head. "I hate to feel useless."

He looked hurt. "I made you feel useless?"

"Not you," she said gently, reassuringly. "Whatever this has become has. I don't know military things, or bombs, or guns, and I'm not sure I care to. I know how to type, and I know how to tell a story. I'm going to go to the paper, Tamás. What do you want me to print?"

"The truth," he said.

She wasn't sure if he meant that. Not all of the truth cast him in a favorable light. Or them. The truth was not as clean and tidy as that.

"No more lies," she said to him quietly.

He shook his head. "No more lies." He looked at the cloth in his hand. "I don't like the idea of you being somewhere that might be a target."

She reached up and tugged at his collar to get his attention. He didn't move his body, still half-turned from her, but his gaze did move to her, albeit reluctantly. "This whole city," she said quietly, "has made me a target since I was a child. This isn't anything new to me. I know it's new to you, but it isn't new to me."

Surviving was a siege, she almost told him.

But she kept that to herself. She didn't think he'd understand.

His mouth set into a thin, hard line, and he nodded once to say he'd heard her. They were uncomfortably close again, but this time neither of them stepped away. He put a hand on her hip, and she felt the outline of every single one of his fingers and the shape of his palm against her hip bone.

She knew if she tilted her face up at a certain angle, he'd kiss her. It'd be that easy. It'd be that complicated. But she wasn't ready for that. So she left her fingers tight around his lapel and his hand on her hip, and closed her eyes as he touched his forehead to hers.

"Be safe," he said, and it was a statement and a question, any way she took it.

She smiled. "You too."

She felt his hand slide off her hip when she stepped away, and she did not turn around when she walked out the door. If she'd turned around, she knew she'd stay. She knew she'd kiss him. She'd knew she'd let him take her to bed—or desk, or wall, or whatever was closest. She could feel a hunger in her bones, in her body, in the need to get out the energy that was building within her.

And she wasn't ready to share that quite yet.

First, she had to tell the story of what had happened to Gábor, and remind people of what they were fighting for and what they were truly fighting against.

We should end the collectivization of agriculture. We should increase what the government pays farms, and we should end production quotas. This will garner us goodwill with the People. This is outside the scope of my role, but I have written a series of internal memos to the people who may make these decisions. I cannot do my job effectively if I am enforcing rules on people who do not believe in the work we are doing. I believe Imre Nagy is open to discussion. We're meeting next week, after work.

—Simon Tisza, February 9, 1952

CHAPTER TWENTY-NINE

CSILLA

OCTOBER 24, 1956

She walked to the newspaper quickly, ducking around corners and holding the bag of journals close to herself. She was surprised that the front door was unlocked. János, the other guard, with whom Csilla rarely spoke, stood up, frowning at her.

She gave him a weary smile. "Hello, comrade. I cannot believe they're making it so hard for good people to get to their jobs."

He relaxed a fraction. "They are enemies of the People and of the Revolution. It is good to see you."

"And you," she said, giving him the warmest, steadiest smile she could manage. "I hope I was not the only one brave enough to come to work today."

"There are a few other girls upstairs, the printers and a few journalists," János told her. "You should be able to produce the paper."

She nodded, then asked casually, "Did Márton Szendrey make it in?"

He gave her a puzzled look. "He did."

"Thank you, comrade," she said, and walked to the stairs. It was hard not to run up them, but she didn't want János to think there was anything out of the ordinary happening.

Szendrey must have heard her voice, because he was on the second floor, waiting by the stairs for her. He kept his voice low. "János is an informant, but he's keeping his head down right now. They're dragging ÁVH agents into the streets and shooting them in waves, from across the street and other places. Don't be alarmed if you hear shots. Be careful. Aliz is here too."

"It's good to see you," she said, exhaling hard. "I was worried."

He gave her a look. "I saw you last night, Csilla."

"It feels like that was a year ago," she admitted.

He softened, joy, elation, pride and relief blossoming like fireworks across his face, one after another. But then they were gone, and his face was smooth glass, bright and kind, the facade he'd worn, and she'd bought, for so long. "Understandable."

Csilla, too, had to be smooth-faced and strong. "Szendrey, we must produce a paper that tells the whole truth of what's happening out there."

"Even if it makes some of your new friends mad?" he asked gently. "Yes. I agree."

He paused at the doorway to the typists' room. The room fell completely silent. And only then did Csilla remember she'd been wearing the same clothes for two days straight and probably looked like hell.

Aliz stayed still in her seat, staring at Csilla in shock.

"Good luck," Szendrey said as he left her there.

"Aliz?" Csilla said, slipping into her seat.

"What you're doing is dangerous," Aliz snapped, returning to her work. "You understand you put everyone at risk, don't you? If you are arrested, I will be too."

"We won't be arrested," Csilla said, even though she'd just been contemplating that possibility. She added softly, "They won't arrest you."

"I have a son," Aliz said, her hands shaking. "You might be able to go into the streets and think of no one but yourself, but I can't."

Csilla reached over, stopping Aliz's hands on her keys. "We are doing this for Tibor, don't you see? He could grow up unafraid."

"Unafraid of whom?" Aliz said, her hands jerking. She made a mistake, striking the wrong key, and she hissed, glaring at the paper.

"Aliz," murmured Csilla. "I'm the same person you knew two days ago."

"Well, that's true," Aliz said. "I always wondered when you'd do something like this."

Csilla blinked, and before she could stop, she asked, "Because of my parents?"

Aliz snorted. "No. Because of you. You are like a pot ready to boil over." She shook her head. "I don't care what you do, but I must survive this and help my son survive it."

Tamás had said something similar, that her heart was rebellious. Csilla wasn't sure how she felt about that.

"Where's Feri?" Csilla asked, hearing the unspoken in Aliz's words.

Aliz's fingers came to rest on her typewriter keys again. "I haven't seen him. He hasn't been home since the first protest."

And she began typing again, while Csilla's stomach sank. So Csilla left her friend alone, and they worked side by side in silence.

Szendrey reappeared after an hour or so, dumping a pile of papers into her basket. "These are a priority. Bring them to me when you're done."

"Yes, comrade," she managed to remember to say.

He nodded and disappeared.

"Back to the grind," Csilla quipped.

Aliz did not reply.

So she dove into the work. As she read through all of Szendrey's notes, the story began to come together in her head. She learned about what was happening outside of the city's central neighborhoods, what was happening outside of Budapest: The farmers bringing in food to the rebels of Budapest. The riots and protests in cities and villages all across Hungary. She didn't even know how Szendrey got the information, but it was best not to ask questions. She added everything she knew about, everything she'd seen on the streets, the ingenuity of Zsu and the women of Budapest, the children and the adults working together, the flags with the Soviet seal cut out and the way color could be seen through the hole in the flag.

She wanted others to read these articles and feel the same growing sense of possibility she felt.

After an hour, Zsu appeared in the doorway, holding notes written in a hand that wasn't her own.

"From Tamás's men," she whispered, her eyes glittering. She glanced at Aliz and then frowned. "What—"

From the look on Zsu's face, Csilla realized that her friend did not know the fate of her fiancé. She stood and said, "Let's talk in the hall."

And so, in the hallway, she told Zsu, as carefully and sensitively as she could, that she'd seen Gábor attacked by a mob and that she didn't know if he was still alive. Zsu's eyes started to widen, and when they could go no farther, her mouth dropped open. But it was only when Csilla whispered, "I'm so sorry, Zsu," that Zsu let out a wailing, a horrible, animal-like noise, sinking to the floor.

The door to the typists' room jerked open, and Aliz stepped out, eyes wide. She looked at Zsu and then at Csilla, who had tears streaming down her face too. "What happened?"

"Gábor's dead," whispered Csilla.

And as mad as Aliz was at them, she did not hesitate to sink to the floor next to Zsu, wrapping her arms around her younger friend and cradling her. Zsu sobbed into Aliz's blouse, and Csilla cried into her own hands, and it took a long time before the tears ceased.

Aliz walked Zsu home, and then it was just Csilla, alone in the typists' room with the notes Zsu had brought her, trying to remember how to do the work she'd told Tamás she could do.

When she was done with the article, she picked up a stack of paper and walked down the hallway.

In his office, Szendrey shook his head, holding up a finger. He wrote the single word *BUG* on a piece of paper and held it up to her. She kept quiet. He took her stack of papers and gestured for her to walk with him. They went down a back staircase and out onto the street. He walked and read her papers in silence as she strode next to him.

"Should we be out here?" she asked finally.

He didn't look up. "Probably not. But the whole office feels like ÁVH right now. Even your pretty friend Aliz."

"I didn't realize you noticed women," Csilla said without thinking.

Szendrey almost missed a step as he walked. He gave her a narrow sideways look. "What's that supposed to mean? Just because I'm married doesn't mean that I don't notice pretty women."

"You knew that my friend's friend was picked up for being gay, and you asked if my friend needed an escape from Hungary for the same reason. You had contacts," she said. And then she took a deep breath. "And I think you and my father were in love. Before he met my mother."

He slowed and came to a stop. "What makes you think that?"

"He wrote about you," she said. "I put the pieces together in his journals. He was in love with someone he called M in his journals, and he uses entirely different language to talk about M and about my mother. And he names her. So he must have been protecting M."

"He kept journals?"

She looked up at him. "Don't be daft. You're the one who brought them to me, aren't you? You knew my father before, which is how you knew our old last name. And the way he writes about you—the way he *wrote* about you—I think he would have trusted you with his journals. That's how you knew him so well and why you kept mentioning him," she suggested softly.

He looked suddenly so old and so sad. The kind of sad that she didn't think one recovered from. "Yes. He gave them to me in 1952, just before he was arrested. He must have known that they were going to come for him. . . ." Szendrey's voice trailed off, and he looked into the sky, blinking rapidly. He took a deep, rattling breath.

"How did he find you?"

Szendrey smiled sadly. "You knew that he found me. See, you think that you did not know your father, but you knew him."

Csilla wasn't sure how true that was. Children would always see their parents through the lens of being a child, and her memories, she was realizing, were always colored by her memories of the war and the profound loss of her parents.

"We stayed in touch. During the war, I thought—I feared the worst," Szendrey said. His voice was low and soft. "When he appeared at the paper in July 1945, I wept."

Csilla's throat closed in a tight fist, and with a jolt, she realized that she was about to cry. She had not cried for her parents in so many years.

Szendrey continued. "I agreed to keep his journals. I told him he was overreacting, that he was too powerful to be taken down now, and he made me promise to keep them. I admired your father so much. Even when—even when we fought, and that was often, I really thought that he was an incredible man. Perhaps one of the foremost thinkers of our era. You know that Nagy's reforms of '53 came from him, yes? I don't think we ever got to know how brilliant he was. And he didn't leave Hungary. They were all leaving Hungary, you know. In the '30s."

"Did you read the journals?" Csilla asked him.

Szendrey shook his head. "No."

"Why not?" Maybe she wasn't meant to have read them. Maybe that was a mistake.

"I didn't want a version of Simon he didn't give to me himself," Szendrey said simply. "I am happy with the man I had for as long as I had him."

She knew that feeling. It'd been why she threw the journals into the river. She hadn't wanted a version of her father she hadn't experienced in person. She hadn't wanted yet another version of her father. And she had been afraid that it'd be another version she didn't like. Szendrey had been happy with the version of her father that he'd had, but she hadn't been. The version she had found in the journals hadn't solved that quandary for her. He was still a wonderful father and a brilliant dreamer who had made some terrible, inexplicable choices. She wished she could know the version of her father that Szendrey had known.

She swallowed her words and managed to say, "Did my mother know?"

"About our relationship? I don't know," he said, looking down. "I never asked. I was young, Csilla. And I was selfish. I didn't know much about your mother other than that she was religious and quiet and Simon loved her. He loved her. We'd split up before he met her, but we remained friendly. I'll never forget when they met. He was"—Szendrey gestured with his hands like an explosion—"lit up from the inside."

"Why did it end? Between you two, I mean." Csilla didn't know why that seemed important, but she wanted to know.

"He didn't want to take the risk anymore," Szendrey said quietly. He shrugged. "He wanted a political career."

"Not back then he didn't. He wanted to teach," Csilla protested.

Szendrey gave her a sidelong look. "Do you really believe that?"

She wasn't sure anymore. "But he took plenty of risks later."

Szendrey offered her his arm as they stepped off a curb, and she took it. "But as far as I'm aware, he never dated another man. Or was unfaithful to your mother. He loved her. After the war, we met often for coffee. I interviewed him a few times. But it remained platonic between us after he married Éva. I promise you."

Csilla wasn't sure what to think about this and the ways her father kept morphing in her mind. He was a shattered glass image, and every piece of him was different from what she remembered.

"Did you love him?" she asked.

"Very much," Szendrey replied immediately. "I feel his loss acutely. Not as you must, but every day, I think about Simon."

"Do you love your wife?" She wanted to know.

"Very much," Szendrey said. He sighed. "I know it's difficult to understand. Simon loved me and Éva equally, I think, and in the same way. I love my wife. But I do not love her in the same way I loved Simon. We make it work. She must know. But we have a happy life, Csilla. We have two beautiful children, and my wife and I don't need to talk about things that would change that. I care very deeply for her. I would never do anything to hurt her. I would not be unfaithful to her."

Csilla was quiet for a long moment. Her father had nearly made a life for himself with someone of the same gender, and he'd maintained a close and kind friendship with him for the rest of his life. Her father had been capable of thinking and loving outside the rigid confines of society.

Like she wanted to.

She wrapped her arms around herself. "Thank you."

"For what?" Szendrey asked, surprised.

"For loving him," she said abruptly. "For telling me the truth."

Szendrey nodded slowly, then took a deep breath. "Do you want to talk about this story?"

She exhaled, relieved. "Yes. Let's."

When they returned to the office, Csilla went right back to typing, and she was there long after dark. When she finally had a finished draft, she took it over to Szendrey. While he read it, she paced back and forth across his tiny, book-and-paper-filled office.

"Stop," he said more than once, without looking up.

"I can't," she shot back.

He paused to mark something on the paper, still reading, and said, "Simon used to pace too."

She almost stopped, but the itch inside her body burned, and she had to keep moving. "Did he? I don't remember that."

"I don't think you got to see that part of him," he said, without apology. "It was before the war. Before the Party. Before Éva, though I'm sure he did it to her too, poor woman. He was full of frenetic energy. He could barely stay still. I think he instinctively sought out partners who were steadfast as a counterweight."

And Csilla did remember that her father had always moved everywhere with intensity. He didn't do anything in parts. And her mother had done everything after much deliberation. She was cautious and steady, slow and methodical, whereas her father was the one whispering stories of magic and rivers and men made of clay. But Szendrey was wrong. In her memories, when her father was with her mother, he was steady too. She'd been his center.

"Yes," she said softly, because this was a small lie and a small gift for Szendrey, who was a friend to her.

Szendrey's eyes bounced up to hers quickly and then back down to her typed pages. He tapped a pencil against his mouth and said, "It's a relief to speak of him after all these years. Thank you."

It was a tiny jolt to realize that all this time she'd thought she was missing her father alone, there were other people missing him too.

"Me too," she admitted.

Another small smile, and then he marked one more thing on her paper. "This is excellent, Csilla. I hope you're considering a career as a journalist."

She blinked. "Truly?"

"Truly," he affirmed. "You have a gift. I'll get this down to typesetting, and then I'll walk you home. It isn't safe to be out there alone right now."

"I'm not going home," she said. "And I'm fine on my own. I'll see you tomorrow?"

He studied her and then nodded. "Tomorrow, then. Be safe, Csilla."

"You too, Szendrey," she said.

And she closed the door behind her.

The streets were empty, and she could hear sporadic gunfire, explosions and the boom of tank guns. On street corners, she ducked and ran, and sometimes a bullet whizzed past her, cracking into the pavement or walls around her.

She stepped inside the quiet apartment, shutting the door behind her with a soft click. She felt dead on her feet and emotionally drained. Behind her, she heard someone sleepily say, "Fuck. Fuck."

For a split second, she thought she'd walked into the wrong apartment, and froze. But then she saw Azriel and Tamás tangled together on the bed in the corner, half dressed, groggy, hair mussed. Azriel was awake first, and he sat up, swearing and running his hands through his hair while she stared. He yanked on a shirt, kicking at Tamás.

"Csilla," said Azriel, desperation framing the angel's words.

Tamás blearily opened his eyes, blinked at Csilla and then crushed his hands to his face. "Fuck."

"Csilla," Azriel began again.

"I don't really care," she said, though something buzzed inside her chest. She reached for the door handle. She was too tired to deal with this, this loneliness, this sudden sharp pain of being left out of something she realized she wanted to be in on. She was far too fragile emotionally to think past her desire to get out of the room.

"Don't go," Tamás said, kicking off his sheets. At least they were both still wearing trousers. "Csilla, don't go."

"It's fine," she said automatically, because what else could she say? How could she deny anyone happiness now, in a time like this?

"It's clearly not," said Azriel.

"Come," Tamás said gently.

She blinked at him, and so did Azriel. Tamás patted the bed next to him. "Come. You look like you're about to fall asleep on your feet."

Or fall apart completely.

"We'll talk in the morning," he said, and patted the bed again. "I promise."

She waited until Azriel nodded at her, the curious expression he had directed at Tamás changing into something hopeful for her. She didn't know what moved her toward the bed, but she approached, slowly and cautiously. She dropped the bag with the journals and sat down heavily next to Tamás. He helped her shrug off her coat and, for lack of any other furniture, folded it next to his on the floor, while Azriel's nimble fingers made quick work of the pins in her hair. Then she lay down beside Azriel for the second night in a row—had that only been last night?—with her head on the pillow. Tamás stretched out on the other side of her, pulling the blanket over all of them.

She wanted to ask questions, but she was too tired. She wanted to tell them about Szendrey, and how much she wanted to fight for this city, and what was in the journals, and the story she wrote for the paper, but she was too tired. She wanted to watch them as Azriel untangled the knots in her curls and Tamás's hand stroked her cheek, but her eyes were fluttering closed.

And then, with one deep breath, she slipped into sleep.

She woke in the middle of the night, panicked at the feeling of someone touching her, and then realized Azriel's legs were tangled in hers—he'd long since rolled over so his rear end was against hers, and he was facing the wall, snoring softly, and Tamás's arm was thrown over her waist. They were warm and steady, and she wanted to pull them both against her, as if their steadiness and reliability, as if the mere feeling of them could quell the riot in her chest. Tamás was closer, and so she inched cautiously toward him.

His eyes fluttered open a little bit, and he didn't seem to be fully awake, but he scooted closer to her, as if he could tell what she needed, even though that was completely impossible. He let her nestle into his folded arm, chin on the pillow over her head, protecting her in the curve of his chest.

She didn't know what to do with her hands.

She wanted to touch him.

She wanted to be touched so desperately. It wasn't even desire—not like that, anyway. She wanted in some primal way to know and be known by another human through touch, like without touch she might be forgotten, like she might turn into something ephemeral. She was thirsty, parched for touch. Starved for it.

"Good?" he mumbled into her hair.

She shook her head and then slipped her hands beneath his shirt, pressing them against his bare stomach. His muscles tensed beneath her fingertips, and she started to draw back, but he just exhaled, wrapping his hand around her wrist to hold her hand still.

"Just cold. You're cold."

She wasn't really, or maybe she was.

He tugged the blanket higher over her and then reached over her with his foot to nudge Azriel. "Azriel."

"Mmm," Azriel said sleepily.

"Roll over," mumbled Tamás, still sleepy and groggy himself. "She's cold."

"Oh," said Azriel happily. And then the whole bed shifted. He slipped beneath the blankets again, eliminating the draft that had caught the back of Csilla's neck. Then Azriel draped a warm arm over her, and her entire body relaxed.

"There," said Tamás, already closing his eyes again. "Sleep."

And it was an announcement and a command, and she didn't mind either. She closed her eyes and was swept away again.

In the morning, she woke, groggy, to a bright, beautiful blue sky outside the window. She hadn't drifted away from herself at night. She hadn't drifted at all.

She recognized the window. She recognized the bed. She recognized the dark hair on the pillow next to her. She touched Tamás's cheek. He was stretched out, his hair limp and covering his eyes, one arm across his stomach and one over his head. One of her hands was still on his stomach, covered by his hand beneath his shirt.

The other side of the bed was empty, but the bathroom door was closed. She didn't realize angels needed to relieve themselves, or brush their hair, or clean themselves. She didn't realize a lot of things.

She looked up again at the blue sky.

Blue.

That was the color. She knew it because it was instinct to say *blue sky*, but she hadn't seen this color in so long. She felt like it was the brightest, most beautiful thing she'd ever seen. And she wasn't seeing it through a flag. It was simply blue, all on its own.

She whispered, "Tamás."

He turned his face toward her a little, eyes fluttering but falling closed. "Mmm."

"The sky," she whispered. "It's blue."

"Yes," he said sleepily. "So are your eyes."

She blinked at him and sat up. "What?"

He opened his eyes blearily. "Your eyes. I think they're blue too."

She yanked off the covers and scrambled out of bed over him, running with bare feet over cold floors to the bathroom. She knocked loudly. "Azriel, I'm coming in!"

There was a small angelic yelp, and she pushed the door open and stepped in while Azriel was still buttoning up his trousers. She stared at herself in the mirror. The rest of her was still gray, and so were almost all of her surroundings, but her blue eyes stood out in a sea of gray, wide and bright.

Tamás came up behind her, rubbing at his own eyes, which were still dark and black in grayscale.

He peered at her over her shoulder. "That's blue, isn't it?"

She nodded, wide-eyed. "But they weren't always blue. They were dark—I think brown—before the war."

It meant something, the colors. She just wasn't sure what.

Azriel joined them in the mirror, his own blue eyes set deep into his face. They looked worried. "I want to check on the river."

"I want to join you," she said immediately. "And I need to get new clothes. And take a bath. I reek."

"You don't," both men said.

Azriel touched the wound on her head. "Yesterday?"

She nodded, wincing.

Tamás frowned. "It hurts?"

She started to answer and then turned around, backing up until she hit the sink to give herself room from them. "You don't both get to hover over me now. I'm a grown woman—"

"I noticed," said Azriel dryly.

"—so I can take care of myself," she finished, glaring at him.

"Probably true," agreed Tamás. He turned around and walked back into the room, fishing around for his shirt, which he pulled over his head. He stood at the window, staring off at the sky. "There's just so much blue."

"Wait until you're outside," Azriel called to them. "It's going to dazzle you."

> There should be more transparency in government. The work we do is so vital, and I do not think we always communicate it to the People properly. Transparency is key. But this must be done in a way that does not threaten the Revolution or the ideals of the nation. Transparency must be a tool to strengthen the resolve of the People and shore up support for the Party, not a counterrevolutionary measure.
>
> —The Journal of Simon Tisza, May 1947

CHAPTER THIRTY

CSILLA

OCTOBER 25, 1956

It dazzled them, and it felt surreal. The world they stepped into did not feel like the world they'd lived in yesterday.

The river glowed, iridescent in the sunlight, reflecting the blue sky so the sky and the river blurred together, endless and infinite, and it drew Csilla, Azriel and Tamás to itself like moths to a flame. Csilla paused, taking off her shoes so she could feel the earth beneath her feet.

"Csilla," hissed Tamás. "It's freezing. You'll freeze."

She dropped her shoes behind her on the ground, her eyes fixed on the river. She heard Azriel tell Tamás to pick them up, that she'd need them later, but neither of them tried to stop her.

She took one step, then another and then another, the cold pavement beneath her like a wave through her toes to the arch of her foot. This was the walk through the wilderness. This was the pillar of fire by night. It'd been there the entire time, and she hadn't seen it for what it was because it wasn't exactly a pillar of fire, because she'd taken a story to be literal when it was true. She'd forgotten the heart of every story was a truth, and it wore different clothes for every reader, wore different clothes for every generation.

A story wasn't retold to remember the truth it held at the time it was first told, at the time it was created. A story was retold to learn its truth at the time of the retelling.

This was the truth of Budapest, the river turned silver, the girl with the moon in her hair, the boy with the city in his eyes, the boy with death in his hands.

This river was their pillar of fire, their way through the wilderness, their cloud by day and light by night.

She went to the edge and lay down on her stomach, reaching out with her hand.

Ehyeh asher ehyeh, she thought to the river. *I will return to you. I will return to you. I will return to you.*

And the river opened to her.

CHAPTER THIRTY-ONE

There is a city, and through the middle of the city there is a river, and running parallel to the river there is a street. It's crooked like a bent elbow, an outstretched arm, leading from one synagogue to another, an olive branch from which the Budapest Jewish community springs. Once a flourishing community, it was nearly extinguished from the earth. But like the eternal lamps that hang at the front of the sanctuary in each synagogue, the community returned. Quiet and small and cautious. Gray and thin and bright. The familiar streets heard a little less Yiddish, and almost no Hebrew chanting through the windows of the temples, but there were still black hats and tallitot, kippot and quiet murmurs of "Gut Shabbos" as the men passed each other in the streets. And from Friday night until Saturday night, it was the quietest part of the city.

The river runs parallel to the street, like siblings, just as it runs through this community in every city it touches. Vienna.

Linz. Bratislava. Belgrade. And the story was always the same. Devastation, and fire, and then the quiet. A deep, unearthly stillness. And after, the return. Quiet, and sad, and small. Perhaps just one, two people. Perhaps a few dozen. But enough.

Water has a long memory, and though the river was there before the street and will be there long after, the river holds stories in its silt, carries them far away from where they began.

There is a city, and through the middle of the city there is a river, and running parallel to the river there is a street. It is crooked like a bent elbow, an outstretched arm, an olive branch. And on the street, parallel to the river that splits the city, held in the memory of water, is a girl.

On the day she was born, the midwife lifted her free from between her mother's thighs and gasped. She nearly dropped the infant straight to the floor. The midwife gathered herself, wrapping the screaming baby in a clean blanket, rubbing her dry and transferring her to her mother's arms.

The mother, dark-haired and dark-eyed, touched the baby's milk-white hair. Whether she touched the baby's hair in reverence, in fear, in horror or in confusion wasn't clear. And she looked up at the father, dark-haired and dark-eyed, speechless.

As the girl was delivered in water, so did the waters come that night.

The Duna hadn't broken its banks in Budapest in many lifetimes, but it broke its banks that night.

The water ran through the streets of Pest and up the staircases of Buda and into the castle, down the other side.

It went in no open doors. It went in no open windows.

It ran, white-silver like the moon, and the people said they heard it whispering, *here, here, here.*

The young father and the young mother stood at the window of the mother's childhood bedroom, now their own, which was now the girl's. And they watched the moon water run through the streets as they held their baby in their arms, with her moon hair.

When she was grown and they told her this story, they did not tell her what they had spoken about, though surely they did not stand there in silence. The baby was born in 1937. The parents knew, as all Jews know, in their bones that it was time to leave. That a place that'd been safe for so long was no longer safe. They knew that for Jews, *safety* is a word that is temporary. There is no such thing as security. No such thing as assurance of home and belonging. They knew then that they ought to leave.

They must have.

But they didn't.

Later, the girl would imagine her mother saying to her father, "We need to go."

Beneath them, the moon water rose.

She imagined her father saying, "This is our home."

Beneath them, the moon water whispered.

And she imagined her mother saying, "For how much longer?"

And she imagined her father, for once in his life, did not have an answer.

But that was all she imagined.

She didn't know.

And she will never know.

The story of the night of her birth ended with the moon water, the window and her moon hair.

For in many ways, despite the ominous hair that had midwives and old women crossing the street to avoid her, she was just another little girl, living in the city on the street that ran parallel to the river. Human memory is much shorter than that of water, especially that of a river like the Duna.

Before the unsettling quiet blanketed this part of the city, she was just a girl, skipping like a little brook. Her mother, who called for her to walk like a lady. Her father, who chastised her mother for calling for her to walk like a lady. He indulged the girl. The mother curbed her. She needed both. Like a river herself, the girl needed both the rains of her father to nourish her and the banks of her mother to guide her.

CHAPTER THIRTY-TWO

AZRIEL

He held her face above the water in her mind, her chin tilted toward the sky, and he did not panic when her skin grew cold and clammy. He'd let people slip into the abyss, and so he could keep them in this life too. There were no angels of life. An angel of death sufficed for both.

Still, when she surfaced, gasping for air as if she'd fallen into the river, he exhaled in relief.

Not everyone who fell into the waters of their mind surfaced again.

Beneath his hands wrapped on either side of her face, he thought he could feel the seams of her, the stitches of her where she'd had to remake herself again and again, day after day, every day since she and her parents plummeted into the river, surviving what they couldn't have survived.

But then, on her other side, Tamás knelt beside her, his hand going to her cold shoulder. And her seams disappeared, blurring away.

She'd pulled the river into her bones. It'd changed her forever.

And Tamás had pulled the city into his bones. It'd changed him forever.

And in his bones, Azriel carried all of the people he'd ever shepherded to the other side.

This was all they could do together. Stay. For now.

It was not enough.

That was all he could do. Stay with her. For now.

It was not enough.

It was enough.

Dayenu.

CHAPTER THIRTY-THREE

CSILLA

October 25, 1956

The river opened to her and did not close. It ran silver through the veins on the back of her hands, glinting in the light.

"What does it mean?" Tamás asked roughly, turning her hand over in his as they walked through the city.

"I don't know," Csilla admitted. She didn't, but she could feel the river's love coursing through her. They belonged to each other. They spoke each other's languages.

"It doesn't *have* to mean anything," said Azriel, but he looked at her hands with unguarded curiosity.

They avoided the tanks where they could, but it didn't matter—they could not have missed the crowds of people streaming toward Parliament again. Azriel was the first to notice them. His steps kept slowing, and he'd half turn, watching a few people hurry past them north and west, toward the river and to Parliament. Csilla watched him warily.

Then someone recognized Tamás and called out to him. He jogged across the street, gesturing for Azriel and Csilla to stay back.

Csilla watched Tamás chatting with a few other young men across the street, hunching her shoulders against the damp chill in the air. "You are hiding something."

"Deception isn't angelic," Azriel said.

She shot him a look.

He gave her a half-quirked smile. "You have to admit it was worth the try."

She wouldn't give him the reward of a smile, not now. "What's happening at Parliament?"

"I don't know," Azriel said quietly, "but you two shouldn't go."

She leaned sideways a little so their shoulders touched. The river stilled inside her. "But you will."

"I must," said the angel, his voice resigned.

She had made choices. Azriel did not have that luxury.

"What did you tell the river?" he asked her.

She drew a circle on the palm of her hand. "I will return."

He kissed the side of her head.

Tamás came back over to their side of the street. "Protest at Parliament over the fact that Soviet tanks are still here."

"He's been prime minister for a *day*," Csilla grumbled.

"And the tanks are still here," Tamás said. "You think we should just let Nagy off the hook? He wasn't good at standing up to the Soviets last time. We must push him. Wasn't it you who said something about momentum?"

"We're making progress," protested Csilla. "Why must it all be overnight?"

"Csilla," said Tamás, exasperation peering through his words. "The Sixteen Points? That's just the beginning."

"Don't go to Parliament," she said, watching Azriel sliding away from them, a pained look on his face. "Please."

Tamás shook his head. "We have to push Nagy. These tanks can't occupy us forever. You don't have to come, Csilla, if you're getting cold feet."

She was not getting cold feet. She didn't want to die. And she didn't want Tamás to die. If Azriel was being pulled to Parliament, then so was death. She didn't want to argue with Tamás, but she couldn't say he was wrong. There was some part of her, a tiny part of her, that wanted to be comfortable and forget the way the river felt in her veins, that wanted this to be over, for this to be enough. But it couldn't be enough, because it wasn't enough.

Tamás turned, looking at Azriel's retreating back and then at Csilla. He held out his hand, and she slipped her silver-veined one into his.

They followed the same path as the others, crisscrossing the city through apartment courtyards, small street cutaways and empty market corridors.

At Parliament, the crowd was nearly as big as it'd been the night before, and far more diverse. People of all ages joined the chants for Russia to leave, and there were babies sitting on shoulders, children playing among the crowd. Csilla closed her eyes, breathing in the atmosphere. There was something deeply powerful, and terrifying, about a group of people this size. An electric thrill ran through her.

"I am scared," she whispered to Tamás.

He gripped her silver-veined hand. "You think they're going to hold show trials for all of us? You think they're going to deport or execute, what, a hundred thousand people here right now?"

She relaxed a little. He was right. There was power in numbers, as her father said. And they were all committing the same crime.

There was a shift, the people moving like a small tide, and then, abruptly, there was a crack through the air. Csilla's head snapped around as she tried to locate and identify the sound.

Then there was a scream. A single piercing scream that sliced right through the crowd to cut into her. She inhaled, and then gunfire cracked and popped through the air, one shot after another. Someone else screamed, and then people began to stampede, trip and fall. There was no cover in Parliament Square, none except for the large columns of the buildings across the way.

"Csilla," Tamás gasped, his hand sweaty around hers as they ran. "Csilla, I—"

But hundreds of thousands of people could not fit behind the columns, and so the crowd pushed and shifted and turned to the streets.

Tamás's hand was yanked out of hers, and Csilla was swept up in the crowd and had to run, her heart in her throat, to avoid being trampled. There were tanks rumbling down the street, and people screamed, scattering in every direction. Csilla slowed, glancing between them as she tried to figure out where they were herding the people to.

But the tanks weren't herding the people.

One tank pointed its turret at another tank.

Csilla sucked in a breath.

Someone popped out the top of the tank, shouting, "We are the Hungarian People's Army! We protect the Hungarian People!"

Csilla felt her eyes widen.

The officer in the tank shouted to the other tank, "Stand down!"

That tank's turret swung toward the first tank.

"Run!" shouted someone. And the people scattered again. Csilla lost her footing, fell and scrambled to her feet. Next to her, a woman was screaming on the ground, holding her leg.

Another tank fired, and Csilla jerked, the splash in her memories jerking her back to the river, the war and the siege that had raged around them.

The river whispered to her, a warm gentle feeling inside of her, and she exhaled, the world around her rushing back in. She scrambled over the rubble to the woman, finding her hand.

"Can you get up?" she shouted.

The woman shook her head, her face pale, nearly white with pain. Csilla glanced around, but they were the only two out in the middle of the street between the two sides of the same army fighting with each other.

"We have to crawl. I'll help you," Csilla told her.

"It hurts," whimpered the woman, gripping the dark part of her leg below her dress and stockings. Csilla didn't dare look at it.

"Come on," Csilla urged her, crawling on her belly toward a nearby side street. "It's not too far."

The woman sobbed, but Csilla stayed with her, and they inched along, ducking and covering their heads when the tanks fired and rumbled at each other. Csilla smelled the gas before she heard the clink of a Molotov cocktail being thrown toward the tanks. It exploded behind them, setting a nearby car on fire. The heat felt like it'd sear off her skin.

Csilla scrambled to her feet and whispered to the woman, "I'm so sorry. This is going to hurt."

She grasped the woman beneath her armpits and dragged her across the street as fast as she could. The woman screamed until Csilla abruptly stopped, and just as they reached the corner of the side street, the car on fire exploded, right where they would have been.

Csilla collapsed, rolling the woman onto her back. Breathing, but unconscious.

People appeared from nowhere, friendly hands reaching for them. Someone wrapped a tourniquet around the woman's leg. Someone else yelled for a medic or a car to the hospital. Someone pressed a damp cloth to Csilla's forehead.

Csilla leaned back against the wall. Then, through the people, Tamás appeared, pale-faced. He crouched next to her, his palm against her cheek. "Csilla."

"You're right," she said quietly. "They have to leave. Nothing can happen while the city—while Hungary is occupied."

That was what her father had gotten wrong. He'd dreamed of reforms but failed to make a world in which they could happen.

Reforms could not take root in a field sown with fear and violence. The country could not be occupied and move forward at the same time. They could not ignore the injustices of the past and the ones still happening and hope for change.

Her father had wanted open and fair elections, but they needed more. They needed a plurality of thoughts so one truth would not drown out other truths. Her father had wanted more autonomy, but that was not enough. They needed independence. Her father had dreamed of a Hungary he wanted to invent, instead of the one that could exist right beneath his own feet.

Csilla would not make the same mistakes.

PART IV

Did you listen? asks the city.
Do you hear us? ask the people.
Are you listening? asks the river.

CHAPTER THIRTY-FOUR

The river tells a story—it has always told this story. No matter how many times it tells the story, something always changes. That is the way stories are.

The river says that once there was nothing, and then there was something.

It happened all at once, and it took an eternity.

Before, there were no people.

And then there were people.

And then the river forgot what the world was like without people. Without swimmers and without boats, without fishermen and fisherwomen, without children at its banks, without people evolving to find ways of crossing the river without touching it.

They wanted to look down the river, or up it, or across it, but they wanted to avoid it. It was a barrier. They didn't want to touch it. The river was an inconvenience, and it was a life-giver.

It saved, and it took away. The river shaped the land, and the people shaped the river.

Perhaps it'd once been an equal relationship, but it wasn't anymore and hadn't been in a long time. And so the river became the secret-keeper, the storyteller (and all too often those are the same things). The river, of course, like all water, has a long memory. And the long memory of the water kept all the stories for all of time and carried them away for safekeeping.

But it has always told this story:

A long time ago, the people used the river's magic for everything and anything—they asked it to bless their crops for a bountiful harvest, they baptized their children in it for long lives, they used its waters for their mikvahs for purification, they toasted with it for their health, they caught the magical fish and used them for stews that fed armies and children and growing empires alike.

The river's magic was the bounty of the land, and everyone went to the river to pray, to feast, to forgive, to thank, to prosper, and the river's magic existed along with all the other kinds of magic in the world. (There are nearly infinite types of magic in the world if you know where to look.)

But as people built bridges across rivers and as people built below rivers, as they learned to work around the river instead of with the river, the magic faded.

The river asked—many times, eleven years ago, a hundred years ago, yesterday, thirty-three years from now—to save the city.

But a city is not a city without people, and sometimes people do not want to be saved.

Such was the case with the people who could read the writing on the wall and in the streaks of color running to the river and who saw the bodies floating downstream—it happened before, and if the river wills it, it'll never happen again—they saw, and they spoke, but they did not want to be saved. Perhaps they didn't know they needed to be saved. Perhaps they didn't know if they wanted to be saved. Perhaps they weren't sure if they deserved to be saved.

The river deals only with needs and wants. It is all the river understands. It is all the river has ever understood. It doesn't take things such as deserving or sin or potential into consideration.

It is asked, and it gives.

It is wanted, and it gives.

It is a river. That is what rivers do. They give.

But the people must remember that they give.

Forgetting. That is what people do.

And remembering. Well. That's what rivers do.

CHAPTER THIRTY-FIVE

CSILLA

She'd dreamed stories of times she'd never known, but the longer she was awake, the more they faded away from her, and the more she felt like herself again. She didn't drift apart from herself, not if Azriel or Tamás was touching her, and it was strange to wake up and find her hands tucked beneath her cheek on the pillow, childlike, instead of against the window, clawing for the river.

But she still felt the river clawing for her as she and Azriel went to her apartment. The river wanted her to know something. It wanted her to connect something. It wanted. She hadn't known it could want. But maybe rivers were like people and hid their wants, denied them, until they were undeniable.

Listen, urged the river.

She pushed away the feeling.

Azriel had found her at the paper later, looking exhausted,

and she'd taken him back to Tamás's apartment—their apartment now—and they'd all slept there in their crowded bed. This morning, Tamás had been gone by early light, and Azriel had remained subdued and quiet. Csilla hadn't asked him about the children she'd seen at the Parliament protest yesterday, and he hadn't asked about her change of heart.

But the ÁVH's opening fire on the Parliament protesters had changed things. Outbreaks of violence had happened all night, and their effects were visible this morning.

"You have to tell him," murmured Csilla as they wove past charred husks of tanks and armored vehicles, the results of Zsu's handiwork with the bottle bombs and the plates mimicking mines.

Azriel flinched, and a moment later, Csilla heard a tank explode nearby. Azriel's hand went to the small of her back, and they ducked into another street, away from the death that called him.

"I don't want to tell him," Azriel said.

He hadn't told Tamás who he was.

"He deserves to know," Csilla said. And Tamás was going to start to get suspicious if Azriel raced toward violence every time. She didn't say that aloud.

"Csilla, he just lost someone he loved," the angel reminded her gently. "Don't you think that complicates things?"

Everything complicated things. The three of them in one bed complicated things. Living in Hungary complicated things. Ilona complicated things. Tamás's increasing involvement in the military strategy complicated things. The rebellion—revolution, whatever this was—complicated things. The river complicated things. Everything was complicated.

"I'll think about it," Azriel promised her as they arrived at her apartment building and carried bags of food and flour up to Ilona.

Csilla fought the key in the door a little more than usual that day, and when she opened the door, she gasped. Shattered glass covered the floor. Bullet holes pocked the wall across from the window by the—blue!—dining room table, but Csilla didn't get a chance to panic because she heard Ilona humming in the bedroom.

"Tante," she called. "I brought you food." She glanced at Azriel. "And we have a guest."

"Csillagom," said her aunt, appearing in the doorway. "Was that your friends who shot our window?"

Csilla had no way to tell, but she put down the wooden crate she carried and folded her arms around her aunt. Ilona stroked her hair and hugged her back.

"Is it terrible out there?" Ilona whispered.

Csilla thought of Gábor and Zsu and Aliz, and of Elek, and of the bodies next to the tanks on her dangerous walk here, and of the woman yesterday and the children, and of the sound of screams when the shots came from above. She couldn't lie to her aunt. "Yes."

"Will it be worth it?" Ilona asked her.

Csilla nodded into her shoulder, and Ilona pushed her back, pressing her hands to either side of Csilla's cheeks.

Ilona gave her a small smile. "Then it is worth it."

Csilla reached for Azriel and wrapped her hand around his, a signal to Ilona that her aunt did not miss. "Tante, this is Azriel."

She'd forgotten, when she suggested Azriel come with her,

that he'd been Nati and known her, and that he'd been in the gas chambers with her children when they died. But she could tell, when she looked at his face, that he'd not forgotten.

He said, "Ilona," with a touch too much familiarity.

And Ilona said softly, "Hello, angel."

They unpacked the food in the kitchen, chatting about Ilona remembering Azriel's eyes and knowing from the way he moved that he was an angel from the Bible and he was also an angel without the Bible, and Csilla tugged at the feeling inside her chest. It wasn't jealousy that Azriel was not her own—she wanted him to share that part of himself with Tamás, after all—but rather that there were still so many things about Ilona she didn't yet know. And that she might never get time to know. She'd thought of her mother and Ilona as people set in time, so sure of who they were when compared to her father that she'd forgotten that they too contained infinite complexities.

A crack of artillery fire echoed down the street, unnervingly close.

"Tante," murmured Csilla. "Maybe you can go stay with Zsu's family, in Buda. It might be safer."

Ilona tutted. "You think there's anywhere in Hungary that is safer for me than this apartment?"

She had a point.

Ilona set to work, taking out the canisters of flour and yeast from the cupboard. It was, after all, Friday, and tonight would be Shabbat.

"I'm not going to stay for Shabbos," Csilla said softly. "Would you be mad at me?"

"No," Ilona said, giving Csilla a surprising, sly smile as her eyes flickered to Azriel. "I will be lonely, but I will not be angry. But you're denying your angel here my challah, and that is a sin, Csilla."

Csilla froze for a moment, then laughed, delighted. She hadn't heard her aunt make a joke in years, longer than the last time she'd made challah by hand. She rolled up her sleeves and said, "Then we should stay and help you make the challah, at least."

"I can help too," Azriel said, stepping to the counter.

And so the three of them measured out the sugar and yeast and flour. Ilona tapped the back of Csilla's hands with a spoon, eyeing the silver in Csilla's veins, but said nothing when Csilla said nothing. Csilla told her aunt everything that was happening outside the walls of this apartment against the backdrop of the sounds of war climbing into this city once again. Azriel checked the yeast and began to stir in the flour, while Ilona mostly listened to Csilla. She didn't retreat from what Csilla said, and she did not crawl back into bed.

"Did you finish reading your father's journals?" Ilona asked when Csilla had kneaded the dough and they'd set it to rise. It was cold in the apartment with the shot-out window, but bread would rise, given enough time.

"I did," Csilla said. Then she thought of something. "Tante, can I ask you something about the war?"

Ilona leaned against the counter. She nodded, looking at her shoes.

Csilla continued slowly, "He said that during the war, he tried to build something—to protect the ghetto. Do you remember that?"

Ilona looked up, startled. "Yes, of course. We were all there. We tried to help him. We were building a golem. It was my father's—your grandfather's—idea."

"Yes," Csilla said, excitement peppering her voice.

"I remember too," murmured Azriel, wonder in his voice. "I was in Prague for that golem, and I remember the one your father tried to build."

She jerked, staring at him. "Do you remember what went wrong?"

He shook his head. "I'm not familiar with the process. It could have been anything."

"Water, mud." Ilona nodded. "Anything. Golems are dangerous, but they are real. And difficult to build."

"All real things are dangerous," Azriel said quietly.

"And the things that are not real can be too," Ilona replied, spreading her hands wide. "You are creating something out of nothing. It is playing God."

But everything they were doing out there was playing God. It was what Azriel had told her before this started. Every moment was a turning point, and every moment was a life-and-death decision for someone—them, their friends, their lovers, their enemies, strangers they'd never know.

This was no different.

"If you are going to make a golem," Ilona said finally, seeing through to Csilla's true question, "you'll need to know how to write the Hebrew letters. Do you remember?"

Csilla shook her head. "Will you teach me?"

And her aunt taught her, using her finger in the flour left on the table to teach the shapes of a language Csilla knew she must have known at some point in her life.

When Csilla and Azriel left, her aunt was braiding three strands of bread together, humming a song on the edges of Csilla's memory, and Csilla clutched in her hand a piece of paper with three simple letters. Aleph. Mem. Tav. Three letters that she'd braid together to make a man out of clay.

When they found Tamás again, he was working on an inventory. She wanted to touch him, to tease him, but her mind was full of the chattering river, and she was afraid that the sweat from her palm would blur the letters Ilona had given her on the paper.

"Csilla," Tamás said, alarmed when the door slammed behind them. "Azriel."

She paced. "Do you know what the golem is?"

"No," said Tamás, his brow furrowing. "Should I?"

"It's Jewish," Csilla said, flopping on the bed. "So perhaps not."

"Start at the beginning, Csilla," said Azriel.

"You know what she's talking about?" Tamás asked Azriel.

"A golem," she said, closing her eyes to draw the image of her father's journals to the forefront of her mind. "A golem is a protector."

A man made of clay, with the breath of life in him, with no conscience, who will protect the Jews.

Would the golem protect the gentiles of Budapest too? If she asked it?

She had to try. The tanks fired at buildings, at people, at each other. The chaos that reigned prevented progress. They had to defeat the Soviets, force their hand to withdraw.

"We could end the battles," she said, her voice soft. Stillness came to the room after her words. "We can destroy a handful of tanks, but tanks will kill more people than we can kill tanks, even if the Hungarian army begins to fight for us. And I am worried that people's will is flagging. It's been a long three days."

"It has been," Tamás said, after a lengthy pause. "I believe in the people on our side, but ending battles in our favor would save lives. What do we need to do?"

"We need river water," she said. "And clay or mud untouched by humans."

"Where do we find that? Other than digging for it?" Tamás wanted to know.

"At the bottom of the river," Csilla said, opening her eyes. "We need the silt from the bottom of the river. We'll need buckets and a cart."

"Did you ask?" Azriel wanted to know.

She hadn't yet, but she could feel by the sudden, warm calm in her mind that she didn't need to. The river had opened to her, and she could take from it what she needed to save the city and its people.

"I can't swim," Tamás said to her, his voice low.

"I can," she said. And what she meant was that she could swim well enough and she had to trust that the river would protect her.

The crease returned between his eyes, and he stepped forward, his hand gliding as if on ice to stop beside her wrist. "Are you sure?"

She made herself meet his eyes and give him a smile. "Of course."

But he didn't believe her, she could tell from the look on his face, and truly, she wasn't sure if she believed herself.

Azriel shook his head. "This is dangerous, Csilla. You are not God. You cannot make and destroy life. The story of the golem is a cautionary tale. Your father failed."

"I am not going to fail," she said, turning to him. She didn't know that. Her parents and aunt and grandfather had failed, but they had not used water from the river or mud from the bottom of the river. They'd been limited by what was available in the ghetto. And they hadn't known the river the way she did.

She reached for Azriel's hand, and he reluctantly let her take it. "I am not trying to play God. I am trying to save the city."

"It is hard," he murmured to her, "the line between the two."

She did not want to believe that God would destroy Budapest the way God destroyed Sodom and Gomorrah and that there was nothing else she could do for this city. She wanted to believe this was more David and Goliath than anything, that she was the underling with the tool and God at her side, and with a golem she could defeat the undefeatable, unconquerable foe.

"I am not looking to play God," she said.

"You must remember," said Azriel, "that that is all it is. Playing."

She nodded.

He exhaled and dropped her hand, though the worried look in his eyes didn't change. "Very well."

CHAPTER THIRTY-SIX

CSILLA

When night fell, Shabbat began. In Jewish tradition, Shabbat was both outside of time and within it, a time when everyone had two souls, and Csilla felt as if she was navigating those murky waters of space and soul and time as they slipped through the city toward the silver river.

The angel, Csilla and Tamás returned to the river with a wooden cart, buckets and all of the containers they could collect from neighbors and the rebels. They decided that while Csilla dove for the river silt, the boys would take turns scooping river water with buckets to keep the mud wet and malleable.

Csilla stripped down to her underthings and stood at the edge of the Duna.

Azriel stepped up next to her, facing the river. "You know what I've never understood?"

"I imagine that's a long list," she said dryly.

He laughed a little bit. "It is. I meant what I've never understood about you, Csilla."

"Could still be a long list," she added, stalling for time. She didn't want to know what the angel didn't know about her.

"Why didn't you go back to the river?" he asked her.

"What do you mean?"

He studied her in the moonlight. "You might have asked the river to carry you far away from here. Or asked it to save you and your aunt. When they came for your parents, were you afraid?"

She'd been terrified.

But he was right.

"I was," she said slowly. "The morning you saved me, I thought about it. I always saw the river as a last resort. Not going to it to ask it for favors, like with the torches and with this, but leaping into it? I understood that to be a last resort."

"You were still fighting for this city and your place in it, in some way," he murmured, almost to himself.

"I was supposed to leave," she reminded him.

"And yet," he said, smiling, "here you are."

Here she was.

She whispered to the river, *I am listening now.*

And the river murmured, *listen, listen, listen.*

She dove into the silver water, under the late quarter moon, and let the water consume her. She opened to the river as it'd opened to her, listening in a place where time and space didn't exist, where memory was the thread connecting each thought to another thought, braiding them together.

Her father used to hold her hands along the wall as she walked, before the war, before the Party, before they disappeared.

At the end, when her foot wobbled off the wall, he'd cry, "Soar, Csillagom," and she'd leap into the air, the air rushing by her cheeks and streaking through her hair, and he'd catch her. She remembered the way his beard would rub against her cheek, and she wondered at how different the hair on his head was from the hair on his face.

"We're marvels," he'd tell her, if she ever mentioned this.

If her mother was around, she'd add, "Baruch HaShem." Thanks to God.

"Éva," her father would chide her mother.

"Simon," her mother would say in return.

The only time she ever heard them argue—before the war, of course—was about God.

"The river is magic," her father would whisper to her.

"Never listen to your father," her mother would tell her when she tucked her in at night.

And she believed them both.

There was a woman, and her son had fallen through the ice on the river. She'd gone out to save him. She'd fallen through too. This was not a metaphor, it was a story Csilla could feel in her bones that the river carried and was giving to her, like a gift, like an offering, like a sacrifice, but she felt the metaphor nonetheless.

There was a man. He'd been drunk. He'd fallen into the river. He'd felt the cold when he hit it. He'd had one or two blazing seconds of wonder and regret. Then he'd drowned.

There was a person who went into the river because they

couldn't find anywhere else to be themself. Csilla reached for them across the water, but they were already gone. She could just hear their voice in her chest.

She surfaced, gasping. She treaded water, reaching up toward the two anxious boys on the shore. "Bucket," she said.

"Are you okay?" asked Tamás, handing her a bucket.

She didn't reply. She put her hands on either side of the bucket and dove beneath the surface again, going to the bottom of the river. She pushed the bucket into the bottom of the river, and it did not give.

The river soothed her, and the silt gave way, filling the bucket.

She kicked herself to the surface.

Tamás reached for her hand, but she handed him the bucket instead. He pulled it up and out of sight, the night swallowing him. She treaded water, waiting. Azriel silently scooped river water next to her, pouring the silver water into jugs.

"It feels wrong," Azriel murmured, "to steal river water."

"It's freely given," Csilla assured him.

Tamás reappeared, a full-moon face of anxiety at the edge of the river, and leaned down, giving her the bucket back.

She dove again.

The bucket in her hands bumped along the bottom of the river, and she ran one hand along the bottom, searching for silt and dirt instead of rocks and debris. Her palm ran over something smooth and strange, like a stone, the length of a tree branch. Then the smoothness ended, rough at an edge where something else smooth picked up. She felt her way over it, curious, aware she was running out of air. Then her hand glided over something round, and she screamed underwater, kicking wildly to the surface.

She broke into the air gasping and thrashing.

"Csilla," Tamás hissed, shushing her. He reached for the bucket, but it was empty.

She pressed a cold and shaking hand to her face, treading water and trying not to let the cold into her bones. "We need to swim downriver a bit."

"That's closer to Parliament," Azriel commented.

Closer to soldiers, farther from the Jewish Quarter, where they would build the golem, he meant.

Her hair stuck to her cheek, cold curls like the fingers in the river pulling her under. "We have to," she said shortly, and flipped to her back to start swimming. "The silt here is used. We can't have used silt."

"Why not?" asked Tamás. "I mean, who decides what *used* is? What do you mean?"

They scrambled to their feet, but Azriel was slow, like he could see that she wasn't telling them something.

"That's just how it works," Csilla told them. "I don't know why. Ask God."

Tamás said nothing to this. Azriel frowned at her. He knew she was withholding something, he just didn't know what.

She tried not to think about the bottom of the river, but after she swam fifty paces, Tamás insisted that she check again. She dove, holding the bucket in front of her. She could feel her heart pounding in her ears when the bucket bumped against the bottom, but she found nothing but silt and mud. She filled a bucket and surfaced.

Azriel took the bucket this time, still silent.

He dumped it into one of their containers and handed her the empty bucket.

She dove again.

She dove eighteen times in total.

Chai.

Eighteen, the number for life.

The last time she surfaced, her teeth clattered so loud that Tamás hushed her before he realized what was making the noise.

"Out," he commanded.

She would have protested, but she couldn't make the words, and she'd dove into the river eighteen times, so she let him pull her out, his hands under her arms, strong and tense. She let them wrap her in a blanket, and Tamás rubbed her shoulders vigorously, trying to bring heat back into them. But once she was out of the water, the air seemed even colder than before, and her legs started shaking too. Azriel started speaking to her, but she couldn't hear him as she let him drop a dress over her head. It stuck to her skin, damp and wrinkled, and he tugged it down over her hips. He put her feet into shoes.

Tamás pulled his hat down over her wet hair. She protested at that, but half-heartedly. When she closed her eyes, she could feel the debris at the bottom of the river, and she clutched the wool blanket tight.

Tamás tried, but failed, to push the cart with one arm around her and one hand on the wheelbarrow. He nearly tipped out all the hard-won water and silt from the river.

Azriel slipped his arm around Csilla, holding her upright. "Let's go, Csilla."

Tamás picked up both handles of the cart, and Azriel and Csilla shuffled behind him. They snuck through the city, across the tram tracks, up Széchenyi Street to Bajcsy-Zsilinszky Avenue. In the distance, they heard sporadic gunfire.

Tamás stopped near one of the hotels. Csilla looked up and closed her eyes. She knew this hotel. The hotel owner married a Jew, one of the women he'd hidden during the final battle between the Nazis and the Soviets. They'd left three years after the end of the war, when the hotel was seized by the State and nationalized. She thought that woman and her mother were friends. She remembered her mother's fury that her own family wasn't leaving too.

"Csilla," Tamás said, his voice sharp, like he'd been saying her name and trying to get her attention for a while. "Where?"

They weren't going back to the tunnels or Tamás's apartment tonight. She remembered now.

"This way."

CHAPTER THIRTY-SEVEN

CSILLA

OCTOBER 26, 1956

Tamás did not know the Jewish Quarter as she knew it, but it was clear that Azriel did. He remembered it from his time in the ghetto, when they were both here as small and hungry children. As cold as Csilla was, she and Azriel moved through the streets and alleys and connected courtyards of her home until she found the abandoned apartment building she was thinking of, bombed and burned into ruins and never repaired. She remembered all her friends who'd lived in that building. It was still strange to see it unrepaired, like the damaged limb of an ancient tree.

Azriel and Tamás lifted the wheelbarrow over the debris at the gaping mouth of the building. Csilla followed as they carried it to the back to the old water pipe. The remnants of the floor above stretched into the night sky, bared teeth biting into the moonlight.

They would not build the golem that night. They'd build it at dawn, when they were rested and had the benefit of light. They poured some of the water into the buckets of mud to keep it wet overnight. They draped each one with canvas.

Exhausted, Csilla sank to the ground. Now they just needed to wait.

She wasn't cold anymore. She was no longer shivering. She didn't know if that was a good sign. She thought perhaps she should feel the cold. Instead, she felt numb.

She didn't like the way Tamás was looking at her, like there was a question he wanted to ask that they both knew she wouldn't want to answer. But instead, he looked past her, staring around them at the shell of a building. "How'd you know about this building?"

Csilla sighed. "It used to be a Jewish apartment building." She glanced at Azriel. "You remember, don't you?"

She kept his secret. Azriel nodded, and offered nothing more.

"Before the war?" Tamás asked, though he must have known the answer.

"Before," she said simply. For him, it was before. For her, it was during. The distinction was a fine shimmering line between them. She wondered what Azriel's concept of time was.

For a long moment, the three of them stood there in the shell of the building in complete silence. Even the night and the war in the city were silent, as if they were observing a moment for all the people that'd been in the Before. Csilla found her mind wandering to her father's notebooks and his studies. She wondered if it was real. If it'd work. If the river's magic and the mud and the water and the words to a language she didn't understand and was not her own could save this city.

If she wanted to save this city.

"Do you think it'll work?" Tamás asked, as if he could read her thoughts.

She glanced at the wheelbarrow. "I hope so."

"No," he said softly. "I mean the revolution."

When she looked at him, he wasn't looking at her or at the mud that would become a golem if they were lucky. He was looking at the moon. He appeared so young right then, his hands in his pockets, his face washed clean of all its wounds and lines and dark circles.

"I don't know," she whispered. She felt like she ought to lie to him the way her father had lied to her, but she was her mother's daughter, and she felt most prepared when she accepted the reality in front of her: magic was a lie, and it might be the only thing that saved them, and they still might die on the streets of a city that didn't care enough about them.

Tamás turned from the moon to her, his face unreadable. He reached for her then, hands coming out of his pockets so he could drape an arm around her shoulder. "Come on."

She stood, pulling the blanket tight around her. She looked to the silent angel of death. "Do you know?"

He smiled sadly at her. "I wish I could."

"Let's go," she said, because if none of them knew, there was nothing to do other than get some rest.

They walked out of the apartment building three abreast, but quickly had to switch to single file to cross the city. One street would be quiet, but in the next they'd dodge sniper fire. At corners, Tamás would call out *barát* so perhaps their allies would know what side they were on, but still, bullets ricocheted off the stone above their heads.

Tamás swore, and behind Csilla, Azriel laughed, a breathless, adrenaline-filled sound. Csilla just kept her head down, too exhausted for swearing or laughing. Tamás's apartment building was crowded tonight, becoming home to those displaced from the main streets.

Tamás reached behind him blindly, and Csilla slipped her hand into his, letting him protect her among all the men sleeping on the stairs and curled up in the corners.

Inside the dark room, with the blackout curtains pulled across the windows, he turned on a light. It flickered and died. He jiggled the switch, and it hummed back on.

Azriel pushed Csilla into the bathroom. She stepped in front of the sink and looked at herself in the mirror. She was covered in mud, her hair streaked, things from the river caught in her curls, her eyes bright and wide and—dark. They'd changed back to their natural color. Deep abysses had opened in her face, her bottomless pupils blown wide. She looked like an illustration of a monster in a children's book.

Tamás stepped in behind them. He ducked slightly and caught Csilla's dress at the hem, pulling it up and over her head. His hands glided, hot, down her bare arms, but his gaze in the cracked mirror was sharp and critical. Azriel only met her gaze, and she saw her own haunted thoughts echoed in his eyes.

She stepped out of her wet undergarments, standing in front

of them naked. Tamás disappeared briefly, and she could see him in the mirror, searching the floor for clean, dry clothes she could wear. She braided her hair before it could knot worse than it already had.

Azriel said, "You can hear the river's memories."

She met his eyes, and she nodded. "There were stories this time."

In the mirror, she could see Tamás pause, taking in this information. But that wasn't what haunted her.

Tamás brought her a pair of trousers—hers—and a sweater—his—and helped her into them. She looked helplessly lost and impossibly small and pale in the oversized clothes. Tamás pressed an open-mouthed kiss to the cold, clammy skin on the back of her neck.

"Csilla," he murmured against her neck.

She watched him in the mirror. "What?"

He lifted his eyes and met her gaze in the reflection. "It wasn't just the stories. What was in the river, Csilla?"

She swallowed. "Bones. From the people they executed on the banks during the war."

Azriel turned, pushing his way out of the bathroom. She saw him in the reflection as he sank to the edge of the bed, his hands in his hair.

She shuddered then, hands covering her own face, and she'd have retched if there had been anything in her stomach. But she pressed backward into the surety of Tamás. He pressed back against her, reaching around her to turn on the tap. The water ran rusty brown and then clear, but the sound of it made her pull away. Tamás gently tugged her hands down from her face, and when the water was warm, he ran her hands beneath the trickle, rubbing the river silt from them and from beneath her nails.

The whole time, he whispered to her, "You survived. You survived. You survived."

Her tears ran dirty paths down her cheeks, down the line of her neck, to sink like stones beneath the collar of her sweater, like bones to the bottom of the river.

Dear Comrade Ambassador,

I realize that this is an unusual request, but I am hoping you will understand. I do not know Russian, but my niece is learning in school, so she is translating this for me.

My name is Ilona Rosenfeld Frankel, and I was a Jewish prisoner at Auschwitz during the war. I was wondering if I could please be sent some of the dirt from Auschwitz. Enough to fill a jar.

My husband, parents, uncle, aunt, sister, brother-in-law, nieces, nephews and my own three children died there. And I have no bodies to bury. I would like to bury dirt from Auschwitz in their stead.

There are no rabbis in Budapest left to ask—they too went to Auschwitz.

But I believe this does not violate Jewish law. I hope it does not violate Polish law either.

Thank you,
Ilona Rosenfeld Frankel

CHAPTER THIRTY-EIGHT

AZRIEL

Azriel could not watch them play God. It made the space between his shoulder blades burn.

"You don't have to be there," Csilla reassured him.

"Why not?" Tamás asked.

"He's not comfortable with making a golem," Csilla chided
Tamás. "Let him be."

"He should be there," Tamás said grumpily.

Azriel wrapped his arms around himself.

"Where will you go?" Csilla asked, ignoring Tamás.

Azriel wanted to pull the curtains of the apartment shut and
let her sleep the day away. She looked exhausted, her cheeks pale
and hollow, dark circles beneath her big nighttime eyes. She sat
on the end of the bed, her bare feet pressed to the cold floor,
her hands pressed to the mattress on either side of her. She was

351

barely upright. Humans were so frustratingly stubborn, wearing themselves down until they were frayed. It was like they didn't even know how fragile they were.

"Across the river," said Azriel shortly.

"You could just stay here," Tamás offered. "Get some rest."

Azriel shook his head. He could barely stay in the apartment as it was. The itch and pull to cross the bridge, to climb some hill in Budapest following that sensation, was too strong.

Csilla gave him a significant look beneath her uncombed curls, and Azriel sighed. With a glance at Tamás, he jutted his chin at the door. "Walk me downstairs? Let her get ready?"

He loved these moments with Tamás, when he suggested walking downstairs or offered to tie Tamás's tie, when Tamás looked surprised and shy and hopeful. Tamás nodded and led the way out of the apartment, down the stairs, outside to the streets. It was early enough in the morning that the fog still sat in the air, and few people mingled. It was the quietest that Azriel had heard the city all week.

"I didn't mean to get short," Tamás said, his voice low. "I'm sorry."

"I know. Tamás, I'm going to . . . ," Azriel began, and then sorted out the feeling in his chest. "I'm going to go across the river to a hospital, I think. That's what it feels like."

There were other places that felt like hospitals too, crowded, congested places full of dying people, but he didn't think that those were here. Not this time. Though the basement of 60 Stalin, where he'd been detained, had felt like that.

Tamás frowned at Azriel, who kept his face as open and

sincere as he could, like he would if it was Csilla, who knew everything he could share with her, standing in front of him. Tamás looked away first, swallowing hard. "Care to clarify?"

"You know," said Azriel softly, "that I am not from here. You knew it the moment you heard me speak."

Tamás's head jerked. Azriel chose to think it was a nod.

"My name is Azriel, and I am an angel of death."

Whatever Tamás had been expecting, it'd clearly not been that. He jerked away from Azriel, putting space between them in a heartbeat. "What?"

"I'm an angel of death," Azriel said, desperately hoping now that Csilla was right, that Tamás could handle this. "I am called to places, and I go to ease people and their souls."

Tamás swallowed. "Where?"

"Where they need to go," Azriel said.

It was complicated, explaining death to humans who feared death.

Tamás blew out hard, turning away from Azriel and pacing out into the street (proving his point nicely, Azriel thought to himself). When he turned around, he wiped tears from his cheeks with the back of his hand.

"Were you— Did you see?" Tamás's voice broke.

"No," Azriel said quietly. "I'm called to places where children are. Márk was an adult. Tamás, look at me. Another angel would have been with him."

"Promise me?" asked Tamás.

"I promise you," Azriel said, though promises were not things he ought to give humans.

Tamás made a terrible pained noise and pressed his fist to his mouth. Azriel made a move toward him, and Tamás held up his hand. Azriel stopped, his chest splitting open, a river in the middle.

"You said you needed to go," Tamás reminded him, his voice choked and tight.

Azriel did. He very much wanted to stay, but he needed to go.

"Tell Csilla I told you?" he asked Tamás.

Tamás flinched. "She knows?"

"We were children together, in the ghetto."

Tamás looked up then, like he could see into their window. "She told me never to ask her about that time. I didn't know."

"Don't ask her today," Azriel said grimly. "She needs to focus today. Tamás, you'll take care of her?"

Tamás nodded. "Of course. If she'll let me."

Azriel snorted. "Good luck."

They exchanged a smile, and then Tamás reached out, taking Azriel by the elbow and pulling him back into the shelter of the apartment building entrance. He nudged the door shut, casting them back into shadows.

"Thank you," Tamás murmured, his fingers interlacing with Azriel's.

Azriel could feel Tamás's pulse pounding and his hand trembling. He touched Tamás's cheek, then leaned forward and kissed it. Tamás turned his face a little, exhaling against the corner of Azriel's mouth. Their noses brushed.

A shiver ran down Azriel's spine, painful. "I have to go."

He didn't want to move, but Tamás nodded and dropped his hands. "Meet you by the synagogue?"

"I'll be there," Azriel promised.

He really had to stop promising things to humans.

He'd add it to the list of unangelic things he did. Right after loving them.

On the other side of the river there was a hospital. It was carved into the bedrock below the old castle, utilizing the natural caverns once used for storage and as a jail. In the last war, they'd used the castle as a hospital during the siege, and it seemed they'd resurrected it now for the same purpose. Azriel drifted in alongside nurses and doctors; he had to resist the urge to stare at everything around him. When he was there on official duties, people tended to overlook him. That'd always been true, except for Csilla. She'd always seen him.

Every available nook had a gurney or stack of blankets, with the injured piled on them. The place smelled sickly and sweet, like infection and cleanser, and the nurses and doctors looked harried. The air was stale, like the circulation system had long since died. The infections would kill everyone whether he was there or not, but at least he could ease the pain of a few. He watched a doctor scrubbing in the hallway for surgery despite the long odds.

When he finally reached a room full of patients hooked up to IVs, quiet and still, nurses moving among them, Azriel knew he'd found where he was needed. There were dozens of people in here, some wearing Soviet Army uniforms. They were being treated right alongside the rebels they'd been shooting at hours before. Most of the Soviets had burns, likely from Molotov cocktails thrown into the tanks. Rebels had shrapnel and bullet wounds.

But he wasn't there for them.

He moved among the beds, finding the children that he'd been called to serve. He knelt beside them—a toddler injured by stray gunfire, teenagers shot when they took up arms against the occupying force, an eleven-year-old with a head injury. He touched the backs of their hands and whispered what they needed to hear. He placed his hands on either side of their heads, just as he'd done with Csilla when she'd nearly slipped away touching the river, and this time he gently ushered them into the waters and to their own beyond. Only when he felt their souls depart did he let them go.

At the end of the room, he took a breath and pressed a hand to his chest. The world felt heavy and dizzy, rocking inside of him. The cave's air suddenly felt too thin.

He'd let them move on. That was his job. Now he would move on too.

CHAPTER THIRTY-NINE

This is how you build a golem.

You believe in magic enough to dive into an ice-cold river in the dead of night, under the threat of gunfire, touch the bones of your people who died here, the people who left and never came home and the people who died so that your father could live.

You understand that you will never have everything you need. You will never find soil in this earth that's never been dug—if not by a human, it's been touched by a creature, perhaps hundreds or thousands of years before you touched it, but human digging is not valued above or beneath the digging of other creatures. You will never find water where you need it that's never been caught in a vessel before, but you will find water that has forgotten what a vessel feels like. Wild water, unused to boundaries and division.

You will understand that everything you are is enough. You, with your desperation. You, with your hope. You, with your dreams. You, with your secrets. You have never felt like you were enough, for your parents, for your teachers, for your bosses, for your friends, for the strangers. But here, what makes you not-enough makes you enough. You, with your indecision. You, with your fragility. You, with your uncertainty. You, with your immortality. You, with your mistakes. These are what give you the will to shape from mud the semblance of a man. These are what give you the determination to learn what you didn't know.

You learn the words. Unfamiliar and unsure, shapes strange to your tongue and lips, but sounds that are familiar, that sing to your blood and pull it to the surface. You flush as you pull the words into you. Once a word is known, it cannot be unknown. Once a word is learned, it cannot be unlearned. Once a magic is known, it cannot be unknown. Once a magic is used, it cannot be unused. And so you learn the words, you learn the magic. They are one and the same. You will now not forget even if you want to.

You shape each limb. Here is the arm. Here is the leg. Here are the fingers. Here are the toes. Here is the torso, this shapeless clay void. The heart is the press of your palms, a print against the belly, the love and hope in your words, the way you learned them and the way you learned the magic. The lungs are filled with water, the water you used to loosen the clay, to bend it to your will the way that breath shapes a body. The stomach is filled with your hunger, and your hunger is your hope.

You create the joints, flexible like the way the laws governing magic bend in times of desperation. Your fingertips smell like the river. Your whole body feels electric. You couldn't stop now even if you wanted to. You aren't sure if you believe in God, but you believe in God more than ever. Not because God is working through you—no, this is entirely your work—but because who else could create this kind of magic?

You form the head last, setting it on a good strong neck. You smooth the clay over a hairless head, carve cheekbones from nothing, mold a nose that matches your own. Their mouth comes to you, thin and unsmiling. They are no one's friend. If it were Chanukah, you'd call them a Maccabee, for they could be nothing but your hammer. You give them ears, as if they need them to hear you. You, with whom they share a heart. You, whom they will obey until you alone let them sleep.

And into every glide of your hands across their wet clay body you press your memories of another person shaped by this land, by the land and water they loved, and you infuse the clay with all of your love, and all of your memories, and all of your pain, and all of your regrets. You make them not in the image of the man himself but in the image of your memories, callous and kind, cunning and forgiving, thoughtless and optimistic.

You wet your hands one last time. And on the forehead of the clay person who lies inert beneath you, you write the first Hebrew word of your life. Aleph. Mem. Tav. The letters make the word *emet*. Truth.

And here is the truth.

When the golem rises, they look only to you.

And you, you look only to the city.

This is how you build a golem. You believe, you know, you hope, you despair, you determine, you learn, you create. You play God. You build a myth of a person from the instructions that a myth of a person left for you.

You let go.

CHAPTER FORTY

CSILLA

October 27, 1956

Csilla walked her golem through the city. They were made of clay, but they were like her father, tall and silent, the same loping stride, the same warmth radiating from them as she remembered from her father before the war. When they glanced down at her, they smiled, and she felt like a child again.

They were unmistakably her father, and yet they were still a person of clay.

Tamás pressed a kiss to her cheek and disappeared, splitting off to fly through the shadows and tell the rebels that there was an ally, and not to shoot the golem—Csilla wasn't sure what her golem would do if they were shot by an ally.

Csilla walked alone with the golem, and then Azriel appeared from a side street, confident and calm, to join her. Their hands brushed every so often. He said nothing, a silent presence beside her, and for the first time, she really, truly thought of him as an angel of death. Someone not quite like her and not quite unlike her, someone unknowable.

The blue sky against the gray buildings, the gray people and the gray trees looked like an unfinished painting, but where her golem stepped, a brief splash of color ignited, fireworks on the earth beneath their feet. They walked, and where they walked, the city fell silent. People crowded at windows, leaning outside for the first time in days, risking everything. Where there was fighting, it stilled and fell silent.

They waved flags, tentative, small flags made of scraps of fabric or flags with the Soviet seal cut from the center, and Csilla raised her hand, as tentative as they were in their waving, and waved back. Her golem walked on, straight up Stalin Street toward the space where the Stalin statue used to live.

Someone must have alerted the Russians, because the first tank turned the corner and began firing immediately, big resounding thuds, then the scream as the round flew past, hitting buildings. Csilla screamed out of instinct, and Azriel's hand closed around her elbow, his hand warm, dry and sure.

For a moment, she thought perhaps she'd died, finally, and he was taking her away, but he only said to her, "Steady, Csilla."

She took heart from it. She took a deep breath and slipped her hand into Azriel's hand on one side of her, and she slipped her other hand into the hand of the golem. The angel of death threaded his fingers with hers, and the golem closed their hand around her hand, and they walked up the boulevard.

This is the city, she told her golem. *You were made from the river, just as I was. And this is your city. You loved it. You died for it.*

And her golem asked no questions. They took what she said as truth. She was their creator and also their daughter.

This is the city, and there are those who would destroy it. You must protect us.

She did not know what else to say. Her father's instructions included only how to create a golem, not how to use one, and so she could only guess and trust herself.

It was terrifying, to rely on guesses, and hopes, and wishes, and herself.

But it was all she had.

An angel of death, a golem and herself.

Another tank turned the corner on Podmaniczky Street, took aim and fired, and this one hit the golem. She gasped, but it was as if the golem hadn't been hit. Their body absorbed the munitions, and they kept walking. The tank operators panicked.

They fired another round and another round and another round, and all of them hit home on the golem, but still the golem did not fall.

And though Csilla flinched at every boom, she did not flee.

She almost didn't notice when the tanks adjusted their guns to aim at her, and she might not have noticed if Azriel's grip on her hand hadn't tightened infinitesimally.

She glanced sideways at him and took in the way his eyes stayed locked on the street in front of him, his mouth flattened into a thin line. She turned to follow his gaze at the tanks that advanced through the city, at the slight shift in their direction.

She had only one dizzying moment of clarity, realizing that the river was too far away to save her this time, when the next tank fired.

CHAPTER FORTY-ONE

AZRIEL

OCTOBER 27, 1956

He should not have interfered in the affairs of humans. It was—well, it wasn't a sin per se—but it wasn't what angels did. They were observers, recorders, historians, librarians of human history and the human experience, cataloging it and shelving it as appropriate.

But it was Csilla, and the thin golden thread that drove through him still tethered him to her. And so he moved to act—but the golem, that mutable being who shifted from one appearance to another fluidly, familiar and unfamiliar in equal terms, as if their body was still made of a soft and malleable clay, was faster. The golem knelt swiftly, one clay arm swinging up and in front of Csilla, their fingers curled into a fist, and in a thud of clay and dust, they took the impact meant for Csilla. The force of it knocked their arm backward, right into Csilla, and she crumpled like a small bird onto the street.

The golem made a noise then, something Azriel had never heard a golem make before, somewhere between a keen and a growl. They fell to their clay knees, and for a brief and terrible moment, Azriel thought the golem would collapse because Csilla had collapsed, but then the clay creature reached for her with open, trembling hands.

"She's alive," he said to the golem, stepping forward then, his hands up.

Someone shot him, and he ignored it. The golem turned toward him and let out a low growl, the defensive kind, and if they had had hackles, they would have risen, and if they had had pupils, they would have narrowed.

The golem had neither, and still Azriel understood. He stopped moving toward Csilla. He did not have a heart, but something hammered in his chest nonetheless. Csilla did not move. She was so still. But her golem reached out, brushing the hair out of her face with such tenderness as clay exploded around them, as the bombardment continued, that it took Azriel's breath away. Csilla had built this. The golem shifted, morphing as if it were being reshaped by air, by the sky, and Azriel held his breath. They appeared like a woman Azriel had known a thousand years ago halfway across the world, then like Csilla's father, then like a child Azriel remembered from the war and then once again like Csilla's father. Azriel knew well the way it felt to move between bodies and genders and places and times, to be of a place and not of it all at once.

"I know," he told the golem, "that you know who I am." At the golem's glare, he amended, "What I am. But I am not here for her. Not right now. Let me help."

The golem studied him as bullets and shells exploded around them.

"Let me take her," Azriel said. "To the rebels. To safety. The best thing you can do for Csilla, the thing she needs from you, is for you to protect this city."

There was something, he suspected, of Simon in Csilla's rendering of this golem, like the way she'd assembled the myths of her father into a golem in her mind.

He needed that to be true. Because if it was true, then the clay man in front of him would do anything for the girl in a crumpled heap on the ground. If that was true, then the golem would protect the city, the river, the magic of this city, just to save this one girl.

Azriel was not to interfere in the affairs of men.

But he could interfere in the affairs of golems.

The golem slipped their enormous clay fingers beneath her fragile body and lifted her.

Csilla's dress, Azriel realized, was yellow. She was wearing a yellow dress. It dripped sunshine down the golem's fingers, staining them like pollen, and they looked down at her as they lumbered the two steps, their daughter and creator cradled in their palms. Then the golem let her slip from their hands and into the waiting arms of the angel of death.

"I will protect her," Azriel promised the golem. "Protect the city."

And with another one of those strange keening calls, the golem turned back toward the tanks that had begun to encircle them. And Azriel heaved Csilla against his chest, clutching her close, as he turned and fled the front lines with this mortal human in his arms.

CHAPTER FORTY-TWO

CSILLA

Csilla did not wake for an entire day. In that time, the rebels were busy. The golem fought alongside them, taking the blows and shells meant for them, the city, the rebels' tanks, and they pushed and pushed until the Soviets sat on the edge of the city and the guns went silent. And one by one, the Soviets turned east, rumbling for a border far off in the distance.

When Csilla woke, every bone in her body hurt, but she felt the change in the city almost immediately. She opened her eyes, and her body was in one piece.

She was in her bed, in the apartment where she'd grown up, where she'd been born, where she'd been made, where her mother had grown up, under the quilt that she and her aunt shared, heavy and familiar.

Tamás slept next to her, his legs tangled with hers, his head on the pillow beside hers.

Silence.

No guns. No explosions. No tanks firing.

She sat up, pain lancing her ribs as if someone had punched the air right out of her lungs. Azriel stood at the windows, his hands in his pockets, his hair long now, tied back in a ponytail low against his neck. He wore a vest over his white shirt, and he looked as if he were of a different time, a different place, a different gender.

"They're gone," she whispered, and in the complete silence of the room, the words sounded so loud and hopeful.

Azriel glanced at her in surprise and nodded. "Yes. They withdrew to the border."

"Why am I here?"

"I didn't know where else to take you," he said simply.

It was right that she was back here.

"Your aunt is making us breakfast," he added.

"Csilla," muttered Tamás, his voice cluttered with sleep and pain.

"He fought," Azriel added, with a tad too much affection, "all of yesterday and most of the night. He only got in an hour ago."

"Stay in bed," Csilla whispered to Tamás, pressing a kiss to his temple.

Then she slipped out of the bed. She pulled open the bedroom door and stepped into the dining room with its blue table, where she could see her aunt in the kitchen, boiling water for tea.

"Tante," she said.

"Sit," said Ilona, without turning around. "You did too much on Saturday."

Csilla obediently sat at the table.

Only then did she realize that she was wearing a dress that was not gray. If she hadn't been sitting already, she would have gone to the floor. She pressed her hands against her stomach and then against her thighs, against the brightness of the dress she wore. It was—she couldn't describe it. She wanted to press her face against it, wanted to drink it, because she was sure it'd warm her insides.

"It's called yellow," Ilona murmured, setting a cup of tea in front of her. "Do you remember it?"

Csilla did not.

"It's beautiful," she whispered in awe. "What—what else is yellow?"

She couldn't tear her eyes from the dress, the way it looked against her still white-gray skin, or from this color, this yellow, while her aunt listed things that were yellow. Tears ran down her cheeks, but she wasn't sad.

Baby chicks.

Canaries.

Butter.

Lemons.

Daffodils.

Sunshine.

"The tram cars," Ilona added. "Though they're darker than this. More saturated."

"Saturated," repeated Csilla. She'd thought of clothes being saturated with oil or water. She'd thought of saturated sponges. But she'd forgotten, if she had ever known, that color could be saturated too.

Then she remembered. She tore her eyes away from the

yellow dress and looked around. When she found Azriel in the doorway, listening, she asked him, "The golem?"

"Defending the city still," Azriel confirmed. "They're at Heroes' Square. That's what the people are calling the park where Stalin's statue used to be."

Csilla did not want to talk about colors anymore. She only wanted one thing. "I want to see them."

She did not know what to do with the sight of her golem defending this city. It was in fact exactly why she'd built the golem, exactly why she'd created them with all her pain and all the memories she could bear to give away—she had to make them loyal to a city to which she wasn't sure she was loyal—but here they were, in all their clay-and-dust glory, standing at the gates of a city, a creature born of Jewish folklore, defending a city that had tried to wipe the Jewish people from the map, defending a city that'd allied itself with those who would seek to annihilate the Jewish people, to burn them from history, to burn their books and their temples and their businesses so it was as if they'd never lived there, as if they'd never existed.

And the golem saved them all. At their feet, the people of Budapest had scattered flowers and tree branches as offerings, medals from wars, cups of coffee and coins. They wore a flower crown, and on their shoulders someone had draped a flag of the new Hungary, with the center cut out, and it was—she knew this—green, white and red, and their body was not gray but brown in the center of the hole.

The golem was pocked by grenades and friendly fire and

Russian shells fired from tanks that had saved her and her father and her mother from more months in the river.

She ran her hand over their thigh, for their hip was above her head, and she swore they'd grown overnight.

She remembered now that when they'd walked across the city, she'd thought of them like her father, that they'd looked like her father and felt like her father beside her. But they did not feel like her father now. They felt like an enormous clay man, someone she trusted but didn't know. A teacher. A rabbi. A protector.

The golem had been staring resolutely into the distance, but at her touch, they bent their head. They still had a face of stone, but it softened, she thought, when they gazed at her. They knelt then, a single graceful motion that brought them onto the same level with her.

She almost called them Papa. She almost called them Papa. She almost called them Papa.

But her father was dead, and this golem was not her father. She'd shaped them with her own hands. She ought to know.

"Hello, khaver," she said, pulling a word that did not belong to her but could belong to her if she wanted it. *Hello, comrade. Hello, friend.*

The golem touched her cheek with a single dusty finger. *Hello,* they seemed to say.

She smiled and wrapped her hands around their finger. "Thank you."

The golem nodded, as if they understood.

"I know I can't keep you," Csilla whispered to the golem. "I know that it is my duty as your creator to release you before the magic is corrupted."

The golem said nothing.

What was there to say?

Only everything.

And so Csilla spat on her palm and reached up with her wet hand, and she rubbed the aleph out of the word *emet* on the golem's forehead. Now it only read *met*.

In Hebrew, that meant death.

Truth and death were separated by one letter, one glancing raindrop, one teary cheek, one spit-covered palm.

The golem closed their eyes, and they folded to their knees. Csilla's throat closed up, and she started to cry. Part of her wanted to reach out quickly before the clay dried and write the aleph back into their forehead, to keep them for one more moment, but she'd read the warnings in her father's journals, and she knew that one who had fought so bravely deserved a final resting place.

The golem made no sound as the wind began to carry them away, dust brushing off their shoulders, and then in a gust, the street was obscured, flowers from their crown scattered in the wind and the flag whipped in the air, and then the air settled and the golem was gone.

Csilla sank to the street, scooping up a handful of clay dust in her hands. It pitted with her tears and then turned wet, shapeable in her hands, as she wept. A crowd gathered, some angry, and some weeping, and some silent, and some relieved, where the golem had once stood, and they gathered more flowers. They piled them beside Csilla as if this were a grave, and Csilla supposed, in a way, it was. A grave to make up for the ones she'd never have.

*   *   *

Much later in the day, Tamás knelt beside her, reaching out to brush a tear from her clay-stained cheek. "Hi."

She looked up at him, sniffling. "Hi."

He gave her a sad, small smile. "Come on. Let's go home."

He slipped his hand into hers and pulled her to her feet, and she let him drape an arm over her shoulder, tucking her against his side protectively and in companionship as they walked back toward his apartment (their apartment, she realized), Azriel on her other side, not touching her but within arm's reach if she needed him.

In their room, Csilla went to the bathroom and stared at her face. She was not gray anymore. She was not white. Her skin had a faint pink-yellow-brown tinge to it, and her brown eyes were red-rimmed. But Azriel and Tamás were still cast in grayscale. She scrubbed the clay from her hands, crying again as the last bits of the golem swirled down the drain. When she washed her face, the clay water got inside her mouth. It tasted like honey and iron on her tongue.

That was what victory tasted like, she realized. Sweetness and blood.

She stepped back into the bedroom, where the boys were conversing quietly side by side on the bed. "We did it."

Tamás blinked up at her, but Azriel seemed to know what she was asking. "Yes."

Tamás heaved a heavy sigh. "We did it. It doesn't feel real, though, does it?"

It didn't. But they'd bested the Soviets in every alley, and the city's magic had defended Budapest, not the Soviets. If they could keep the proper pressure on Imre Nagy, the new prime minister, Csilla thought to herself, the interim government had a chance of surviving. They had shown that Hungary would not be held by a foreign government, or by a corrupt domestic one. They might make mistakes, but they would be their own mistakes, not those made because their leaders hadn't been their own but handpicked by Moscow.

She remembered her father's optimistic, naive words at the end of the war.

Everything from here on out is ours. We own it. The good, the bad, the ugly, the beautiful, the tragic and the heroic. Isn't that wonderful?

Countries were made by the stories told about them.

Csilla had learned that from her father.

And people shaped the events around them, for better or for worse.

Csilla had learned that from her mother.

This was the story she could tell her children.

This was a country that chose the wrong side of every world war. This was a country that lost every war it deserved to lose. It was also a country that forged its own identity under the thumb of colossal superpowers. It was a country that found itself in the mountains and plains and the edges of a magic river. It was a country that clung to its own language, surrounded by languages unlike it, for thousands of years. This was a country that welcomed strangers and that participated in a genocide that nearly annihilated its Jewish population. This was their country, beautiful and imperfect, troubled and cruel, diverse and complex. It had no path to stray from, and yet it strayed anyway.

Like the river, they were magical and wild and the architects of their own stories.

The days of telling themselves that they deserved the cruelty and rules inflicted on them by their oppressors were over. The days of deciding what they deserved and what they could work to earn were upon them.

Csilla sat between the boys on the edge of the bed, wiggling her hips so they would shift to make room for her. Tamás leaned into her, as did Azriel, and one smelled like wet clay after a rain, the other like woodsmoke.

She could see then: this boy who stretched her future forward, bright with an endless horizon, and this angel who had known her when she was a small girl whose world had shrunk to the ghetto, who saw magic in a piece of small glass held to the light. She didn't want to let either of them go.

She laced one hand with Tamás's hand and one hand with Azriel's. "You should both wash. We ought to start cleaning up this mess."

Tamás lifted their hands to his mouth. It was not quite a kiss, just a press of his lips to her bloodied knuckles. "Do you ever slow down?"

"I was stuck for so long," she told him slowly. "Now that I'm moving, I'm too afraid to stop."

He lifted his head and looked at her. There was red dust on his beautiful lashes. Red, the first color she'd ever seen on him.

"Csilla." He kissed her, two fingers beneath her chin. Then he whispered into her mouth, "It would be a terrible revolution if it lived and died by one person. It'll go on without you, and without me."

He was right, and yet he didn't understand. And how could he? She barely did. The revolution did not need her. But she needed the revolution.

The revolution exploded like a wayward firework, bright and spectacular, unpredictable, though not as sudden as some expected, delighting some and shocking others and leaving most bewildered. But in those sparks of light against the dark night sky, she'd found a way forward out of the war she'd still been fighting in her head, in her efforts to survive and in her struggle to stifle herself. The revolution around her had been the mirror to the revolution within her.

"What do we do now?" she asked.

"First?" Tamás asked.

She nodded.

"You tell me what color this is," he said, and lowered her hand and his gaze to her yellow dress, covered as it was in dust.

"Ah," she said. She looked to her other side, at Azriel. "This," she said softly, "is yellow. Like butter." She turned back to Tamás. "Like butter. Like daffodils. Like canaries."

He looked up from the color only briefly, then back down, touching it with just his forefinger, as if he were mesmerized.

She whispered on, "Like lemons. Like sunshine."

"Sunshine," murmured Tamás.

Azriel said softly, "Sunshine."

CHAPTER FORTY-THREE

AZRIEL

OCTOBER 29, 1956

The night was cool and dark and clear. The stars glittered above the river. He traced constellations with his finger, a habit of his for as long as he could remember. He wondered if there were angels that covered the heavens too, and how that worked on a purely logistical level. He had questions.

He had too many questions.

He waited, sitting on the windowsill while Tamás and Csilla slept in the bed. For the first time, they looked soft and peaceful while they slept. Csilla tended to sleep curled up like a pill bug, but Tamás sprawled, all limbs and length. Azriel breathed out. Some part of him hoped to leave without having to say goodbye. Csilla would understand, he thought. He wasn't sure if Tamás would.

He waited, watching the now-peaceful city from the window.

He waited to feel the pull in his chest to another place, but it didn't come. Maybe he wasn't ready to leave Budapest yet. Maybe there was nowhere else that needed him yet. Maybe he'd be lucky and he'd get the time he hadn't got here with these two beautiful humans.

He wanted to believe that was why. *It could be,* he reasoned. *It could be.*

He waited and waited until light crept over the city, and then he crawled back into bed.

CHAPTER FORTY-FOUR

CSILLA

October 30–31, 1956

It rained the next morning. A torrential downpour, the biblical kind of rain, the kind of rain that drowned out all other noise and made people shout to be heard. And wherever a raindrop landed on Budapest, color returned.

It began in the streets, and as the asphalt was gray, it took minutes for people to notice. But then the raindrops began to reveal the green in the grass and the yellow and orange and brown of the fallen leaves of autumn. People poured out of their apartment buildings for the first time since the rebellion began, and the streets of Budapest were full of people, standing in the rain and getting soaked to the bone. They cried and they laughed. Someone brought out an accordion.

Csilla watched from the blasted-out window in her apartment's living room, at the little blue table, holding her aunt's hands, while Zsu swept up the broken glass around them.

"You don't have to do that," Ilona said to Zsu.

Zsu gave Ilona a smile. "I want to."

Ilona watched her for a moment, and Csilla watched her aunt, but eventually Ilona turned from Zsu back to the window. A smile trembled on her lips when she watched children dancing around below, splashing in puddles and splattering color everywhere.

"Come down," Csilla murmured. "It's beautiful outside."

Ilona squeezed her hands, and to Csilla's surprise, she nodded. They walked together down the stairs, Zsu and Csilla on either side of her, to where Azriel and Tamás waited in the doorway. Csilla introduced Tamás to her aunt, and though Ilona curled in on herself, she smiled and shook their hands. Csilla wrapped an arm around her aunt, and they stepped out into the rain together.

It washed over them, aunt and niece, and Ilona's gray hair streaked with a dark auburn. Her dress was blue with little white and yellow flowers. The buttons were iridescent. The numbers on her arm turned dark blue against her skin, which turned peachy and bright in the autumn rain.

Csilla thought she might cry when she watched Ilona turn in a small circle, her arms falling from where they'd been clutched over her chest, as she took in Budapest with a wide, wondering, hopeful look.

"Csillagom," said Ilona. "Do you remember how to dance?"

Csilla shook her head.

But Zsu took Ilona's hand. "Teach me."

Ilona showed her and Csilla how one foot crossed in front of the other and then behind, braiding their splashing, rainbow footsteps across the street. Azriel joined them, taking Ilona's hand, and Tamás joined them on the other side. The circle widened to neighbors they knew, the other Jews who still lived here in Budapest who knew the steps and those who didn't—István, to Csilla's surprise—and strangers.

Zsu tipped back her head and laughed, breathless when Ilona guided them into the center, their hands in the air, and Csilla couldn't help but laugh when she tripped as they changed direction.

The colors around them couldn't be contained by single words, and so the adults named them for the children too young to remember a time when the world was in rainbow. The rain came down and down and down, washing color back into the city, everywhere except the river.

The river stayed silver, like Csilla's hair.

She didn't mind, though. She wanted to drink in this beautiful, colorful city, and so she did.

Just before sunset, Ilona went back upstairs, tired, she said, from dancing. And just after sunset, Csilla, Zsu, Tamás and Azriel decided that they couldn't walk around and stare at everything anymore and that the intensity of the colors was starting to give them all a headache, and so they went about the work of building the world they'd fought for, they'd done magic for, they'd imagined into possibility.

They discovered, almost immediately, that there were already those who would steer Hungary in the wrong direction, who were ready and able to pervert this revolution for their own ends, to satisfy their own image and dream of Hungary, one that was limiting instead of infinite, one that closed doors rather than opened them. They spoke of purges, of quotas, of knowing who was a real Hungarian and who was not.

"Jews," Csilla murmured angrily to Tamás in the back of one such room of people where she, Zsu and Tamás stood against the wall. "They mean to purge Jews. Kill us, arrest us, whatever. They don't care what."

"They don't," Tamás began to protest. Then he saw her face and paused, sitting back to listen to a part of the conversation he'd dismissed because it hadn't mattered to him before, when it hadn't touched him. He blinked as he heard speaker after speaker argue exactly what Csilla had said they'd argue.

He tilted his head toward her so his words were for her and her alone. Then he reached up and straightened the knot of his tie, which she was wearing around her neck, so his fingers grazed her throat and chin. His expression was solemn. "I hear you."

He pushed his way to the front of the room and put himself in the conversation, arguing against the efforts to identify Russian assets within their ranks. He didn't call out their antisemitism outright, and Csilla understood why, but he stopped them from weaponizing it.

No more bureaucrats like her father and mother would die for reasons no more or less specific than their Jewishness.

"He's good," Zsu said softly to Csilla.

Csilla squeezed her friend's hand. "He is."

Zsu leaned her head against Csilla's shoulder. "Gábor would have liked him."

Zsu had only started to talk about Gábor. She'd been moving

too much in the wake of his death, Csilla thought, to compre-hend the loss. Not that she'd slowed, either.

"Gábor was good too," Csilla whispered back. She and Tamás would always disagree on this point, and that was okay. But she knew Gábor was good. "He would have liked the work you're doing."

Zsu was leading a commission on women's roles in the up-coming elections. Hungary had not been as egalitarian in its po-litical processes as it had purported to be.

When Zsu told her this, Csilla had said, "But the stance of the Party is—"

And Zsu had held up a hand and said, "Csilla, we can't stop here. No more comrades. No more Party."

And they'd argued about it into the wee hours of the morn-ing over a cake Ilona had baked them, and when they were tired of arguing, they decided it didn't matter if they disagreed on how far to push the revolution. They agreed on the next steps, and that was what was important.

When Szendrey appeared in the room, Csilla wasn't sur-prised, but she was surprised that he wasn't there for the stories the men and women in the front of the room were trying to in-ject into Hungary's new process. He pointed at her and gestured for her to come into the hallway.

She looked at Tamás in the front of the room and lifted her hand to catch his eye. He looked up at her, and she gestured that she was leaving. He frowned, a question written so plainly on his face that he might as well have asked it aloud. *Are you okay?*

She smiled reassuringly. *Yes.*

She didn't need to give him more than that, but she owed him at least that much. He nodded and returned to his conversation, and she made her excuses to Zsu. Then she stepped out into the hallway to meet Szendrey.

He looked quiet and old, gaunt but not thinner, as if all his weight had shifted down, pulled to the earth by gravity and sadness and the weight of Hungary's troubles. His trousers sagged. His shoulders slumped.

"You look terrible," Csilla said in greeting.

The corner of his mouth tipped upward. "I think the revolution might have made you bolder than ever."

"How can I help you?" she asked.

"You don't want to be in there," he said, nodding to the door behind you.

"On the contrary," she said, surprising herself with a laugh. "I very much want to be in there." She wanted to be writing the narrative.

But he shook his head, insistent. "No, you don't. Your father thought he did too, and it was the death of him and everything he thought was true to this country."

She stared at him. He gestured for her to walk with him, and for a reason Csilla wasn't quite sure how to name, she did. "Where would my father have gone instead, if he'd listened to you? That's what this is about, isn't it? You think he should have listened to you."

Szendrey shrugged. "He should have done a lot of things. But I can't blame the dead for ending up dead. But if he'd listened to me, he might have become a writer. A poet. A photographer.

Something that captured the story of Hungary and what makes Hungary Hungary. He thought he wanted to shape Hungary, but Hungary," said the journalist, pushing open the side doors of the Parliament building and stepping out into the square full of sunlight—yellow, bright, illuminating the pale gray stone— "Hungary already has a shape. And one person can't change the shape of Hungary. It takes all of us to shape Hungary again and again. We mold it like clay with every choice we make."

Clay, like he'd heard about her golem. Clay, like he'd known she'd made it. Clay, like he'd known she'd killed it.

They stepped out into the sunlight together. There was a burned-out tram car behind them, rubble everywhere and bullet holes in all of the walls. But children skipped by, splashing in a puddle, swinging between the hands of their parents, and two teens, guns over their shoulders, rode their bikes across the plaza, weaving around and goofing off.

"Csilla," Szendrey said, "I want you to write about what happened here. The truth of the war."

"War?" she asked.

He glanced at her. "You don't think it's a civil war?"

"I like the etymology of *revolution* better," she admitted.

He laughed. "Revolution, rebellion, civil war. They'll be arguing over what to call it for years to come."

It didn't truly matter, Csilla thought, as long as they made change. There was always the risk that in a big shift, people expected too much too quickly, and the change failed. Or, and she could feel this already happening in the room where Tamás remained, that the change was too incremental, and people lost faith in the power of change. Or that the change was too much, and people were frightened. In times of trouble, people clung to what they knew, even if what they knew was terrible. The enemy they knew was better than the enemy they didn't. And it was easier to hate the Russians and blame them for everything than to grapple with the fact that Hungarians, too, were not perfect and often created their own nightmares.

But that would be something yet to come.

"Do you think that we'll succeed?" Csilla asked Szendrey, watching life resume in the city.

"Oooh," he murmured, then sighed through pursed lips. It came out like a whistle. "What are you calling success?"

Csilla hesitated. She, Tamás and Zsu would all have different definitions. But he'd asked about only her definition. She admitted, "I don't know."

He patted her hand, making her bristle a bit, but his words soothed her. "I didn't expect you to know. We're all figuring it out as we go, Csilla. That's the secret. We're figuring it out as we go. But at least we get to figure it out, yes?"

"My father said something like that in his journals," Csilla said.

"Yes, he's the one who used to tell me about how important that was. That we make the decisions, good or bad." Szendrey sounded impossibly sad in that moment, the saddest Csilla had ever heard him.

She did not know how to comfort him. She was still getting used to the idea that other people missed her father too.

The river glittered at her, the bright, shining silver ribbon around the neck of the city. She heard the river whisper to her *daughter, daughter, daughter,* and she dearly wanted to go to it, to touch it with her hands and whisper her thanks, her gratitude, her apologies, over and over. She'd be thanking it and apologizing to it for the rest of her life.

"Are you ever going to tell me why you and the river share the same coloring?" Szendrey asked.

She blinked at him. "How do you know I don't just have very light-colored hair?"

"I would have thought it, but neither of your parents did, and I know your father didn't cheat on your mother with another woman." His face darkened. "And because I have never seen another person with hair quite like yours."

She hesitated and said, "The night I was born, the river ran over its banks."

He looked thoughtful. "I remember that night."

She reached out and touched one of her silver curls. "That's all I know."

"Perhaps that's all there is to know," Szendrey said. Then he said carefully, "And is that how you built your clay man? With river water?"

"Yes, and river silt," said Csilla, surprised into honesty. "You saw them?"

"Everyone knows about your clay man," Szendrey said.

"Please don't write about them," murmured Csilla, thinking of the antisemitic sentiments she'd heard all morning.

"I won't. You'll be doing the writing, Csilla."

She wanted to. She didn't know where to start.

"They're called a golem," Csilla said to fill the silence. "They come from Jewish folklore. My father tried to build one during the war and failed. I don't know why."

She did know, though. They'd been missing the river's gift of water, and the untouched silt at the bottom of it.

"I am glad," Szendrey said after a long pause, "that you succeeded."

She leaned against the wall to steady herself. "Do you think he'd like me? Who I turned out to be?"

"Yes," Szendrey said immediately, loudly, profusely. He reached out to Csilla, gripping her hands so tight it hurt. "Yes, Csilla. He'd love you even if you hadn't done all the things you've done over the last few weeks. Nagy said that this wasn't counter-revolutionary, didn't he? I think your father would realize the same thing. I think he'd be so proud of you."

She wanted to believe him. She did. She just didn't know if she could.

Szendrey continued, "But I don't know if that really matters, Csilla. Because I'm here, and I am proud of you. And that boy you made eyes at is proud of you. You can see it all over his face. And I am sure your aunt is proud of you. There are people here who love you and are proud of you. We're right here."

She had to pull her hands from his to wipe the tears off her face. "I didn't know."

"I know," he said simply. "And I'm sorry. I wish I'd thought to be there for you earlier. I didn't know you needed me, and I didn't know I needed you. I'm sorry, Csilla. But I am so proud of you."

She nodded and leaned sideways, her head against his shoulder. He wrapped an arm around her.

"I think," Csilla said softly, "that I could write something."

That night, she sat at the window, brushing out her hair, while Azriel, who had returned looking tired and pained at the end of the day, listened to Tamás work on a statement for the student union, which had decided to hold fast to its Sixteen Points, which hadn't been addressed yet by the new government under Nagy. Nagy was a moderate, but, Csilla thought, too willing to see the good in people. Not unlike Tamás.

In front of her, on the windowsill, were a typed-up story she'd written today and a pencil. She hadn't started to edit yet. She didn't know if she could.

Azriel had been so quiet when he came back from his walk, and he had shrugged off their hands, their touch, their comfort. His hair was long, and he touched his lips with some rouge Csilla had brought from her apartment when she'd visited her aunt. He looked beautiful, and she wanted to touch his reddened lips with hers.

He looked over at her like he could feel her gaze. "It isn't going to edit itself, Csilla."

"Maybe I'm not supposed to be a journalist," she said quietly. "I don't know how to do it."

"Do what?" Tamás asked, putting down his speech.

"Tell the truth," she whispered. That wasn't quite right. She tried again. "Everything I write seems inadequate. How can I even say what happened here?" She shook her head. "I can sew. And type. Perhaps someone else would hire me. Perhaps I could work at a university. I could be a typist. Surely they have typists."

The boys exchanged glances. Then Tamás climbed off the floor, unfolding himself without grace, and went to her. He brushed his thumb over her mouth.

"Where is that courage, rebel heart?" he murmured.

She pulled his hands down. "I don't know what happens to me now. I don't know where I fit into this new world. I knew where I fit before."

"You didn't," Azriel said softly. "You just knew where you were supposed to try to fit."

She flinched at the truth.

Tamás tried to look her in the eye, but she wouldn't meet his gaze. "Avoiding the truth because it's hard belongs to the world before the revolution. Is that what you want to go back to?"

She closed her eyes. "It'd be easier."

"Yes," he agreed. He leaned forward, touching his forehead to hers.

She whispered into the small space between them, "How can you just go back to where you were before? You are so different now."

"Am I?" he mused.

She didn't want more questions. She just wanted answers. But it was clear she wasn't going to get the answers she wanted from him. She didn't know what answers she wanted from him.

She leaned against the cold window, a little breathless.

"I want to collect our stories," she said aloud.

"Whose stories?" Tamás asked her, without judgment in his voice.

"Our stories," she said. "Hungarians. I want to know about the things they believe in but don't understand. And Jewish Hungarians. Those of us who are left."

The stories that had shaped them and that would shape them, make them better than they'd ever been. The stories that would save them. The stories that felt shameful. The stories that felt glorious. The stories that seemed small and inconsequential, and the ones too big for words.

Tamás's eyes were so soft Csilla ached. "Good. You can do that. I believe in you."

"Even when you don't understand me?" she asked.

His smile was like a glint of sunshine on her skin. "Yes. Even when I don't understand you."

Azriel's fingers fell into her silver curls. She could feel him turning her hair around his fingers in a manner that likely looked lazy to any onlookers, but really could not have been anything short of deliberate and curious, as he always was.

Tamás leaned forward, straightening her Magen David necklace. She'd put it on again for the first time since the war. He traced the interlocking triangles with his finger. She watched his eyes following his finger. She wanted to watch him for the rest of her life.

He looked up at her. "It's important to you, isn't it? These stories. From people you've never met."

She leaned into Azriel's leg. "Yes. And the people I've lost."

She reached out and pulled one of Tamás's hands to hers, playing with his fingers.

They were building a country on stories. They were building this—whatever was happening between her, Tamás and Azriel—on stories too. The stories they'd tell each other and others about each other. Her, the girl with moon hair and an abyss in her heart. Tamás, the bookish boy with the gun in his hand and a dream for the world. Azriel, the angel of death with tears in his eyes and his heart on his sleeve.

"Yes." She tugged at his hand, though, as she rose and climbed into bed beside Azriel. She lay down with her head in Azriel's lap as Tamás obediently followed. He curled up on the other side of her, his head against Azriel's side. "Can I tell you two a story?"

"Of course," murmured Azriel, his fingers in her hair.

So she told them about a little girl with hair the color of the river, who remembered the ghetto in bits and pieces, fragments of light cutting across dust suspended in the air, refracting off shattered glass across the floor. She told them the way her mother cried each time her father was taken to the river, and she told them the stories her father told her about the river's magic. She told them about walking across the bridge to be deported, and about the way her father had grabbed their hands and leapt into the river. She told them about the end of the war and waiting for everyone to come home, and how her aunt was the only one to return. She told them all the things she missed about her cousins and her grandparents, and all the things she missed about her parents.

When she wept, they held her.

He's all bright eyes and impish smile in the photograph his mother hands me. On the other side of the room, Péter flushes. I've withheld their last name for safety, a holdover and habit ingrained in me and Péter's parents, but beyond that, Péter and his parents are open books, telling their story of the revolution.

Péter was eleven on October 23, when the students marched. On October 25, he turned twelve, and he picked up a gun and joined them. His parents were afraid for him, but his father says they were also proud of him.

"Sometimes," his father says, his voice a little hoarse, like he is trying not to cry, "it is the children who show you what action must be taken, that we do not need to live the way we've always lived."

There are dozens of stories like Péter's. Hundreds, perhaps. Thousands and thousands across all of Hungary. The revolution was not limited to the confines of Budapest, but rather spread everywhere. We know that tyranny can thrive anywhere. We forget that hope can too, and hope feeds rebellion. Hope and rebellion shake us from our winter slumber.

Adults have grown uncomfortable with being uncomfortable. Fear becomes a comfort because it's a known entity. But hope—that is uncomfortable. That is an unknown. And we must all become more comfortable with the uncomfortable. We cannot accept things as they were and believe that they must be that way. We must question the moral and practical underpinnings of every element of society so we can move toward a better world. A just world. A more truthful world.

I hope I get to vote for Péter one day, or for his sister, Erzsébet, just one week old. She was born on the day the tanks left the city.

> —Csilla Weisz Tisza, in the inaugural issue of *Népszabadság*, the successor newspaper after the revolution, November 2, 1956

CHAPTER FORTY-FIVE

CSILLA

November 3, 1956

It lasted seven days. Seven entire days. Seven days of fearlessness. Seven days of arguing and infighting and brilliance and people rising to the occasion. Seven days of farmers dragging their produce into the city so its residents could eat and thrive while the city rebuilt its infrastructure. Seven days of Csilla coming home exhausted from walking the city with Szendrey and learning how to ask questions of people so they would spill their hearts into her hands. Seven days of her collapsing into bed and wiggling her way between Azriel and Tamás, who almost always beat her to bed, and both of whom welcomed her with gentle hands, warm bodies and tangled limbs.

The busier Tamás and Csilla grew, though, the more withdrawn Azriel grew, and it bothered Csilla. She woke one night that week to find him missing from bed, and so she pulled on a coat and slipped her feet into her boots and walked out to see if she could find where he had gone.

He was outside smoking, a human sin he occasionally partook in, and he looked small and frail against the empty street. He opened an arm to her silently, and she slipped into his embrace, letting him keep her warm against the early November chill.

For a long time, they said nothing at all as she searched for the words to try to understand this quiet, uncertain angel. She tipped her head back and rested her chin on his chest. "It must be lonely. What you do."

He gave her a look that crossed between gratitude and warning. "*Lonely* isn't quite the right word for it, but it works."

"Does it help, then? Falling in love with us humans?" she asked him.

He tightened his arm around her. "For a little bit."

And she realized what he wasn't saying. That he was always losing people. He fell in love to escape the gaping canyon in his heart carved by the work he was compelled to do, day after day, and then he was called somewhere new, or they died, because they were mortal and he was not.

She pressed her hand to his chest. "You love us."

He closed his eyes, and she wanted to kiss his eyelashes, his eyes, the line in his cheeks, his mouth. "I do." Then he opened his eyes and looked at her with questions in his gaze he couldn't quite ask.

She answered them anyway. "I love you both too."

He dropped his cigarette to the ground, crushing it beneath

his shoes, shoes too fancy for the coming winter. He wrapped both arms around her, pulling her close.

"I will miss you two," he whispered, so quietly she had to strain to hear him, rising on her toes as if that'd help her, "more than anyone I've missed before."

She imagined he'd said that before, that he was constantly missing people more than the people who came before those people, that he fell in love deeper and faster each time, because that was the way love worked. Love grew easier with practice. And letting go grew harder with practice. Anyone who said the opposite was lying to themselves.

But she found that she didn't mind that he'd used that line before and that he'd loved people before her and that he'd love people long after her. She only wanted to make her love soothe him in the time that they had.

"Come," she said, and fitted her hand into his. She pulled him inside, back up into the apartment building. She pulled him up the stairs and into the bedroom, where Tamás was still asleep.

This time, they folded Azriel between them, instead of putting Csilla in the middle, and Tamás pulled all the quilts and blankets over them. Azriel sighed and nestled his face into the crook of Csilla's neck, pulling Tamás's arm around him.

"Thank you," whispered the angel of death, his voice sad and heavy.

Csilla wished they could press that pain out of his voice, but she could only absorb it from him, stroking his hair and his cheek and letting him draw whatever strength he found from their touch.

They got seven days.

Six days after the Russians withdrew from Hungary, Csilla heard the radio announcer say breathlessly that there were Soviet tanks on the border. Azriel was sitting on the sink in their bathroom, his legs casually hooked around the back of Tamás's legs as he held Tamás in place, his razor gliding softly over Tamás's cheeks, shaving him as carefully as he could.

Csilla froze, her hands halfway through the knot in the tie she'd stolen from Tamás. Then the announcer repeated it, and she blinked, unfreezing.

"Tamás. Azriel," she said, her voice low and tense. The way she said their names immediately caught their attention, and Azriel managed to pull the razor away just in the nick of time before Tamás whirled toward her.

"What?"

She turned up the radio.

The Russians have massed thousands of tanks at the borders, according to our sources. They continue to say they are negotiating with Prime Minister Imre Nagy, however—

Tamás swore, then grabbed his shirt off the floor and yanked it over his head. He bolted out the door, slamming it behind him. Csilla stared at Azriel, still on the sink, still holding the razor.

He looked so lost, so sad and so unsurprised.

And then she remembered that he would not stay forever. He was an angel of death, called to where he was needed. He did not stay by choice.

"You knew," she said softly.

He swallowed hard and put down the razor. "Csilla."

"You knew," she screamed, and launched herself at him.

He slipped off the sink and caught the brunt of her impact with his chest, catching her arms and pinning them behind her though she flailed and fought to hit him. She screamed and slammed her head into his, seeing stars, and then hit her head against his collarbone. He held her firm but didn't fight her off.

"Csilla," he said, tears in his voice. "I didn't know. Listen to me."

"But you're still here," she sobbed, collapsing against him. She was furious at herself for loving that he was there more than thinking about why he'd stayed.

"I know. I didn't know what would happen, though," he whispered, loosening his grip on her wrists. He let her go when it was clear she wasn't going to hit him, and slipped his arms around her body. When she returned the gesture, accepting the embrace, he sighed a deep, bone-tired sigh. "I just knew it wasn't over. I can't see the future, Csilla, and I can't change what will come."

She could have, though, because she was human. If she'd spent even two seconds thinking about why the angel of death was still there when they thought the war was over and they were at peace, perhaps they wouldn't have been caught unawares. Perhaps Tamás wouldn't have been running off to the war, to certain death.

Thousands of Russian tanks.

Thousands.

"You could not have known what it would look like either,"

he murmured to her, rocking her slightly. "Stop blaming your-self."

"It's an awkward time," she managed to say, "to reveal that you can read minds."

His chuckle was a warm, low thing that rippled through her, pushing back her tears and darkness. "I can't. I just know you well enough."

She sobbed into his chest. "I will always want more time."

He kissed the side of her neck softly. "I have all the time, and I can promise you that it is still not enough."

She curled her hands into fists, gathering his shirt in her sweaty fingers. "I can't lose more people."

She'd lost so much, and she'd lose so much more. And she didn't want that to be the hallmark of her life. Loss after loss.

Azriel whispered, "I'm sorry, Csilla. I'm so sorry."

And she understood the pain in his voice and face from the night before, that he'd known what was coming.

"Will you be there?" she asked.

"Yes," he said immediately.

"Will it hurt?" she whispered.

She felt him shake her head against hers. "No, my love."

She did not care that he might be lying to her, only that he loved her enough to lie about this and give her one last gift.

PART V

We are listening.

CHAPTER FORTY-SIX

CSILLA

Everyone knew that they could not hold off an invasion. It didn't mean they wouldn't try, but people were preparing for the worst. Almost everyone Csilla knew had lived through the siege during the war. They all knew the city's weaknesses. So people were leaving the city, trying to escape Hungary while the borders were less protected, while it was unclear who was truly in charge of Hungary at the moment.

Csilla was running out of time.

She went to Szendrey first, coaxing his address out of an older woman at the paper who sat in the personnel office as if there wasn't a war outside and a power struggle upstairs in the journalists' offices.

She appeared at his door, where a gangly boy, caught between childhood and adolescence, answered.

He called for his father, and his father came. Szendrey's eyes widened when he saw Csilla there, and he sent his son away from the door.

"Csilla," he whispered.

"I won't be long. I don't have much time." Csilla handed him the four black journals, again wrapped in paper. Szendrey took them like he wished he didn't have to. Csilla swallowed past the lump in her throat. "Those are yours as much as they're mine. You should—you should read them. I think he'd want you to."

Szendrey shook his head, but he held the journals to his chest. "Csilla. Come in."

And she thought he was offering her an out, a way to escape the things she'd done, an opportunity to return to her old way of life. She couldn't do that. She couldn't imagine doing that. Not anymore.

Every moment was a turning point.

And she chose.

She shook her head. And they embraced, kissing each other on the cheeks.

"Good luck, Csilla Tisza," Szendrey whispered again.

"Please call me Csilla Weisz," she said.

He smiled. "Csilla Weisz. I'll write about you, Csilla. I promise."

But he wouldn't, she thought. Because he needed to stay alive for the children in this house. He'd go back to exactly what he'd done before at the paper. Maybe he'd say the rebels had forced him to write what he had over the last week. She didn't mind.

"Thank you," she whispered, because it was true.

She realized, somewhere between the walk from Szendrey's apartment to her own, that she'd never be able to know her parents fully. Not only because they'd been taken from her too soon, before she was old enough to know the right questions to ask, but because she could only ever know them as a child knew their parents. People were made up of all the ways they were seen by others: as friends, as lovers, as spouses, as parents, as children, as siblings, as colleagues, as bosses, as employees, as voters, as leaders. People got only fragments of each other. No one ever got the whole.

She climbed the hill to her parents' grave, in a gentile cemetery her mother would have hated.

She told her father that she forgave him.

She told her mother that she loved her.

She placed a small stone from the riverbank on each of their headstones.

At the apartment of her birth, of her family's entire life, Ilona was in good spirits until Csilla told her the plan. "We can get you to Austria."

"Austria!" Ilona spat to the side. "They hate Jews."

There were so few places where they were loved, Csilla wanted to remind her.

But she held her tongue, because her aunt's life was worth more than a point well made in an argument. "You can get to Israel, or America, from there. Tante, listen to me. Please. You should leave while you can."

Ilona narrowed her eyes. "I will not leave without you. That was the deal. We agreed to leave together. I said I would not go without you."

For a brief moment, Csilla thought about lying to her, promising to meet her over there in a few days, but she couldn't. She gripped Ilona's fingers. "You helped the revolution, Tante. And while I want to see it through, I won't see you arrested and in a show trial and in a gulag. You survived one camp. It would do my heart good to see you somewhere else."

"You could come too," Ilona said.

Csilla shook her head. "But I don't want to."

Ilona worried at her lower lip and then sighed, her shoulders slumping. "I suppose those train tickets aren't good anymore."

"No," Csilla admitted. She wished that her aunt had been on a train a few days ago, but that hadn't been possible. The trains weren't running. Austria was the only way out. "But the money is still good."

"I will be alone," Ilona said to no one in particular.

"Jews," Csilla said, blinking her tears away. "We are meant to be together. You will find a community of Jews, and they will welcome you."

"You don't know that," Ilona said helplessly.

"I believe that," Csilla amended.

Ilona looked up and said quietly, "I suppose that'll have to be good enough."

When Ilona agreed, Csilla went to find Zsu, because for the next piece, she'd need Zsu's help. She couldn't do it alone. And though Zsu was swamped with committee work, she put down her pen, her paper and everything else.

"I'm sorry to ask," Csilla began again.

Zsu took her hands. "Don't be."

They walked together to Aliz's house, and as they approached the apartment building, Zsu said, "Csilla, let me do the talking."

"It's for my aunt," Csilla argued.

"Yes, but sometimes you have all the tact of a bomb," Zsu said, rolling her eyes. "And Aliz doesn't want to see us. This will require tact."

Aliz opened the door, saw them and hissed, "What are you doing here?"

Tibor was stacking blocks in the room behind her. Csilla realized with a start that though it'd been just two weeks since she had seen him, he looked like an entirely different little boy. Aliz did not look older, but she did look more tired than Csilla had ever seen her before.

"We need a favor," Zsu said softly. "Will you let us in?"

Aliz bit her lip, glanced up and down her hallway, then opened the door. Zsu and Csilla slipped inside. The apartment was dark and small, but cozy and quiet. Aliz put on a pot of tea and then came into the living room, keeping a careful eye on Tibor.

"Feri?" Csilla asked softly.

Zsu shot her a look, but Aliz relaxed. "He came home last night. He's been . . ." She hesitated and then said, "He's been with the rebels."

"The Russians are invading. They've got tanks at the border," Csilla said quickly. "If I see him, I'll send him home."

"Csilla," said Zsu.

But Aliz looked relieved. "Thank you." She looked at Zsu. "What did you need my help with?"

"Csilla's aunt—she needs a ride to the Austrian border, or as

411

far as you can take her," Zsu said quietly. "And you are the only ones we know with a car."

"She's leaving?" Aliz paused to accept a block from Tibor and add it to his tower. Csilla watched it fall over, and her throat closed up. The boy didn't seem to mind, though. He knocked his hands through the pile of blocks, picked one out and started again.

"I was going to leave," Csilla said quietly. "Before. I had money to buy papers. *We* were going to leave. We were going to go to Belgrade and from there to Israel. Maybe to the West."

It was a treasonous thing to say aloud, and now she'd said it twice.

"I'm not leaving," Csilla said. "But my aunt should. They'll punish her for what I did, and she ought to get the chance she should have had after the war to live somewhere where she's happy."

Or at least happier. Somewhere where the stones around her didn't carry memories that haunted her.

"It would be treason to help," Aliz said. She looked down at her baby's head.

"You don't have to see her escape," Csilla said quietly. "Just drive her as far as she can go."

"I thought she was unwell," Aliz said. "Can she get over the border on her own?"

"I hope so," Csilla said honestly. That part she'd have to leave up to Ilona.

Aliz did not look up. "Which crossing?"

"Everyone I know is going to Andau," said Zsu softly.

Aliz nodded a bit, pressing her mouth against her fingertips and staring at her son. "That's not too far."

Zsu and Csilla exchanged a look. Csilla started to open her mouth, trying to find more arguments to convince Aliz, but Zsu shook her head, holding a finger up to her mouth quickly.

Finally, Aliz sighed and looked up. "All right. I'll ask my mother to watch Tibor. When do we leave?"

"Tomorrow." Csilla breathed. She reached forward and pressed her palms to Aliz's knees. "Aliz. Thank you."

Aliz smiled, and it wasn't grim or nervous, but reluctant and sweet. "I'm glad I can help, even if it's in a small way."

"It isn't a small way," Csilla said softly. "Not to me."

The next morning, after seven days of freedom, Csilla sat on the bed, braiding her hair, listening to the distant boom of tanks. Somewhere out there, Zsu was holding Ilona's hand in the back of Aliz and Feri's car as they drove toward Austria. Zsu said she wasn't crossing the border, but she'd stay with Ilona as long as she could. Csilla hoped Ilona could change the younger woman's mind. If she closed her eyes, she could imagine the look on her aunt's face, and it crushed her heart. She should be there with her. And she still could not imagine being anywhere but here.

Tamás appeared in the doorway, Azriel right behind him. They'd gone to scope out the situation early this morning, when the light was still low.

Csilla said softly, "It's time."

"It's not," said Tamás roughly.

He crossed the room and pulled her to him, a little harder than he needed to, but she let him. He just rested his forehead against hers, his arm tight around her waist, his breath a little shallow. He wore his hat pulled low over his worried brow, but he'd gone out without a coat, and he smelled of early winter air, crisp and fresh. There was a part of Csilla that wanted to pull them both back into bed, pull a blanket over their heads and pretend they had another day.

But there was not another day.

They'd been playing with borrowed time, and Csilla supposed that in a way, she had always assumed this would happen. The Soviet Union would not let this dangerous, bold revolution stand. But winter was coming, and in a few short weeks, she would be lighting the Chanukah candles in the dark of her aunt's apartment, on the floor of the kitchen, where no one would see the glow of the candles in the windows, and they'd hold their hands over the flames and they would thank God.

There was still enough light in this world to thank God.

Their room was as quiet as it'd ever been, but in the distance, Csilla thought she could hear tanks approaching.

On the radio, a shaking but clear young voice said, "Nations of the world! Help! Soviet tanks and guns are coming! SOS. Help us! Not with councils or words but with action! SOS."

She moved to turn it off, pulling out of Tamás's arms, but he caught her wrist. "Don't you think we have an obligation to listen?"

What could she say?

For seven days, they'd held this city in the palms of their hands. They breathed the current into the river and stoked the fires in every home. They held the hand of every citizen, cut the pain of the past from every flag. They traded one blindfold for another. Simmering anger for translucent hope.

"We didn't fail," Csilla told him.

Tamás pushed her away, his hands curling into his hair. "Stop it."

"You didn't fail," she insisted.

"Did you?" he snarled.

She flinched, though she knew he wasn't angry with her. "Yes."

His fingers uncurled, and he shifted, peering at her around the corners of his sharp wrists. He had more angles to him than the streets of Budapest. She wanted to look away from him, from this boy who believed so hard that it'd fractured his heart, a rift that could not be bridged. But she knew she couldn't. "A golem won't be enough. I was foolish to think it would be."

"It'll buy us time," he said quietly. "As the first one did." He reached out for her again, and she let him draw her against him again. She felt the tension leave him as he breathed out, his breath warm against her cheek.

"We don't have enough time," she said. "And I don't have it in me."

She expected him to be angry with her for admitting that. But he didn't say anything for a long time. Then he whispered, "What now, rebel heart?"

She wanted to tell him that she didn't know. But she found the words stuck in her mouth. Instead, she turned to him and said, "If I'm going to die today, I will die in the streets. Find your coat. It's time to go."

There is a river that cuts through the heart of Budapest. It is a street for the magic. But here, they are the magic in the streets. They are the defiance and the rebellion, the hope and the dream, the future and the past, the Party and the People, the forgiveness and the apology. They are all the mistakes this country's ever made and all the potential it's ever had. They are the loved and the hated, the believers and unbelievers. They are the survivors and the victims.

Azriel parted ways with them, called to another part of the city. He pressed a kiss to Csilla's cheek and promised to return before the end.

She said, "I'm going to hold you to that, angel."

A radio played in a café.

It wasn't that shaking young voice anymore.

It was an older man saying, "SOS. Please send help."

At a street corner where they paused, rebels were carrying arms, getting ready to fight to the very last minute for their city. Tamás moved into easy conversation with them, and one of them let him take one of their extra guns, as if that would help. She watched him and his cool, calm confidence. He clapped the smaller boy on the shoulder, and the smaller boy's face lit up like he'd just met one of his heroes. Perhaps he had. She wondered if she and Tamás would have found each other if her parents hadn't been murdered. She wondered if they would have found each other if not for Márk Dobos, the boy who died. She wondered if they would have found each other if not for Tamás's heart.

His brave, brave heart. His belief that they could win.

Someone ran past them, gun in hand. Elek, Csilla realized with a start.

"A thousand tanks," he shouted. He jumped into a truck, hands coming out to catch him and pull him up. He loaded his gun in one simple, swift motion. He turned back and lifted a hand to her.

She lifted her hand in response.

She watched his truck until she couldn't see it anymore.

On the east side of Pest, the tanks rumbled over rubble, pausing only to fire. Buildings fell apart.

They pressed on.

Csilla wondered what came after this for Hungary.

She wondered if they'd ever be free.

Azriel reappeared when they were finally walking alone in the city, when the rebels had gone to the front and they were staying behind, the three who would take the place of the golem for as long as they could. She didn't ask him where he'd gone or what he'd seen or what he'd done.

He kissed her cheek and kissed Tamás on the mouth. Tamás glanced around, panicked for a moment that someone had seen them. But then Azriel murmured, "If you can't kiss someone you love in the street now, when can you?"

And Tamás kissed him again.

The river reached for her, frantic waves against her breastbone.

She whispered back, *I will return to you. I will return to you. I will return to you.* But she did not turn away.

When they walked, she could hear the sound of their footsteps, it was so quiet on the streets of Budapest. The sound of the feet beside her strengthened her heart.

"Ready?" she whispered to Tamás.

His long lashes brushed his cheeks, and then he slipped his hand into hers. "Ready."

And Azriel slipped his hand into Csilla's other hand, warm, cool and knowing. He would not die. He could not. But he'd be with her then, just as he had been all those years ago, and he'd be with her whatever came next.

Everything she'd ever been stretched back behind her through her hand in Azriel's hand, a long, meandering rainbow path. And everything that might have been, everything that could still be, stretched ahead of them, a golden path spilling ahead of them from her hand clasped in Tamás's hand.

Two rebels and one angel stepped out onto the avenue and faced the tanks together. And somewhere behind them, the river began to rise.

There is a city, and through the middle of the city, there is a river, and running parallel to the river, there is a street. It's crooked like a bent elbow, an outstretched arm.

Water has a long memory, and though the river was there before the street, and will be there long after, the river loves the stories the street carries to it, cradles the stories in its silt, and ferries them far away from where they began. The river is a historian, a keeper of stories.

This is a story in its silt.

Sometimes, though it is very rare, the river runs over its banks twice in a lifetime.

AUTHOR'S NOTE

The revolution in *This Rebel Heart* is real.

What had started as a protest by young people for the future of their country spiraled into a violent uprising against a police state controlled by a world superpower. On one side, there were tanks, bombs, and the immense military strength of the Soviet Union. On the other side, Hungarians with spray-painted dinner plates, kitchen grease, Molotov cocktails, and some light weapons. On one side, a state that had ruled through fear, and on the other, people who knew that those streets were their streets.

The Hungarians won.

Briefly. The Soviet Union retreated, withdrawing troops to the border, around October 28, 1956. They invaded again on November 4, and had control again by November 11.

After the Soviet Union reinvaded, it would be another thirty-three years before Hungary had its freedom, and thirty-five before the last Russian tanks withdrew from Hungary.

I traveled with my father to Budapest in February 2018 to research this book. We visited sites from Hungary's Communist past, World War II, and the Holocaust. We walked the exact path the students marched from the university to Bem tér, across the bridge, and to Parliament. On the pillars outside Parliament, there are still bullet holes from the massacre on October 26, 1956.

All governments and nations struggle with defining the truth and how to speak about and with the painful, violent parts of our past. It is vital that we engage with that struggle instead of ignoring it. Without truth, we can have no justice. Without justice, there is no peace.

The golem, Azriel, the river's magic, and the color of Budapest are fantastical elements in the book, rooted in fantasy, and folklore, and possibilities. I am always drawn to the glimmers of magic in real life that can be magnified in fiction. But in Budapest, it is easy to believe that the magic might really exist. It is a city of winding roads and ornate doorways, layers of the city that unfold and surprise you. Cities are made of people, and stories, and this is a story of Budapest. But it is only one of them.

I was fascinated by this revolution in part because it, for all intents and purposes, failed. And yet. . . .

I believe there's power in movements that don't immediately succeed—or whose success cannot be measured in political points or changes in power structure on paper. In Hungary, though many of the rebels were tried and most were punished in some way, including prison time and execution, the revolution did lead to changes in the secret police and how they operated.

Hungary liberalized, such as it was, as a result of the revolution, and the quality of life for people improved.

In Hungary, the 1956 Revolution has taken on almost mythic proportions—which can be both good and bad. It has been used as a cornerstone in post-Communist national identity, and that's fed the ultra-nationalist right-wing movement that holds power in Hungary now, and it's fed antisemitism. The revolution itself struggled with antisemitism, and Hungarian Jews participated in the revolution on both sides.

I was interested in this revolution because it was a bottom-up revolution started by young people—university students—with children as young as eleven fighting in it. It was driven by the hope of youth.

I took some liberties with history by tightening up the timeline of events and skipping the slow build from February 1956 through the summer of 1956. I also decided that I wanted to reclaim the revolution from its antisemitic modern proponents by centering a Jewish girl, without having her experience more antisemitism than what she survived as a child.

I also wanted to center it on students and non-military personnel, but I would be remiss if I did not mention that several key Hungarian military personnel defended the Hungarian People against their own units and commanders. Without this defection, the Hungarian rebels would not have had access to weapons, weapons training, and skilled armed personnel, which undoubtedly made a difference. Pál Maléter, who led that effort, was executed after the Soviet invasion, along with Imre Nagy, the interim prime minister.

In this book, I also did not touch on the role of the United States and the CIA in fomenting rebellion in Hungary. Through Radio Free Europe, the United States actively encouraged the Hungarians to rise up against the Soviet Union and made implicit promises that the West would back the effort with military support. This support did not materialize. It's unclear if it was ever going to happen, or if it was possible but not during the Suez Crisis tensions. That part matters less than the fact that Hungarian rebels believed that it existed and would come, and they took risks and chances with their lives, convinced that America would back them.

If you are interested in some of the books that I read while researching this book, here is a short list:

The Bridge at Andau: The Compelling True Story of a Brave Embattled People by James A. Michener

Budapest 1956: Locations of Drama by Bob Dent

Castles Burning: A Child's Life in War by Magda Denes

Failed Illusions: Moscow, Washington, Budapest, and the 1956 Hungarian Revolt by Charles Gati

The Faith of Fallen Jews: Yosef Hayim Yerushalmi and the Writing of Jewish History, edited by David N. Myers and Alexander Kaye

Journey to a Revolution: A Personal Memoir and History of the Hungarian Revolution of 1956 by Michael Korda

No More Comrades: A Message from the Freedom Fighters of Hungary by Andor Heller

Survivor Café: The Legacy of Trauma and the Labyrinth of Memory by Elizabeth Rosner

Twelve Days: The Story of the 1956 Hungarian Revolution by Victor Sebestyen

I chose to use the Hungarian names for the bridges and the river, which you may know as the Danube. I am indebted to the Hungarians and Hungarian Jews who spoke to me about their experiences in Hungary and their family's experiences in Hungary, before, during, and after the revolution. All mistakes concerning the experience of the revolutionaries or of Hungarian life are mine and mine alone.

Jewish scholar Yosef Hayim Yerushalmi wrote that "the memory of the past is incomplete without its natural complement—hope for the future." And that's the imperfect, and yet vital, spirit with which I wrote this book: that events of the past, including ones of deep despair, flawed people, and many perspectives, can give us the road map and the light we need to see the path forward.

Ken y'hi ratzon.

Let it be so.

ACKNOWLEDGMENTS

This Rebel Heart is a book that lived so long in my head and in my heart that I thought it might never see the light of day. I wrote this book in a void, sharing very little of it with anyone else until it was a draft, and even then, I kept it close. So for me, I must start these acknowledgments with gratitude to the story itself, for trusting me as much as I trusted it, and for clinging to my bones, so even when I was tired, I could not stop.

This book happened, through dark times and light, because of the path carved by the readers, librarians, and booksellers of my previous novels. For those fans, educators, and book lovers, I am forever grateful. I hope you love Csilla and her story too.

Thank you to my family, for hearing about this book for years and years before they ever got to read it, and a special thank-you to my dad, who traveled with me to Budapest for research in 2018, and who read, and loved, one of the earliest drafts. Thank you to my siblings, for being so wonderful that it felt distinctly weird to write my first book about an only child. I could never.

Thank you to my friends and beta readers, especially to Dahlia Adler, Katherine Welsh, Ashley Poston, Kaitlyn Sage Patterson (whose name I didn't misspell in *these* acknowledgments), Rebekah Campbell, Christina June, Kate Johnston, Alex London, Miriam Weinberg, Lauren Magaziner, Jen Bragan, Heather Tran, and others I undoubtedly missed who carried this book, and my angst about it, without complaining (to my face) all this time. I love and appreciate you all so much.

Thank you to Lara Perkins, my agent with the sharpest, keenest eye for story I've ever known. I am so grateful for your kindness, empathy, wisdom, and brilliance. And to everyone behind the scenes at Andrea Brown Literary Agency, thank you for taking me under your wing and supporting my stories with so much enthusiasm.

And a very special thank-you to Marisa DiNovis, who not only helped this story shine, but did so with bottomless empathy, thoughtfulness, openness, and kindness. I loved your love for these characters. It made me fall in love with the book all over again. Thank you for making me laugh, for your gentleness in hard times, and for your positivity in dark ones.

Thank you to everyone at Knopf who believed in this story and helped it become a book (with the world's most beautiful cover!). Jake Eldred, Cathy Bobak, Ray Shappell, Artie Bennett, Janet Renard, Rick Wright, Jonathan Morris, Josh Redlich, and Caitlin Whalen, thank you for joining me and Csilla in the streets.

I spoke to a number of Hungarian Jews (here in the United States) about their family's history and experience, before, during, and after the Hungarian Revolution. Their stories helped me shape the story on these pages. I am grateful for those who spoke to me, especially about time periods and events that were very painful. Thank you to Dr. Paul Hamosh for his early support, wisdom, clarity, humor, and knowledge, which informed my research and direction.

When I was completing edits on this book, my aunt Meryl died unexpectedly. She was a devout reader, a teacher, an artist, a surveyor, an author, a lover of nature and history, a proud Jew and granddaughter of immigrants. She was smart and kind and endlessly generous. She read every one of my books and got them into her rural community's public library, and her pride in me was something I treasured. I miss her more than I can possibly say in words, and words are my job. I can only try to be as generous, genuine, and curious as she was. If you are struggling with thoughts of suicide, please know you are not alone. You are loved, and you are important. Please stay. There are stories yet to tell.